NOWHERE TO RUN

"It's just Liv . . . please . . . and, yeah, someone's after me."

"Who?"

He was studying her in a way that made her extremely uncomfortable.

"I don't know, but it's always been there. I've always known it, felt it. I think this—*massacre*—has something to do with me." She raked her fingers through her hair. "I can't explain it. I don't have any proof. I know you won't believe me. Why would you? But it's a feeling I have, and it's *real.* . . ."

Books by Nancy Bush

CANDY APPLE RED
ELECTRIC BLUE
ULTRAVIOLET
WICKED GAME
WICKED LIES
SOMETHING WICKED
WICKED WAYS
WICKED DREAMS
UNSEEN
BLIND SPOT
HUSH
NOWHERE TO RUN
NOWHERE TO HIDE
NOWHERE SAFE
SINISTER
I'LL FIND YOU
YOU CAN'T ESCAPE
YOU DON'T KNOW ME
THE KILLING GAME
DANGEROUS BEHAVIOR
OMINOUS
NO TURNING BACK
ONE LAST BREATH
JEALOUSY
BAD THINGS
LAST GIRL STANDING
THE BABYSITTER
THE GOSSIP
THE NEIGHBORS
THE CAMP

Published by Kensington Publishing Corp.

Nowhere
To Run

NANCY
BUSH

ZEBRA BOOKS
Kensington Publishing Corp.
www.kensingtonbooks.com

ZEBRA BOOKS are published by

Kensington Publishing Corp.
900 Third Avenue
New York, NY 10022

All Kensington titles, imprints and distributed lines are available at special quantity discounts for bulk purchases for sales promotion, premiums, fund raising, and educational or institutional use.

Special book excerpts or customized printings can also be created to fit specific needs. For details, write or phone the office of the Kensington Sales Manager: Kensington Publishing Corp., 900 Third Avenue, New York, NY 10022. Attn. Sales Department. Phone: 1-800-221-2647.

Zebra and the Z logo Reg. U.S. Pat. & TM Off.

First Printing: August 2012
ISBN-13: 978-1-4201-5732-1
ISBN-13: 978-1-4201-2833-8 (eBook)

15 14 13 12 11 10 9 8 7 6

Printed in the United States of America

Prologue

Then . . .

He stood outside the house, staring at it from the backyard. They didn't know he was there. They didn't know that he stood in the backyard of many houses, watching, thinking, plotting.

He could see her outline through the kitchen window above the sink. Her figure was hazy beneath a dress, but he smiled to himself as he watched her. He knew what she was like, what they were all like.

A yellow square of light from the window set in the back door fell onto scraggly grass. As he watched, she moved from the window above the sink to the one in the back door, peering out. For a moment his heart squeezed with the thrill of the hunt. Could she see him? Could she *know*?

But no. She couldn't know. She didn't know about the others though the newspapers and television reporters were squawking about the missing women whose bodies had yet to be discovered. She didn't know about *him*. How close he was . . . how she was in his sights . . .

His eyes burned and he wondered if she could feel his desire and fury, but she turned away, her back to him. The

curve of her white nape was beautiful as she tilted her head
as if listening.

Do you hear me, bitch? Do you?

He felt himself harden as he thought of her, and his cruel
smile widened as he reached down inside his pants and
began rhythmically stroking himself, part of the ritual, part
of the beginning . . .

Do you feel me?

I'm coming for you . . . now. . . .

Livvie Dugan looked in the mirror and said, "I'm six
years old today." She was missing one of her front teeth and
she dragged her lips back in a snarl and stuck her little
finger through the hole, just to see what it looked like.
Pulling her pinkie back out, she next stuck her tongue
through the space, squinted one eye and said, "Arrrgh, me
mateys!" Just like pirates did.

It had been a grand day. Mama had gotten her a big cake
with pink roses on it, and she'd blown out all the candles at
once! Her brother, Hague, who was only two and a half and
didn't know diddly-squat, according to their dad, tried to
blow them out first, which made Livvie so mad that she'd
stomped her foot. Livvie knew Hague was special; Mama
said he was even though he seemed like he couldn't do
diddly-squat but that didn't mean he got to blow out *her*
candles! No way! She'd pushed him out of his chair and he'd
toppled to the floor, and started crying like a big, big baby
and Livvie kinda thought that's what he was, anyway, a big,
big baby. But Mama had scooped him up and soothed him
and then shot Livvie *that look*—the one that said she was
really mad but would hold it in till later.

Then Mama sat Livvie in front of the cake and she
sucked in tons of air and blew with all her might. The candles

had flickered and gone out. All of them at once! It was grand, Mama said. Grand. But she'd still been mad about Hague, though, so she didn't smile too much. She got Livvie and Hague each a paper plate with a slice of the white cake with the pink filling and a small cup of milk. Livvie had asked for apple juice but Mama hadn't seemed to hear her, so she'd said it louder and Mama got it for her, kind of like one of those robots, like Mama didn't know what she was doing. Then Hague had gone down for his nap with a loud, "Noooooooo!" as Mama carried him away, which was what he always said. Livvie thought he deserved to be put to bed and left there forever. After all, he'd tried to blow out her candles.

Livvie had finished her cake and smashed the crumbs with her finger and sucked them into her mouth. But Mama never came back, so Livvie had finally left the kitchen and wandered into the den and that's where she'd found Mama, just sitting on the couch. "What are you doing?" Livvie demanded. Mama had just left her in the kitchen and gone to the den! And the T.V wasn't even on! It was just a dark square, but Mama was staring at it anyway, as if it were playing *General Hospital,* her favorite show.

"Why aren't you watching TV?" Livvie asked, upset. It was *her* birthday! Mama hadn't answered, so Livvie declared, "I want to watch cartoons!"

Mama got up from the couch and stuck a tape in the machine. They had a videotape of some of her favorites though Mama said it wasn't going to last much longer and that was because Hague had grabbed it and pulled out some of the dark ribbon. Livvie had wanted to *kill* him, but Mama had put it back together and swept up Hague while Livvie wailed that Hague had ruined it! Well, he *had.* But the tape still worked okay sometimes.

Livvie settled herself onto the couch and though Mama

usually left her to watch alone, today Mama had stayed and sat with her a long while which was kinda weird, but then Hague woke up and she went to get him. Livvie had expected Mama to come back and shoo her outside because Mama didn't like her watching cartoons too long, but today she didn't. It was Livvie's birthday, after all. When the tape ended, Livvie rewound it and watched it again. After that, she was kinda bored, so she grabbed up the new box game she'd gotten for her birthday, Hungry Hungry Hippos, and because it was no fun playing by herself, she went back to the kitchen and asked Mama to play with her. Mama was just standing at the sink, staring outside like she was in a trance. (That's what happened on cartoons, too. They went into trances sometimes and sort of floated around.) Hague was on the floor by her feet, playing with some blocks, pounding one on top of another.

Mama said she couldn't come play right then, but maybe Hague could play with her? "No way!" Livvie yelled back, then quickly scooted back to the den. She played the game by herself, then watched some more cartoons. After a while Mama called her in for supper and she ate a Swanson's turkey TV dinner. Mama knew it was her favorite, and Hague saw it from his high chair and said, "Um, um, um!" 'cause he wanted some, so Mama gave him some leftover mac and cheese from lunch which he threw on the floor, of course. He pointed to Livvie's plate but Mama ignored him, for once. Livvie then smushed around her food when Mama wasn't looking and asked if she could have more cake.

She was kinda surprised when Mama brought her a piece, but she had to clap her hands over her ears when Hague, seeing Livvie's piece, started howling.

"Stop it!" Livvie yelled at him. "Mama, make him stop! It's my birthday! He's ruining it!"

"He's not ruining your birthday," she said as she gave him some cake, too.

Livvie was upset. "He can't have my cake. He's too little. And he didn't eat his mac and cheese!"

"He can have a bite."

"That's a whole piece! It's *not fair!*"

But Mama went back to the sink and stared out the window again. She kinda stood there, her hands braced on the counter, like she was having trouble staying on her feet.

Mad, Livvie glared at Hague who smacked away on his cake. Livvie dug into hers, too, but she couldn't quite eat it all because Mama had cut her a very big slice. A *grand* slice. Then, when she couldn't eat anymore, Livvie slid from her chair and left the room, and Hague said something to her. He couldn't talk right 'cause he was too little, and anyway, he didn't know diddly-squat, but it sounded like he said, "Kill you."

Mama turned and stared at him and he grinned at her with his little teeth.

Livvie then wandered back to the den and turned up the volume, loud. Mama rushed in and said, "Turn it down!" in that hissy whisper she used when she was really, really mad. "I'm putting Hague down for night-night and it's too loud!"

"Sorry," Livvie mumbled, but she really wasn't.

Mama switched down the sound and left in a hurry. Livvie heard her putting Hague to bed and his wailing, "Noooooo!" and she crossed to the dial and turned it up again, just a little. She waited, listening, but when Mama came out of Hague's room she went right past the den back to the kitchen.

Hague howled for a while, then finally quieted down. Livvie rewound the tape and watched some of the cartoons again, but after a while she got bored and wandered down the hall toward Hague's room. She kinda still felt mad at him. It was her birthday. Hers! Not his.

"He doesn't know any better," she said to herself, pausing outside his door.

She almost knocked. She kinda wanted to wake him up. Or, she wanted Mama to come back and sit down with her in the den but Mama never did. After a while, she walked backward to the den, trying not to look around and not to run into any walls. She wondered if Mama was going to put her to bed soon, too. That thought turned her around and sent her scurrying back to the den couch where she flung herself face down. If she was really, really quiet, maybe Mama would forget.

Then Mama cried out. Livvie lifted her head. What was that? She got to her feet and went to the den door, opening it a little.

"Mama?" she called softly, peeking out from the den. She wasn't too far from the kitchen, just down the hall and around the corner, but she felt really scared all of a sudden. Carefully, her heart jumping around in her chest, she tiptoed toward the kitchen. She could just see Mama; she was sitting at the table and her leg was shaking. When Livvie came up to her she saw that Mama was holding the side of her face with one hand. Underneath her hand the skin looked red and she was staring toward the open back door. There were tears in Mama's eyes.

"What happened?" Livvie cried, alarmed. "Mama, what happened? Why is the door open? Is someone there?"

Mama looked around the room in a kind of scary way, Livvie thought, but when the policeman asked her later if when she said "scary" she really meant "blankly" Livvie just clammed up. She didn't know what he meant.

The policeman had also repeated, "The back door was open," to Livvie, like he didn't really believe her, and Livvie had pretended she couldn't hear him anymore and just sent herself away into a quiet world where no one else was. A place she went sometimes 'cause it felt safe.

But at that moment Livvie cried, "Mama! Is there somebody out there? *Who's out there?*" Mama had used her mean voice and said, "Go back to the den, Olivia!" Livvie had started to cry. It was *her* birthday! Why was everyone so mad?

She'd run back to the den and slammed the door, still crying, waiting for Mama to come charging in and send her to her room or something. But when that didn't happen, she got mad, too. She stuck out her chin and crossed her arms. She sat down on the couch and stared at the door. She was going to stare at it and stare at it until Mama walked through.

But then . . . Mama never came and Livvie sorta forgot . . . and fell asleep. 'Cause suddenly she woke up and it was a lot later than she usually stayed up, she could tell. She'd drooled on the couch pillow and that reminded her of her tooth, so she went into the bathroom and stuck her tongue through the hole, squinted one eye, said, "Arrgh, me mateys!" and ran over the rest of the events of the day in her head.

She concluded that a pirate probably deserved another piece of cake, maybe even with ice cream this time.

She tiptoed back to the kitchen. But as she got close, her arms broke out in goose bumps. She stopped short. Her heart was speeding up, and she felt scared. "Mama?" she whispered.

No sound.

She stepped into the kitchen, looked, and started screaming. Screaming and screaming.

Because Mama was hanging in the air, her face all puffy and her tongue sticking out like she was joking around.

But she wasn't.

Livvie knew she was dead.

Dead. That's what it was.

Mama was dead.

Livvie kept on screaming and went to her safe place and that was the last thing she remembered for a long, long time. . . .

Chapter 1

Today . . .

Liv swam up from the nightmare, soaked in sweat, an aborted scream passing her lips. Heart racing, she blinked in the faint, early-morning light sneaking beneath her bedroom window shade. What time was it? Five? Five-thirty?

Closing her eyes, she willed her galloping heart to slow down, aware of the fragments of her dream but unable to completely grasp them. Didn't matter. She'd had enough nightmares to know this wouldn't be the last one—far from it—and though the dreams weren't exactly the same, they represented a deep trauma that years of therapy had never completely uncovered and erased.

At Hathaway House Dr. Yancy, who'd had enough compassion and understanding to actually make Liv believe she was really trying to help her, had once said, "I think it's something you saw."

Like no shit, Sherlock. She'd seen her mother after she'd hanged herself.

But Dr. Yancy had shaken her head slowly when Liv had been quick to point that out. Liv was always quick to defend herself. One of the problems, apparently, that had landed her in Hathaway House in the first place.

Dr. Yancy had then added, "You saw something else. Something you can't—or won't—let yourself remember."

That had caused a quickening in Liv's blood. An inner jolt of truth that had sent perspiration instantly rising on her skin as if she were having a hot flash. Her mind had clamped down hard, or so Dr. Yancy had told her, when she'd insisted she couldn't remember anything other than the horror of her mother's suicide.

But, though Liv denied Dr. Yancy's claim, she didn't completely disagree with it, though she never said so at the time. There did feel like there was something she did feel. And with it was the sensation that she was being followed. Stalked.

Now, years later, the question of whether her stay at Hathaway House had helped or hindered her still remained unanswered. None of the other so-called doctors and quacks at Hathaway House would have ever committed themselves to the kind of bold statements Dr. Yancy put forth; they all hid behind compassionate expressions and deep frowns and not much else. At the time even Dr. Yancy hadn't really wanted to show her hand to her contemporaries because they would have undoubtedly berated and dismissed her. Liv knew enough about the institution's politics to read between the lines and consequently she thought they were all a bunch of chickenshits with minimal understanding of the human condition and maximum interest in hanging on to their jobs.

But that wasn't really the question, was it? The question was: had Olivia Dugan been "cured" of her sweat-soaked nightmares and dark depression—the very reasons why, as a teenager, she'd been shuffled off to Hathaway House in the first place? Had Olivia Dugan learned to combat the triggers that sent her heart palpitating, palms shaking, thoughts colliding around inside her skull like pinballs, firing the wrong neurons, causing her to make wild, unreliable choices?

The answer? A resounding no. Though she had lied and pretended and acted and done every damn thing she knew how to do to be released from Hathaway House, as far as a cure went, the answer was still no. She didn't know how to combat the triggers that started the nightmares and increased the depression. Even if she knew what they were. Even if she told herself to stay away from them.

Because last night, one of the triggers had been pulled. A blinking red light had welcomed her home. The answering machine. A warning beacon. A voice from a stranger. She'd reluctantly picked up the receiver and listened to the phone message.

The phone message . . .

Now, Liv threw off the covers, shivering a little. She climbed out of bed and padded to the kitchen, a journey that took about ten steps across the tired carpeting of her one-bedroom apartment.

The phone message.

Lawyers had found her home phone number and left her a message. That was the trigger for her nightmare. She'd tried to ignore the blinking light when she'd tossed her keys on the counter. She'd asked herself for about the billionth time why she kept the phone and voice mail at all. Most of the time she liked the idea of being off the grid completely. That's why she didn't carry a cell phone. If that made her a Luddite, then so be it. She *was* a little frightened of technology anyway. She didn't want to be on someone else's radar. It just didn't feel safe. Dr. Yancy had told her she was hiding from something, and she supposed it was true but she didn't care.

Still, Crenshaw and Crenshaw had found her phone number, so she'd phoned back and the lawyer—Tom

Crenshaw—had asked her for her address. She'd been
reluctant to give it to him. Not that he couldn't find it, she
supposed; he was just asking to be polite.

He said he wanted to send her something—a package.
But he was cagey as hell about what that package contained, and only when they'd gone back and forth and he'd
finally convinced himself that yes, she was definitely the
Olivia Margaux Dugan whom he was searching for, did
he come through and say that his firm had a package for
her—from her mother.

Her *mother*?

After that Liv had simply dropped the phone receiver,
stumbled into bed and fallen into a coma-like sleep that
she'd just woken up from.

Now she wondered if it was all a mistake. Her mother
was dead. Had been since Liv's sixth birthday. The package
could *not* be from her mother.

She gazed at the phone receiver. It dangled along the side
of the cabinet, tethered to the base unit by a long cord,
hanging in a way that made her stomach wrench. She could
still see her mother's softly swaying body, the protruding
tongue; an image that didn't fade with time.

Sucking in several deep breaths, she squeezed her eyes
closed, then opened them again, picked up the receiver and
placed it back in the cradle. More old-school technology.
She didn't have a hand-held receiver. She didn't even have
a satellite phone in the bedroom. Her brother, Hague, had
real issues with paranoia—worse than Liv's by far—and
some of his paranoia had definitely penetrated her way of
thinking as well. There *was* a bogeyman out there. Maybe
more than one. Better to be safe than sorry.

She did, however, have voice mail and that nagging,
blinking red light on the base unit meant she had another
call. The lawyer had undoubtedly phoned back. For a
moment Liv considered the paradox that was her life. Here

she was running away from almost all technological communication and yet she worked for a *software* company that made simulated war games mainly played by adolescent boys. Okay, she was little more than a low-level bookkeeper for Zuma Software; she'd always been good with numbers. But the irony of her situation did not escape her. She smiled faintly to herself, screwed up her courage, and pushed the answering machine's button.

The lawyer's disembodied voice came through the speaker: *Ms. Dugan, this is Tom Crenshaw again, of Crenshaw and Crenshaw, Attorneys-at-Law. Please call us back so we can send you the package from Deborah Dugan addressed to her daughter, Olivia Margaux Dugan. Per our earlier conversation, this package was left in our care to be sent to you on your twenty-fifth birthday. As that date has passed, we need to make certain you receive this package soon.* A pause. As if he wanted to say a lot more, then simply, *Thank you,* and a return phone number and the law firm's hours.

Liv pushed the button a second time and listened to the message again. It was too early to call Tom Crenshaw back. She didn't even know if she wanted to anyway. She felt hot and headachy and strange just thinking about receiving something from her mother. *Her mother.* Nearly twenty years after her death.

Putting the number to memory, she got ready for work, then drove her Honda Accord by rote to the business park which housed Zuma Software. The company was situated in a private cul-de-sac, separated from the other buildings by a long drive bordered by arborvitae, isolating it, giving it the illusion of more importance than it truly deserved. Or maybe it was more important. Zuma's owner, Kurt Upjohn, certainly projected an "I'm better than you" attitude.

Liv skirted the front parking lot and drove to the west side of the building, the unofficial employee parking lot.

The building itself was concrete on all four sides, with a glass atrium entryway complete with double doors and a guard of sorts, Paul de Fore, a total tool, in Liv's biased opinion.

Liv parked nose out, climbed from the driver's door, remote locked the Honda and started around to the front of the building. She didn't even think of using the back door as Upjohn wanted all his employees to enter through the front. The back door automatically locked whenever it was used, and could only be accessed from inside. Upjohn was very, very cautious about anyone learning anything about his newest game models created by the nerds/techies who worked in the upstairs office with its glowing screens and simulations and miles of computer code. Liv had only peeked in once when Aaron, Kurt's son, had practically dragged her up the stairs with him, and she'd been half-awed at the way the room looked like a control room straight out of some high-tech adventure movie.

Now, as she entered through the mahogany front door— a door surrounded by windows—Paul gave Liv a narrow-eyed once-over, as if he'd never seen her before. Liv clutched her purse harder, an automatic reaction she couldn't quite repress even though she would never bring her handgun to the office. She wasn't *that* crazy.

Jessica Maltona, Zuma's receptionist, smiled at Liv as she entered, then slid a sideways look toward Paul who was still standing by the front door, arms crossed, watching Liv walk across the polished floor to her cubicle on the far side of the large room. Though the two women weren't friends exactly—they didn't know each other that well, Liv's fault mostly—they shared a silent communication about Paul whom neither could stand.

Liv smiled at Jessica as she passed. *He's a tool, all right.* To which Jessica, as if hearing her, nodded emphatically.

Settling herself at her desk, Liv stuffed her purse into a

lower cabinet with a lock. She twisted the key and pocketed it, then settled down to the night before's bookkeeping entries. It wasn't an exciting job. It was rote, by and large. But rote work was exactly what kept her from thinking and imagining and worrying. No, she wasn't bipolar. No, she wasn't schizophrenic. She was just . . . damaged . . . for lack of a better word. From the moment she'd discovered her mother's body, she hadn't been the same.

An hour into the job, safely ensconced at her work station, which was about a hundred feet from the front doors and the floor-to-ceiling windows splayed with the Zuma Software red neon logo in script, backward from inside the building but dramatic nonetheless, she picked up the phone and dialed the number before her brain, with its strong governor, could stop her.

"Crenshaw and Crenshaw," a woman's voice answered in that slightly bored, slightly snooty tone that seemed to invade the better law firms.

"This is Olivia Margaux Dugan returning Tom Crenshaw's call."

"Mr. Crenshaw is not in yet." There was a small rebuke there, as if she felt Liv should know someone of Mr. Crenshaw's importance wouldn't deign to get to work so early. "Would you care to leave a message?"

"Just give him this address." She told the woman Zuma Software's street address and finished with, "If he wants me to have the package in his care from Deborah Dugan, he can send it here."

"May I tell him what this is concerning? Something further?" she asked, sounding a bit miffed by Liv's high-handedness.

"He'll know what it's about." And she hung up.

Two hours later the package arrived by special messenger. Liv looked up from her computer first with annoyance, then surprise at the speed, then trepidation, as Paul de Fore walked toward her, holding out the 8 ½ x 11 manila envelope. Liv had been inputting figures into a computer program, compiling information to be turned over to Zuma's account- ant, who in turn would pore over the data as if it held the answer to the universe's deepest questions, who would then pass it along to Kurt Upjohn, the original developer of the war-game-type video games that had put his software com- pany on the map. Her head was full of numbers and seeing Paul coming her way pulled her out of that world and into the present at hyperspeed. She almost felt motion sick.

Paul slapped the envelope on her desk without so much as a word. He was no conversationalist, which suited Liv just fine.

Gingerly picking up the package, she looked it over, her gaze jumping to the return address of Crenshaw and Cren- shaw. She'd been alarmed when Tom Crenshaw had asked her birth date, where she grew up, the names of her parents, and a myriad of other questions. She in turn had demanded to know to whom she was speaking. How had he found her number? What did he want really? What were his creden- tials? He explained about Crenshaw and Crenshaw and what a long-established, trusted firm they were. Then he told her about the package and when he invoked the name of Deborah Dugan she dropped the receiver.

But now here it was. The package from her mother, nineteen years after her death. It was a large manila envelope with her name typed on a label affixed to its center. She laid it carefully on the desktop. She almost wanted to poke it with a stick, though it was clearly just some papers. Papers about what, though? She couldn't think of anything that—

"Hey!" Aaron Dirkus snapped his fingers in front of her face.

Liv sat bolt upright, as if goosed. "Aaron," she said tightly to Kurt Upjohn's son, her only "friend" at Zuma.

"Didn't mean to scare you," he answered affably,

though he clearly didn't care one way or another. Aaron's last name was different than his father's, due to some undefined wrangle between Kurt and Aaron's mother—Kurt had only managed to marry her after Aaron was born and that angered her but good, so much so that she'd given her son her maiden name rather than Upjohn. Then later, she and Kurt had divorced anyway. The story went something like that. Liv had never quite got it in full detail, but it didn't really matter. She'd never wanted to question Aaron further because that would have given him carte blanche to ask her about herself and she didn't want to go there. Ever.

"You're kinda in a fog. C'mon, let's go out back and have a smoke," Aaron said.

"I've got some work to catch up on." She wasn't interested in smoking anything, especially Aaron's type of cigarettes.

"Bullshit. You work too hard as it is. You're giving the rest of us slackers a bad name."

"The boss is your father. You can get away with it. I can't."

"People are starting to hate you around here, you know that? You gotta come with me."

He wasn't going to take no for an answer, and he'd been known to actually pull her out of her chair to get her to comply, so she reluctantly got to her feet. Truthfully, she really didn't take enough breaks, according to the law, so she followed him to the back door on the first floor and outside to the enclosed patio-type area, with its overhang and its gate that led to the employee parking lot. Her blue Accord was three in, facing out as if ready to take off.

Aaron normally stuffed a brick-sized rock in the door to keep it ajar, but today he actually pulled out a key and unlocked it from the outside, so that the door would stay open until he relocked it.

"Where'd you get that?" Liv asked.

"Kinda lifted it," he admitted. "Don't worry. I'll lock up before we leave tonight. I just can't stand walking by that asshole de Fore every time I want to breathe some fresh air." He shot her a quick smile as he pulled a joint and lighter from his pants pocket.

Aaron liked to smoke "maree-wanna," as he called it. Liv stayed away from all drugs; she'd been encouraged to take enough during her yearlong treatment at Hathaway House to last her a lifetime and then some. She liked a clear head and, apart from a very occasional drink, mostly steered clear of alcohol, too.

"You don't say much," Aaron observed with a sideways look as he belched out a lungful of smoke. "I like that about you. Although you're kind of shut down."

Remembering her six-year-old self, Liv felt a pang of sorrow for the loss of the independent, headstrong little girl she'd once been. That girl had apparently died along with her mother.

She stood to one side, leaning against the gate to the parking lot, gazing out. Occasionally she'd left the building this way when Aaron had propped open the door. She completely agreed with him that bypassing Paul de Fore was worth breaking some rules. Paul was just one of those guys no one could stand, the type who took his job too seriously and made it hell on everyone else.

Being too serious, though, wasn't Aaron's problem.

"Tell me something about yourself," Aaron said now. He had long hair and wore a plaid shirt over a T-shirt, slacker-style. It hardly mattered since his dad was the boss, but truthfully the programmers and game designers who were on the upstairs floor kind of dressed the same way. Slacker, hacker, computer techie, video game designer . . . there seemed to be an unspoken dress code with them that thumbed its nose at accepted business attire.

Only Liv and Jessica Maltona dressed in legitimate office wear: skirts or slacks, blouses, vests, jackets, sensible shoes, tasteful jewelry and makeup. Paul de Fore wore a navy shirt and pants as if it were a security uniform though there was really no such dictum.

"Well, I'm a Leo," she said. "I like Italian food and expensive coffee and live in an apartment with a three-hundred-pound cat."

Aaron coughed out some smoke on a laugh. Liv had never so much as hinted that she might have a personality and she'd taken him by surprise. She wasn't even sure why she'd said it. She'd just wanted . . . to not be so serious for once.

"Cool. What's the cat's name?" he asked.

"Tiny."

He grinned at her and Liv smiled back at him. It was the most playful conversation they'd had to date and though Liv was simply talking to talk, Aaron peered at her as if she were something he'd just discovered.

"Who are you?" he asked. "You're too good-looking to be this mousy bookkeeper you want us all to think you are."

Too good-looking? She had straight brown hair, hazel eyes and a mouth and jaw that were set too tightly, or so she'd been told. "I'm kind of average-looking."

"Look in the mirror, sometime."

She shook her head. Whenever she looked in the mirror she saw a woman with anxious eyes whose personal life was nonexistent and whose professional one was practically invisible, too.

He flapped a hand at her and sucked in his last toke. "You're good-looking and you're too serious. You should have some of this." He held out the teensy little end of the joint.

"Nah."

"Or a glass or two of wine, or a few mojitos, or some

Xanax. You just need to let go." He pushed on the gate and let himself into the back parking lot.

"You're going to piss off your father by ignoring security," she warned him.

"A guy's gotta do what a guy's gotta do. You go out this way sometimes, too."

It was true. Though Liv generally played by the rules, there was this inner part of her that occasionally liked to flout authority. Most of the time she pretended it wasn't there. But sometimes it stretched and peered around like a waking beast, looking to prowl. Was it because she'd spent time constrained by others? Or, the fact that the police had left an indelible impression on her since her mother's death, and not a good one. Or, maybe it was just a side of her personality that she mostly ignored and that surprised her and others now and again when it suddenly popped up. She wasn't the meek worker bee everyone thought she was, though she took pains to make others see her that way. A kind of camouflage, like an animal's coat or a bird's feathers.

By the time she left work she still hadn't opened the package and when she got back to the apartment she dropped it on the kitchen counter while she threw together a quick meal—a microwavable TV dinner with limited calories and limited taste; her eating habits hadn't evolved over the years, either.

She went to bed at ten-thirty and stared up at the ceiling through the dark. She could hear the comfortable sounds of the refrigerator humming and the tinny voices from her neighbor's television, which seemed to be right behind her head, set against the paper-thin wall that separated their units, her bedroom butting up against theirs.

She fell asleep, then came to abruptly at midnight, wondering what had woken her. There was moaning from behind the wall. It had been her neighbor Jo's last climactic shriek during lovemaking—something that happened regularly enough—that had penetrated her sleep.

Sleep . . . That's what some people called it, though Liv was pretty sure her sleep was different than others'; she'd learned that over the years. Hers was disturbed by images that kept coming back, creeping into a dream that had nothing to do with whatever the dream was about, images burrowing inside, memories from her childhood that simply wouldn't go away. Gruesome visions. The kind that had sent her to Hathaway House, a place for troubled teens who were recovering from serious issues: drug addiction, suicide attempts, self-mutilation . . . whatever. She'd been sent there because she was "disturbed," or so said her evil stepmother—yes, she really did have one—who had convinced her father to seek help for his nutso daughter. Only it hadn't helped, apart from making Liv realize that her problems were small compared to some of the other kids' at Hathaway House.

But because she was underage and had no choice, Liv put in her time there and finally, much to the evil stepmother Lorinda's dismay, had been pronounced "in recovery" sometime in what would have been her senior year of high school. She was released into her family's care and she went on to earn her GED. She'd learned by then that the best thing to do was just not to tell anybody about the powerful images she had of her mother's body hanging limply from a noose that had been attached to the rustic kitchen rafters of their old home. Images that stole her sleep. Images of a suicide that had left Deborah Dugan's two children, Liv and her brother, Hague, in the hands of a stunned father who quickly took a new bride.

Liv blinked in the darkness. The television next door was now tuned to an old sitcom that ran in the off hours and every so often the canned laughter would burst out in little fireworks of *har, har, har.* Liv listened to it and thought of the couple who lived adjacent to her in Apartment 21B. Young and in love, around her own age, they seemed to live on pizza and Diet Coke. At least the girl did. The guy had a penchant for beer. "Whatever's on special," he told Liv one day when she met them on the outdoor balcony and he was lugging a six-pack of Budweiser. They were trying to hug, kiss and giggle with each other while he also was threading the key into the lock and then they sort of fell inside and slammed the door shut behind them.

Liv had opened her own door and was greeted by the scent of loneliness and lost opportunities.

The next-door couple's name was Martin and though they hadn't formerly introduced themselves she knew the shrieker was Jo. His name started with a T . . . Travis, or Trevor, or something kind of cowboy-sounding to Liv's mind. She should know what it was as she'd heard Jo scream it out enough times while they were making love, but it always made her feel like an auditory voyeur and therefore Liv covered her head with her pillow whenever they went at it.

The worst of it was that their lovemaking reminded Liv of the two times she'd gotten close to sex and the third time that she'd actually gone through with it and had been left wondering, what the hell? Where were the bells and flowers and rainbows and endorphins? She'd mostly felt sort of depressed and wondering if sex, too—touted as a supposedly wonderful expression of love—was just another part of life that she wasn't able to experience like everyone else.

Cynical. That's what she was. And afraid . . . afraid to open a package from someone who'd sent it to her long, long after her death.

The following morning she went through the shower, dressed in black slacks and a black, long-sleeved T-shirt, drank a glass of orange juice and ate a piece of peanut-butter toast, her gaze on the envelope. She grabbed her purse and keys and headed out the door, then turned around abruptly and went back for the package, ripping it open while her heart pounded. She fought the crippling anxiety that sometimes overtook her and left her gasping for air and practically in the fetal position and shook the package's contents onto the counter.

Out tumbled several pictures and a couple of folded pages.

She saw her mother with several other people in one of the pictures, and she staggered backward to the couch and sat down hard, the photo in her hands; the other papers flew to the floor—someone's birth certificate among them . . . hers.

Drawing a long breath, she tried to stem a tsunami of coming panic. Her ears roared. She couldn't think. Couldn't see. Could scarcely recall where she was.

Her vision went inward, to the memory of a long ago, cool, summer evening, the air breezing inside the kitchen through the opened back door. The toes of her mother's shoes drifted from side to side . . . her face purple . . . her tongue fat and sticking out. . . .

Liv squeezed her eyes shut. Attempted to shove the image into blackness, but it shone white on the insides of her eyelids like a negative. Her eyes flew open again, and for just a moment her mother was standing right in front of her.

"I'm done," Mama said, then the mirage *poofed* into mist.

Chapter 2

Liv drove home from the office during her noon hour, even though there really wasn't enough time, even though she would probably skip lunch entirely. She'd left the package opened and spread across the coffee table. She couldn't look or touch any part of it when she'd left for work this morning, but the way everything was exposed had haunted her inner vision all morning.

Now, she took the steps up from the apartment parking lot to the second level of the L-shaped building where her apartment lay one in from the end unit. She threaded the key in the lock and pushed open the door before she felt someone behind her.

She screamed. One short, aborted shriek and stumbled into the apartment, turning, facing the intruder.

"Whoa, whoa! Sorry!"

It was her neighbor, Trevor or Travis or something. He was standing there in shock, holding up his hands. Liv felt the energy drop out of her and she leaned against the wall, near collapse, quivering inside.

Worried, he grabbed for her and said, "Geez, sorry."

She flinched away. "I'm okay. What . . . are you doing?"

"Come on." His arm was around her shoulders and he started to help her to the couch against her protests, her legs moving forward, but feeling detached from her body.

"What do you want?" she asked, trying to keep all traces of fear from her voice.

The pictures from the package were scattered across the coffee table as was her birth certificate and the note from her mother. She glanced at them, then at him, but he was only looking at her. "Just wanted to invite you over tonight," he said apologetically. "Didn't mean to freak you out."

"Oh." She didn't know what to say. She was working to get her pulse under control.

Then his gaze swept over the photos and he focused on one where an angry-looking man was stalking toward the cameraman, his hand up as if he were about to rip the offending camera away. The same man was in several other photos with Liv's mother, but he was always turning away, frowning, as if he didn't want his picture taken.

"Who's that?" he asked.

"I don't know," Liv said stiffly.

"Looks really pissed. This an old photo?"

The color had leached out of the print and the women's permed hair and over-the-shoulder tops and black stretch pants, straight out of *Flashdance*, spoke volumes about the date of the picture. "Yeah."

"Huh." He turned back to her. "So . . . Jo and me . . . we're just havin' some drinks and pizza. We don't get goin' till late. That work for you?"

"Thanks, but I've already made some plans." It wasn't exactly a lie. She'd determined over the course of the morning that she was going to show her brother the contents of the package. Hague had his issues, but he was strangely insightful as well.

He'd only been a baby when their mother died, but

maybe there was something buried in his psyche that could offer some explanation. "Another time, maybe? I've gotta run. I'm on my lunch break."

"If you change your mind, just stop by," he said.

"I'll do that." She went back to the office for the rest of the afternoon, wondering how her brother would react.

The apartment where Liv's brother, Hague, lived was on the third/top floor of an older, industrial building on the east side of the Willamette River that had been converted into loftlike units during the '60s. Those lofts had subsequently grown tired and in need of maintenance over the intervening years, but the place still had a spectacular view toward Portland's city center, its westside windows looking back over the river. Hague's unit was in the northwest corner and would have commanded an amazing slice of Portland skyline had he ever opened his blinds.

Liv parked her blue Accord a block and a half from Hague's building, the closest spot she could find. She hurried toward his apartment, the package tucked beneath her coat, feeling unseen eyes following her, though there were probably none. It was more likely her own paranoia, always on the prowl. She usually could hold it at bay, but there were times when it simply took over and she was powerless to do anything but feel its paralyzing grip.

She wished fervently, like she always did, that she could change the past, but it was impossible. She'd lost her mother and huge parts of her life—days, weeks, months, years—and there was no getting them back. She could still remember the policeman's probing questions after she'd woken from her trauma-induced coma. She was in a hospital with its bad smells and gray walls.

* * *

"*Did you see anything when you were in the kitchen?*" he'd demanded. She didn't know he was a policeman at first. He didn't have the clothes of a policeman.

"*I saw Mama.*" She forced the words out. Her lips quivered uncontrollably.

"*Anything else? Something?*" He threw an impatient look toward the woman who'd come with him. A social worker of some kind, she knew now, but she hadn't understood at the time.

Livvie's quivering lips were replaced by out-and-out sobs.

"*Useless,*" he muttered.

"*She's just a child,*" the woman responded tautly.

He turned back to Livvie. "*The back door was open. Did you notice that?*"

She nodded jerkily.

"*Did you walk outside? Look outside?*"

"*NOOOOOOOO!*"

"*Calm down,*" he told her. "*Was there anyone— anyone—around?*"

"*H-Hague was in his bed,*" she stuttered, plucking at the covers. "*He—he started crying. . . .*"

"*Any* adults!" His mouth was smashed together like he was holding back something mean to say.

She felt the tears rain down and the woman walked over to her, patted her hand, glared at the man and said, "*Let the poor child be!*"

"*Maybe her mother killed herself because she knew something about those dead women out in the field behind her house.*"

"*Shhhh.*" The woman's mouth was a flat line, too, but

*Livvie was glad to see it, understanding that it was for him,
not her.*

*"Or, maybe somebody thought she knew something and
decided to take care of her himself?"*

*The woman marched right over to him and said in a
low voice, "This child found her mother! It was suicide,
and it was tragic, and she's been terribly traumatized. Try
to remember that."*

*He gave her a mean, mean look, and said, "I'm trying to
catch a killer. You should try and remember that."*

With the hindsight of age Liv now realized the man had
been a plainclothes policeman with the small Rock
Springs police force and completely out of his realm
working with children. But that didn't excuse him. And he
hadn't given up after that first interview. Oh, no. He'd
come back to the house as soon as she'd gotten out of the
hospital. By that time she and Hague had a neighbor
woman taking care of them but Liv would not go into the
kitchen. She was in the den when the officer came to interview her, and this time she was on her own with him . . .
and the panic started to rise.

He tried a little harder, but Liv had lost trust completely.

*"Try to think back to the night your mom died," he told
her, smiling at her through his teeth. She recognized that he
was trying to be kind, but his smile just creeped her out all
the more.*

"Okay," she said in a small voice.

"Don't think about your mom. Think about the kitchen."

*Panic swelled. She saw the table and the sink and the
window. "It was really dark. The outside was coming in,"
she said.*

"Yes. The back door was open," the officer said, nodding. "Do you know who went out the door?"

"My dad?"

"You think your dad went through the door?"

"Mama was holding her face."

"Your dad told me they had a fight. Do you know what the fight was about?"

That made Livvie think hard, but she shook her head.

"Have they fought before?"

"Yeah . . . Mama hit him once."

"Your mama hit your dad?"

"I think he hit her, too," Livvie said solemnly. "That's why she was holding her face." Then, remembering Mama, she started shaking and hiccupping.

"Now, be a big girl and stop crying. I need your help. Your mama needs your help."

"Mama's dead. Mama's dead!!!"

"You can help her."

"You're lying! Mama's dead!" Livvie wailed and clapped her hands over her ears and the policeman left the den, said something mean to the neighbor lady and slammed the front door.

After that the police gave up trying to interview her, though the social worker questioned Livvie further about her parents' relationship, which created havoc for her father and was probably partially to blame for their chilly relationship ever since. The police questioned Albert Dugan thoroughly, and he'd been furious with Liv for telling tales. Still, he admitted that he and Deborah's relationship had been tempestuous. He might have slapped her . . . once . . . or twice . . . but she'd hit him, too. He admitted to slapping her the night of her death before he'd stalked out the back door.

Deborah had bitten him and he'd struck without thinking.
But he was so sorry. So, so sorry.

It was also why Mama had said, "I'm done," Liv was
pretty sure.

Even so, to this day Liv wasn't sure what the truth had
been between her parents. Her father swore they'd loved
each other . . . well, at least he'd loved her . . . but then she'd
taken her own life and there had to be a deep-seated reason
for that, and he just couldn't understand it. He'd never
agreed that Deborah had committed suicide. Wouldn't talk
about it. Within the year after her death he married Lorinda,
and the whole family moved from the house with too many
memories to another one across town. Employed by the
forestry department, Albert pushed his old life behind him,
and made a new one. Liv understood he was as haunted by
the events of that night as she was, maybe in a different way,
but in one just as powerful. Deborah's death had affected
and shaped his life from that day forward.

As it had Hague's . . .

Now Liv climbed in the rattling elevator with the accor-
dion door, slamming the handle shut, watching the floors
pass as she headed for the third story. She let herself onto
the hallway with its scarred wooden surfaces and scents of
floor wax and dust and overcooked vegetables, and walked
quickly to Hague's door.

After their mother's death, the policeman had interviewed
Hague, too, for all the good it did. Hague had babbled about
"that man." The authorities had looked around for help but
no one seemed to know what he was talking about. Liv
asked him later, when they were alone, and he squirreled
under the blankets of his bed and said, "Zombie man. Kill
you. Kill you!" And he was crying and laughing and crying
some more.

He'd scared the living daylights out of Liv, who ran to

her own room, hiding beneath her covers. Later Hague said Mama had a friend. "A friend!" he'd yelled at the authorities. "Mama's friend!"

They, in turn, labeled "the friend" Deborah Dugan's Mystery Man.

Liv never mentioned Hague's zombie man comment to the police, nor that he'd also said *kill you* in the same reference, like he'd said when he'd been sitting in his high chair, if that's what he'd said that day; she'd never been completely sure. And she didn't know then that his words were the first inkling of the behavioral changes that would send Hague down, down, down in a descending spiral that would last until his life to date.

"Hello, Olivia."

Della Larson, Hague's companion, stood in the open doorway, answering Liv's knock. She leaned her head back and crossed her arms, assessing Liv suspiciously; behind her the place looked like a dark hole. Hague didn't like lights, or fresh air, or anything remotely *different.* Unless, of course, he chose to do an about-face himself, which happened occasionally.

Della was older than Hague by about a decade and was a nurse-cum-attendant-cum-friend and maybe lover. She'd been with Hague for most of his adult life, ever since his release from Grandview Hospital, the mental institution for teens where he'd been sent briefly while Liz was at Hathaway House. Even though Liv had been adopted by the Dugans—a fact the birth certificate she'd just received spelled out clearly—and wasn't related to Hague by blood, it sure seemed like mental illness relentlessly plagued their family. Hague was a genius with a 160 IQ but it didn't mean he knew how to live in this world. *Maladaptive* was the word often used to describe his behavior. On that, Liv was way ahead of him, though her problems had been diagnosed as derived from mental trauma, not from a mind that moved in ways the rest of the so-called normal humans couldn't understand. As the German philosopher Arthur Schopenhauer once said—as quoted by Della more often than Liv cared to count—"Talent hits a target no one else can hit; Genius hits a target no one else can see."

That and a dollar would buy you a newspaper. Maybe.

Della's white-blond hair was scraped into a bun at her nape and her icy blue eyes raked over Liv as if she were someone she'd never seen before. It irked Liv, but then she knew it really was a reflection of the suspicions her own brother held inside himself as well.

"You didn't call ahead," Della said.

"Hi, Della," Liv said. "The last time I called the line was disconnected."

"It's been reconnected for over a month."

"Under whose name?"

She hesitated briefly. "Mine."

"No matter what you may think of me, I'm no mind reader," Liv said. "I'll leave that to Hague."

Her nose twitching in annoyance, Della stepped aside and Liv was allowed into the dim recesses of her brother's den. The place smelled like bleach and lemon and everything clean, which was a relief given the fact Liv's eyes were adjusting to a whole lot of clutter. Hague might be a hoarder of sorts, but everything had to be squeaky clean, per his decree and by Della's hand.

"He's in his room," Della said, leading the way to the northwest corner of the apartment. She knocked on the door panels and when he barked, "What?" she said, "Your sister is here."

A long silence ensued, before Hague bellowed, "Well, let her in!" as if Della's interference were just that, interference. She ignored his tone and opened the door and when Liv crossed the threshold, Della was right on her heels.

Hague sat in a brown leather chair that nearly swallowed him whole. He was lithe to the point of wispiness but he was tall like Albert—his biological father and Liv's adoptive one. He looked a lot like Deborah, too, Liv realized, seeing those hauntingly large blue eyes of her dreams stare at her from Hague's thin face.

"What do you want?" he asked gruffly.

"Nice way to greet me. I came to find out if you know anything about this." She held up the manila envelope and his eyes followed it, a frown creasing his brow.

"What is it?"

"Guess that answers my question."

"What is it?" he demanded more loudly and Della moved to his side and laid a comforting hand on his shoulders.

"It's from the law firm of Crenshaw and Crenshaw. Ever heard of them?" Liv asked.

"No."

"They were directed to send me this package when I turned twenty-five."

"Last Friday. Happy birthday."

She smiled faintly. Hague didn't live by the world's time line though he understood it perfectly. "It had pictures of our mother and some other people inside." She handed him the series of pictures she'd pored over throughout the last two days. This morning she'd decided to go visit her brother directly after work and see what he made of the package's contents. "And it has my real birth certificate and several other papers."

"Who directed the lawyers?"

"Our mother."

His eyes caught hers. "What?"

Liv explained how the lawyers had gotten hold of her and sent the package. "She—Mama—wanted me to have this, but I don't really understand why. My birth certificate, okay, and personal stuff, but who are these people?"

"That's our father."

In one of the pictures Albert was standing beside Deborah in a grassy field, possibly the one behind their old house.

"But who's this?" she asked, pointing to the man trying to grab for the camera.

Hague was ignoring her as he selected a piece of paper, holding it up between his thumb and index finger, away from his body, as if it might bite him. He glanced at her expectantly.

Liv had read the missive, knew what it was. She said carefully, "It's a note from Mama to me."

Hague was utterly silent. Liv gazed at him and her heart squeezed. Framed by his scruffy hair and beard were a pair of glittering blue eyes and a handsome face that he would never—could never, apparently—let the world see.

"Read it," Liv urged him gently.

Hague brought the note closer and stared at it hard for several seconds, then he said in a monotone: "*Livvie, my sweet girl, if you're reading this then everything I've feared has come to be, and I'm not around to tell you these things for myself. You know you were adopted. Your biological parents are listed on your birth certificate. I've enclosed some snapshots for you to have of me. Know I love you. . . . Mom.*" He peered at the photographs, then up at her quizzically. "Why these pictures? They're not even that good of her. I have better ones."

"Do you remember anything about those other people?" Liv asked.

Hague glanced at the photographs again, zeroing in on the one Liv had pointed to with the angry man. His shoulders tucked in and his head tilted back, his gaze glued to the photo.

"There he is again," he said in a strained voice.

Liv looked at the man in the picture. "*Again?* You've seen him before?"

"Zombie," he said.

Kill you . . . Kill you!

Liv's head spun a bit. "This is the zombie man?" she demanded, pointing to the picture.

"They keep their hands in their pockets and wear rigor smiles." His eyes rolled away, stretching wide as he looked into some distant horror only he could see.

"Hague," Della said uncertainly.

"He follows me," Hague said in a harsh whisper. "If I look, he's always there. Out of the corner of your eye. Just there . . . almost . . . there . . . *there!*" He jerked violently and Liv and Della both jumped, too.

"Hague," Liv said sharply, recognizing the signs that he was leaving reality. She hoped to keep him with her. "Hague!"

But his eyes closed and he drifted away. Into one of his fugue states.

Gone . . .

Chapter 3

"You put him in a trance!" Della snapped.

Liv looked at Hague with resignation. She wanted to call him back, but it was too late. It was futile to try to rouse him when he disappeared into his own world.

She slid a glance at the photograph. *Zombie man* . . .

Della fussed over Hague, tilting his head back in the La-Z-Boy recliner he practically lived in. Hague didn't trust computers or telephones, especially cell phones; he was more of a Luddite than Liv. He was absolutely certain malicious groups bent on evil and destruction were tracking him. He spent hour upon hour calculating figures on lined yellow paper with an ink pen. Della worked part-time as a care assistant at a nearby assisted living/nursing home facility. Hague, who'd never been able to keep a job, received government assistance, and she thought maybe her father subsidized them as well. However, that would only be if Lorinda, the evil stepmother, didn't know about the tap on Albert's finances, which was questionable.

As if she could read Liv's thoughts, Della said, "Albert's coming by."

Liv reached for the pictures, note and birth certificate and she saw that her hands were trembling. She felt guilty enough for sending Hague into the trance; Della's accusation hadn't been necessary. "He is?" Liv couldn't remember the last time she'd seen her father.

"*He* called," she said with a certain satisfaction.

Ignoring that, Liv asked, "Does he see Hague often?" Since Lorinda had entered their lives, both Liv and Hague's relationship with Albert had suffered, and in Liv's case it had become basically nonexistent.

"Now and again. He's not good with Hague, either."

"When is he showing up?"

Della shot a glance at the old grandfather's clock, which stood against the living room's far wall. It was the kind that was wound with a key. Hague liked to limit their amount of electricity use in any way he could, and it wasn't that he was trying to lessen his carbon footprint, he just wanted to make himself smaller and more indistinct in the world, and therefore less traceable. The less information the "government" or "powers that be" had on him, the better.

"Anytime, now," Della answered.

"I've got to be going," she said.

"Oh, no, stay. Maybe Hague'll come out of it. . . ."

Liv arched a brow. She and Della both knew Hague's fugue states were unpredictable, but it was rare that he snapped back within a few minutes.

Della added, "We could go down to Rosa's Cantina and talk. Hague has his own table there."

Rosa's Cantina was on the street level of the apartment building. Liv had seen its bright green and yellow neon sign when she'd entered. She knew Hague went to Rosa's; his only habitual place of business, and she suspected his "own table" was the establishment's way of appeasing him, and wondered what would happen were someone already at his table should Hague arrive. An ugly scene, no doubt.

In any case, he wasn't going to make it there tonight, and

Liv wasn't interested in going there with Della. "Is Albert bringing Lorinda?" she asked.

"I'm sure." Della made a face. Their mutual dislike of Lorinda was the only thing Liv and Della totally agreed upon. "Can I get you a cup of tea?" Now she was accommodating with a capital A. "Have you had dinner? No, you're just off work. I could make up some sandwiches. Tuna. Hague doesn't really like meat, as you know. Or, grilled cheese?"

"I appreciate it, but I really should get going."

"I'm sorry I was a bitch," Della said suddenly. "But with Hague like that . . ." She glanced toward him where he sat with head lying back, his eyes now open and staring sightlessly toward the ceiling, "I don't really know what I'll say to Albert. We don't have a lot in common except your brother."

Liv didn't have a lot in common with her father, either. "I've got groceries in the car," she lied.

"Tell me more about this package. I can talk about it with Hague and it'll be easier coming from me. I know him."

"He already read the note and saw the photos. There's not a lot more to tell." Liv glanced at her brother. "He was a toddler when our mother committed suicide."

"I want—"

But what she wanted was interrupted by the sound of the doorbell, a deep *dong,* like a ship's tolling bell.

"He's here," Della said. She lifted her chin as Liv girded her loins.

Della walked briskly to the door and threw it open. Liv followed after her, a few paces back, and when she looked past Della she saw her father and Lorinda appear inside the open freight elevator as it bumped to a stop on their floor. Albert slid back the metal bar, stepped into the hallway in front of his wife, then looked up to see them.

"Liv," he said, stopping short in surprise.

Lorinda quickly moved out of the elevator and half stood in front of him, as if she were protecting him. "Olivia?"

"Hi," Liv greeted them.

"What are you doing here?" Lorinda demanded and Liv inwardly sighed.

Lorinda Dugan hadn't changed much in the almost twenty years since she'd married Liv's father. Same dyed black hair that looked even more unnatural than it had then, same line between her brows, same flat mouth and lack of expression. If Albert had been in the market for a shrew, well, he'd hit the jackpot. Liv didn't like her then, and she didn't like her now, and the feeling was mutual. Della might be a pain, but she was good for Hague. What part Lorinda played for Liv's father was a mystery that had no reasonable answer, but then, since the terrible night of Deborah's death, Liv hadn't been all that comfortable with her father either.

"I was just visiting Hague," Liv answered.

Lorinda sniffed. "Yes," she said, as if Liv merely stating the obvious were one more horrendous fault.

"How is he?" Albert asked, his jaw tight.

Della said, "He's in one of his states. Come in."

"He was last time, too," Lorinda answered with a sniff, her dark gaze snapping between Della and Liv.

"Stress brings them on," Della responded as she and Liv both stepped back, making way for Lorinda and Albert to enter the small apartment. Having them crowd into the room as well only made the place seem darker, the air denser. Liv felt anxiety crawl around under her skin and surreptitiously glanced toward the grandfather's clock, wondering how many minutes of them she would be able to stand before she needed to bolt.

"What's that?" Albert asked, his gaze on the envelope in Liv's hands.

Liv couldn't think of how to respond, but Della had no

such qualms. "Pictures of Deborah and some documents," she said. "A note from her."

Albert blinked. "*What?*"

"Oh, my God," Lorinda murmured, recoiling as if the package could somehow jump up and bite her.

"It's nothing bad," Liv assured them. "Just some snapshots of my mother with some friends."

"Show him," Della said.

"Her friends?" Albert asked.

Lorinda turned her face away and stared over their heads, lips pressed together as if she had a lot to say but was taking herself out of the situation.

Feeling like she was leaving herself bare, Liv reluctantly reopened the package and handed the envelope to Albert. "The package came to me at work," she said, then explained about Crenshaw and Crenshaw and how they'd found her and sent the package to her.

Albert's fingers were faintly shaking as he pulled out the pictures and examined them carefully. "Who are these people?" he asked.

"I thought maybe you'd know," Liv said.

He shook his head. "She . . . your mother . . . had a secret life."

Lorinda had deigned to look back and was now gazing raptly at the photos. She seemed to keep her own counsel with an effort. "There's one of you with her," she finally said tightly to her husband, but Albert merely grunted at that.

Liv glanced toward Hague, whose eyes were still open. He remained utterly still and she didn't know if he was aware of them or not. To her father, she said, "Do you think . . . is it possible . . . that she didn't commit suicide? That maybe these people know something about what happened, and they—".

"We've been over this," he cut her off. "Deborah was sick and unhappy."

"Who told the lawyers to send you the package?" Lorinda demanded.

"Well, my mother, of course. . . ." Liv had thought the answer was self-evident, but now saw both her father and Lorinda react with shock. "She set it up before she died."

"It's upsetting," Della said, shooting a worried glance toward Hague. They all followed her gaze, but Hague didn't respond in any way.

"You brought this to *Hague?*" Lorinda asked, as if Liv had lost the little bit of mind she still possessed.

"Goddammit, Liv," Albert muttered, his face red.

"I thought Hague might remember something," Liv defended herself. "Remember what he said about the zombie man?"

"No," her father stated flatly.

"How *old* was he at the time of Deborah's death?" Lorinda reminded them. "One? Two?"

"You shouldn't have brought this to him," Albert chastised her.

"Should I have brought it to you first?" Liv asked tightly. "There were other women killed about the same time that Mom died, remember? Strangled. One of them in the field practically behind our old house. That's a fact."

"That woman was a prostitute," Albert bit out.

"So?"

Lorinda said, as if Liv were dense, "Your mother committed suicide. *That's* a fact. You shouldn't be digging into this!"

"This came to me for a reason," Liv said, holding onto her temper with an effort. "I'm sorry that I want to look into it. I'm sorry that I still want answers. I see her, you know. In my nightmares. Hanging there. Sometimes she even talks to me." They both looked at her sharply. "I've always found it hard to believe that she would kill herself. Especially that way, with me in the other room. She wrote me a note and put it inside."

"A note." Albert, holding the photos, reached inside the package again to pull it out, but his wife snatched the package from his hands before he could. She would have grabbed the photos back too but he jerked them out of her reach.

"Stop all this," Lorinda snapped, shoving the package back into Liv's hands. Upset, she told her husband, "Give Olivia the photos."

Liv put out a hand and Albert, very reluctantly, handed the pictures back to her. "I think my mother was afraid," Liv said, tucking everything back inside the manila envelope and closing the clasp. "Those women's deaths scared her." She hesitated, thinking over whether she should reveal her thoughts to them or not. "Most of the victims were strangled . . . and hanging's a form of the same thing."

"Some maniac strangled them with nylons. That's how he killed them, not by a noose," Lorinda said. "And they were all whores, anyway."

"Not all of them," Liv said levelly. Lorinda's prejudices never failed to rile her.

"It doesn't matter, does it?" Della whispered harshly. "If Hague wakes up, I don't want him to hear this."

"All I'm saying is she was scared of something, and she sent me this package for a reason," Liv said.

Albert stalked over to Hague and looked down at his son, then he turned to gaze hard at Liv and stated flatly, "You don't really think she was scared of the strangler."

Liv frowned. "What do you mean?"

"You're still blaming me," he spat out. "Just like you told the police."

"I don't—"

"Deborah and I had that fight," he interrupted angrily.

"That's all. It got physical. I told the police all about it after you turned them on me."

"Turned them on you," Liv repeated. "I was six years old!"

"Those bastards ran me through the wringer, all right," he growled. "Didn't matter that Deborah gave as good as she got."

"You're making this about you, and it's not. It's about my mother. I think she was scared of the strangler, and she sent me this because she was . . . I don't know . . . scared for me, too."

He lifted both arms and tossed them down as if he were completely through with Liv and her issues.

"Can't we ever put this to bed?" Lorinda asked tiredly.

"She hanged herself," Albert said. "That's all there was."

"You shouldn't have brought this here," Lorinda declared, waving a hand toward the package.

"I didn't expect to see the two of you," Liv reminded them. "Like I said, I thought maybe Hague would remember something."

"It's just so disrespectful of you to bring all this up again!" Lorinda declared.

Liv counted silently to ten. *All this* was her father and mother's physical fight. Her parents had been furious with each other that night and Albert had left in a silent rage, banging out the back door. He told the police he didn't remember leaving it open, but it hadn't been locked, either, so the consensus was the door stayed open after he left. Liv half-believed someone had come back inside after she'd been banished to the den, and *that* someone had then killed her mother and staged the suicide. And Liv still thought it was a good bet the killer was the same one who'd left several women's bodies in the rocky foothills of the Cascades twenty years earlier, too. That's where she wanted to start looking for her mother's killer. That's where this trail led.

She hadn't realized she was planning to reopen her own

past, but since the package had arrived, the thought had been coalescing in her mind. That's what she wanted to do. And with the new information her mother had sent, she was going to find out what really happened to her. Good, bad or ugly. Suicide, or something more malevolent . . .

She said as much to Lorinda, Della, her father and Hague, if he understood, and they looked at her as if she'd truly lost her mind.

"You're seriously going to investigate this?" Della asked in undisguised disbelief.

"My mother sent the items in this package to me for a reason," Liv said. "I've always wondered. Maybe it's time I got some answers. Investigators are opening up cold cases and catching killers all the time. Why not this one?"

"But it was a suicide. There was no crime!" Lorinda declared. "Why can't you let this go and give your father and brother some peace!"

"I don't think it was suicide," Liv argued. "Maybe I'm wrong, but I have to know. I thought Hague might be interested in helping. We've talked about those unsolved strangulations, and whether Mama was one of them. Hague's the one who first questioned whether she committed suicide. You remember what he said when he was little? About Mama having a friend?"

"Deborah Dugan's Mystery Man," Albert said darkly.

She pulled out the picture of the angry man again, the one where he was stalking toward the camera. "Hague said, 'There he is again,' when I showed him this."

"He said 'zombie,'" Della reminded her. "And he said the man followed him."

"Hague says a lot of wacko stuff. None of it means a damn thing," Albert growled.

Liv didn't want to go into the whole "zombie" thing. "Do you think this guy could be the 'Mystery Man'?"

Albert's eyes slid toward the photo again. "I don't know him."

"Did you put Hague into this state with these photos?" Lorinda asked Liv, throwing a thumb in Hague's direction.

"I wanted to talk to him about the contents of the package," Liv said, defending herself.

Lorinda lifted an "I told you so" eyebrow to Albert, who ignored her.

"None of you seem to care about Hague at all," Della said angrily. "None of you! Maybe it's time you all left. When Hague's like this, it's pointless to try and talk to him anyway." She bustled them toward the door and Lorinda, Albert and Liv reluctantly moved into the hallway.

"Tell him I'll come by again soon," Liv said, just before Della slammed the door shut behind them. Not wanting to deal with Lorinda and Albert any longer than she had to, Liv headed quickly toward the lift. She wanted to get into it before her father and Lorinda could join her. She didn't think she could stand being squeezed into that small space with both of them there as well.

As Liv was lowering the elevator bar Albert and Lorinda moved slowly her way. If they wanted to climb in with her, they sure didn't act like it, and they let her take the rattling cage down on her own, which was a relief. When Liv reached the street floor, a young mother with three children traded places with her, and by the time Liv got past them, out of the building and into the street, she gulped down fresh air as if she'd been strangling.

She was nearly run over by a guy racing down the sidewalk in a rush. He jostled her and she grabbed the envelope closer to her chest as he put out his hands to steady her.

"Sorry. Are you all right?" The dark-haired stranger peered into Liv's face. "You look familiar?"

Liv pulled herself together and tried to sidle away.

"Can I buy you a beer to make up for it? Please?" He

inclined his head toward Rosa's Cantina with its glowing green and yellow script. "I promise I'm not a homicidal maniac. I own the place and I'm late. Come on in."

"You own the place?" Liv asked cautiously. She'd been planning how to blow him off, but maybe he wasn't trying to hit on her.

"With my better half." He moved toward the bar. "I am really, really late."

"Do you know my brother? Hague Dugan? I think he comes here . . . sometimes?"

"Hague . . . ah . . ." One hand on the door, he peered at her through the gathering gloom from drifting fog off the river.

Liv could feel the censure, and she could well imagine why. "I'm not like him . . . much . . ."

He smiled faintly and inclined his head as he opened the door and happy music and loud voices spilled from inside.

Liv followed after him, but he strode quickly forward and was already pulling up a section of counter of the brightly tiled bar as she entered and looked around for a seat. He swooped up a woman whose dark hair was pulled back into a bun and gave her a big, sloppy kiss. She grinned, then snapped a towel at him and pretended to be angry.

Liv took a seat at the bar. "La Cucaracha," or "The Cockroach," was playing from speakers hidden by a raft of piñatas hung from the ceiling. Twice a year the cantina had an afternoon party for all the neighborhood kids who slammed away at the piñatas until all the candy spilled across the floor. The owners then replaced them for the next bout of pounding. Once a night, Rosa's Cantina also played the Marty Robbins classic, "El Paso," from which they'd taken the name for their bar. At least that's what Hague had told Liv, but now she heard the owner calling his wife Rosa, so it looked like there were other reasons as well.

From her viewpoint Liv could see through the front

window to the stretch of sidewalk outside the cantina's doors. As she settled herself onto a stool, she saw her father and Lorinda pass by. Albert glanced in but Liv didn't think he noticed her on the far side of the rectangular, center bar as she was squeezed up tightly against the young couple on the bar stools to her right.

The bar owner was pulling glasses down from the overhead rack. "What'll you have?" he asked Liv. "My treat." He pushed two empty margarita glasses toward Rosa. "I'm Jimmy."

"And I'm Rosa. His better half," the woman said, grabbing up the glasses. "What'd he do? If he's buying you a drink, he did something."

"He can buy me a drink," the man next to Liv said. "And Nicole here, too."

Nicole looked up from under her date's arm and said, "El Grande Margarita."

"I nearly ran her down," Jimmy said to Rosa. "She deserves a margarita." He gave Nicole a mock glare through narrowed eyes. "You don't."

"Yes, I do!" she declared. "I'm your best customer!"

"You're not even close," Jimmy snorted.

Her date said, "She's close. Maybe she's not first, but she's close."

Jimmy gave them both a look that said, "Bullshit," but he relented, and Rosa whipped up two margaritas and slid one to Liv and one to Nicole.

Liv was pretty sure she abhorred tequila, but the drink was free and she was desperate to shake off the bad feelings meeting with her family had brought on.

Rosa slid a small bowl of chips and salsa Liv's way, and Jimmy revealed that she was Hague's sister. "The Hague?" Rosa asked.

It was a nickname that had followed her brother throughout his life, a reference to the city that is the governmental center of the Netherlands. It seemed that anyone who got to know Hague, even marginally, called him The Hague.

"If someone's in *his* seat, he gets worse than upset," Rosa said. She jerked her head toward the northeast corner of the bar, where a man and woman were staring at each other and holding hands, he with his back to the booth, she across from him in a chair. "That's Hague's place, and he makes sure everyone knows it."

"It's not that bad," Jimmy said.

"Hah," Rosa snorted. "We're just lucky The Hague's not here tonight, otherwise those two lovebirds would have to move. He's not coming, is he?" She looked a bit stricken.

"No," Liv said. She felt like apologizing for her brother, but knew it would do no good. Hague was Hague. He couldn't be changed.

"He mutters to himself, and then shouts, then waves his arm, then goes into a trance," Nicole said.

"He swears at people that pass by," her boyfriend offered up.

"Stop it. Stop it." Jimmy waved a towel at them. "You'll make her want to leave." To Liv, he said, "Don't listen to them. The Hague's just part of the colorful group that makes up our clientele."

Liv nodded. She couldn't think of anything to say, but when they clearly expected her to add something, she asked, "Does he come in here alone?"

"That nurse is with him sometimes. Or, whatever the hell she is," the boyfriend said.

"Caretaker," Nicole clarified.

Rosa shook her head. "I think he likes to get away from her. He mostly comes when she's out, but then she always comes looking for him."

This little insight into her brother's life gave Liv some hope. At least Hague seemed to want to escape Della's smothering sometimes, maybe even often. In her mind, she couldn't see how that was a bad thing.

Forty-five minutes later, and after refusing another margarita several times, she thanked them all and headed out. Jimmy and Rosa urged her to come by again soon, and Liv promised to stop in the next time she visited her brother.

As soon as she was outside the establishment again, however, she felt her skin prickle as age-old fears crept up again. Talking about her mother with Hague first, and then her father, had jarred something loose that wouldn't go back into its place. With one eye looking over her shoulder, she hurried to her Accord and jumped inside, driving a circuitous route home, wondering if her paranoia was overtaking her good sense once and for all.

When she got back to her apartment Jo and Travis . . . Trask . . . whatever . . . were out on the balcony and they invited her to have a drink with them. She almost said no, but decided she needed to foster neighborly relations since Trevor, or whoever he was, had seen the contents of the package. It just felt rude not to.

"Come on in," Jo said, and as Liv entered, she added, "Get her a drink, Trask! We're having gin and tonics, or just gin, as in martinis. Whaddya want?"

The smell of cannabis was thick in the air, but neither one of them was smoking a joint at the moment. "Gin and tonic," Liv said.

"Comin' right up," Trask said, dropping ice into a glass, splashing in a healthy dose of gin, then topping it off with tonic. He added a lime wedge and handed it to Liv, who was committing his name to memory.

Jo was half-drunk and dancing to some rock music with a lot of bass that Liv thought might bring the downstairs neighbors up and pounding on their door. As if reading her mind, Trask turned down the volume.

"How ya doin'?" he asked.

"I'm okay. How about you?"

"Can't complain," he said, nodding as if they were involved in a truly meaningful conversation.

"Doesn't anybody wanna dance?" Jo asked.

Liv shook her head and sipped her drink, which was way too strong and made her feel like her bones were melting. She stopped about halfway through, knowing she had work in the morning.

Still, she stayed at their place until past midnight. Trask gallantly offered to accompany her the ten feet from their door to hers. She tried to decline but he insisted, saying, "Trask Martin always walks a lady home." At her door, he looked over his shoulder, focused a bit fuzzily on the parking lot below, and said, "Hey, y'know, I saw this dude outside your door a couple weeks ago. He was just standin' there and I asked him, 'What's up, dude,' and he just turned and left."

A cold jolt of fear ran through Liv. "*My* apartment?"

"Uh huh. Acted kinda weird, I thought."

"What did he look like?"

Trask screwed up his face like he was really thinking hard. "Wore a hoodie and jeans. Didn't turn my way. Headed down the stairs to the lot and went over there. . . ." He gestured to the far end of the parking lot which was lined by thick Douglas firs. "Gray truck. GMC. 2005. I know 'cuz I had one just like it once," he said wistfully. "Now, I've got a piece of shit with a bad alternator. One of these days I'll get it fixed."

"How old was the guy?" Liv asked. She was coiled and tense.

"Don't know. Young? With that hoodie, I kinda thought . . . Hard to tell, though."

"And he was at my door? Just mine?"

"Maybe he was sellin' somethin'. You just seemed kinda freaked out earlier, so I thought maybe you should know."

"Thanks," she said with an effort.

"No problemo." He headed back toward his door and Liv hurried inside hers and slammed the dead bolt shut. The apartments didn't come with dead bolts as an option; she'd had hers installed when she'd moved in. Now, she wondered if she should move out.

Was someone looking for her?

There was no reason for someone to be looking for her. No reason at all. That was her problem . . . this deep-seated fear that could never be fully quashed. She just couldn't help feeling like she was being watched. Like someone wanted something from her.

She rechecked the locks on her door, then made sure all the windows were closed, then rechecked everything again before heading to her closet, pulling out the shoe box on the floor, the one she'd buried beneath a pile of shoes that she never wore. Placing the shoe box on the bed, she lifted the lid, then gently reached inside for her handgun. She hadn't purchased it; Della had confiscated it from Hague years before when he'd been suicidal and had found it at some gun show. Back then, Della thought Liv was an ally, that they were both interested in Hague's well-being, but she'd slowly lost faith in Liv over the years. Now, Della only warmed to her when they had a common enemy like Lorinda. Liv had gotten the .38 out of the deal, however. Sometimes she asked herself why she had a gun. She knew how to load and unload it, but she wasn't proficient in its use. Still, it made her feel secure, just knowing it was at hand, and tonight she put the .38 under her pillow and fell asleep wondering if she should load it, never wakening to do so.

Chapter 4

Friday morning Liv was late for work and caught the stink-eye from Paul de Fore as she hurried through Zuma Software's front door. She'd almost parked her car in front of the building instead of the employee lot on the west side, just to save time, but she sensed that might come back to bite her somehow, so she backed into her usual spot and walked around to the front, taking the heat from Paul as she strode quickly to her desk. Paul had no serious authority to admonish her, but that never stopped him. She listened with half an ear for his footsteps, expecting him to follow after her to give her a good tongue-thrashing, but he got tied up at the door when Jessica Maltona slipped outside for a coffee on an unscheduled break.

"Hey," he yelled after her. "You can't leave without authority! Mr. Upjohn will hear about this!"

Definitely a tool.

Liv ducked down below the half-wall of her cubicle, switching on her computer and locking her purse in the drawer as she settled into her rolling chair and wheeled up to the desk. She laid down the package from her mother, eyeing the manila envelope thoughtfully as she waited for the machine to click and burp its way to "ready."

It was the envelope that had made her late, or more accurately, the contents within. She'd pored over the pieces again this morning while she was drinking her coffee and the time had swept by so quickly that she'd looked up at the clock and gasped, and then raced to the office.

Was the stalking, angry man in the photo Hague's zombie, and therefore the person the police had dubbed Deborah Dugan's Mystery Man? Was he her mother's friend? Her lover, maybe? Why was he in the photos? And what was its meaning to Liv?

What did she know about her mother, really, she asked herself now. Only vague childhood memories that had been tainted and colored with time.

About lunchtime Aaron came around her partition and rapped his knuckles on her desk while she was on the phone with a supplier missing an invoice. She shook her head at him, and he motioned for her to meet him outside. Nodding, she waved him off, and as soon as she finished her call and hung up, she grabbed her purse from its locked cabinet, got up from her chair, straightened it, threw a glance at the package which she'd now stuck in the slot of the message holder at the side of her desk, then turned—and nearly ran smack into Kurt Upjohn, owner of Zuma Software.

"Hi," Liv said in surprise.

"Are you leaving?" he asked.

Upjohn was a short man with a tight mouth, a smoothly shaved head and one earring. He wasn't all that bad looking, but he was always filled with tension, like a coiled spring, and it invariably made Liv feel uncomfortable.

"Just . . . getting ready for my lunch break." She picked up her mother's package and stuffed it into her purse, deciding she didn't want to leave it at her desk after all, then slung the purse strap over her shoulder.

"Kinda late for lunch." Upjohn frowned. He liked his employees to take their meals at noon and be back at one P.M. sharp, one of his personal quirks that didn't seem to be grounded in anything that made sense.

"I've been running late all day," she admitted.

"Phil said he gave you the financials from last quarter. . . ." He sounded cautious, his brows pulled together.

"Um, no. I don't think so. I haven't seen them." *And why would he give them to me, anyway?* Liv thought. Phillip Berelli was Zuma's internal accountant whereas she was an inputter, not an analyst.

"Okay." He seemed relieved. "Maybe he said something else."

Liv lifted her shoulders and after a moment Upjohn walked off. She'd heard rumors about Zuma, about how they could be in financial trouble, but if they were she didn't know anything about it. She had pieces of the financial mosaic, but getting the whole picture was way above her pay grade.

She'd heard other rumors as well, though. Like how Zuma's war games were so accurate and well thought-out that there was some military connection—the think-tank guys upstairs being secret government employees—and that Zuma Software itself was merely a cover.

Even with her paranoia, Liv didn't buy that one. She'd seen the guys upstairs when they came out of their locked room, walked down the stairs, and passed by her with barely a look as they headed out the front door. Invariably, their conversation made her feel like she was listening to the goings-on inside a thirteen-year-old boy's mind; mostly they talked about other games and popular movies and their eyes darted quick looks at Jessica Maltona's breasts when they thought she wasn't looking. Jessica was the only other woman on the main floor with Liv. Count in Aaron, Paul and Kurt Upjohn, and that was the extent of the business staff, except for Phil, the accountant, whose office was upstairs with the game builders.

Aaron was just stubbing out a cigarette when Liv opened the unlocked exterior door and met him on the side patio. "Man, this place is boring," he said, punctuating his statement with a yawn.

Liv merely nodded. Her mind's eye wouldn't stop going over the papers from inside the package whenever she had a free moment. The birth certificate named her biological parents. She'd never known who they were. Hadn't really cared. But now she wondered if she should make an attempt to meet them . . . like maybe that was important to Deborah? Did that sound right? It was much more likely that her mother had just wanted Liv to have the information in case anything happened to her. . . . Maybe she was toying with the idea of suicide when she'd made up the package? Or, maybe she'd sensed something else . . . something coming toward her . . . something—

"Hey." Aaron snapped his fingers in front of her face. "Come back."

"I was just . . . thinking."

"I could see that. Did you hear what I said?"

She tried to run back the last few minutes, but it was useless.

"I said," Aaron reminded her in a measured tone, "that I think I'd like to meet Tiny and get to know her on a more personal basis."

"Tiny . . . oh, the cat. Yes. Well, about that—"

"You don't have a three-hundred-pound cat."

"Well . . . no." She smiled.

"Figured." His answering smile was faint. "Just thought maybe you and I . . . could do something? Before I'm gone for good." He made a face, as if he'd tasted something bad.

"What does that mean?"

"My father . . ." He looked back inside through the glass door with an unreadable expression. "He and my mom don't get along. At all. Ever. She hates it that I'm here. Says it's too dangerous."

"Dangerous?" Liv repeated.

"Oh, it's all bullshit. She doesn't even mean it. She just mainly wants to irk my father any way she can. And it works, 'cause he starts yelling that he should just fire me to get her off his ass. And she tells him where to stick it, and blah, blah, blah. It just goes on and on. God. They can't stand each other."

"But you're leaving Zuma?"

"I overheard the old man tell her that he was really gonna do it this time. By the end of the week." Aaron shrugged. "Maybe he will, maybe he won't. But if he does, I'll survive. Just wanted to make sure we could stay friends." He peered at her through heavy blond bangs. A scraggly beard darkened his jaw. His clothes looked like they'd come straight from the clothes hamper and his pants rode low enough on his hips to make her wonder exactly when gravity would win and puddle them around his ankles.

She liked Aaron. She really did. But not in the way his eyes said he was hoping for. "We're friends," she said lightly.

"Olivia . . ." he said, disappointed. "Give me something more than that."

"Good friends?" To his crushed look, she added, "Maybe later, we could talk? I'm just on my way to lunch now. I'm late already." She half-turned back to the building.

"Sneak out this way," he invited, opening the gate.

Now, this was definitely against all the rules. "Paul won't like it."

"Paul doesn't have to know."

Liv felt a stirring of rebellion fueled by the encouraging

light in Aaron's eyes. Add to that, she didn't want to turn him down again, for anything. She hesitated a moment, then shrugged her shoulders and said, "All right."

He swung open the gate. "I'm not trying to push you, or anything. I just would like to . . . keep things going between us."

"Okay."

He smiled and swung the gate shut behind her, satisfied.

"But when I come back through the front door, Paul's going to rip me a new one," she said.

"Call me on my cell. I'll sneak you back in."

"I don't have a cell."

"Oh, God, that's right." He shook his shaggy locks. "I'll leave the door propped open."

"Nah, I'll go through the front and just take the heat."

"Check the side door. If it's open, it's open. If it's not, the old man or somebody caught me."

"You don't have to do that."

"Hey, I'm a short timer. I want to."

"Okay, then." Liv waved to him as she headed out. Aaron was a slacker and a truant and a bit of a slug, but at least he amused her. Everybody else on the main floor seemed to have had the humor centers of their brains lobotomized.

She went to a local deli whose chicken salad was to die for and ordered a chicken salad sandwich, Diet Coke and a packet of Miss Vickie's Jalapeño Chips. She sat at a bistro table and watched the passers-by outside the window, her mind flitting back to the packet and Hague and his comments about the zombie man.

If I look he's always there. Out of the corner of your eye . . . there!

Gooseflesh rose on her arms beneath the three-quarter-length sleeves of her V-necked shirt. It was late August and hot, and she could feel her skin break into a sweat.

Since she'd pushed her lunch break till after one, it was

two-twenty by the time she made it back to the building. This time she did park her car in the front, way in the front, so no one saw her car return so late. Then she hurried around to the right edge of the parking lot. She might be able to sneak by as a pedestrian if she kept the parked cars between her and Zuma's main doors and therefore screened herself from Paul's line of vision. As she ducked along, she peeked a time or two through the glass windows of the front atrium but she saw no one. She found her way to the side entrance and saw that the door was firmly shut. Uh-oh. Somebody was onto Aaron.

Sighing, she retraced her steps to the front doors. She had five different excuses to tell Paul, none any good, and decided to just breeze in as if she owned the place and let him rain the litany of her transgressions down on her head. Take the bitter pill and get it over with.

Drawing a breath, she strong-armed the mahogany front door and wondered why Paul wasn't standing at the ready, poised to berate her. As the door swung shut behind her she stepped through the atrium and turned toward Jessica's desk, a question on her lips as the door swung shut behind her, and then she saw the carnage in the office.

Paul de Fore was splayed on the tile floor face down, blood pooling beneath his open mouth from a gunshot wound to the back of his head. She could hear moaning from beyond him. In a dream state she stepped over Paul and went to Jessica's desk, giving a quick look over the top to see the receptionist on the floor behind her chair, curled up in the fetal position, blood blooming around the mounds of her breasts from a wound to the chest, small mewls issuing from her lips.

A roaring started in Liv's ears. She glanced to the partition of her own desk, her blood pounding, a voice screaming loudly. She clapped her hands over her ears to stop it and realized the shrieking voice was coming from her.

She clamped her jaw shut; her lips trembled violently. Heart beating so hard she could see it jumping through her clothes, she cautiously stepped forward, half-expecting the gunman to leap from behind the partition. She was quaking so much she could scarcely stand. From around the corner that led to the executive offices, she saw the outstretched hand of a man wearing a white, long-sleeved shirt: Kurt Upjohn.

Liv staggered toward him, peeking reluctantly around the corner. Upjohn was lying half-in, half-out of his office. Beyond lay Aaron's body. Both of them were riddled with gunshot wounds.

Kill you. Kill you!

Backing away, she threw a glance toward the stairway and the geeks upstairs and Phil. That door was always locked. Shivering as from ague, her brain unable to process, she staggered back to Jessica's desk and hit the main phone line, punching out 911.

"Nine-one-one. What is the nature of your emergency?"

"There's—been a shooting," she said in a stranger's voice. She gave the address, then the receiver clattered from her hand as the operator begged her, "Don't hang up. Don't hang up," and she didn't. She simply let the receiver drop to the ground just like she had in her kitchen a few nights before.

She stood frozen for the space of five rapid heartbeats.

Then with a cry she ran back out the front door, her thoughts pinging around in her head as she considered how close she'd come to being gunned down as well.

It's you they're after. You! Always you, the paranoid voice in her head warned. *Go home. Get your own gun. And RUN.*

"Nine!" Detective George Thompkins bellowed from his swivel chair at the far end of the squad room.

Detective September "Nine" Rafferty, named and nicknamed for the month she was born, jumped as if goosed. She'd been filling out some paperwork but the tone of George's voice drove her instantly to her feet. She was a newly minted detective and so she stood ramrod straight. "Yes?"

"Just talked to D'Annibal. He's on his way in." George cast a glance to the darkened glass cubicle that was their superior's, Lieutenant Aubrey D'Annibal's, office. D'Annibal was on the last hours of his vacation and that left George in charge, a dubious honor for a dubious commander. George liked to squeak his heft in his swivel chair and remain at his desk and that was about it. Now he swiveled around and said, "Jesus Christ. There's been a shooting at Zuma Software. Patrol's on the way. Get over there and see what's what. D'Annibal's orders."

"And me?" Detective Gretchen Sandler demanded in her nasal tone. She was slim, dark-haired and dark-skinned, a gift from her Brazilian heritage, with almond-shaped blue eyes that raked over September as if looking for flaws. She was also September's partner, a fact Gretchen didn't like much at all. But then she hadn't liked her previous partner much, either. Gretchen and George had also tried to work together and that had not worked out. Gretchen's stormy resentment and George's deep, long-suffering looks had forced Lieutenant D'Annibal to prudently break them apart and that was how September had become Gretchen's partner. As soon as they heard her nickname, to a one, the detectives and Lieutenant D'Annibal of the Laurelton Police Department called her Nine. None of them knew the nickname's origin; they'd just taken it on.

"Of course, and you," George growled at Gretchen, then swatted at them both as if they were gnats buzzing around his head. "Get outta here."

September dropped everything except the wallet she kept

in her back pocket that held her identification. She wore gray slacks and a matching gray shirt, buttoned to her neck. Gretchen had on a pair of denim jeans and a black sleeveless sweater with a matching cardigan that she snatched from the back of her chair and threw over her arm as they headed toward the front of the building. Gretchen walked ahead of September and ignored her as they passed by the front desk and outside into the shimmering heat. "You gotta dress for the weather," Gretchen told her as September felt sweat gather along her hairline and the back of her neck.

"This is cotton," she answered, gesturing to the gray shirt as they climbed into an unmarked black Ford Escape.

"Nobody wants to see you sweat." Gretchen threw the SUV in reverse and wheeled them around, then slammed the vehicle into gear and they lurched forward.

Realizing the gray material was light enough to show moisture, September filed that away for future reference. She'd just moved to homicide from property crimes and it was a whole different ball game. She'd followed her brother into law enforcement but he was currently working with a gang task force in conjunction with the Portland PD and hadn't been around to congratulate September about joining the Laurelton PD—the same police department he was also based out of—and still wasn't.

She glanced back as they headed onto the street. The Laurelton Police Department was on the northern edge of the city, a squat, rectangular brick building that the idiots from the Laurelton City Council had demanded they paint white because it was in the original specs. Now, years later, that white paint had turned a dirty, yellowish beige. So much for city planning. Farsightedness was not their forte.

The walkie-talkie buzzed and Gretchen grabbed it. September heard squawking and Gretchen snarled back, "Yeah, yeah. We'll be there in ten." She switched off and added,

"Four people shot. All on the first floor. Shooter didn't go upstairs, or if they did, the steel door was locked."

"What were they after?" September asked before recalling that Gretchen hated rhetorical questions.

Gretchen shot her a cold look and said, as if Nine hadn't even spoken, "One's dead. Three on their way."

"To the hospital . . . ?"

"To the Pearly Gates, is my guess," she said dryly.

After that September kept her mouth shut until they reached Zuma Software, which was a two-story building of modern design in glass, wood and metal with two ambulances parked in front. A woman was being carried out on a gurney and loaded into the first one. A man was being carried toward the other. Both ambulances turned on their lights and started screaming out of the lot, past Gretchen and September, at the same time.

September had to race-walk to keep in step with Gretchen as they headed to the front door, a monstrous piece of mahogany stained almost black surrounded by floor-to-ceiling translucent windows. Gretchen pushed on the partially opened door and it slowly swung inward to an atrium and the office floor beyond. September stepped carefully after Gretchen and saw that the tech team was already at work on a man who was clearly a corpse.

"Coroner's that way," one of the techs said, inclining his head.

"Who's this?" Gretchen asked, gesturing to the body at her feet.

"Name's Paul de Fore. He was some kind of security."

"Fat lot of good it did him," she remarked.

September scanned the room, her pulse running fast. Her head felt light and she clamped down on emotions that had no place here. Gretchen could see through her too easily and she needed to keep a cool head. Easing around the dead man, she walked past a desk and chair covered in blood. Ahead was a partition and she peeked over it gingerly, but the workstation was unstained. Then she walked toward the office the tech had indicated and saw another man on the floor, his chest and neck sporting two or three bullet holes. His shaggy hair was thick with blood. His eyes were open but as she watched, the coroner closed them with thumb and index finger.

"Aaron Dirkus, the owner's son," the coroner, Joe Journey, known to all and sundry as J.J., said. "His father was conscious. Kurt Upjohn. He's on his way to the hospital."

"How bad are his injuries?" September asked.

"This one's dead."

"I meant Upjohn."

Journey stood up, giving September a long look. He was heavyset and jowly with muttonchops that appeared to be his pride and joy. "They each took three bullets. If you can talk to Upjohn, I'd do it soon."

Gretchen appeared. "Two dead, two on their way to Laurelton General. A whole group upstairs who heard popping sounds, or didn't, depending on whether they were wearing headsets apparently. Nobody up there knew anything was even wrong until we showed up, or so they say. Doesn't look like the killer even attempted to break in."

"Who put the call into 911?" September asked.

She spread her hands. "Mystery guest, or maybe the missing employee."

"Who's missing?"

She inclined her head toward the undisturbed desk area. "Bookkeeper behind the partition. Know-nothings upstairs say her name is Liv something."

"We should get to the hospital and check with Upjohn," September suggested.

Gretchen lifted her brows, threw a glance to the coroner, then gave September an assessing look. "Why is your nickname Nine, again? Did you tell me?"

"No." So there it was. The first person to ask. Not that it was a huge issue, but she was trying to avoid any reason for her coworkers to tease her. "Month I was born."

"I thought it had something to do with you being almost a ten."

September wasn't quite certain how to take that. Was it a compliment, or a put-down? She knew she was pretty enough—auburn hair and blue eyes, slim, almost boyish, but still with enough curves to catch sideways glances—but Gretchen wasn't known for courtesy and compliments. She decided she didn't care what Gretchen meant and ignored the comment entirely.

Gretchen nodded her head, as if coming to a conclusion. "We're going to head to the hospital. We'll come back later and go through things. Make sure nothing's disturbed."

"That's our line," the coroner said and he looked damn serious. September understood. The techs and coroner's office were constantly screaming about how the police first responders always screwed up the evidence. But the officers on this one had gone upstairs to interview the other employees—the know nothings, according to Gretchen—as soon as the tech team had arrived so there wasn't anything to complain about, as far as September could see.

As if her thoughts had willed them, she heard footsteps on the stairs and one of the employees, a young man with long, floppy red hair, most of which was tied back in a rubber band apart from two hanks beside his white face, was walking on rubbery legs down the last steps. The officer with him was someone September didn't know, a young guy with an equally white face. She understood completely. The gory scene around them was like something out of an art director's vision, except this one was real.

"I—I—I heard it. The pops. I—I—thought it was the game. Kinda. But it couldn't be. I looked around but everyone was on their screens and nobody moved. And then Officer . . ." He gazed vaguely toward the young policeman.

"Lomax."

"Officer Lomax was just there. And I asked what the hell he was doing upstairs. Mr. Upjohn doesn't let people just walk upstairs. We're careful, y'know? Piracy, and all that . . ." He looked from September to Gretchen and back. "Where is Mr. Upjohn?"

"The rest of the employees still upstairs?" Gretchen asked Lomax. The officer nodded. "How many?" she asked.

He looked to the red-haired man, who said, "Um . . . twelve? And Mr. Berelli. Phillip Berelli. The accountant."

"Berelli came downstairs," one of the techs said. "He's puking in the bathroom."

Gretchen looked to September, who said, "I'll go check on him."

As she walked away, Gretchen asked the redhead what his name was and he responded, "Ted," and then started hyperventilating. September glanced back as he collapsed on the floor. She caught Gretchen's eye.

"Security tapes?" she asked, and Gretchen asked Ted, "You got any cameras on this building?"

"Oh, sure. I—I—yeah. Piracy. Gotta worry about that. . . ."

Gretchen said, "Who's in charge of security?" and Ted looked at the body nearest him and pointed with a shaking finger at the facedown man near the front door, blood pooling under his head.

September left them in search of the accountant, circling Kurt Upjohn's office and finally discovering the door to the unisex bathroom in the short hallway behind it. Rapping her knuckles on the panel, she then tried the handle when there was no answer. The door was unlocked and she pushed it in slowly and carefully. "Mr. Berelli? I'm Detective Rafferty. Are you all right?"

"Yes . . ." he quavered.

"Is it all right if I come in?"

"Yes . . ."

She stuck her head inside and found him propping himself up at the counter, his head drooping on his neck, his forearms taut and shaking with the effort.

"You might want to sit down," she suggested.

"I didn't know. I was up there. I heard the noise but I thought somebody's computer volume got switched up. It was like a *blam*. And then *blam*. And then . . . after a little bit, *blam, blam, blam, blam, blam!* A lot of 'em. Too many! I walked into the control room—that's where it all happens at Zuma, y'know—and the guys were all working on their computers. Most of 'em had headsets on so they didn't know, and it was weird, but I . . ." He exhaled hard. "He said they were shot . . . the officer . . . was it . . . *all of them?*"

"I don't have any answers for you yet," September said. "We're sorting through it. Can you come out and talk about it with my partner?"

"The whole first floor?" he asked, looking panicky. "Jessica and Liv, too? The women?"

"What are their names?"

"Jessica Maltona and Liv Dugan."

"Which one's which?" September asked as they walked slowly back to the main room. Phillip Berelli looked like he could fall over at any time.

"Jessica's the receptionist. Dark-haired and has the big chest. Liv's pretty . . . younger . . . brown-haired, too. She's the bookkeeper. Is she okay? She and Aaron are friends. . . ." They were passing Upjohn's office and he looked inside, an automatic reaction. The coroner and another tech were zipping Aaron Dirkus's corpse into a body bag. He stopped and goggled. "I saw Paul and Aaron and Kurt. . . . They're all dead, aren't they?"

"Mr. Upjohn is on his way to the hospital." *Liv Dugan had gotten lucky somehow*, September thought.

Gretchen crossed the room toward them. "Mr. Berelli?"

He gazed at her with horror-stretched eyes.

"Who should I ask about the security cameras?"

"Paul . . ." His eyes turned toward the man's bloody remains.

Gretchen followed his gaze and said, after a quiet moment, "Who else?"

Chapter 5

Liv threaded the key into her apartment door lock with quaking fingers and a field of vision that had narrowed to a two-inch square. Blackness was creeping in on all sides. She'd made it home. To her apartment. In her Accord, which was parked a bit cockeyed in the lot. And now . . . and now . . . the familiar panic from her youth was taking her over.

"I can't . . ." she whispered, shaking her head furiously. *No, no, no!*

No.

The police. She should call the police.

But the officer from her youth invaded her thoughts, followed quickly by the memory of the supercilious policeman who'd come to Hathaway House over a disturbance during her teen years and had treated them all like criminals.

No. No police. She couldn't trust them. She couldn't trust anyone!

Why? Why Zuma Software?

You know why. It's not Zuma. It's you.

She clapped her hands over her ears, hyperventilating. This was her own paranoia talking. Talking, talking, talking.

Always talking. Always convincing. But she knew better. She—knew—better. Didn't she?

Didn't she?

She'd slammed the apartment door behind her, and now she leaned against it, eyes ravenously searching the room. Maybe Kurt Upjohn was into something she knew nothing about. Maybe there were financial concerns. Bad debts to the wrong people. Maybe Aaron was involved in more drugs than she knew.

It's about you, Liv.

Maybe there was some military connection after all. War games. Sensitive information running beneath the guise of computer games.

But no one went upstairs to the control room, where it all happens.

Or, did they?

Her heart seized. Maybe the killer had still been there. When she returned. Maybe he thought she'd seen something and was *coming after her!*

"Don't . . . don't . . ." she whispered aloud, willing her vision to expand outside the shrinking box closing in on her.

You have to leave. You have to go. Now. Get your things. Go. Drive. No, walk away.

Blindly Liv searched through her closet for her backpack, something she could carry. Her hands closed upon it and she squeezed her eyes shut and offered up a silent prayer, asking for what? Help? For a wild moment she thought about calling Dr. Yancy. They hadn't spoken since Liv was at Hathaway House but the doctor had been kind; she'd talked straight.

But Liv had no number for the doctor. She would have to call Hathaway House to reach her.

With that thought in mind she crossed swiftly to the phone. She reached out and it suddenly rang shrilly beneath

her hand. She screamed, a short, aborted sound that may
have been in her own head. Heart galloping, she counted the
rings but didn't answer, was afraid to.

Someone was leaving a voice mail.

A voice mail.

She waited three minutes that felt like an eternity, her
ears filled with a dull buzzing that wouldn't go away.
Then, with unsteady hands, she picked up the receiver and
retrieved the message.

"It's Lorinda. I know you're at work, but I just wanted to
call you about . . . your father. He's with your brother. It's
not good for him. He and Hague aren't good for each other."
Her voice rose. "If you could just try to help me," she said
harshly, as if growing angry with Liv. "I don't ask for much,
and you're making this so hard!"

Liv's brain ran in a circle. *How did she get my number?*,
she thought first. *Does she know where I live? Does the
killer know?*

"It's because of *you* that he's not listening to me," Lorinda
went on in a complaining voice. "And Hague. I've been his
wife for nearly twenty years, but you and Hague . . ." She
broke off, sounding like she was about to cry, and the line
went dead.

*She doesn't know about Zuma . . . she hasn't heard.
Maybe no one knows yet.*

With that thought in mind, Liv quickly catalogued what
she would need for a long trip away. Money. She had cash
in an empty ice cream carton in the freezer. Quickly she retrieved that roll of bills, then found the jacket of her running
gear and zipped the money inside a pocket. She needed her
gun. Running shoes. An extra shirt and pair of jeans. Under-
garments. A raincoat even though the sun was shining like
it would never stop. The manila envelope.

She stuffed everything into the backpack, the gun on top.

Rummaging through the bathroom drawers, she grabbed her toothbrush and several hair bands, then looked in the mirror at solemn hazel eyes flecked with gold as she snapped her hair into a ponytail and then smashed a baseball cap with a Mariners logo on her head, drawing the ponytail through the back hole above the adjustable strap.

Erasing the message from Lorinda, she unplugged the phone. She did a fast but thorough search to assure herself she hadn't left some scrap of paper with information about her family. Let it take whoever was out there as long as possible to learn whom she might contact.

Unless they already know . . .

She was running on instinct, and a sense of being the prey. She wasn't going to sit down and try to think it through. There was time for that later, when she was somewhere safe, wherever the hell that might be.

Five minutes later, she was out the door. She had the keys to her car in her hand, but she left the Accord in the parking lot, heading for the street. Just another pedestrian. Walking slowly—strolling, really, to avoid drawing attention—she wound along a newly revitalized street in this suburban, hoping to be urban, part of Laurelton, with its new cobblestone crosswalks and lampposts and shops with green awnings and outdoor seating. A place to mingle and maybe sit down and catch her breath.

Somewhere, if not safe, at least saf*er.*

With an effort she kept her mind off the images of her friends and coworkers at Zuma sprawled across the floor, blood oozing beneath them, the life force draining away. If she thought about it, she was lost. If she remembered Aaron . . .

Swallowing hard, she moved into a late afternoon crowd just beginning to gather at their favorite bars and bistros for happy hour, merriment spilling onto the street from open doorways.

Aaron, she thought, a smothered cry wrenched from her throat.

Shhh . . . don't think . . . don't think . . . don't draw attention . . .

Blinking back cold tears, she turned into a sandwich shop with a long line of customers at their counter service and a smattering of tables.

It had grown hot outside and she was overdressed, but she was shivering like she was consumed with fever as she took the only empty table, situated in the center of the room with a good view of the door and street.

She collapsed into the seat like she'd just completed a marathon.

It fell on Phillip Berelli to show September and Gretchen where the security tapes were. The man was fast losing what little control and backbone he'd ever possessed and was sprawled like a limp rag in a chair in Kurt Upjohn's office, where there was a videotape monitor and a number of tapes. Upjohn had been taken in the ambulance earlier, and Aaron Dirkus in the coroner's wagon. September and Gretchen were left with blood on the floor and asked by the techs to step around it, which they all did.

"Mr. Upjohn is cautious," Phillip said in a thready voice. "Paul . . . Paul de Fore gives him the security tapes . . . I think they look at them. It's old-school technology but Kurt liked that. No one really thought it was that important. I mean, the door to the upstairs is always locked. That's where everything is and you have to know the pass code. Kurt . . . Mr. Upjohn was vigilant about it."

"What about the main floor?" Gretchen asked.

"Paul was . . . he cared . . . but it just wasn't that important.

Not really. There's no reason to care. There's nothing here. There's nothing here." He cut himself off on a hiccup.

September had called in Ted, one of the techs, and he'd hit the rewind button on the tape currently being recorded. The tape stopped and he then pressed PLAY and they could see only one camera angle, but it encompassed most of the front parking area.

"You can't see the side door," Berelli said on a swallow.

"It's all right. He came through the front," September said.

"Aaron was lax about the side door. They had a fight about it, Aaron and Kurt. Aaron just didn't think keeping it locked mattered."

"But Mr. Upjohn felt it was worth keeping locked?" Gretchen asked.

"He didn't like the side door. I think that's why . . ." He trailed off.

"You think that's why, what?" September asked.

"I think that's why Aaron was so lax about it. He just kinda wanted to needle his old man, and it worked." He rubbed a hand viciously over his face as if to rub the whole tragedy away. "Aaron took the side door key and Kurt was mad."

"There he is," Ted said.

They all looked at the monitor. There, indeed, he was. The killer was one man. At least it looked like a man, dressed in navy pants, lace-up boots, a navy shirt like the kind security teams sometimes wore. A black vest. A black ski mask and a gun.

"That's a Glock," Gretchen said.

"He just walked up as boldly as you please," September said.

They ran it back again and watched it three more times. There was no sound and as soon as the man entered the building he disappeared.

"Can't see what vehicle he came from, but he sure didn't walk far looking like that," Gretchen said.

"Does he seem nervous to you?" September asked.

Gretchen considered the question. "No. He seems like he came here to kill some people, and that's what he did."

"He sorta has a stutter-step. Right there." September pointed to the screen where the man did a bit of a shuffle about three paces from the steps. "Like he's hesitating."

"Maybe," Gretchen conceded. She looked at the puddle that was Phillip Berelli. "We'd like you to come to the station, Mr. Berelli."

"Am I under arrest?" he squeaked out.

"No, sir. We just want to talk to you somewhere—else," Gretchen said.

"I need to call my wife," he said, his gaze sliding around the room.

"We'll call her on the way." To the tech, she said, "See if you can get a close-up on that uniform. I don't believe for one minute he'd be idiotic enough to wear something that connected him to a job, but maybe it's a costume? From a costume shop? Or, like Goodwill or something?"

"I'll see what I can do," Ted promised, as he pulled the tape from the recorder.

"Did J.J. leave?" she asked, looking around.

"With the Dirkus and de Fore bodies," September answered her. She'd watched through the front windows as the coroner and an assistant had slammed the back of the wagon closed and pulled away, feeling slightly sick to her stomach.

Phillip Berelli shivered and suddenly leapt up and ran for the bathroom again.

Gretchen almost yelled something after him but thought better of it. To September she said, "How're you doing?" but her voice held a hint of disparagement that did not foster honesty.

"I'm okay," she said, and felt Ted's gaze slide over her quickly. She wasn't fooling anyone.

A few minutes later a white-faced and weak-kneed
Phillip Berelli followed them out to the Ford Escape.

The café was crowded, noisy and exposed. Liv would
have liked a table in a corner, her back to the wall, with a
view of the street instead of this one in the center of the
room, but it was not to be. Her brain felt too big for her head
and her pulse beat like angry, tribal drums inside her ears.
Boom, *boom*. Boom, *boom*. Boom, *boom*.

It was surreal. A dream. It wasn't reality. She'd had a
taste of that once before, of believing in lies and visions. It
was a defense mechanism, Dr. Yancy had told her. Her own
invention. A protection against her darkest fears.

Protection? That wasn't going to help her now. *Now*, she
needed to think about truth.

Why? she asked herself, seated in the uncomfortable café
chair. There was a table of three teenaged girls between her
and the window to the street. The girls were looking through
the glass and talking about someone named Joshua, who
may or may not have been right outside. One of them blew
the paper off her straw at one friend who seemed the most
obsessed with this guy. They were laughing and teasing and
just hanging out. The kind of thing Liv might have done as
a teenager if the bright, sassy six-year-old she'd once been
hadn't found her mother's body hanging from the kitchen
rafters.

To Liv's left was a table with a middle-aged man in John
Lennon glasses and spiked hair, a style way outside of his
era. Instead of looking hip, he seemed a little pathetic. He
was drinking a Widmer beer and absorbed in the sports page
from the day's paper. The Portland Timbers, the city's soccer
team, had won two nights before in an exhibition game of
some kind.

Liv could feel pressure building inside herself. Looking

past the girls and through the window, she could see a lighting store across the cobblestone crosswalk, chandeliers ablaze in the windows. A coffee shop sat next to it: Bean There, Done That. She knew that coffee shop. It had booths with brown leather seats and a dimmer ambiance. She'd already ordered a cup of soup and a can of Diet Coke, however, and when the waitress brought her order, she had her money ready.

A tempo was beating inside her ear: *Get out, get out, get out.*

She couldn't stay. Couldn't. Taking a sip of the Coke, she carried the can to the recycle bin, dumped it, then left the rest of the food untouched. She was out of the café, across the street and inside the coffee shop before she had another conscious thought. She took the booth one in from the door, as the couple who'd been seated there were just leaving. Then she realized she would have to stand in line to order. She needed a cup of coffee in front of her so people would know the booth was occupied. She debated leaving her backpack on the table to save her seat, but couldn't risk it.

Chafing, she found her place in line, and saw her booth immediately taken by a young couple who slid inside it on one side, laughing together. Damn. Now what?

The boy got up and stood in line behind her.

She felt herself start to sweat. A row of glass pendant lights in red shades lined the top of the counter, sweeping a slash of color over her. Garnet red. Blood red.

Her pulse beat in her head. Boom, *boom.* Boom, *boom.*

I'm going to faint, she thought, just as the customer in front of her paid for his order and moved aside, allowing her to step toward the barista.

"Coffee," she said in a voice she didn't recognize as her own.

"Latte? Mocha?" the girl asked brightly.

"Black coffee. Large."

"I guess I don't need your name then," she said cheerily,

plucking a to-go cup from a stack and turning to the machine behind her to serve the coffee immediately.

Liv felt the boy's eyes on her neck like daggers. She dared not turn around. Facing forward felt like a supreme effort. As soon as the barista took her money and handed her the brimming cup, the boy shouldered past her and said, "A latte, and a double mocha."

"Names?" the girl said, a Sharpie poised over the paper cup.

"Alana and Mike." He turned and grinned back at his companion in the booth. "She's the latte."

Liv moved away. To the station that held the lids and cream and nonfat milk. She poured a quick shot of cream into her cup and then reached for a plastic lid. It was all a ploy to pass time until there was a seat. Her hands felt disembodied but at least they'd stopped violently shaking.

Two men and a woman filed into the line at the counter, but her gaze swept past them as she looked for somewhere to sit. Finally a table opened up. Not a booth, but a table. She hurried over, pulled back the chair and seated herself so she could look out the door and front window.

"Do you mind if I join you?"

The male voice brought her up short. She did mind. Very much so. But she couldn't afford to cause anyone to remember her. Her heart resumed its heavy beating.

"No, go ahead," she heard herself say, sounding breathless. No wonder. She felt strangled for air. Suffocating.

Her new companion was probably around forty, she determined, and looked like he worked out. He was losing his hair and seemed to be sensitive about it because he kept swiping a hand over the front wisps, smoothing them back in place.

She didn't want him at her table. She didn't want his eyes on her. Kind eyes? Or knowing eyes? What those eyes *weren't* were indifferent.

Does he know who I am? *Is he after me?*

She tried to act normally, if she could remember what normal was with all the physical reactions wildly coursing through her body: rocketing pulse, shaking legs, fevered brain, hysteria climbing up her throat.

Stop. Stop. Calm yourself.

At Hathaway House she'd learned to control her bouts of panic, and she'd believed, wrongly, it appeared, that she'd put them to bed for good. The pictures of Aaron and Kurt and Paul and Jessica's bodies sprawled over the floor were right behind her eyes.

A sound on the street caught Liv's attention and she glanced past the man to the window and the sunny street beyond. A man's shadow traveled by. She watched fearfully, but it was only in her imagination; gone in an instant. There were, however, people outside stopping to witness the results of a fender bender across the way, from the side of the street she'd just crossed. Two people, a man from one car, a woman from the other, were stepping stiffly toward each other to exchange insurance information.

Her mouth was dry. The shadow . . . was she being watched? It felt like she was being watched. Gooseflesh rose on her arms.

"You're wearing a jacket," the man observed. *He* was watching her. They all were. Everyone in the coffeehouse.

"I run cold," she murmured. She was sweating inside, though. She hoped it didn't show on her face.

The line had grown longer; the barista unable to keep up with the demand, so a sullen-looking, male coworker with dark, suspicious eyes joined her. Liv tamped down the tide of fear threatening to wash over her and picked up her coffee, drinking a slug of liquid as if it were water to a lost desert traveler.

Her companion's eyes were on her face. "I'm fine," she said.

"You don't look fine. You don't have any color, at all."

"Did you hear about the killing at Zuma Software?" a voice called from somewhere in line.

Liv whipped around. It was a woman's voice. She was standing at the counter, digging through a coin purse for change, making small talk. The sullen helper was waiting for her to count out the coins, a peeved expression on his face. The two men in line in front of her had already been served.

"It's breaking news," another woman answered her, now several people behind her. "Broke in while I was watching TV. The owner, Kurt Upjohn, is in critical condition. Somebody else, too."

"There were two women," the first lady said, turning around to gaze at the second. "One got shot, but one wasn't there. They think maybe she did it."

Liv nearly gasped. *Who? Who thinks that?*

"She killed all her coworkers? Mowed 'em down?" the second woman sounded disbelieving.

"They're looking for her. That's all I know."

The man across from Liv was staring at her as if he knew—*knew*—who she was. Liv warred with herself as several more people went through the line. She wanted to bolt out the door. She needed to escape. They were looking for her. Of course, they were looking for her.

But she didn't want to be caught. Couldn't be caught.

Carefully, she took several more swallows of her coffee, then she scraped back her chair, picked up her backpack and stood.

"Leaving so soon?" the man asked her, his lips smiling, his eyes cold. Or was that her imagination?

She didn't answer, just sidestepped around the tables toward the door that seemed miles away even though it was only twenty feet. She reached the handle, and it burst inward, and she was nearly mowed down by two policemen in uniform.

Her vision blurred. She couldn't turn around. She heard them address the barista: *We're looking for someone. . . .*

Panic licked through her again. She stepped out. On the street it was hot. The sidewalk sent up a wave of heat. A dark gray Jeep was parked directly in front of her. A man was circling the front of it, unlocking the doors, sliding into the driver's seat, balancing a cup of coffee.

She walked toward the passenger door and flung it open just as he slammed the driver's door shut and was in the act of putting his drink into a cup holder. "Hey," he said, gazing at her in surprise.

She slid inside and closed the door behind her, clutching her backpack, her heart jumping crazily inside her chest. "I need you to take me somewhere."

"Yeah?" he asked cautiously, looking for all the world like he was about to throw her out.

With deceptive calm, she withdrew her .38 from the backpack and leveled it at him. "I'm a pretty good shot. I'm sorry. I really am. You just need to drive me away from here."

He was good-looking. Black hair, blue-gray eyes, a strong jaw and maybe the hint of a dimple as he clamped his teeth together and stared at her gun. Thirtyish. In dusty jeans and a faded gray T-shirt with a list of words crossed out across its front.

"You are kidding me," he said slowly.

"You think so?" she asked, a lump building in her throat. "I might not be able to kill you. But I could hurt you. I could do that, I'm pretty sure. If you won't help me, I could hurt you." She glanced at the coffee cup and read his name: AUGGIE.

She felt tears building in the corners of her eyes.

He stared at her another long moment, as if assessing the truth of her statement. Then he sat back in his seat, switched on the ignition and silently guided the nose of the Jeep into traffic.

Chapter 6

She kept the gun leveled at him. It wasn't loaded, but he didn't know that. She had ammo stowed in her backpack, for all the good it would do her. Not that she wanted to actually hold a loaded gun on someone. For all her words she didn't think she could hurt him or anyone else. But again, he didn't know that.

They were driving east, away from Laurelton toward Portland. She felt like she was in some improvisational acting scene where each player just keyed off the situation and made up their own story.

She was crazy. Flat-out nuts. This definitely decided it. This was a crazy thing to do. And yet she wasn't sorry. They rode in silence. The man—Auggie—seemed intent on the road but Liv could just imagine the thoughts rattling around in his head.

It felt like an eternity, and was probably only a matter of minutes, when he drawled, "Did you have a place in mind?"

"Just drive."

"I have a quarter of a tank. I can drive for a while, then I'm going to need gas."

She looked at the gauge, saw he was telling the truth and wanted to rail at him. How could he be so irresponsible?

She wanted to scream and cry and pull out her hair, but that made her think of the unfortunate ones at Hathaway House who sank into that kind of behavior and were moved to other facilities. She'd always felt more grounded than they were, more capable, more sane, but maybe she was as wacko as they were. *This* was crazy.

But right now, she was putting miles between her and her apartment, and for the first time since she'd seen the bodies at Zuma, she felt almost safe. Still, she couldn't prevent the shudders that wracked her body. Auggie shot her a sideways glance, aware, so she lifted the .38 a bit, just to remind him.

"Would you seriously shoot me when I'm driving?"

She glared at him, resenting his insolence. "Where do you live?"

"Uh . . . not far from here. Toward Portland."

"Are you lying?"

"No."

"You took a while to answer my question."

"I was just thinking about the exit I need to take. It's coming up."

They were driving on Sunset Highway and getting close to the junction at 217. "Do you live alone?"

"Yes."

"Then let's go there."

She wanted just to keep driving and driving and driving, but that wasn't prudent, either. She wondered, for a moment, if she could ditch him and just take his car. But what would she do with him?

He passed 217 and turned off at Sylvan, winding the car up the hill. Liv gave a glance around his vehicle, thinking hard, noting the dark clothes he'd thrown into the back and the toolbox. A length of twine was wrapped around the Jeep's back hatch, holding it down, as if maybe it popped open unexpectedly from time to time.

They drove in silence for about twenty minutes, taking

several side streets until they reached his place, a small bungalow that needed some serious repairs if the cracked sidewalk and sagging gutters were any indication. There was a breezeway between the house and one-car garage. The door to the garage was open and he pulled inside, put the Jeep in park, and switched off the engine.

"Now what?" he asked, pulling the key from the ignition.

"Stay in the car. Hands up. I'll come around." She opened her door, the gun still trained on him, then walked around the front of the Jeep and stood outside the driver's door, her muzzle aimed at him through the window. "Let yourself out," she said.

Carefully, he opened the door, his hands raised in front of him. She took the keys from his hand.

"Get the twine from the back of your car."

"The twine?"

She nodded.

"You're not going to tie me up," he stated flatly, challengingly.

"Yes. I am."

"It won't work. What are you running from? They'll find you."

"No."

"Don't take offense. But I don't think you're good at this."

Liv barked out a harsh laugh. "I'm only as good as I need to be."

He thought that over, then walked around to the back of the Jeep and pulled up the hatch as far as the twine would allow. He untied the twine, gathered it together and put it into Liv's outstretched hand.

She said, "I'm going to put this gun into my jacket pocket now, but I'll shoot you through it if you do anything while we walk across the breezeway to the back door."

He made a movement of acquiescence and then headed

out the garage's man-door, across the breezeway and up two concrete steps. At the door, he said, "I'm going to need the key."

Carefully, she put the full set in his upturned palm.

"I usually close the garage door," he told her.

"I'll do it later."

There were no neighbors directly across from him. In fact this stretch of road was winding and covered with fir trees, with a wide stretch of sun-scorched lawn beside the cracked cement driveway. If she had to stay out of sight a while, it was not a terrible hideout.

He threaded a key in the lock. Twisting the door open, he stepped inside, but Liv was right on his heels, just in case he planned to slam the door in her face and lock her out.

They were in a kitchen with a small wooden table and two chairs. "Sit down," she ordered, holding the length of twine.

He eyed the twine and said disbelievingly, "You plan to tie me to a chair?"

"Yes."

"Oh, come on. I'm not going to do anything. I don't really care what you've done. Let's just sit down and talk about it."

She gestured with the muzzle. "Sit down. Put the keys on the table."

He eased himself into one of the chairs, set the keys on the table, then slid them away from himself toward her. She picked them up and put them in her pocket.

"This must be a first offense," he said.

"It's not," she lied. "Put your arms behind you."

"Oh, come on."

"Just do it," she snapped.

"So, you're a hardened criminal? Is that what you're saying?" He put his arms around the back of the chair, though it was clearly hard for him to comply.

"That's what I'm saying."

With his arms behind him, she threaded the twine through the lathed spokes of the chair's back and around his wrists, tying them tightly, testing the twine's strength.

"This is gonna get damned uncomfortable real fast," he muttered.

"Be quiet. Please."

"First offense," he said. "You're way too polite."

"Shut up."

She'd set the .38 on the table out of his reach while she tied him up, but if he made a move for it, she was pretty certain she could beat him to it. He might be able to take her down with brute strength, but there was the chance she could get a shot or two off were it loaded, and since he believed it was, he let her truss him to the chair with no resistance though the dark, mutinous look on his face didn't bode well if he should chance to get free. With that thought in mind, she tested his bonds a second, then a third time until she was satisfied that he was contained.

Finally, she checked his pockets and found a cell phone, which he clearly wanted to protest about but kept his mouth a taut, grim line. She saw that it was turned off, but when she tried to switch it on, nothing happened.

"Out of juice," he said, stating the obvious.

"Where's the charger?" she asked.

"Not here. Why? You wanna use my phone? Where's yours?"

"I don't own one." He looked at her as if she were an exotic species, which annoyed her. "Not everyone has to have a cell phone," she said with a touch of asperity.

He shook his head and changed the subject. "What's your plan?" She could discern a faintly mocking tone to his voice and decided he wasn't taking this seriously enough.

"If you try anything, I will shoot you."

"I'm having serious trouble believing you."

The image of Aaron Dirkus's body and the blood—all the blood—crossed the screen of her mind again, and she had to look away, tears welling. She drew a quivering breath and swallowed hard, several times. "I will," she said with more conviction and her desperation must have penetrated because his expression grew more serious.

Needing to get outside his range of vision, she walked behind him, obsessively testing the twine yet again. When she was convinced it would hold him but wouldn't cut off his circulation, she backed away until she felt the kitchen counter behind her. Leaning against it, her legs seemed to lose all strength and she sank to the floor, wrapping her arms around her knees, the .38 hanging loosely from her hands. Tears ran down her cheeks and she stared into space, reviewing the scene at Zuma though she'd told herself she wouldn't.

"What's your name?" he asked. She could only see the back of his head.

Blinking hard, she cleared her throat. "Livvie," she said, invoking the name of her younger self.

"Well, Livvie, I don't know about you, but I'm kind of hungry. I hope you're not planning to starve me."

It took her long moments to pull herself together, but finally she got to her feet and wandered to his refrigerator. Inside were some sliced deli ham, a loaf of bread, mayonnaise, mustard and some dicey-looking iceberg lettuce. She put together a sandwich, leaving off the lettuce, put it on a plate, found a steak knife in a drawer—he hardly had any utensils or kitchenware of any kind, she noticed—and cut the sandwich in half.

Sliding the plate in front of him, she asked, "What do you drink?"

"Beer. Coke. Water. Occasionally a semi-nice glass of wine."

She went to the sink and poured him a glass of water,

placing that in front of him, too. They stared at each other and she picked up the sandwich and held it to his mouth.

"Actually, I'd like a drink of water first."

"Take a bite." When he pressed his lips together in rebellion, she added, "Please."

"You're a very polite kidnapper," he pointed out again.

"You were right. It's my first time," she admitted.

"Wow. I'm shocked." Then, "The police after you?"

"Probably. By now, anyway."

"What did you do?"

"Take a bite," she said again, and he bit into the sandwich with white teeth, his gray-blue gaze never leaving her face. When he was finished chewing, she held the water glass to his lips and he took a long swallow. After that, they sat in silence while she fed him the rest of the sandwich.

After he'd swallowed the last bite, he said, "What about you? Hungry? I don't have a huge selection, but I think there's enough for another sandwich."

"I'm going to go close the garage door."

She was happy to get out of his presence for a moment. Her head was crammed with thoughts. She needed to see the news. She needed to know what was going on.

God, what have I done?

The realization that she was a kidnapper sent a shockwave through her body. What had she been thinking? Now, it didn't matter what the situation at Zuma was all about, she was a criminal of the worst kind.

Shutting the garage behind her, she looked around quickly and found the source of the twine in a roll in the extremely empty garage. There were no rakes or tools or lawn chairs or whatever else people kept in garages. There was nothing but the Jeep, the twine and a pile of black tarp.

Reaching upward, she grabbed the handle for the garage door, looking out to the road just as an older-model Buick cruised by with an elderly man at the wheel. He didn't even bother to glance over, but panic filled her anyway as she slammed down the door. She grabbed up the roll of twine.

Returning to the kitchen, she set the twine on the counter, then stood in front of Auggie and asked, "Is this really your house?"

"Yes. Why?"

"It doesn't feel like anyone lives here."

He assessed her silently for a few moments, then said, "I just moved here and I don't have a lot of stuff."

"Where'd you come from?"

"Canada," he said.

"Canada," she repeated with an edge to her voice. "You don't sound Canadian."

"Yeah? Well, I've been oot and aboot all day, eh? That good enough for you?"

She almost laughed. Hysterical laughter, for certain, but the irked look on his face was almost comical. Almost. "Not really."

"I didn't say I was Canadian. I've just been living in British Columbia a while, that's all. I'm a fishing guide."

"Really?"

"Really. What are you, besides a fugitive?"

"I'm . . . I'm . . ." She closed her eyes for a moment, then asked, "You have a television?"

"Basic cable. In my bedroom."

"Can you walk?" she asked. She hadn't bound his feet.

"You want me to come watch TV with you?"

"Just the news."

They stared at each other another moment or two, then he got awkwardly to his feet, carrying the chair on his back as Liv preceded him across the living room toward the west end of the house. Directly ahead was a bathroom and there were bedrooms to the right and left of a short hallway. She could see the television in the bedroom to the right—the room toward the rear of the house—and headed that way.

Auggie followed after her, banging the chair into the wall several times and swearing softly in the process.

By the time he'd slammed his chair down near the door and sat upon it and Liv had perched on the end of the bed, it was five forty-five. Had it really only been hours since the attack?

The remote was tossed on the bed beside her. Liv snatched it up and hit the POWER button. The Channel Seven news came up and it was the weather. They both watched in silence as more sunshine was predicted, and more, and more. "It's been a beautiful week so far and there's more to come," the weatherman said with a smile.

"Beautiful week," Liv repeated as they went to commercial, her voice breaking. She wanted to lie down on his bed and bury her face in the covers and never come up.

"What started this?" Auggie asked her, a note of concern entering his voice, which nearly did her in.

She turned down the volume but kept her gaze on the commercial—something about being ultra-fit with the use of a "miracle product"—but her thoughts were far removed. At length, she asked him, "Do you know about what happened at Zuma today?"

A pause. "Someone shot up the place," he said carefully.

"I was out to lunch, literally . . . but I came back and they were all dead, dying, injured, *shot*. . . ." She looked over at him and saw he was staring at the .38 she'd laid on the bed beside her. "It wasn't this gun. This one hasn't even been fired . . . yet. I just went home and got it and then I ran out."

"You work there."

"I'm the missing employee."

"You should call the police," he said immediately. "If what you're saying is true, then—"

"That's just it. They won't believe me. They never believe me."

"Never believe you?"

"I don't trust them. I don't like them and I don't want them." She shook her head. On a half-laugh, she gestured to his trussed-up state, "And now, it's too late anyway."

"I wouldn't press charges."

"Oh, sure," she said with a snort of disbelief.

"Livvie, they'll help you. They want to get in touch with you."

"Of course they do!" she said emphatically. "And they'll throw me into an interrogation room and try to wring out a confession and use my past against me and before you know it, it'll all be my fault. And maybe it is anyway!"

"I don't know what you're talking about."

"You're not meant to."

"What did you mean about 'my past'?"

"Nothing!"

"Well, why the hell did you say it was your fault? I believe you, that you didn't shoot those people at Zuma," he added.

"I didn't."

"Why were they shot? Do you have any idea?"

She shook her head slowly.

"You do have an idea, Livvie," he argued, watching her closely.

"It's just Liv . . . please . . . and, yeah, someone's after me."

"Who?"

"I don't know, but it's always been there. I've always known it, felt it. I think this—*massacre*—has something to do with me." She raked her fingers through her hair. "I can't explain it. I don't have any proof. I know you won't believe me. Why would you? But it's a feeling I have, and it's *real*." She paused, then added, "I'm not . . . completely nuts."

He was studying her in a way that made her extremely uncomfortable. She was about to say something to break the tension, when he said, "We'll go to the police together. I'll take you and we'll tell them—"

"NO!"

He drew in a breath and exhaled it slowly. "If you would just—"

"Shhh." The news had come back on and Liv turned up the volume. The anchorwoman was saying, "—just learned that there are two confirmed dead at the Zuma Software shooting this afternoon, Paul de Fore and Aaron Dirkus." Liv made a sound of pain. Aaron. She'd known he was dead. She just hadn't wanted to believe it! Turning away, she curled up on the bed like she'd wanted to before. But her ears could still hear: "Zuma's owner Kurt Upjohn has been taken to Laurelton General Hospital in critical condition as has Jessica Maltona, one of the company employees. Police are looking to question Liv Dugan, another Zuma employee who was apparently not at the scene at the time of the shooting and appears to be missing. They want to talk to Ms. Dugan. If you've seen her, please call the authorities."

A picture of a much younger Liv flashed on the screen. Her hair was shorter and she recognized the steps of Hathaway House in the background. She realized the picture was one that her father had from her teen years. Lorinda, she thought, swallowing hard. Lorinda had given the police her picture.

"They've got my picture," she said.

"Doesn't look much like you. How old were you? Thirteen?"

"Sixteen."

"Was that your high school in the background?"

"Something like that," she said tiredly.

They watched the rest of the report and then Liv dragged herself to her feet and headed back to the kitchen where she sank into the other kitchen chair, laying the gun on the tabletop in front of her. Auggie followed after her, clomping along with the chair on his hunched back. He banged it down, and they stared across the table at each other.

"Looks like someone wanted to take out Kurt Upjohn," he said. "This was about Zuma Software, not you."

"You're wrong." She wanted to believe him. She really, really wanted to believe him. But the timing of the package . . . and Dr. Yancy saying she'd buried the truth . . . and something about Hathaway House.

"Why do you say that?" he asked.

"Because I just know. I've always known."

"What have you always known?"

"Stop humoring me. I know what you think. That I'm crazy, or deluded, or misinformed. And you think I'm wrong about these killings. That I'm egocentric, maybe, that it has to be about me, when it's obviously not. That I'm a drama queen. That I have to make this about 'my stuff' when it's clearly a different matter entirely."

He didn't respond, which was a telling admission in itself.

"They're after me," she said in an unsteady voice. "That's why I jumped in your car."

Phillip Berelli was slouched in a chair inside D'Annibal's unoccupied office. He'd needed somewhere to sit outside of the squad room, which, though mostly empty, had a feel of interrogation and criminal processing that scared honest citizens and felons, hopefully, alike. Those under arrest were brought in through a back door to a general booking area that led to several holding cells and then the squad room, which held some of the more raucous accused felons away from those at the station for other reasons, but that didn't mean much to Berelli.

He'd called his wife, then barely said another word on

the ride over, looking for all the world like he might pass out at any moment. Since they'd been at the station, he'd mostly just sat, staring straight ahead. After half an hour Gretchen had left them and gone to find someone to complain about Guy Urlacher, the man at Laurelton PD's front desk. Guy took his role seriously enough to piss off everyone. He wasn't really *wrong* to make everyone identify themselves; he was just too eager and had turned following regulations into an art form. The good news? Guy's attitude was the only thing Phillip Berelli had reacted to thus far. Berelli said that Paul de Fore, who'd been hired at Zuma as a kind of security guard, suffered from the same overzealous need to control. Since that admission, the man had simply sat in a blank-staring funk, so September had left him for a few moments and just returned.

"Here," she said, handing the man a cup of coffee strong enough to melt steel.

He took the cup reluctantly and cradled it in his palms. Not an encouraging sign.

"So, Paul de Fore," September said. "Tell me more about him."

"Paul . . ." he murmured, shaking his head dolefully as his breath caught on a sob.

"Take a drink, Mr. Berelli," September said.

As if he needed someone to tell him what to do, Berelli obliged, sucking in the dark liquid and coughing a bit as it went down his throat.

"I know you want to go home, and we want to take you home, too. We just need some help. A little background. That's all," she said.

"I don't know anything. Kurt . . . Mr. Upjohn . . . he's . . ."

"He's in surgery," September told him. "Miss Maltona, too."

"Paul's dead," he said, as if trying the words out, disbelieving them.

"Yes."

"So's . . . Aaron . . ."

September nodded. "But Mr. Upjohn and Miss Maltona are still alive, and the other employee, Miss Dugan."

"She called 911."

"Yes," September said. The security tape had captured Olivia Dugan's return, shock and phone call. If it was an acting job, it was a damn good one.

"She's lucky she wasn't there," he said. His face crumpled as he added, "She and Jessica didn't like Paul much."

"She and Jessica were friends?"

He shrugged. "Maybe."

"You said Paul took his job too seriously?"

He nodded. "He kinda wore his own uniform. No one asked him to," he added softly, as if by saying it quietly he could keep from maligning the dead.

"His duties were . . . ?"

"Nothing specific, I guess. He would go upstairs a couple of times a day and just patrol around. And he'd go outside and check the grounds. Mostly, he stood by the door." He stared down at his shoes and admitted, "Nobody much liked him. He kinda took things on himself." He made a face. "I overheard him tell Kurt that Jessica took off on her break. She left the building."

"That's not allowed?"

"Well, you can't really stop anyone from leaving on their break, legally. Kurt just likes to know where every employee is at all times. He wants the girls to go at noon and be back at one."

"The girls . . . Miss Maltona and Miss Dugan?"

"Liv musta gone to lunch late," he said. "I was upstairs. I came down and she wasn't there and Aaron had unlocked the side door."

When he trailed off, September encouraged him, "The side door's generally always locked."

"Yeah. But Aaron got the key and unlocked it, and Kurt found out and they had words."

"Why did Aaron unlock the door, do you know?"

"Like I said, he just likes messing with his dad. His mother and Kurt don't get along. She uses Aaron to get to Kurt, and Kurt doesn't really know what to do with him. Aaron's kind of a slacker and . . ." He cut himself off, his eyes filling with tears.

"Can you tell me a little more about Olivia Dugan?" she asked as Gretchen returned, her mouth a grim line.

"Liv is quiet. Keeps to herself. I think Aaron likes her, but she's careful."

"Careful, how? With his feelings?" September sipped from her own cup of coffee, hoping Berelli would drink up as well. He needed something to keep him going.

"Careful in every way," he said, looking into his coffee cup. "Afraid to say too much."

"Afraid?" Gretchen jumped on the word.

"Not . . . like that . . ." he said. "She's just . . . quiet."

Gretchen frowned. "Was there anything different in the last few days? Something you can think of that might have precipitated this event?"

Berelli turned to September. "Can I go home now? I can't think of anything else. I'm just . . . tired."

Gretchen looked irked, but she gestured to September and said, "Detective Rafferty will give you a ride home."

"My car's still at Zuma," he said.

September said, "I'll take you to it."

Berelli tossed a look toward Guy Urlacher as he and September passed by the front desk and pushed their way through the two sets of glass doors that led outside. "Liv isn't involved in this," he said. "I know she took off, but she was just scared, y'know."

"Uh huh."

"She's just lucky she wasn't there. Really lucky." When September didn't respond, he added, "I mean it. I'm right about Liv. She's just one of the meek ones, y'know?"

September nodded.

Liv stared at her gun, which rested on the table beside her left hand. She was still seated across the table from Auggie. Each of them was working through their own thoughts, but it had been quiet a long time and Liv finally could stand it no longer.

"What do you do down here?" she asked him.

"Down here?" he repeated, as if he weren't really listening.

"In the States."

"A fishing guide. Same as Canada."

"Where's your boat?" she asked.

"At a marina on the Columbia River," he said, frowning. "You think *I'm* lying to *you?*"

"I don't even care if you are," she said. "Unless there's someone else coming to this house."

"Look in the other bedroom. I live alone," he stated flatly.

"I need to figure this out," she said.

What had precipitated the attack on Zuma? Maybe Auggie was right and it had something to do with Kurt Upjohn and his war games, or his finances, or maybe even his personal life. Or, maybe it was somebody else at Zuma? One of the geeks upstairs? But the upstairs hadn't been compromised. At least she didn't think so. She hadn't gone up there herself, but the door at the top of the stairs wasn't easy to breach. It was everyone downstairs who'd been gunned down.

Maybe Jessica or Paul or even Aaron had some desperate enemy willing to kill innocent people to get to them.

But why now? She was the one who'd gotten the package from her long-dead mother.

But what would the package have to do with anything? It was benign, really. A few photographs, a message from her mother, her birth certificate. Yet . . . yet . . . there was *something* there.

The pictures . . . the zombie stalker . . . it felt like there was a door cracking open inside her mind. Dr. Yancy had told her she'd buried her memories.

Who knew about the package? Hague. Della. Her father. Lorinda . . . the lawyers at Crenshaw and Crenshaw . . .

Was it about the package? *Was it?* How could it be?

How could it not be?

Last night she'd told her father and Lorinda and Della that she was going to look into the past. She'd declared and/or intimated that she was going to learn more about the serial strangler who'd been killing women in their area about the time her mother committed suicide. That she wanted to know who the people were in the photographs. That she might follow up with her birth parents.

Hague had called the man in the picture the zombie, the man who was always there, just out of the corner of his eye. But then Hague had mentally disappeared. He knew something. Something that had sent him away from reality.

Kill you.

And then today the gunman had come to Zuma.

"What?" Auggie asked when Liv suddenly jumped to her feet.

"I've got to go talk to someone."

"Now?"

"Yes."

"You're not going to leave me tied here," he warned her.

She pulled the keys from her pocket. "I'm going to have to." She looked around, yanked out a drawer, then another, until she found a small knife, then cut off a hank of twine from the roll while he tried to reason with her as she lashed his legs together and to the chair. "There's no need for this. Take me with you. I want to help you. Do you hear me?"

She wasn't listening. It was all just noise in the background as her mind moved ahead. She tested the ropes and ignored his darkening expression as she grabbed her backpack from where she'd left it by the kitchen table, stuffed the knife inside, and, more gingerly, her gun, then gave a last look around the kitchen. The oven was freestanding with a bar for the handle. Following her gaze, he said, "No."

With all her strength Liv dragged a struggling Auggie in his chair to the oven and then tied the chair to the handle of the opened oven door.

"This is dangerous," he said through his teeth.

"Yes, it is." She went through his pockets. Nothing. His cell phone was on the counter. "You don't have a wallet," she said, wondering where that was.

"Yes, I do. I—" He cut himself off, thinking hard. Swearing beneath his breath, he said, "If it's not in my back pocket, I must have left it at the coffee shop. Damn." He threw her a fulminating look. "Maybe you can get it for me?"

She tightened her lips, silently telling him that wasn't possible, then she opened the back door, keys in hand. The last thing she saw was Auggie, glowering at her, clenching his teeth as if to keep himself from blasting her. She closed the door behind her, listened for the satisfying sound of the deadlock shutting tight and the ear-blistering sounds of Auggie swearing a blue streak. Then she headed to his Jeep with a length of twine to tie down the back hatch.

My brain is full of worms. It is failing me. What I did today . . . crazy. Crazy. Like fuckin' Rambo . . .

My heart is pounding triple-time. I have to hide the gun. Hide my clothes.

Hide.

But she has to die. She knows too much. It's planted deep inside her.

I have to kill her. I have to find her and kill her.

I can feel the need overtake mè. Hot and smothering. My hands reach into the darkness, and I dream of that soft, white neck. Crushing the hyoid bone at her throat is almost like sex.

But what I did today! Fuckin' Rambo. Too desperate and reckless and she wasn't even there*!*

I've let her live too long.

Too long.

I need a new plan. Something less BIG, but it's getting harder to keep my thoughts in order.

My brain is full of worms . . . it's failing me.

I must finish what I started . . . accept who I am . . .

Before it's too late . . . and little Livvie catches up to me.

Chapter 7

"Detective. Rafferty . . . ?"

September was in the process of striding back through the station's main entrance and past Guy Urlacher after taking Phillip Berelli back to his car. She gave Guy a long look, just daring him to ask for her ID.

"Yes," she said in a tone that warned him not to get in her way. It was like an uncontrollable obsession with him and though he contained himself with Gretchen most times as she would glare ice at him if he should even speak to her, he did not feel the same restraint when it came to September.

This was the curse of being the newest detective on staff. No uniform. No name tag. Guy Urlacher didn't know how to handle it.

It was dark outside and she was tired. Too tired to deal with him in any professional way. She could feel the cloud over her head as she stepped around him with a dark scowl, then marched down the hall to the squad room.

She overheard Gretchen saying to George as she entered, "The guys upstairs didn't know what went down. They don't leave unless they absolutely have to, apparently. Someone takes a lunch order for them and otherwise they're just there."

"Who took the lunch order today?" George asked.

"A guy named Rad. Yes, Rad. He went out about twelve, got back about one, and then went upstairs. The accountant, Berelli, has an office in one corner, and Rad got him something, too."

September already knew this as she and Gretchen had walked through the "control room" and spoke briefly to the nine or ten programmers. To a one they were slack-jawed with shock. Their world, apparently, was inside the games they developed, games that were rife with violence. But they were just games after all, and the programmers didn't seem to know what to think about life and death events in the real world.

Rad had insisted he was the only one who'd gone in and out of the upstairs door that day other than Berelli, and September was inclined to believe him. Backgrounds were being checked but on first glance it appeared none of the computer geeks was connected to the grisly massacre that had taken place on the first floor.

Gretchen's desk phone rang and she swiveled around to answer it, smashing the receiver to her ear. September, who, at a request from Gretchen, had stopped at a deli on the way back, plopped the brown bag on Gretchen's desk. Gretchen was tapping her fingers and staring up at the ceiling, clearly irked at some delay on the other end as September pulled out tuna fish sandwiches for herself and her partner.

George said, "Nothing for me?"

"You gotta put in an order," September said.

"Tuna," he said, spying the sandwich and wrinkling his nose. He made a sound of disgust and turned back to his work.

"Yeah, well, tell me something I don't know!" Gretchen snarled into the phone and crashed the receiver into its cradle. She picked up half of her sandwich and waved it at

September. "Everybody's an asshole," she declared, before taking a bite.

"Everybody?"

"Everybody," she stated firmly.

"What was that about?"

"The lab. Nobody can get jack shit done unless it's an act of Congress."

They munched on their sandwiches and Gretchen washed hers down with cold coffee. September got up, walked into the hallway and to the water cooler and poured herself a small paper cupful. She returned just as Gretchen demanded, "Where's this Olivia Dugan person?"

George spoke up, "D'Annibal sent someone to find her. Wes, maybe."

"Why hasn't she called us?" Gretchen asked. "She should have called us by now."

September shrugged. "Maybe she's scared? Maybe she still doesn't know we're looking for her."

"She'd have to live on another planet not to know, with all the press that's come down. And she should know to wait for the police. Where'd she go after she left Zuma?"

September shook her head. No one had that information.

"Did you get through to the de Fores?" Gretchen asked George, who'd been tasked with finding the man's family.

"Finally," he said, exhaling heavily. "Mom and Dad live in Medford and are flying up, so they'll be here in an hour or so. You gonna be at the morgue when they arrive?" he asked Gretchen.

She grimaced. "Yeah." She turned to September. "How'd you do with Upjohn's ex?"

"I talked to Camille on the phone. Camille Dirkus. She was at the hospital earlier, maybe still is," September answered. "She took back her maiden name, but Aaron was their son together. Camille's beside herself about Aaron's death, and I don't know . . . I think if Kurt Upjohn lives she could actually try to kill him." She was half-serious.

George said, "Hmmm."

"She blames him?" Gretchen asked. At September's nod, she said, "We'll go see her tomorrow."

"What about the receptionist? Maltona?" George asked.

"Maltona doesn't appear to have anyone but the boyfriend, a Jason Jaffe who's an artist of some kind," Gretchen said in a tone that suggested what she thought of artists in general. "I started leaving messages on Jaffe's cell phone this afternoon and he's texted me back stuff like 'ok' and 'at hospital.' I don't really know if he's telling the truth; nobody at the hospital's seen him. He's first on my list tomorrow to track down."

"Upjohn's first on mine," September said.

Gretchen stretched her arms over her head. "It's six-thirty. After the de Fores, I'm done for today." She scooted back her chair and gathered up the second half of her sandwich.

"I hear ya," George said and Gretchen shot September a sideways look. George did as little as possible when it came to dealing with people, especially bereaved people.

September thought of her rented condo. She'd lived there for three years, ever since the owners had bought it, and a number of other units, out of foreclosure and turned them all into rentals. When she'd first moved in she'd painted all the rooms and bought new towels and an overly expensive couch, but since that first flurry of pride of house, she'd spent more time advancing her career than caring about hearth and home. Now, she didn't really relish going back to her empty rooms.

"I think I'll stick around a little bit longer," she said.

"Suit yourself," Gretchen responded as she took a left out of the squad room. George hefted his bulk from the chair and headed down the hall after her in the direction of the staff room.

After they were gone, the squad room was nearly empty and had a strange echoey feel that didn't exist during the rest of the day. She thought of her family—two brothers, one sister, her autocratic father and stepmother—and decided she didn't want to talk to any of them, either.

Detective Wes "Weasel" Pelligree stuck his head inside the squad room from the hall to the lockers. A tall, lean, black man, he had a killer smile, a slow-talking manner and a dry wit. He made September's heart race a little faster whenever he appeared, but he was firmly entrenched in a long-term relationship with his high school girlfriend and had been for fifteen years or so, so the rumor went. He was also on a mission to arrest every crack and meth dealer he could find, a result of the death of his older brother, a user, who'd nicknamed Wes "Weasel" long before Wes had grown to his full six-foot-three height.

"How ya doin'?" he asked her.

"Been a long day," September admitted.

"Sandler's a bitch, but she knows what she's doing," he said.

"I guess that's a recommendation of sorts."

He grinned. "Look forward to the day when someone says it about you. Then you'll know you're a detective."

"Oh, joy." When he ducked back out, she yelled after him, "Aren't you on the trail of Olivia Dugan?"

"The Zuma employee? Uh-uh. Probably somebody D'Annibal thinks'll look good on TV. Channel Seven's all over this."

"All the stations are," September said.

"Well, try to stay away from Seven's Pauline Kirby. That woman's a barracuda." He gave a mock shudder. "*And* a bitch."

"So, she's good at her job?"

He snorted. "You *can* be a bitch and a lousy detective," he allowed. "You just don't last long."

"How about nice, or at least personable, and good at your job?"

He flashed her his pearly whites. "Never happen."

September was still smiling after he was gone. "Then I guess I'll just have to be a bitch," she said to the empty room.

Trask Burcher Martin was a pothead. And a drunk, kinda. And definitely a slacker. But he was a good guy inside. Ya just had to look a little harder, sometimes, to see the good of it all. At least that's what he told himself whenever he thought hard about the whole thing, like now.

He exhaled a lungful of smoke, lost in a bit of a weed dream-state. He liked Jo. Loved her, maybe. She was his woman and they were *together*. Taking another toke, Trask relaxed into the couch cushions. A little MJ from time to time kept him from noticing that he and Jo didn't have too much going for them, really. Not cash-wise, anyway. Making the rent payment every month was kinda tricky, and well, his job pumping gas wasn't gonna make them rich anytime soon. Jo was a clerk at the local convenience store, but she would only work the daylight hours because of all the sick fucks who held up places like hers late at night, so that kept her from any serious greenbacks.

Still, it was okay. Pretty okay. Kept Jo safe and that was good.

He squinted an eye at the television cable box. If he didn't pay that bill soon, it would shut off and be over. But for right now, he could read the time: eight-thirty.

So, where was Jo, huh? It was getting damn dark.

"Jo," he said aloud. And then burned the end of his fingers with the last ember of the doobie. "FUCK!" He dropped it and stamped it out with his foot, waving away the smoke. Lucky for him, his neighbor, Liv, was spooked by about everything so if she smelled anything she wasn't likely to call the authorities down on him. Like the landlord. Or the police. Or anybody.

Shaking his head, he sucked on his fingers, then ran them through his hair and stepped outside onto the concrete balcony that fronted the parking lot side of the L-shaped building. A wave of August heat burned up from the pavement below; he could feel it rising beneath his bare feet, too. It was just barely dark, but still fuckin' hot. He could see the faint glimmer of stars above the fir trees at the back of the lot.

And the GMC truck was there. The 2005 one that . . . was kinda like his old one.

Trask blinked. Tried to remember. What was that about? Oh, yeah. The lurking asshole in the hoodie outside Liv's place who wouldn't show his face.

He wondered if Liv was home. Maybe Jo was with her?

"That . . . would be . . . unlikely," he said to the parking lot below, working on the thought to keep it from flying around inside his muddled brain.

But the truck . . . ?

Oh, yeah. The dude. He'd been in a truck like that. Asshole.

Trask lurched along the balcony toward the stairs. Whoa, man. He musta kinda overdid it. Was havin' a few problemos with his equal . . . equality . . . equilibrium. Yessirree. Equilibrium. Maybe he should just talk to that dude? See what was on his mind. Ask him what the fuck he was doing hangin' around Liv's . . . place . . . room.

Nodding, he worked his way slowly down the outdoor stairs to the ground level, his soles scraping along the concrete steps. Shoulda put on some shoes, he realized belatedly.

He slipped down the last couple of steps, had to grab the

metal rail. Whoa. Head rush. Pulling it together, he strode right over to the truck. "Hey," he yelled, then was incensed when the bastard fired up the vehicle like he was gonna race away.

"Hey!" Trask yelled again. He pointed his finger at him. *I see you. You fucker. I see you!*

To Trask's surprise, the guy slid down his window . . . and pointed the barrel of a handgun at him.

"What . . . whoa, man." Trask backed up, holding his hands in the air. Fucker! Geez . . . God.

Bang. Bang.

Two shots. No hesitation.

Pain exploded in his chest. In disbelief, Trask staggered sideways, staring down at himself. "You shot me. You fuckin' shot me!"

The GMC sped out of the lot with a roar, tires burping on pavement. Through a haze Trask tracked its progress. He lurched and fell to one knee, looked around wildly, then gazed across the parking lot to the line of doors and windows of the apartment building. Silence. No one around. No one busting out of a door to help him.

"Hey . . ." he said feebly.

Wrapping one arm around his chest, vaguely aware this was gonna hurt like a son-of-a-bitch later, completely in denial that this was anything serious, Trask staggered across the lot and reeled and stumbled his way up the apartment steps.

He made it all the way to Liv's apartment before he sank down in front of her door and died.

Driving to Hague's apartment, Liv kept her eye on the speedometer, careful not to drive too fast, careful not to drive too slow. She wasn't used to Auggie's Jeep, but she didn't want to show it on the road. She didn't want to give any quota-anxious cop a reason to stop her.

She crossed the Willamette and wound down the narrow eastside streets to Hague's apartment building, passing in front of it once to get the lay of the land, spying the green and yellow neon script of Rosa's Cantina as she went by. She parked at the end of the block, left her backpack behind the front seat after a moment's thought, removed the envelope to take with her, pulled down the brim of her baseball cap to hide her face, and headed toward the building's entrance. She nearly ran into the same woman with the three children from the night before and turned away quickly so the woman wouldn't be able to see her face.

Up the elevator she went. She hurried to Hague's door, rapping so hard against the panels she bruised her knuckles in the process.

Come on, come on, come on. Time was running out. She'd left Auggie tied up and if anything should happen, like an unforeseen disaster, like a fire, or . . .

She shook her head. No. She just had to make this quick and get back and—

Della yanked open the door, a sour look on her face. "You."

"I need to talk to Hague," Liv said, trying to step inside, but Della was planted firmly in the door.

"He's not here."

"What? He's not?"

"He's at the cantina. Holding court. I'm about to go down and get him."

"No, let me. I'll find him and send him up."

She laughed harshly. "Won't do any good. He doesn't listen to anyone when he's in one of his moods. He's talking. Ranting. Telling the whole world that it's fucked up and he's not gonna take it anymore. He just has to wear down."

Liv didn't care. It was a chance to see Hague without Della. An opportunity. "I'll do my best."

"It won't be good enough," she predicted, then closed the door with a firm thud in Liv's face.

She headed back down the elevator, out to the street and to Rosa's front door, reflecting that Della hadn't commented about the Zuma killings. She would have, if she'd known about them, because she knew it was where Liv worked. But Della, because of Hague and his fears, stayed away from the news; more government conspiracy, according to Hague. So, at least that was a good sign. Fairly soon, however, if Liv didn't turn herself in, someone else would.

She just needed a little more time.

Pulling her hat down yet further, Liv entered the cantina and looked around. Jimmy and Rosa were behind the bar, busy on a Friday night, and didn't notice her arrival.

Hague was seated in his corner and practically bellowing at a small group of people who were sitting nearby, raptly listening. His rant was about government interference in everything, particularly, for some reason, how it was influencing the medical profession. By the sound of it, Liv half-expected him to launch into his theories about secret studies on humans without their knowledge or consent. Hague definitely believed he'd been subjected to tests and drugs at the hands of various mental health professionals over the years.

Liv walked toward the gathering slowly.

"The government plans these things," one of the men in the group was agreeing with Hague. "They don't see us as individuals. We're like crash test dummies. No feelings! No thoughts! Available and expendable."

"The government keeps a lid on this stuff so we can go about our daily lives," Hague stated. "But it's the hospitals you have to worry about." He wagged his finger at his listeners. "That's where the mindbenders are. That's where experimentation takes place. Hi, Livvie."

She hadn't thought he'd even noticed her. "Hello, Hague."

"This is my sister," Hague told his followers and all four of them gave her a hard once-over. She was glad for the baseball cap and the jacket. Did they watch the news? Maybe. Maybe not. This was dangerous territory, but she desperately needed to talk to her brother.

"You're the one who works for the government," a woman with a long face and stringy gray hair said.

"No," Liv answered, surprised.

"War games," the man next to her said knowingly. He had eyes that didn't quite focus properly.

"It's that company," another man, younger and rail thin, said, clearly rolling the idea over in his mind.

Liv's anxiety level spiked. If they came up with Zuma Software . . . "Could I talk to you for a minute alone?" she asked Hague.

He slid a darting, birdlike look at her. For a moment she thought he was going to refuse, then he gestured to a chair while his four listeners reluctantly scooted their own seats back and walked a few steps away. They perched just out of earshot, apparently waiting to return at the first indication that Hague and Liv were finished.

"What?" he asked.

"I'm in trouble. Someone could recognize me."

His gaze narrowed on her, cataloguing the way she was dressed. "What kind of trouble?"

She leaned toward him. "There was a shooting earlier today . . . did you know about it?" Hague shook his head, so she quickly brought him up-to-date on what had taken place at Zuma, finishing with, "I know it sounds crazy, but I think they were after me."

"We're both crazy, Livvie. Everybody says so."

"And as a result, I've done something—irresponsible."

She lightly tapped one fist against her teeth, seized with anxiety.

"What?"

"I've . . ." She couldn't bring herself to tell him about Auggie. How she'd kidnapped him and tied him up. Every moment she spent away from him and out in public felt like an eternity.

"Who did the shooting?" Hague asked in a low voice, matching her tone. His eyes darted around the room suspiciously.

"I don't know."

His eyes came back to hers, holding her gaze tautly. "Yes, you do."

"No, I don't."

"You know who they are," he insisted.

She shook her head. "Really, Hague, I don't. But this has got something to do with the package from Mama. It's about my past. *Our* past. Yours and mine."

"Our past," he repeated.

"I've had this feeling for a while, that someone's stalking me. And then when I got the pictures from Mama yesterday and then today. . . ." She swallowed hard. "I just want to know what you think. Have I got this right? Do you believe me?"

His eyes were dark pools of an emotion she recognized as fear. "It's us," he agreed. "They're after *us.* Could be any one of them," he added, glaring tightly at his disciples, who were still waiting for Liv to leave.

"Not them."

"I told them about the package. I told them yesterday."

"You weren't here yesterday."

"I was. I came later. They said you'd been here . . ." He glanced over to Jimmy and Rosa and the bar. "I told them. I told all of them." Now he looked at his four listeners. "There were more here last night. *They knew.*"

Liv's heart clutched. Though she felt his paranoia as if it had jumped to her like a spark of electricity, she didn't agree with him. It wasn't these people. Quixotically, and like always, the more he agreed with her, the less she felt certain of herself.

"I think it's the Mystery Man who knew Mom. He's at the center of it."

"It's not these people?" He glared at them, turning his head suspiciously as he looked at all their faces individually.

"I think it's about the zombie," she said.

"The doctor," he said.

"The doctor?" she repeated. He nodded, waiting for her to continue and she questioned him, "The man in the picture? The one who's stalking to the camera?" She drew the picture from the envelope and slid the photo to him again. "He's a doctor?"

Hague pulled back from it, as if the paper were covered in germs, but his gaze was zeroed in on the man. "He looks like . . ."

"Who?" Liv asked when he trailed off. "I got the same hit. Like I knew him."

"We both know him. From when we were kids."

She gazed at him helplessly. "How can you know him from when we were kids? You were so little."

"I grew up though," he said, his eyes starting to lose focus.

"No, Hague. Don't leave. Please."

"He's always there . . . out of the corner of my eye." Slowly his head turned and he focused on the bar and Jimmy and Rosa and the red pepper lights looping around the glasses hanging upside down.

His hand shot out and grabbed her upper arm and Liv yelped in surprise. "Don't let him get you, too."

"The stalking man?"

"He'll drill holes in your head. And he'll put receivers inside the folds of your brain. And you'll be a zombie, too."

She saw his eyes start to roll.

"Wait. Hague, *wait*." He was going into one of his fugue states again. "Don't . . . don't . . ."

"We saw him again, didn't we?" he asked in a drifting tone.

"Hague!" she hissed harshly.

But he was gone. Into that distant place. His eyes becoming slits and then closing altogether. Liv looked around for help and the four acolytes rushed back.

"What'd you do to him?" the woman with the long face and straggly hair asked.

Liv edged away. "He does this sometimes."

"But you sent him there!" the younger man accused her.

She shook her head vaguely as she backed toward the door. Della had been right: she wasn't able to get Hague back to the apartment. Especially not now.

With thoughts of letting Della know about Hague, she stumbled toward the cantina's entrance but when she got to the door Della was already there, blocking her exit. She glanced past Liv to Hague, muttered something furious, then pushed on past her.

Liv didn't have time to care. She was filled with wriggling eels of anxiety herself. She needed to get back to Auggie and away from places and people who might recognize her. She needed a place to hole up and think. Time.

How long would it take? How many hours, or days? *Or weeks?*

She'd embarked on this crazy journey and now she didn't quite know what to do next.

"Groceries," she said aloud, halfway back to his place.

Exiting Sunset Highway, she wound the Jeep down Sylvan hill and toward a strip mall with a Safeway as the anchor store. Keeping her head low, she hitched her backpack over one shoulder, grabbed a shopping cart and headed inside the brightly lit grocery, winding through the aisles, grabbing items for more sandwiches, her mind far away from the errand at hand.

In line at the checkout, she heard the checker behind her talking over the Zuma massacre with a male customer.

"Two of 'em are dead," the female checker was saying in a conversational way. "They're not saying who yet. Gotta inform the family first and stuff."

The man answered her: "How many were shot?"

"Half a dozen, maybe?"

Four. Liv swallowed hard and carefully perused the rack of magazines at the end of her checkout stand. Her mind's eye flew through the faces of her coworkers: Paul, Jessica, Kurt and Aaron. *Aaron . . .*

"Are you all right, miss?"

Liv's checker was looking at her with concern and Liv realized she'd made some kind of whimpering sound. She swallowed, shook her head, and said in a forced rasp, "Dry throat. Got a cold."

"Yeah. Been going around." Liv focused on the woman's name tag: JEANNIE. She kept her eyes lowered so Jeannie wouldn't spend too much time looking at her face, then reached in her backpack for her wallet, careful not to let anyone see her gun. She then counted out the cash for the groceries, and watched as a helper put the sacks in her cart. He insisted on wheeling the cart out toward the Jeep, though Liv would have preferred to do it herself. A scream was building up inside her head, one she just managed to tamp down as she thanked the young man and climbed behind the steering wheel, letting out a pent-up breath.

It took another fifteen minutes to drive the rest of the way to Auggie's house. She'd left the garage door open, but once parked inside she leapt from the vehicle and ran around to the rear, yanking the door down behind the Jeep, cutting off the view from prying eyes, throwing herself into pitch dark. She stopped for a moment, gathering her bearings, then she opened the driver's side back door and hefted out the two bags of groceries, noting how clean his car was except for the gray hoodie flung across the other back seats.

Juggling the bags, she was closing the Jeep's back door when her brain kicked in. Setting the bags down, she kept the door ajar to keep on the interior light, then she circled the front of the vehicle and opened the passenger door. Punching the button on the glove box, she held her breath, expecting . . . what? Some big reveal about him?

The glove box was locked.

He's careful, she thought. But then so was she.

Still, she was disquieted. Quickly, she sorted through his keys but the one for the glove box wasn't there.

What are you doing, Liv? What are you doing?

Shutting all doors to the Jeep, she waited until the interior light switched off, grabbing her backpack and leaving the groceries in the garage for the moment. Then she cautiously slipped into the breezeway and across to the back door, unlocking it and stepping into the kitchen. It was dark, but she could see Auggie still tied up to the chair by the oven door. Moonlight filtered in and touched his face, glistening on his open eyes.

"Where the hell have you been?" he demanded.

Chapter 8

"I got groceries," she answered automatically, setting down her backpack on the counter. "It took a while."

He made a big show of looking all around her. "Huh. I don't see any."

"They're still in the garage," she said.

"Afraid to walk in here carrying something? Cause I might be free and jump you?"

"I get that you're upset," she stated flatly.

"You go off for hours and leave me tied up and you 'get' that I'm upset? What if there'd been a fire? I could be dead. Then you really would be a killer."

"Shut up," she muttered, heading back to the garage. She returned a few moments later and thumped the grocery bags down on the table. Then she switched on the overhead light and they both blinked in the sudden onslaught of illumination.

His blue eyes were stormy. He may have been a somewhat willing captive earlier, but that moment had passed.

"I just need a little time," she said, mentally cringing at the faint pleading tone in her voice.

"Take all the time you need," he said expansively. "Be

my guest. I'll just wait right here." He glanced at the bags. "Planning on making us dinner?"

"I picked up a few things. I'm not much of a cook."

"A ringing endorsement," he said. Then, "How long do you intend to keep me here? Or, have you figured that out yet?"

"Not really."

"Honest," he stated. "Unhelpful. But honest."

She opened her mouth to retort, but there was nothing to say, really. Instead, she reached in a bag and pulled out the wheat bread, deli turkey and roast beef, Havarti cheese, romaine lettuce and two different kinds of mustard that she'd picked up. Even though it was after nine P.M. she started to make two sandwiches, one of roast beef, one of turkey, until he said tightly, "I'm not hungry. Thanks."

Instead of responding she finished making the turkey sandwich and ate half of it before her appetite died completely away. She could feel his eyes on her with every bite and it was unnerving, as no doubt it was meant to be.

"I have to use the bathroom," he said when she'd finished putting things away and cleaning up.

She gazed at him, starting to feel overwhelmed. "I'll untie your legs from the chair again."

"Better give me use of my hands, too, unless you want to get really personal," he pointed out.

"Okay, but I'll have to follow you in."

"Hell, no. You can leave the door cracked if you want. Keep the gun on me. But I'm going in alone."

"I'm sorry."

"You're sorry," he repeated on a strangled note.

"Will anyone stop by?" she asked suddenly.

"I told you already. No."

"Nobody? No one?"

"No one," he said. "No one will stop by."

"Why should I believe you?"

"They haven't stopped by yet. They're not stopping by later. Because no one knows I'm here, but you."

"I don't know why I'm doing this," she muttered, more to herself than him.

"You can still get out of this," he said after a moment. "No harm, no foul. And, if you're as innocent as you claim—" he started to suggest.

"*If?*" she cut in.

"—then you should contact the police right now. Let them take care of this. They're good at it."

She shook her head in disbelief. "I can't even make *you* believe me!"

"I believe you. I do."

"Oh, bullshit."

"I believe you think someone's after you, and that's why we're here now," he corrected himself. "You might even be right. The police could help you. Or, if you'd let me, I could help you."

"You could help me," she said without inflection. "And why would you do that?"

"Because I think you need help."

"You're not a very good liar, Auggie."

"I'm a *very* good liar," he disagreed with an edge, as if it were a matter of pride. "But I'm not lying to you."

"What kind of name is Auggie anyway? A nickname? Is it short for something?"

His lips compressed. "Are you going to untie me? Take me to the bathroom?"

She pulled the .38 from her backpack, looked at it a moment, then walked his way. He sank back at the sight of the gun, but she merely laid it on the counter before untying his chair from the oven handle. When she released his feet, she quickly stepped back, snatching up the gun again and leveling it at him. His hands were still tied behind him and he gave her a look that said she was half-crazy if she thought he was a threat. She felt dark amusement at that but held it inside. After a moment, she undid the twine wrapped around his hands, then, sweeping up the gun again once he was completely free, she took five steps back.

Rubbing his wrists, he eyed her thoughtfully. "You're not going to shoot me."

"I don't want to," she said.

"You won't."

He sounded so positive it rankled her. "I think I could shoot you. It's just a matter of displacement. I'll pretend you're a wall, or a rock, or a bull's-eye I'm shooting at. Pulling the trigger would be easy."

"You can do that? Displacement?" When she didn't respond, he said, "Been through some therapy, I guess. Displacement. Got any other psychobabble buzzwords?"

"How about crazy, wacko, nutso, psychotic, borderline personality, breaks with reality, delusional, paranoid. . . ." She trailed off. "Dr. Yancy tried to help me, but most of it didn't take."

He nodded, not quite certain whether she was putting him on or not, she could tell. "Dr. Yancy is your therapist?"

"Was my therapist."

"What would he say about this?" He motioned toward the weapon she had leveled at him and the bonds she'd just untied.

"*She* would try to get me to think about the trigger," Liv said, realizing it was the truth.

"The trigger of the gun?" he asked cautiously.

"The trigger that set this all in motion."

"Ahhh . . ." he said. "Fear. You saw a horrible scene."

Images flashed behind her eyes of the Zuma slayings. Blood. Sprawled bodies. Then she saw her mother. Hanging. Eyes closed. Tongue out.

And then Mama slowly lifted her lids and stared at Livvie.

I'm done.

"Hey!" Auggie called.

Liv snapped back to the present. She blinked, realizing she was fast losing control of the situation. "The trigger's something else," she said, licking her lips and feeling slightly faint. "From way back in the past."

When she didn't go on, he said, "I'm listening."

"No . . . No . . ." She shook her head. She wasn't going there with him. Deciding it was time to return to safer subjects, she asked, "What's your real name? I can't keep calling you Auggie."

"Why not?"

"It's too . . . personal."

"Somehow I think the worry about 'too personal' is way over," he said dryly.

"Then give me your last name. Something."

"Planning on sending me a Christmas card?"

She gritted her teeth. "It's pretty convenient that you lost your wallet."

"Convenient," he repeated, annoyed, as he got to his feet.

His size alarmed her a little and though she refused to retreat another step, she couldn't help leaning back, away from him. Lips tight, she kept a steady grip on the .38. He was tall and lean and muscular, and damnably good-looking. And dangerous, she decided.

She didn't like him one bit. "I thought you had to use the restroom."

"I'm heading that way." With that he strode out of the room, Liv on his heels. When he entered the bathroom, he tried to shut the door. She held it open with one hand. "Fine," he said through his teeth, turning to the toilet and slamming up the lid.

She kept her eyes staring at the profile of his face as she

held the gun on him. It was silly. Stupid. Of no importance, in the larger scheme of things, but she kept her gaze averted anyway. She was running on reaction rather than logic. Had been since the massacre at Zuma.

She heard the toilet flush and the sound of him zipping up. Then he moved to the sink and washed his hands. Finally, he turned to look at her, lifting his palms, as if for inspection. "All done."

She stepped back and waved the gun to indicate he should walk ahead of her, back toward the kitchen.

"I could have overpowered you," he pointed out.

"But you didn't."

"If that gun's loaded, one of us could get hurt."

"It's loaded."

He paused, gazing at her speculatively. "Maybe. So, tie me up again. Do whatcha gotta do." He walked into the kitchen, but suddenly grabbed up his chair and started striding back toward her.

She stopped short at the table. "What are you doing?" she demanded, rattled.

"I'd like to watch TV. And the TV's in my bedroom." He stepped around her.

Hurriedly, she grabbed up the twine on the counter, then race-walked after him, standing by as he set the chair down in the bedroom and picked up the remote. She stood over him as he sat down, feeling like an idiot. "I don't like this," she said.

"I'm having the time of my life," he muttered.

"I don't know how long this is going to take. But I'm committed now. I'm just—not sure what to do next."

"Contact the police," he said again. "Would you mind moving? You're in the way."

She automatically sidestepped. "They won't believe me."

"What happened that made you a cop hater?" he asked.

"I'm not a cop hater," she said. "They've just never

shown the least interest in helping me. They're just another wall." She hesitated, then lifted the twine and ordered, "Put your arms around the back of the chair."

He sighed, set the remote on the bed and got to his feet again. "Save yourself some effort and tie me to the bedpost. I'm not sleeping in that chair tonight."

His highhanded manner irked her; he seemed intent on making her feel like he was in control. If it was some kind of psychological tactic to keep her off balance, it was a good one.

He sat on the edge of the bed, pulled off his shoes, then leaned back, draping his arms over the back of the headboard. "This is gonna be a pain," he said in a long-suffering tone.

She lashed his wrists to the bedposts. It was an older double bed that appeared to have seen better days, but it served the purpose. He was ahead of her in his thinking, she realized.

One of the older *Law & Order* franchises was on the television. The one where one of the main characters unsterstood and dug into a criminal's psyche.

"Just like you, the police will think the murders are because of Kurt Upjohn," Liv said as she checked the strength of her ministrations; the twine was taut and tight. "People think Zuma's involved with the military because of their video war games. Mr. Upjohn likes the rumors. Keeps interest in his product."

"But they aren't true." Auggie's blue eyes were watching her as she perched at the end of the bed. The show ended and she picked up the remote and lifted her brows, but he shook his head. "I'm over it," he said.

"They're just rumors," she answered his earlier comment.

"And you would know."

"What happened today wasn't about Kurt Upjohn. But if it were," she said, when it looked like he was about to object, "it would more likely have something to do with his personal life, than professional. His son, Aaron, was working there, and now he's . . ." She pressed her lips together, then said, forcing herself, "Dead."

He didn't look convinced. "Okay, we'll put Upjohn aside for the moment. What about the others? Could the shooting have anything to do with them?"

"This is about me," she insisted quietly. "Whoever shot them . . . they were looking for me."

"Just . . . okay. Could you just take a moment and consider another angle?"

"This is why I can't go to the police," she said tiredly.

"You could use a little perspective," he insisted.

She wanted to scream at him, take all her pain and frustration out on him. Instead, she said firmly, "None of this has to do with Aaron Dirkus. He's too . . . disorganized and . . . unfocused."

"Maybe you don't know him as well as you think you do."

"I *didn't* know him well at all. But I knew that much about him."

"He could have been into drugs," he suggested. "Or, something that got him caught up with the wrong people."

"No. Aaron smoked some weed, but that's it. Nothing else."

"The fact that you liked him isn't a reason to take him off the list. You don't know—"

"I do know! This isn't about Aaron. I don't care what you say! And, it wasn't about Paul de Fore, either. Paul was . . ."

A tool.

She couldn't bring herself to say what she'd thought of him in life, now that he was dead. The image of his sprawled body was imprinted on her brain. Finding herself suddenly close to tears, she turned away from Auggie's scouring gaze and said diffidently, "He was too into the rules."

"A rules guy. The kind that gets on top of you. Controls you. Forces his way."

She shook her head. "He wasn't the way you make him sound. Not like that, anyhow."

"Then, how?"

"I don't know," she expelled in frustration. "He was pissy about it."

"Ahh. Petty. Into small victories."

"That sums him up pretty well," she had to admit.

"It's not a crime to not like people," he said after a moment of watching her.

"I don't know why I'm talking to you." She got up and paced to the other side of the room, pulling at the curtain and looking outside the bedroom window.

"I know you believe the Zuma shooting was about you. I don't want to totally piss you off, but couldn't this attack be about something else? I mean, can you entertain that idea, for just a few minutes? Maybe get a dialog going?"

She lifted her hands and tossed them back down. "Go ahead."

"It's Upjohn's company. That's where the money is. Chances are the killer was after him."

"I suppose."

"It doesn't really sound like you're agreeing with me."

"I just want you to stop talking," she said. "Stop theorizing. It makes me feel . . . I don't know. Like this is simply an exercise. Like I'm not . . . I don't count."

"You count," he said.

She threw him a look, aware that he was just humoring her, trying to get on his captor's good side. Wasn't that what all hostages did? "Shut up," she told him.

He opened his mouth to argue, then pressed his lips together, as if physically holding back his next comment. She marveled that this was the guy she'd chosen to take hostage.

Why hadn't she taken a woman? That might have worked better.

But then, it wasn't like she'd planned any of this.

Walking back from the window, she perched at the end of the bed again, aware of his feet in their dark socks just inches away. "You said you're a fisherman. From Canada."

"Fishing guide," he corrected. Then, "Oh, sorry. You wanted me to shut up."

"So, where's all your stuff?" Liv asked, ignoring the jibe. "There wasn't anything in your garage. Nothing."

"It's all with the boat. Some's still in Canada," he clipped out. "You want to know about me? Here's the short version: my wife left me, so I moved to Canada. Had to come back to sign the divorce papers and decided I wanted to stay. Saw this place for rent. I've been here exactly thirteen days. And now I don't have a wallet or any ID and lucky me, I've got *you*."

Liv stayed silent for the lack of something to say. She didn't like the fact that he was making sense. She didn't like arguing about it. She knew *she* was right. But all this talking made her head hurt.

"What about the woman?" Auggie asked. "The employee that went to the hospital? Believe it's all about you, if you want, but let's work through it. The woman that was shot . . . what's her name?"

"Jessica," Liv said with an effort. "Maltona. She's the receptionist. She's . . . benign."

"Maybe she thinks you're benign, but . . ." He inclined his head toward her. She squeezed her eyes closed and tried to close her ears, but he went on, "Maybe this Jessica was having an affair with Upjohn or your friend, Aaron."

"Jessica has a boyfriend. An artist. Anytime I talked to her about anything, she brought him up, almost like a compulsion. It was one of the reasons I avoided her," Liv said, realizing it for the first time. She opened her eyes again.

"How about a disgruntled employee? Somebody Upjohn screwed over. Or, a customer who was taken for a ride."

"I got this package, okay?" she finally burst out. "Lawyers sent it to me by special messenger at work. It was from my mother. Who's been dead for almost twenty years. That's what happened. That's what started this. That's why he came for me!"

Auggie's attention sharpened. "Who? Who came for you?"

"*Him.*"

A pause. "Him, who?"

She jumped to her feet and moved to the open doorway. "I don't know. The bogeyman. The one you see out of the corners of your eyes."

He gave her a long look. "Could you be a little more specific?"

"This is why I can't go to the police. They won't believe me any more than you do. They probably already think *I* shot the place up! They'll look into my history and there it'll be: Mental problems. A year at Hathaway House. Crazy as a loon!" She glared at him. "Have you ever been in therapy?"

He slowly shook his head.

"You're just too squared away, right? Fishing guide. I bet you're good with people. People like you. Trust you. That's why you want to talk me off the ledge. You're trusting and compassionate and willing to really go that extra mile to make sure the crazy lady thinks she's being heard!"

"I don't think you're crazy."

"Well, I am," she snapped back. "And I'm through talking."

"Where are you going?" he demanded when she stepped through the doorway.

She was heading to the couch in the living room, such as it was. "Somewhere else," she said aloud.

"What happened when you went out?" he called after her. "Did you get done what you needed to do? Where'd you go?" He sounded desperate to keep the conversation going, but she was deaf to him now. She needed to get away.

"Livvie?"

She flopped down on the couch, burying her face into the dusty cushions, closing her ears to him. She wished she had a gag, too. Auggie was like a devil on her shoulder, talking, talking, talking. Confusing her.

"Go to sleep," she yelled at him, her voice muffled by the cushion.

"I can't."

"Figure it out!"

With that she clapped her hands over her ears and blocked out all sound. Everything. She needed sleep, though she doubted she would find it. But she was through discussing anything more with *him*.

The call on her cell came in a little after nine P.M. September was at home, curled up on the sofa beneath a quilt her grandmother had made for her mother and that had been handed down to her. Her head was full of the events of the day and she planned on watching TV shows she'd taped to her DVR as a means of clearing her mind. She'd half-expected her plan might fall apart with the Zuma killings, but she'd hoped she'd at least make it till morning. But glancing at her cell, she saw the number was from the station. Steeling herself, she answered, "Rafferty."

To her surprise Lieutenant Aubrey D'Annibal himself was on the other end of the line. "There's been a shooting," he clipped out. "The victim was found shot to death on the top-floor balcony of a two-story apartment building. I need you to get down there. Can you get hold of Gretchen? She's not answering her cell." Quickly, he rattled off the address, which seemed familiar to September though she couldn't immediately place it.

It wasn't like D'Annibal to call her, or anyone, directly. He normally left that to George, if other detectives were out of the office, or he just assigned cases to whoever was available when they were in the office. But George, apparently, wasn't picking up, either.

"Do we have a name?" she asked.

"Not yet. One of the uniforms picked up the call. His name's Waters. He's on scene, so if you'll just get there, he'll fill you in." D'Annibal sounded rushed and a little anxious. Totally unlike the put-together lieutenant with his smooth hair, creased pants and expensive shoes.

"I'm on my way."

She tried to reach Gretchen but her cell went directly to voice mail. Failing that, September dug through her closet for a pair of jeans, a black shirt and a black vest. It wasn't cold, but she wanted something to cover the Glock she was going to place in the small of her back, once she got to the scene and climbed out of her silver Honda Pilot.

She was rolling in ten minutes, driving with controlled speed to the apartment complex. Something about the address . . . she thought.

As she cruised onto a side street, she could see the red-and-blue reflection of a cop car's light bar splashing against the sides of an L-shaped apartment building. She turned into the drive at the northwest corner and around the short end of the L into the parking lot, grabbing the first available spot she saw. Apartment numbers were visible in white paint on each asphalt slot. Too bad if the people from 14A came home, she thought, sliding her Glock under her back waistband and climbing from the vehicle into the dark, hot night. The uniform—Waters—was standing on the second-floor balcony and a group of people were hanging back at the base of the outdoor stairway on the far end away from him. September skirted the group to take the stairs and as she started to climb, Waters yelled at her, "Stay back."

"Detective Rafferty," she called firmly, and, reaching the upper level, she held her ID in front of her as she walked toward him.

"Thought Rafferty was a man," he said, holding a flashlight beam into her eyes and then focusing it on her extended ID. Behind him, lying on the ground in front of an apartment door, lay a man, face down, in blue jeans and bare feet, his hair a dark, unkempt tangle to his shoulders.

"The other Rafferty's my brother," she told Waters, her gaze still on the victim. "We're both detectives."

"Huh."

She glanced around the place, noting the exterior concrete walkways and the line of doors, all closed. "Do we know who he is?" she asked, nodding toward the victim.

"No ID. One of them might know." He glanced to the gogglers down below. "He's not wearing shoes."

"He either lives here, or he's visiting someone he knows pretty well." She turned to the group of bystanders and yelled down to them, "There's been a shooting," then began to walk their way.

"Is he dead?" a young man yelled back, cupping his hands over his mouth. He had short, dark hair and it looked as if a tattoo of some kind were trying to escape the neck of his gray T-shirt.

September stopped at the top of the stairs, getting a good look at them. "The medical examiner is on his way," she said.

"He's dead," the man beside the yeller stated positively. He was older, his face looking heavily lined in the illumination cast by the overhead light attached beneath the second-floor gallery. She could hear a moth beating itself into the glass.

One of the two women shivered. She was young and skinny and held her arms hard around her torso like she was freezing even though the night was hot and surprisingly humid for Oregon. "God, I hope it's not Trask. I think it's him, but God I hope it's not."

"Trask?" September asked.

"He lives in the end unit. Just past where he—his body's—laying."

"Check the end unit," September called over to Waters but he was already on his way, having overheard.

He knocked, then tried the door. "It's open," he yelled back.

September headed back his way, skirting the sprawled victim. There was that pesky thing about walking into a place without a warrant. She shook her head to Waters, who reluctantly stayed outside the threshold. "Helllooooo. Police officers," he called into the crack of the now-ajar door.

"You're certain Trask lives in the end unit?" September yelled back toward the crowd. She looked over the rail.

"Well, maybe he lives at the unit he fell in front of," another woman, older and more heavyset, said.

"No! The end unit." Skinny Girl was certain of it.

"That single gal lives where his body is," the older man said. "That's her car over there." He pointed to a blue Accord.

September followed where he was pointing. And that's when it hit her. Blue Honda Accord. The missing employee. This was Olivia Dugan's address.

Oh, my God.

"Stay down there," she ordered the group at the base of the stairs as the younger man had one booted foot on the bottom step. He instantly moved back and September hurriedly returned to the victim's body. To Waters, she said quietly, "This could be the address of one of the Zuma Software employees. The one that was at lunch."

"You're shittin' me." He moved from the end unit to September, staring at the door to 20B.

"Give me a minute." Impatiently, she tried Gretchen

again. No answer. When the cell went to voice mail, she said tersely: "I'm at Olivia Dugan's address. There's been a homicide." She rattled off the address, then hung up and re-called George. When she failed to rouse him, she phoned dispatch and told them who she was and that she needed to talk to D'Annibal directly.

The lieutenant called her back in less than three minutes.

"Detective?" he asked.

"Who did you assign to Olivia Dugan?" she demanded. "Do we know where she is?"

"The missing Zuma employee?"

"Yes."

A pause. Then, "You're at *her* address?" He inhaled a long breath.

"Pretty sure. What the hell's going on? Want me to pound on her door? Is she there? Her car's here."

"She left earlier today. Walking. With a backpack."

"Lieutenant," September asked carefully. "Who's following her?"

"Your brother."

"He's undercover on the Cordova drug czar case," she said automatically.

"He's out of that. Arrests are coming down and he needed to leave. I put him on Dugan's trail this afternoon. I'm expecting his call."

"I've got a dead man lying in front of her apartment door."

"Okay. Okay . . . I'll order a warrant to search her place and the victim's. I'll let you know when they come through. You think this guy's connected to her?"

"He seems to be the next-door neighbor." September was having a little trouble processing all this. Her brother was following Olivia Dugan?

Waters was watching her, waiting for her to get off the phone.

D'Annibal said, "Let me know when the ME's there."

"Just arrived," September said, seeing the medical examiner's white van turn into the parking lot.

"I'll call you back when I know something more here." And he was off.

September hung up as Waters asked, "What do you want to do?"

Without answering him, she placed another phone call. When it went to voice mail, she stated hotly, "Auggie. Pick up your goddamn phone. I've got a dead body at Olivia Dugan's place. Call me back. NOW!"

Chapter 9

In the dark Detective August Rafferty tested the twine wrapped around the bedposts and debated his next move. She'd tied him fairly tightly, but he believed, if he tried hard enough, he could work himself free. After all, she was an amateur at this; he'd known that from the first moment she'd waggled that gun at him, staring at him through hollow, hazel eyes, her face white, drawn and horror-filled, as if she'd seen the devil himself.

He'd known who she was. Olivia Margaux Dugan. Employed by Zuma Software. Missing since she'd found the bodies after her lunch break.

He'd been instructed by his boss, Lieutenant D'Annibal of the Laurelton Police Department, to cruise by her address and check if she was home. While cruising, he'd seen her lam out on foot, carrying a backpack, scurrying down the street and into a café. He'd reported to D'Annibal that he was following her, then had driven past the bistro for a quick reconnoiter, and was circling back when he saw her suddenly exit the bistro, dart across the street, and enter the coffee shop. He'd cranked the Jeep around, but of course, there'd been no place to park. Not wanting to draw attention to himself, he'd driven slowly down the street, momentarily double-parking with an eye on his rearview, then had driven farther, jockeyed around, turned back and, lo and behold, a spot had opened up right in front of the place.

Lucky.

He called D'Annibal again right before his cell quit on him and said he was going to tail her and that he would phone again when he could. Then he cruised right into Bean There, Done That and ordered up a coffee. His quarry was in line ahead of him, jittery, but trying hard to conceal it. She got her drink and sat down and after he got his, he strolled out toward his car, head turned about forty-five degrees, keeping her in his peripheral vision.

And then suddenly she was *right there.* He pretended to be getting into his vehicle and she suddenly slid into the passenger seat, with a gun, and ordered him to drive.

Wow. So he let her take him "hostage." Seemed like a good way to keep tabs on her.

Now, he was wondering about the wisdom of those actions. He hadn't been able to contact D'Annibal again, and the department had since put Liv's picture on television. An expected move by the police, he supposed, because no one, not even D'Annibal, knew he'd connected so tightly with her.

He sighed, staring up at the ceiling. If he catalogued his exploits since being a detective, this move might be number one in the lame-brained column. Sure, he was open, brash, full of piss and vinegar, as his older sister, July, was wont to say, and burdened with oodles of arrogance that had gotten him into more than a few scrapes as a kid and had helped him develop a serious hero complex as an adult—and had been the ruin of several romantic relationships—but he was generally sane. Generally able to make good choices.

He shook his head at himself. Maybe it was because he'd just gotten off a long-term, joint drug-and-gang task force with the Portland PD and had been happy to move out of his fake address—the house where he'd been living under his alias, Alan Reagan—and hopefully back to his own home. He'd been at the fake house for nearly a year while he'd infiltrated a really nasty, homegrown drug czar's clutch. Geraldo "Jerry" Cordova was a pain-in-the-ass small-time dealer who'd connected with a couple of Portland gangs and thought he was Scarface now. Auggie had helped root him out, along with some seriously bad dudes, and as soon as that had come down he'd beat feet as Alan Reagan, planning to pick up his possessions at the house, such as they were, and get out. Then D'Annibal had called as he was checking on his duplex on the outskirts of Laurelton. (He was in the process of evicting the tenants on the other side as he was the owner of the building and they were young, loud and had a tendency to leave the tail end of one monstrous truck or another over his driveway. Pissed him off, no end.)

D'Annibal had explained about the lovely Ms. Dugan and, as Auggie headed over to her apartment for some further reconnaissance, she suddenly appeared, backpack over her shoulder, heading quickly away from the premises.

He'd immediately done a quick assessment of his own state of readiness. He was good to go. He hadn't yet bothered with peeling his wallet from beneath the driver's seat where he'd strapped it with duct tape along with his Glock, a precaution he employed whenever he was playing the part of Al Reagan, or whomever, as he couldn't afford for anyone to find out his true identity.

So, he'd followed her. He knew from D'Annibal that she was employed at Zuma Software where a gunman had come in around one P.M. and shot all the employees on the first floor. Except Ms. Dugan, who hadn't been there, but who had apparently returned to the crime scene and phoned 911. D'Annibal told Auggie to go to her apartment and find out if she'd been there.

He'd been a little ticked off, eager to get back to his messy duplex with all his own things. The last thing he'd wanted was to have to maintain his false identity at this damned, near empty house. It was Alan Reagan's place, in case anybody came looking, a house really owned by the Laurelton PD that had been used for various reasons, the last being a safe house for a wealthy criminal's abused wife and children. That asshole was firmly behind bars now, and so Auggie had used the place as his new home when he started surveilling, and then finally working for, Cordova, just in case the gang boss came looking, which he never did.

When Liv had suddenly jumped in Auggie's Jeep and told him to drive, he'd unconsciously headed to the house. He'd decided to go with the whole hostage thing and though he was both irked and amused at being tied up, he was intrigued with his attractive and self-proclaimed nutso female captor. He didn't quite know what to make of her.

Not that she wasn't screwed up; he could certainly see that. But then, who wasn't?

Only now he wasn't quite sure what to do.

He turned his head to listen. She was sleeping on that crappy couch. How, he couldn't imagine. He felt jazzed and antsy. Earlier, when she'd left him tied to the oven, he'd been aware that he could probably drop his fetters; he'd almost done it, thinking he could call D'Annibal and give him an update. But he wasn't certain he would be able to put the twine back in place without her knowing, so he'd passed on the opportunity, at least for the meantime.

He thought about his cell phone. He'd lied to her about the charger. It was here, in his glove box. He'd meant to charge the battery as soon as he got home; he wasn't much on car chargers, had heard they weren't good for the phone. But he carried an extra charger in the glove box, so if he worked himself free he could certainly get the thing working. Could call D'Annibal. But did he want to give up his act yet? He wasn't sure.

Hmmm. Had to think about that. If she found the charger, she could plug in the phone herself and if someone called him from the department, the jig could be up anyway.

He wondered if he could get her to fall for the bathroom trick again. Not that he couldn't use every opportunity to relieve himself, but there was no emergency imminent yet.

Again . . . hmmm . . .

She needed to go to the police. He believed in her innocence. She was paranoid, too, but maybe there was something worth checking out. If he stayed with her, could he get her to trust him a little? He felt a tweak of interest in her and was annoyed with himself. Down boy . . .

Having decided that waiting was a better option, Auggie closed his eyes and willed himself to sleep, at least for a few minutes. He wasn't certain what was going to happen next, but he might as well be prepared.

J.J., the medical examiner, scrutinized the body and made plans for it to be shipped to the county coroner's office. He glanced at September, who was watching from the sidelines. "Helluva day, huh?" he said.

"Helluva day," she answered. This was the second time today they'd been at a homicide together, and it was looking like the crimes were related. Her cell phone buzzed and she answered it to learn that they had the warrant to enter 20B, Olivia Dugan's apartment, and 21B, Trask Martin's. Hanging up, she signaled Waters, who then kicked in the door to 20B.

She and Waters did a quick run-through of Dugan's premises. The place had that unlived-in feel of someone who had few personal possessions. The closet looked as if Olivia had been home and ransacked it, and one of the drawers was half-open. September plugged in the answering machine on the way out, but any messages had been wiped off. She and Waters then headed back outside where J.J. and his crew were covering the body they'd lifted onto a gurney. September was getting ready to go to 21B when a woman pushed herself past the group at the bottom of the stairs, to their shouts of dismay, then barreled past one of the techs climbing the stairs, who yelled, "Hey!" at her as she practically threw him aside in her headlong rush.

September stepped in her way before she got to the gurney. The frantic young woman clawed at her as she tried to get to the body, screaming, "Trask! Trask! Oh, God. *Trask!*"

"This is a crime scene!" September clipped out, grabbing hold of her flailing arms. "Who are you?"

"Is that . . . is that . . . please, God, tell me it's not Trask!"

"He's not been identified yet," September declared, though it was a pretty good guess it was indeed Trask Martin who lived at the end of the balcony.

"My . . . my apartment," she murmured, looking past September toward the door to the end unit. "I'm Jo." Then she slumped as if her bones had suddenly turned to liquid.

September caught her, then pulled her aside as Journey and his team wheeled the gurney toward the stairs. Jo suddenly jumped forward and pulled at the cover, exposing one male, bare foot. Seeing it, she started crying and ripping at her hair. "Oh, my God. Oh, my *God!*" She jerked around, her eyes wild. "I've got to go with him. I've got to be with him!"

"You live in apartment 21 on this level?" September asked her.

"Yes. With Trask!"

"May we go inside?"

"No." She was stumbling after the body, crying, but now she turned toward the door to her unit. "He needs shoes," she said, staggering past September and through the door to 21B.

September followed her to the entry and looked inside. She could smell the leftover scent of marijuana.

"You can't come in!" Jo declared.

"I have a warrant. I'm just being polite." Jo was crying and hiccuping, and September added, "I don't care about the dope smoking. But I need to find who did this."

"Okay," Jo said, gulping. "I—I—is he okay? He's gonna be okay, all right, yeah?" Her eyes were pleading.

September's silence was enough of an answer. Jo stifled another scream and fled into the bedroom, ripping through the shoes in the closet and pulling out a pair of men's worn leather boots. "He never wears shoes. He needs to wear shoes. I always tell him, 'Trask. Put on some shoes. You never know when you might need them.'" Tears puddled in her eyes. "He needs them. . . ." Then she ducked her head and sank to the ground and the tears started dropping onto her chest.

"Would you like me to take you to the coroner's office?" September asked gently.

She flinched at the word.

"His name's Trask?"

"Trask Burcher Martin." She gulped and looked at September. "Who are you?"

"I'm Detective Rafferty."

"Who did this? What happened?"

"There was a shooting. That's all we know, so far."

"Why? Why . . . was he in front of Liv's door? Is she there?"

"No."

"Did she do it?" she asked in a horror-filled whisper.

"When we get something, we'll let you know." September's heart clutched. Here, she'd been upset with D'Annibal and her brother for keeping her in the dark, but what if something had happened to Auggie?

"Do you think these boots will work?" she asked September seriously.

September fought back her own rising anxiety, "They'll be fine," she assured her, then held out a hand to help Jo to her feet.

Liv tried to surface from a deep sleep. Uncomfortable sleep. Sleep surrounded by nightmare fragments that swept in and out of her consciousness. Fingers of dream fog that beckoned her reluctantly forward.

Through the mist she saw Aaron . . . his quirk of a smile . . . his joking mouth. He opened that mouth to speak but it grew into a dark hole where black blood started spilling toward her. And there was Paul de Fore, with only half a head, leering and jolting forward on stiff robot legs.

She wanted to scream but couldn't. There were rags in her mouth. Pieces of something that kept her mute. A gag. But then the gag was over a man's mouth. Her hostage. Auggie. But his eyes burned with an angry blue flame. Liv turned away, sobbing.

A cat strolled through her legs. A very fat cat with yellow tiger stripes and a long, curving tail that switched and twitched. She reached for it, but it too disappeared into the sneaking fog.

Cat, she called. *Cat!*

She was screaming. Screaming at the top of her lungs but the cat was gone and couldn't hear her. *CAT!*

"HEY!!!" a voice yelled loudly.

She jerked as if pulled by strings, her eyes flying open. She could hear the echo of her own voice fading away.

"HEY! WAKE UP!"

Auggie. Auggie was yelling at her.

"Stop," she told him, struggling to her feet. "Stop yelling. I'm awake."

"You were dreaming. Whimpering," he called out.

She struggled to get her bearings, then finally drew a breath and walked to the open doorway of his bedroom. She could just make out his form in the dim light.

"You said 'cat,'" he told her.

"I know."

"What does that mean?"

"I was dreaming about a cat."

"Do you have one?"

"No. It was just something I said to Aaron."

"What did you say?"

"I told him I had a cat. A very fat cat. It was a joke, of sorts."

"A joke?"

Liv turned away. Sadness and fear vied for control of her senses and she felt tears form in her eyes. She didn't know what the hell she was doing. Making a worse mess of things.

"Hey," he said, but she walked quickly away, to the kitchen, where she poured herself a glass of water and drank half of it down in two gulps. It stemmed the tide of tears. For now, at least.

"I could use a drink!" his voice found her from the other room. She poured another glass and took it back to him. A part of her just wanted to untie him and have him drink it himself, and she was debating that, when he said, "And another trip to the bathroom."

That did it. She just didn't care anymore. She set down the water on the TV stand, untied him, then gestured for him to have at it, whatever it was. Then she returned to the couch, where she sank into the cushions and stared straight ahead.

He came into the room, rubbing his wrists, eyeing her speculatively in the near dark. There was a crack in the curtains where a strip of moonlight crept in, and it was enough for her to see his expression. He looked confused.

"I don't care what you do," she said, before he could speak. "Call the police. Run away. Do the chicken dance. I just don't care."

"Tell me what the dream was about."

"This isn't about the dream," she snapped back. "Not in any way I can explain. Just . . . I don't care."

For the first time, he seemed at a loss for words. Well, good. She was sick of talking to him anyway. "Why are you called Auggie?" she asked him again.

"Because I liked dogs. My Dad called me Auggie-Doggy."

"Is that true?"

"Why would I lie about it?"

She shook her head in frustration, looked away from him, then sighed. "I'm sorry I dragged you into this and growing sorrier by the minute."

"At the risk of being redundant, why don't you contact the police? Do you have some deep dark secret? Some lawlessness that's caught up to you? Some crime you don't want discovered?"

"The police have done me no favors," she mumbled, wishing he would just go back to sleep.

"They catch you shoplifting? Pick you up for a DUI? Give you a speeding ticket?"

"My mother hanged herself when I was six and I found her body, and they treated me like I was stupid and a liar and they treated my brother the same way."

Silence.

That, finally, had the power to shut him up.

And then she remembered what Hague had said about the doctor.

The doctor.

We both know him . . . from when we were kids . . .

The stalker. The zombie. The doctor.

We both know him.

She sat up straighter.

"What?"

"I went to see my brother tonight."

"Your brother? What—"

"Yes, Hague. He said it was the doctor."

"It?" he repeated.

"The bogeyman." She abruptly got to her feet, thinking hard.

"Which doctor? Your Dr. . . . Yancy?"

"Another doctor. But he was there. He came to Hathaway House and he *stalked!*" She paced toward the kitchen, felt for a light switch on the wall, changed her mind at the last minute and left the room illuminated by only faint moonlight. "Can't remember his name. He was a visiting doctor, and I saw him a time or two. I'm sure of it. Almost sure of it . . . He must've had contact with Hague, too. Who *is* he? Could he have known who we were, even then?"

"Not following," Auggie said.

She pressed her hands to her head, dragging at memories long buried, ones she'd hidden from herself maybe. "The man in the photo," she said to herself with conviction. Then, "The doctor in the photo. *Maybe* . . ."

She tried to force herself to think back to Hathaway House, when she'd lived there, but the memories scorched her and she shied away from them. Was he the man in the photo? The one stalking angrily toward the camera? Was he the visiting doctor at Hathaway House? Was he?

And does this have anything to do with the murders at Zuma?

"Any chance this revelation is going to send you to the authorities?" he asked.

She looked back at him, blinking several times. "No. Not yet."

"Not *yet*," he repeated. "Progress."

"I need—to be alone. To sort some things out." Seeing him unfettered, she asked lamely, "Would you mind just going to bed?"

"I can help you," he said.

She couldn't stand it. She needed to *think*. And having him *right there* wasn't helping.

The gun was under the couch where she'd tucked it. Momentarily she thought of pulling it out, but she was past threatening him with it.

"Tomorrow," she said.

He seemed to want to argue. He stood there for a long, long time.

"Please," she rasped.

She had no idea what he was thinking, but in the end he made a sound of frustration, headed for the bathroom, and then back to his bedroom. If he changed his mind and decided to walk out the door in the middle of the night there wasn't anything she would do about it.

She made a trip to the bathroom herself, then lay back down on the couch, certain she would never fall asleep, and then promptly did.

The medical examiner's office was located in a squat brick building on the grounds that held the Winslow County Sheriff's Department and other government offices. J.J. was a busy man at the best of times, and today was closer to the worst. He was brusque and had tired lines around his eyes and Jo Cardwick's histrionics were starting to get on his nerves.

Upon having the drape pulled from Trask Martin's bloodless face, Jo had collapsed into keening wails and swaying motion. September had pulled her away upon seeing Journey's tightened lips and obvious displeasure. Now they were in an anteroom just outside, and Jo was collapsed in an orange plastic chair, her head between her knees, sobbing and shaking.

September walked to the water cooler, grabbed a small paper cup and poured Jo a drink. The girl could really use a stiff one, she thought, but plying alcohol was not accepted protocol. "Here," she said kindly, holding out the cup.

Jo tried to stem the flow. She truly did. She lifted her head and looked at September through glazed eyes. "He's dead. He's really dead." She took the cup but didn't drink from it, just held it out straight as if it were poison.

September nodded. "I'd like to ask you a question or two, if you're up for it."

"She killed him. She must've." Jo hiccupped, looked at the paper cup as if seeing it for the first time, then brought it to her lips. She drank it all.

"Do you mean Olivia Dugan, in apartment 20?"

She nodded, gulping.

"Why do you think that?"

"'Cuz she's the only thing different. Everybody loves Trask. Everybody. And she was always so shut down. And then he was over there and saw some pictures and she was kinda crazy about them, he said."

"Crazy about the pictures?"

"That's what he said."

"What were the pictures of?" September pressed.

"I don't know. Old pictures of people, I think." She suddenly looked angry. "She had a few drinks with us, but she was cold. Really cold."

"When was this?"

A pause. Fresh tears welled. "Last night!" she cried, as if she'd just remembered.

"And that's when Trask saw the pictures?"

She shook her head. "Sometime before. I told you. He saw 'em at her place. And I don't care anyway!" Then, "Are you going to arrest her? Throw her ass in jail! DO *SOMETHING*?"

"Yes. I'm going to do something," September assured her.

She was going to get through to her brother if it was the last thing she did.

Chapter 10

Liv watched dawn creep across the horizon. She was at the living room window, peering out through a gap in the curtains. Pink streaks ran across the sky and a golden arc was forming to the east.

Her thoughts had turned to Hathaway House. She'd been there less than a year. The dreams had started before that; "repressed memories," Dr. Yancy told her later, but her father and Lorinda just wanted her "fixed." They didn't care whether Hathaway House was the right choice. They just sent her there and she could envision Lorinda dusting her hands of Albert's crazy adopted daughter. Somehow Lorinda had then convinced Albert that Hague was as messed up as Liv and away he'd gone to Grandview Hospital, which actually had a reputation for treating more serious mental patients. Should she feel grateful that they hadn't assumed her problems were as bad as Hague's, and that's why they'd sent her to Hathaway House instead? Or, was it a money issue: Hathaway House was mostly funded by donations whereas Grandview was a private mental hospital. Maybe it was just simply that Hague, being Albert's own flesh and blood, was more a son to him than

she was a daughter—an idea undoubtedly fostered by
Lorinda's disinterest in both of them.

Whatever the case, when she was a girl the dreams of her
mother's hanging form . . . mixed in with some kind of
bogeyman chasing her down . . . and sometimes dead bodies
rising from graves outside, from the fields, and stalking
toward her house, zombie-like . . . intensified over the years
until finally Liv had woken up screaming nearly every
night. That's when she was sent to Hathaway House and
assigned to a room with three other female patients, all of
them teenagers.

She was regimented from the start and there were house-
hold chores. Before breakfast: room cleaning. Breakfast.
Group therapy. Lunch. Rest time. One-on-one with Dr.
Yancy. Dinner. Quiet time in your room or in the main hall
with its soothing blue chairs and empty shelves, save for
books. Lights out at nine.

Dr. Yancy . . . She was in her fifties with gray hair and
deep brown eyes and a quiet way about her that was the first
thing Liv always noticed. They had sessions four days out
of five. On Thursday, Liv was given the option of an hour
of television in one of the rooms upstairs, where an employee (guard) watched over her and the other inmates, or
she could take a walk around the fenced yard. No, it did not
have razor wire across its wall, but there was a watchtower.

"Very medieval," Liv had told Dr. Yancy after the first
time she chose the walking yard. "Like a rotting prison."

"A rotting prison?" Dr. Yancy asked.

"The wall looks like it's from some castle. I can half-
believe there's a moat on the opposite side."

The doctor half-smiled. "There's a creek on the north
end. Otherwise, it's a fir-lined cliff down to the highway
below. We're not that far out of the city limits."

Liv knew where Hathaway House was: on the west side
of Portland, not all that far from Laurelton. She'd lived in

Rock Springs until they'd sent her to Hathaway House, and after her incarceration ended, she'd returned to her family only briefly; she wasn't part of it any longer. Albert and Lorinda had moved to east Portland, nearly Gresham, and she'd made a stab at finishing her senior year, getting her GED in the end. As soon as she could, she got a job at a restaurant and moved into low-cost student housing next to the nearest campus of Portland Community College, where she took business classes.

But that was later . . . after her sessions with Dr. Yancy, who'd offered up the repressed-memories theory about a month into their therapy. "You saw something about the time of your mother's death," she told Liv on that rainy Monday afternoon. "Something else. You don't want to look at it, so it's coming to you in your dreams."

"I saw my mother," Liv stated carefully. She didn't like treading this road.

Dr. Yancy nodded and tilted her head, considering her. "And something else, too."

"No."

"Until you look at it, it will keep coming back."

Liv shut her mind down. She would rather keep the dreams than go back down that hall and see her mother's body. She knew the zombies were from Hague's description. She suspected the women from the fields were the strangulation victims from the serial killer that had terrorized the area before disappearing; she'd read about his actions later, going through old newspaper accounts, but it hadn't sparked any repressed memories, either.

And as far as a bogeyman chasing her. She still believed that was real.

Dr. Yancy had kept trying to break through Liv's resolve, but fear, and a large dose of stubbornness, had kept Liv from responding.

Now, however, thinking of the doctor—the zombie,

stalking doctor who might be the man in the photo—she felt a flutter of awareness. *Until you look at it, it will keep coming back.*

Dropping the curtain, she walked back to the kitchen and sat at the table. Screwing up her courage, she closed her eyes and envisioned those moments when she'd found her mother hanging in the kitchen.

I'm done. . . . She'd seen her mother's vision say those words, but now, holding herself tightly, her eyes squeezed shut, she believed they were meant for her father. Her mother was done with the marriage. There was nothing more sinister than that in their meaning.

But there was something else . . . some intent . . . something. Carefully, Liv allowed her inner vision to move past her mother's hanging form, toward the back door and out into the moonlit field beyond . . . something was there. Someone was there . . . watching . . .

"Liv?"

Her eyes flew open at her name. For a moment she didn't know where she was. Then she saw a man's form.

A man.

Her mouth opened on a silent scream and then Auggie bent down in front of her and gazed into her eyes.

Letting Liv know who he was had to happen, Auggie had concluded, but he needed the right moment to spring it on her. Looking at her horror-struck face, he determined this wasn't the time.

He was good that way.

And he just hadn't expected to care about her as much as he already did. It was a conundrum to be sure. But it wasn't the first time.

He was a sucker for women, that was the problem. Not

in the long run, he supposed; not when it really counted. But in the short run he was definitely a sucker. A modern-day knight in shining—maybe tarnished—armor who couldn't help himself whenever some damsel in distress crossed his path. And as path-crossing went, Liv Dugan was a doozy.

He definitely was a sucker for her. Those soulful hazel eyes filled with a raft of emotions: anxiety, mistrust, worry and fear. Though sometimes she seemed to look at him with longing, too. Not sexual longing, although he'd certainly felt faint glimmers running along his own nerves. No, she was longing for friendship, and understanding, and maybe the truth of cold, hard reality.

The fact was, he *wanted* to help her.

But if he told her he was the police, how would that go? Not well, he suspected.

She was coming back to herself with an effort. The gun was on the table beside her right hand. He wondered how advisable that was, given the fact it looked as if she'd put herself in a trance.

"You all right?" he asked.

She shook her head and looked away from him. He followed her gaze. His cell phone was on the counter.

For reasons more personal than smart, he suspected, he was going to keep up the charade and see what he could learn. Luckily, his cell phone was out of battery. If at any time she'd seen fit to take it from him and check him out, it might not have been pretty. But Liv Dugan was living in her own hellish world inside her head. She was fighting paranoia and wasn't paying attention to the details in the real world. She didn't trust anybody, but she wanted to, even though she might not know it. She'd spent too many years of her life not trusting anyone and didn't know how to.

She said, "I need to go to Hathaway House. Where I was—put—to straighten out my head."

"Looking for 'the doctor'?" he asked.

"Hague said we both knew him and he seems familiar. . . ."

"I'll go with you," he heard himself say.

She gave him an "oh, sure" look. But then she looked at him and said, "You want to go to the police."

"I do. But, I want to follow where this leads."

"Why?" she asked him. There was something defeated about her. She'd given up her kidnapper routine, and it had taken her backbone, too.

"I don't completely believe you. I don't think you're right about Zuma, but you got the package from the lawyers and things started happening, so yeah, I want to follow along."

It sounded lame even to his own ears. But Liv looked faintly hopeful. She wanted someone to believe her so badly, it made Auggie feel like a heel.

"I need to go to Hathaway by myself." She worried her lower lips with her teeth in a way that focused his attention on her. "I want to talk to them."

"I'll drive."

"No." She wasn't willing to go that far.

Thinking of his cell phone, and the charger in the glove box, he said more certainly, "Let me. I'll stay in the car. I'll wait outside for you."

She gazed at him uncertainly. He could tell she was thinking it over: was it safer to leave him at the house, or take him on her expedition?

"Okay," she said.

"Okay?" He held out his palm and she stared at it. "The keys. I'm driving, right?"

"No, I . . ."

"You can hold me at gunpoint, if it makes you feel better," he said dryly. "And is there any chance we can get breakfast on the way? Drive-thru McDonald's sounds fantastic."

The look on her face was priceless. "McDonald's?" she asked.

"I'll buy. Oh, wait . . . no wallet."

She grabbed her backpack, zipped it open, put the gun inside and pulled out her wallet and the Jeep's keys. "I'll buy," she said.

Then she dropped the keys in his palm.

Hathaway House was just as Liv remembered it: respectable. The buildings were simply brick and mortar surrounded by trimmed oak trees and several stately Douglas firs and a boxwood hedge and azaleas, which were months past flowering, their green leaves gleaming dully in the heat of the sun. In Liv's dream-mind the windows were eyes and the front door a yawning mouth. Today, it looked carefully tended, if a bit tired, as if all the scrupulous landscaping couldn't disguise the darkness inside.

Shaking her head at her own paranoia and what it had driven her to, Liv trudged up the front steps, glancing back once to where the Jeep was parked at the curb across the street. She could see Auggie through the driver's window, drinking from his McDonald's to-go coffee cup. He was looking at her and she wondered if he would just drive away once she was inside. Why wouldn't he?, she asked herself. If the situation were reversed, she would.

She just irrationally hoped he would wait for her. She'd had a helluva time getting him to stay in the car; he'd insisted on coming with her. But she'd been adamant that she was going in alone, and in the end he'd reluctantly agreed.

With a faint prayer to the powers that be, whoever or whatever they were, she pulled open one of the institution's dark green double doors and stepped inside the administration entry hall.

The place smelled like floor wax and dust and took Liv zinging back to the time she spent here. She inhaled and exhaled slowly, as she walked toward the reception area at the end of the short hallway. The overhead lighting was dim and made pools of illumination along the polished linoleum, like a fuzzy string of pearls, which led to a more modern counter that hadn't been there when Liv was a patient.

A woman with a grayish shag hairstyle sat behind the counter, wearing a headset. She didn't look up at Liv's approach. Liv surreptitiously glanced down the hallways that radiated both left and right behind the counter. Those were the same hallways she'd traversed when she'd been a resident, although there had been a wide wooden desk, mahogany maybe, that had gleamed like the floor where the counter now stood. Hathaway House had prided itself on its sense of period, circa 1940s as far as Liv could tell, but that had apparently finally given way to modern times. There was an electrical conduit running along the edge of the wall and it burrowed through a small hole in the counter to feed the computers, telephone and other electronic equipment.

The woman said into the headset, "Dr. Knudson will be back on Monday." By her tone it sounded like she may have already delivered this information to the caller at least once. "Yes. Monday." A pause. "You can leave a message on his voice mail. Yes. I'll connect you." She quickly stabbed a few buttons and then darted Liv a look. "How can I help you?"

"I'm looking for a doctor who once worked here. Maybe still does. Dr. Yancy?"

"Dr. Yancy retired."

Liv absorbed that. "Is there someone else I could talk to?"

"I'm afraid not. Our director will be in Monday."

"Dr. Knudson?"

She smiled tightly. "Yes."

"Maybe there's someone else on staff I could speak to?" she asked, but the woman shook her shaggy gray hair.

"It's Saturday. I'm sorry," she stated flatly in a tone that suggested she wasn't in the least. "Dr. Knudson is the one you should talk to."

Realizing she wasn't going to get any information by going through the correct channels, Liv thanked her and turned away. She didn't want to draw too much attention by being a nuisance. She was just going to have to wait.

She returned outside and felt a rush of relief at the sight of the Jeep. Letting herself in through the passenger door, she slammed it shut. The interior still smelled like sausage and hash browns from their breakfast on the go. It took her a moment to realize how tense Auggie was.

"Thanks for waiting," she said. Then, "What's wrong?"

"Nothing."

"Bullshit. What happened? Something happened?" She looked around the car wildly, her gaze falling onto the glove box. Without any clear thought she pressed the button and it snapped open, the wires of an electric charger popping up.

"Don't—panic," he warned.

"What is this?" Her brain wasn't connecting. "You had the glove-box key?"

"It . . . was under the mat."

He was staring at her, and she realized he was expecting her to say something else. And then she finally woke up. "That's your cell charger. It was in the car all this time?"

For an answer he pulled his phone from his pocket. "I plugged it in while you were inside," he confessed.

"And made a call?"

"You didn't give me enough time."

"I don't believe you. Hand it to me."

"It doesn't have enough power. I had to rip it out of the charger when you came back." He placed the phone in her hand, and she stared at it, wishing she knew one damn thing about cell phones. She pressed on the phone but nothing happened.

"It's not going to work until it gets some power," he said.

"You were going to turn me in." She felt betrayed. Ridiculous, but true. She sank back against the seat and covered her face in her hands, struggling for composure.

"No, I want to help you," he said again.

"If I had any energy left, I'd laugh," she said behind the protection of her hands. She was moving to a strange psychological place, she realized distantly, the place where you just give up completely.

"I think there's something there," he insisted again. "With the package the lawyers sent you from your mother."

"Why would you help me?"

"Because you need it."

He sounded sincere and she dropped her hands to look at him through eyes that were watering. She wasn't crying, exactly. She was just . . . done.

He reached over and caught a bit of the liquid that fell from the corner of one eye. "I'm kind of a sucker for women in need," he admitted. "Just ask my last ex-girlfriend. It was on the top of her list of complaints. Well, at least number three or four. She also said I was uncaring, uncommunicative and dog shit, not necessarily in that order."

"Don't be cute. I can't stand cute."

"One thing I'm not . . . is cute."

His blue eyes regarded her with warmth. Kindness, even. In another time, she might have argued that fact. He was a hell of an attractive guy and she was pretty sure he knew it.

"I thought it was an ex-wife," she said.

"That," he admitted, "was a lie."

The starch just went out of her. Surrender. Capitulation. The aftermath of too much adrenaline. Whatever the case she felt her body start shaking as if she had the palsy and her watering eyes flooded in a rush of tears she found embarrassing.

"Hey . . ."

"Shut up," she said through a thick throat. "I mean it."

Silence fell between them. Fighting emotion, she lowered her gaze, focusing on his cowboy boots. "Go ahead and call the police. Charge your phone and call them."

He didn't answer, just started up the Jeep.

"Where are we going?"

"Don't worry. I'm not turning you in," he said, on a long-suffering sigh. "We're going back to my house. Then, we're going to take it from the top. Figure out what to do. We'll start with what happened at Zuma. That's where it all began. That's why you and I are together now."

The mood around the station was tense, and Lieutenant D'Annibal had actually said, "Damn," which was way outside his usual vocabulary. He was the face of the authorities and looked good on camera, and he was as careful off camera as on.

It was a testament to his own anxiety when he used the word, and he used it when September questioned him, a bit tensely, about her brother.

"I just got a text from him," the lieutenant told her and Gretchen after September asked to speak to him and Gretchen followed her quickly inside his office, as if she'd been invited. "He's been with Olivia Dugan since about five o'clock last night."

"With?" September asked. "What does that mean?"

Gretchen said, "So, she wasn't involved with the Martin murder?"

"Doesn't look like it," D'Annibal said.

"Well, where are they?" September demanded. "Why

doesn't Auggie bring her in for questioning? What's the big secret?"

"What does he think about the Martin shooting?" Gretchen asked.

"I don't know if he knows." D'Annibal was crisp. "I told Channel Seven I'd give them an update. Maybe he'll see it on the news."

"Update." Gretchen snorted. As if she were reporting, she said, "Person or persons unknown shot him in the residential parking lot of Zuma Software's employee, Olivia Dugan, missing since yesterday's massacre."

"Have you tried calling him?" September asked the lieutenant. "'Cause he's not picking up for me."

"He's not picking up for me, either," D'Annibal admitted. "For the moment, I'm going to trust he knows what he's doing. Dugan apparently went straight to her apartment after she fled the homicide scene. Then she grabbed up some belongings and headed out on foot. Rafferty picked up her trail at that point. He was in his Jeep, and he caught sight of her and called it in. He was going to keep with her."

"Well, that was yesterday." September couldn't stem the irritation in her voice. "And then he texted you today? You sure it's him, and not her with the phone?"

"You think she took Detective Rafferty's phone off him, found my cell number, and texted me an *alibi* for herself for last night's murder?" The lieutenant gazed at her calmly and September felt her face heat up as she heard how improbable that sounded.

"From what we know of Olivia Dugan, that's not likely," she admitted.

"From what we know of your brother, it's quadruple unlikely," Gretchen said. "He doesn't let women get the upper hand on him."

You don't know him as well as you think you do, September thought, but she'd said enough already.

She and Gretchen were dismissed from D'Annibal's office and September said, "Where were you last night?"

Gretchen made a sound of disgust. "On a date. With a man with grabby hands. Slid 'em over my ass about ten times while we were waiting for a table. So, I ordered the most expensive things on the menu and stuck him for a huge bill. He liked the idea of taking out a cop, but got pretty nasty when he realized the night was ending at my front door. Told him I'd arrest him for sexual harassment if he didn't let up. He believed me and left." She made a face. "Turned my phone off. Sorry. Would've rather been with you. So, the girlfriend blamed Olivia Dugan?"

September had given her the highlights before they walked into D'Annibal's office, and now she gave her a more complete report. Gretchen listened closely, then nodded a couple of times.

"All right, let's go see Kurt Upjohn and the ex, if she's still at the hospital."

"Camille. What about Maltona's boyfriend . . . um . . . Jason?"

"Jason Jaffe." She humphed her annoyance. "Slippery bastard. Yeah, I'm gonna track him down after the hospital. When's the interview with Channel Seven?" September shrugged and Gretchen said, "Probably soon. They'll put it on like a teaser. D'Annibal looks good on camera and so does the viper."

"Pauline Kirby? Wes called her a barracuda."

Gretchen smiled thinly. "You're bound to have a 'moment' with her sooner or later. You'll find your own adjectives."

Liv watched the landscape flash by outside the window. "Actually, this started long before Zuma," she said to Auggie, picking up the conversation where it had dropped off. They were almost back at his place.

He shot her a look. "You're thinking it started with your mother. Her death. Or, maybe something to do with the things she sent you?"

"Her death . . . And there were other deaths at the same time of my mother's supposed suicide."

"Supposed," he repeated.

"The official version is she hanged herself, but I've never been able to make myself believe that. There was a serial killer, just outside of Rock Springs. Twenty years ago. He strangled them, and left their bodies in fields. And I think it's connected to my mom's death."

"You think he's responsible."

"It's a theory."

He asked, feeling his way, "You lived in Rock Springs at the time of the killings?"

"Strangulations. Yes."

He thought in silence for a few moments, then said, "I remember some about that case. They never got the guy, and the killings seemed to stop."

"The theory is that he's either dead or in prison for something else."

"You don't believe that," Auggie guessed.

"No. I don't. Like I don't believe it was suicide. Mama's death. I always thought it was . . ."

A long pause fell between them, and then Auggie said quietly, "The bogeyman."

"The bogeyman," Liv repeated.

The old hag put me in a rage today.
She asked about the truck.
It is hidden away, but I couldn't think up an answer and I felt the need rise in me, hot and hard. My hands clenched. Did she know? Does she know?

I could feel the worms inside my brain, feeding on me. I'm getting sicker, that's what the doctors will say.

Sicker and sicker.

I just need to be careful. And keep with the plan.

The bitch may have to be killed, too. It would be a pleasure.

But first Olivia.

Liv . . .

I'm coming for you.

I will throw you down and shove deep into you, my thumbs at your throat.

And you will scream.

Chapter 11

Laurelton General Hospital sat on a hillside, its north side sporting two more levels than its south. The main entrance and emergency were on level three, which was street level except for the north end where the slope added two levels beneath it. September and Gretchen walked toward the main front doors together. The outer glass doors slid back to allow entry and started closing behind them while the inside set whispered open.

A middle-aged woman sat at a semicircular desk. She looked up at the two women and September could practically read her thought: Cops. Maybe it was the way they walked, she thought. Shoulder-to-shoulder. Determined. No emotion visible. Maybe it was something more indefinable.

"May I help you?" she asked. Her hair was short, dyed dark and thinning.

Gretchen took the lead, explaining who they were and what they wanted. Both Kurt Upjohn and Jessica Maltona had been whisked into surgery at Laurelton General; Upjohn for two bullets through the abdomen, Maltona for a shot to the chest that, surprisingly, hadn't killed her outright. Both were stabilized and had brief moments of lucidity, though the jury was still out on their long-term prognosis.

No one was saying anything but September sensed it boiled down to two words: "not good."

"Dr. Denby's on rounds," the receptionist told them, as she pushed a button on her phone. "I'll let him know you're here."

With extreme patience, Gretchen said, "He's expecting us. Which room is Mr. Upjohn's? We'll meet him there."

"North wing," she answered sourly. "Fourth floor."

Gretchen gave her a cold smile of thanks. Knowing she was bound to get in trouble for it, September pointed out, "You set out to piss people off."

"Not consciously."

"Consciously," she argued.

Gretchen slid her a look. "I've been the only woman on this team until you, Nine. I've developed a style that works. Watch and learn."

September didn't respond. She'd been watching and she'd been learning, and she knew that Gretchen really irked people, coworkers and witnesses and perps and victims alike.

Dr. Denby met them at the fourth-floor elevator. He was a short, slight man with a pencil-thin, blond beard that traced the length of his jawline and made his head look a little too large for his body. His brown eyes were stern and when they locked onto Gretchen's blue cat-eyes, they grew sterner.

September suspected Gretchen was about to piss him off as well and braced herself.

"Dr. Denby?" a woman's voice asked, before a word was spoken. All three of them turned to the nurse approaching in the pink uniform.

"Yes," Denby snapped out.

The nurse gave Gretchen and September a harried look. "Four-twenty-seven. Mr. Upjohn? You said to tell you when he woke up?"

"Good timing," Gretchen said, and Denby simply brushed past the nurse and strode with short, fast, irritated steps to Upjohn's room, with September and Gretchen following behind. At the door to the room, Denby blocked their entrance. "Wait here," he commanded, before going the rest of the way inside.

"Prick," Gretchen said. She waited about a minute and then walked in the room anyway. September slipped in behind her—*watch and learn*—and caught the fulminating look on Denby's face, but mimicked Gretchen, who'd already turned her attention to the patient. Denby bit back whatever he'd planned to say, though it was hard for him.

Kurt Upjohn looked at them through bleary eyes. His skin was sallow and his hair stuck out from his head. The blankets covered everything but a hint of bandage by his neck. If she hadn't known about the surgery, September might think the man had been on a bender. She'd seen his corporate image picture: big smile, smoothed bald head, something was a little feral about his smile. Now, he just looked fragile.

"Mr. Upjohn, these women are from the Laurelton police," Denby said tightly. "They would like to have a few words with you. If it's too much of an effort, we can postpone it."

Gretchen said, "These women are Detectives Sandler and Rafferty."

Denby blinked, a bit shocked at Gretchen's open hostility. September guessed not many people took him on, certainly not many women.

Upjohn's tongue rimmed dry lips, then he croaked out, "Ask away."

"The big question on everyone's mind is why Zuma?" Gretchen began without preamble. "Why did this guy attack your company?"

"Don't know." With a pained twist of his lips, he rasped, "My son . . . is dead?"

Denby cut in, "Your wife was here. Do you remember?"

"Um . . . Camille, yes . . . she told me."

"Can you think of one reason . . . any reason . . . for this to happen?" Gretchen persisted. "Sour business dealings? Anything personal?"

"No . . . Are they . . . is the second floor still working? The gamers?" he clarified.

"The business is shut down," Gretchen said.

"Where's Berelli? What happened to Berelli?" His eyes rolled around as if loose in his skull.

"He's fine. We've spoken with Mr. Berelli," Gretchen assured him.

"I want to see him." He focused on the doctor. "I want to see him."

"Mr. Berelli . . ." Denby repeated, nodding.

Gretchen intervened, "I can contact Mr. Berelli and tell him you wish to see him."

"I want to see Phillip today," Upjohn said. His voice was fading out and he cleared his throat with an effort.

Denby said, "It's time to leave."

"I have a few more questions."

The doctor practically stepped on Gretchen, who stood her ground for a moment, but Upjohn's eyes had closed and Denby didn't look like he would be put off. She finally acceded, and September and Denby followed her into the hallway.

"Is Camille Dirkus still here?"

"I don't know. His wife was here this morning."

"She's not his wife," September said.

"Ex-wife." He looked irked that she'd corrected him.

September wondered if they would get anything further from the officious doctor, but Gretchen wasn't intimidated.

"What about Jessica Maltona?" she asked Denby.

"I'm not responsible for her. She's under Dr. Egan's care." He seemed delighted to be able to throw that out.

Gretchen didn't hesitate. She dropped Denby cold and strode to the fourth-floor nurse's station, asking for Jessica Maltona's room number. Denby was torn between the desire to charge after her and get in her way some more, or turn on his heel in a show of pique and disgust.

He chose the latter, practically clicking his heels as he stalked down the hall in the opposite direction.

"Dr. Egan is Ms. Maltona's doctor," the nurse at the station said.

Gretchen showed her badge. "I need to talk to her. Just tell me which room."

The woman bristled, but another, older nurse dropped the file she was perusing and came to the first one's rescue. "That's for Dr. Egan to decide."

"Then find him." Gretchen stared at her and she stared back. After a moment, she picked up the receiver, practically shoving the younger nurse aside, and punched in a number. "Please call the fourth-floor nurse's station," she clipped out. "There's a policewoman insisting on seeing Ms. Maltona." She hung up and said, "It'll just be a moment. . . ."

A moment turned into five minutes and Gretchen said, "You can turn this into a war, or you can work with me. Either way I'm going to see Ms. Maltona."

The younger nurse was gazing at Gretchen with a sort of fear mixed with awe. "Dr. Egan usually answers his page fairly quickly."

The older nurse flashed her a look of fury, as if she'd given away state secrets. Gretchen simply nodded and turned her back on them.

A few minutes later a good-looking doctor with dark hair and eyes came their way, his lab coat billowing behind him. He had a smile on his face and he looked at Gretchen, then

September, then back to Gretchen. "You wish to speak to my patient, Ms. Maltona?"

"That's the plan." Gretchen's eyes narrowed as she sized him up. He appeared more genial than Denby and she was feeling her way.

"She's in room 505. We'll take the elevator." He'd already turned toward the bank of elevators, which was a short walk further down the corridor. "I'm not sure what good this'll do you. She's surfaced once or twice since yesterday's surgery, but she hasn't completely come back to consciousness." He gave them a considering look as they crowded into the elevator car. "The bullet did extensive damage to her heart. You understand she may not recover."

September's stomach did a slow somersault. She swallowed and nodded as Gretchen said soberly, "We understand. We just want to see her."

The elevator *dinged* and the doors opened and Dr. Egan led them down a hall and around a corner to Jessica Maltona's room. She lay white-faced against the white pillowcase, barely a shade's difference between her flesh and the pillow. A bandage wrapped around her chest was visible as the gown gapped in the front. Her eyes stayed closed and her breathing seemed low and faint.

She's not going to make it, September thought.

They only stayed a few minutes then headed back to floor three, street level and out to Gretchen's Jeep. Once inside, September asked, "What do you think?"

"I got nothing. Upjohn's sad about his son and worried about his company. He wants to talk to his accountant, and maybe there's some book-cooking, or something, but he didn't act like a man who felt real danger."

"He doesn't think whoever did it is going to strike at him again, while he's laid up in the hospital," September clarified.

"That's my hit. What about you?"

"I don't know. If Camille Dirkus doesn't call me back soon, I'm going to have to track her down."

Gretchen made sounds of annoyance low in her throat.

"What did you think about Jessica Maltona?"

Gretchen sent her a sideways look as she drove out of the lot. "What did you think?"

"Doesn't look good."

"If the shooting had anything to do with her, she's paying a heavy price. Maybe her squirrelly boyfriend got her into something. I don't know."

"Could the boyfriend have done this, do you think?"

"My opinion? Not a chance. Jaffe's hiding something, though. I don't know what yet. I'll figure it out, but it doesn't feel like it's germane to the killings. We'll see."

"So who does that leave?" September asked.

"I don't know. De Fore? One of the gamers? Olivia Dugan?"

"Auggie's with her." September felt that same faint touch of betrayal that her brother hadn't contacted her. "And what about Trask Martin?"

"Somebody killed him right outside her door." Gretchen considered that. "I don't believe in coincidence, do you?"

"No," September said.

"Then Martin's death is related to the Zuma shootings, too. You said the girlfriend blamed his death on Dugan."

"Jo. Yeah. But D'Annibal doesn't believe that."

"Only because your brother texted him that he was with Dugan," Gretchen said. "Man, Auggie sure didn't get any time off between the task force and this job, did he?"

"No." September felt irrationally irked.

"Huh," Gretchen said, "I asked D'Annibal about him, but he fobbed me off some more."

September didn't want to talk about Auggie. He was her twin and she sometimes felt closer to him than anyone else in the universe, but at other times he was beyond annoying. What the hell was he doing? She'd known his work with the task force was winding down. Though his cover hadn't been blown, he'd said he needed to get out while the getting was good, and besides, he'd gathered as much intel as he could, or so he'd told her.

She knew Gretchen had hoped he would come back and partner up with her, but she'd gotten the feeling that would never happen. September suspected Gretchen had a little bit of a thing for him, but she kinda thought Gretchen wasn't his type. As if she'd asked the question, September said aloud, "My brother tends to go for broken women."

Gretchen made a retching sound. "Sounds like Olivia Dugan's right up his alley."

"Yeah . . ."

Detective August Rafferty was in a quandary. He'd managed to plug in his car charger for a few minutes while Liv was inside Hathaway House and text his lieutenant, but then Liv had come out and he'd scrambled to hide the evidence, to no avail. The wires had been in plain sight.

She hadn't said anything about it much, and he'd driven them both back to the "safe" house after filling the Jeep's tank and now . . . what? What should he do next? He wanted to follow along the path of Liv's zigzag investigation because this whole thing seemed to be morphing into something different than what it had first seemed. Did he think it was all about her? Not completely. But he did believe something was going on. Whether it was part of the massacre at Zuma Software, or something else entirely, he wasn't sure. But he wasn't truly the investigating officer on the Zuma case; D'Annibal had told him his sister and Gretchen Sandler were in charge.

He was just an extra player. He wasn't even really supposed to be working. This time was supposed to be his own, a decompressing period after the infiltration of Cordova's gang. In a perfect world he'd be back at his duplex, getting ready for football season and evicting his aggravating next-door tenants.

But instead . . .

He glanced at Liv, who was sitting at the kitchen table. He'd asked her if she'd like a sandwich, but she'd shaken her head and was just staring straight ahead, involved in some inner pathos. He'd made a sandwich for himself and felt like he'd been eating them forever, even though it had only been a few days. Even this morning's Egg McMuffin hadn't been much of a break.

"Maybe I'm wrong and it doesn't have anything to do with me," Liv said as Auggie grabbed the seat across from her and bit into a mouthful of turkey and mustard. "Maybe Kurt Upjohn's involved with military games, or his company's in debt, or he's a gambler or a thief, or something. Or, maybe they were after someone else there. Paul de Fore, or Aaron . . ." Her throat closed. "Or Jessica, or one of the computer wizards. Or Phillip Berelli."

"Phillip Berelli?" Auggie mumbled, reached for a napkin to wipe his mouth. "There's a name you haven't mentioned."

"He's the firm's accountant." She waved an arm. "Oh, yeah. It's definitely him. He's probably laundering money and hiding it in the Cayman Islands, or something."

He fought a smile and took a couple more bites, making short work of the sandwich half. Then he wiped his fingers and looked squarely into her hazel eyes. There was mistrust there, and a kind of simmering rebellion, as if she felt he were going to school her for her actions.

"Okay, let's say it is about you. For argument's sake," he added quickly when she looked about to protest his sudden change of tactics. "You think someone's after you and you ran from Zuma because you think this someone—the shooter—found you and your place of work."

"The lawyers found me. They called me on the phone," she reminded him. "I don't know how the shooter found me, exactly."

"Well, how did the lawyers find you?"

She spread her palms upward. "Trial and error. They were looking for Olivia Margaux Dugan and they got my home number. It probably wouldn't be that hard. I mean, I have a phone . . . electricity . . ."

"Did the package come to your apartment?"

"No, I asked them to send it to the office. The lawyers messengered it to Zuma."

He thought about that a moment. "And you're pretty convinced the package set off the massacre."

"I . . ." She exhaled, thought a moment, then said, "Convinced . . . I don't know. But it's the one thing that's different in my life."

"What was in the package that would have threatened the killer?" He could hear how carefully he was choosing his words and hoped she wouldn't think he was simply humoring her. He wasn't. Not really. But he also wanted to lead her down a logical path. Maybe there was some truth buried in what she was saying. If so, he wanted to mine it.

"Nothing, really. There were just some things there that my mom apparently wanted me to have when I turned twenty-five." She made a sound of impatience. "The more I talk about it, the more I realize how crazy it was to run. I was just—*scared.*"

"I know you don't think so, but the police will get that."

"I'm not ready to go yet," she said firmly.

He picked up the other half of his sandwich. "Back to the package. Your mother put it together and set it up so that you'd receive it when you turned twenty-five. That's a lot of foresight . . ."

"Yeah." She half-laughed. "What was she trying to tell me? What was happening in her life, that she felt the need to put the package together? I've asked myself these questions, believe me."

"What was in the package, specifically?"

"Pictures. A personal note from my mother. My birth certificate with the names of my birth parents."

"You were adopted." She nodded, and he added, "You knew you were adopted. It wasn't a secret."

"It wasn't a secret," she agreed.

"What were the pictures of?"

"People. My mother. And my father. And some other strangers who looked like maybe they were my parents' friends? There's one man who was stalking angrily toward the camera who I think is the doctor my brother was remembering. I showed the photos to Hague, and he said the man in the picture was the zombie."

"Zombie?"

"It's what he called him when he was two. He talked about the zombie. And then . . . last night, when he saw that picture, he said he was the zombie. Maybe this guy is a doctor, who either treated him, or me. I went to Hathaway House this morning to see if I could talk to my old doctor, Dr. Yancy, but she's no longer there and Dr. Knudson, the director, won't be in till Monday."

He munched on the second half of the sandwich and asked, "You sure you don't want one?"

"No, thanks."

"Something to drink?"

For an answer she got up to pour herself a glass of water. "I can get it. Want a refill?" she asked him, as he'd nearly finished his drink.

"Sure." She picked up his glass, filled it from the tap, then set it down in front of him as she retook her seat. Her own glass was full and though she placed it in front of herself, she didn't immediately take a swallow.

"Who else saw the pictures?" Auggie asked.

"My father and his wife, my stepmother, Lorinda. And Della, she lives with Hague." She paused, thinking a moment. "And my neighbor saw the picture of the stalking man, too."

"Your neighbor?" he asked.

"In the apartment next to me. He stopped by at lunchtime on Thursday and I had the pictures out. He just noticed the guy looked angry and that the pictures were old." She finally picked up the glass and took a delicate swallow. "Trask," she said.

Auggie lifted his brows, and she added, "My neighbor. He lives with his girlfriend, Jo, in 21B. They were there before I ever moved in. They're not involved with this."

Auggie finished his sandwich, then carried the plate to the sink and rinsed it off. Turning around, he leaned against the counter, curling his hands around the edge. "Did the lawyers say when they originally received the package from your mother?"

"Umm . . . no, I guess not. I just assumed it was right before her death. I don't know. . . ." She trailed off, her brow furrowing.

"What?"

"It was the blouse. She's wearing the same blouse in one of the pictures that she was wearing when, when she died. I think she got it for her birthday. Or, maybe she was just wearing it on my birthday. . . ." She shook her head, as if trying to clear out the cobwebs. "But it was around the same time, so she must have given the package to the lawyers right before she died."

"You've never really believed her death was a suicide."

"No. At Hathaway House they really tried to get me to believe. I think beneath all the therapy, that was the real goal: Liv Dugan needs to face the awful truth of her mother's suicide. I finally pretended like I did believe it. It's what it took to get out of there. But it was a lie."

"You think the serial strangler hanged her."

She pulled her shoulders in when he put it like that. "There were some things that just didn't seem to add up. The timing was such, that I've thought, off and on, maybe the killer had something to do with my mother's death. Maybe he strangled her first and then made it look like a hanging. . . ." She shook her head. "But apparently there was no evidence to support that."

"Your mother's death doesn't follow his m.o., at least not in the strictest sense."

"Maybe they never really looked to see," Liv said. "The police just took her hanging as a suicide. Maybe they never checked for other evidence. I don't think they wanted to add her to their homicide list. They had their hands full and a lot of public pressure building."

"Or, it wasn't a homicide," he pointed out.

"My mother's death doesn't fit the pattern," she agreed. "She was inside the house and so was I, and so was my brother. And she wasn't killed and left in a field. She was . . . hanged."

"After her death, what happened to your family?"

"We moved to another part of town. Dad met Lorinda and they got married. Nobody talked about Mama anymore. And then we moved out of Rock Springs and then I went to Hathaway House, and later, Hague went to Grandview."

"And your family didn't talk about your mother's death after that."

"They didn't talk about it at all. Until I got to Hathaway House, then it seemed like it was the only subject we talked about. Dr. Yancy thinks I saw something that I've repressed."

"What do you think?"

She lifted her hands. "Sometimes I think, if I could just reach a little further, I might get it. I don't know."

He thought that over, then asked, "Your neighbor, your father and his wife and your brother and his girlfriend were the only ones who saw what was in the package? That's it?"

"Della's my brother's caretaker, not his girlfriend. Well, maybe she is. That distinction's kind of fuzzy. But I don't think any of them would say anything. And my neighbor, Trask, wouldn't even know what he was looking at."

"You're completely sure about that?"

"Yes."

"And your brother's caretaker, Della?"

"Well . . . no . . ." she admitted. "Della's been with Hague for years and she's devoted to him. She's older than he is, by about a decade. I think she met him at Grandview, and then later, when he was out, they kept in contact and he needed help and . . . there you go. Maybe she is just his caretaker. I really don't know what their relationship is, but I do think, overall, she's good for him."

"You just don't like her much," he said, reading between the lines.

"I like her better than Lorinda," she admitted honestly. She sighed heavily. "Maybe I should just go with the prevailing theory that the shootings were because of Kurt Upjohn. It was a *massacre,* for God's sake. All of my stuff . . . is just maybe . . . my stuff."

"I don't know if you're right, exactly. About Zuma. But I think with the timing of the package, and your own history . . ." He pressed his lips together a moment, not wanting to give her too much to believe in, but also needing to bolster her trust. "Count me in on the investigation."

Liv's eyes searched his face. He could see she didn't trust him one iota; she couldn't figure out his motivation. "Who *are* you?" she asked.

He thought about telling her. The words leapt to his

tongue. But her mistrust of the authorities stopped him. "You picked me," he reminded her. "I'm in between jobs. My ex-girlfriend's still in Canada. Not a wife, but close enough. We lived together quite a while." The lie tripped off his tongue. Lies he'd used when he was Alan Reagan. "We broke up and I'm starting a new life." When she didn't say anything, he said, "Tell me from beginning to end, who saw the package."

She inhaled slowly, then exhaled. "I got it at work. I took it to my brother's apartment."

"After your neighbor saw the pictures."

"Yes." She nodded. "Then my father and Lorinda stopped by Hague's. They thought it was strange that my mother had sent me the photos and documents, and we talked briefly about the strangler. I told them I was going to do some investigating on my own, that I never believed Mama had committed suicide. Della was mostly concerned about Hague, who had gone into one of his fugue states, a trance, so I don't know how much she was really paying attention to the package contents. Maybe she was, maybe she wasn't."

"This was how long before the attack on Zuma?"

"The night before. Thursday."

"Go on," he said, when she stopped.

"There isn't much more to tell. I went to work, went to lunch, came back and saw—the bodies. Then I ran and eventually got in your Jeep and held you at gunpoint."

"Is there anything else—anything—that would make you suspect the Zuma killings had to do with you?"

She shook her head and gave him a resigned look. "No. I told you, it's just a feeling I've had for a long time. All my life really, since my mother's death. Like there's something out there. Someone out there, who means me harm. Yes, I know. This could probably be the result of finding my mother's body. I've heard it all before. It just doesn't go away and it doesn't matter how rational I am, or how much I try to talk myself out of it, it's always there."

"So, if the strangler had something to do with your mother's death, and the Zuma killings are related to that, you think he struck again now because you got the package?"

"He came into Zuma shooting," Liv said. "That doesn't follow his m.o. I know. It doesn't make sense."

"Been a lot of years," Auggie said. "Anything's possible."

"Are you playing devil's advocate?"

He couldn't tell her that he'd seen a lot of criminals whose crimes morphed from one thing to another for various reasons.

"He killed three more women after my mother's death," she said. "Most of them were prostitutes out of the Portland area, but not all. There was a woman from Malone, the town over from Rock Springs.

"It just feels like someone's after me," she went on. "Maybe they think I now know something about my mother's death. The doctor . . . if he knew what Dr. Yancy thought, that I'd repressed something, something I'd seen . . ." She worried her lower lip with her teeth. "And then the package contents scared him. Jump-started him, or her, or whoever. If it's not the strangler who's after me, it's still *somebody. That's* what I feel."

"Okay."

"Okay, what?" she asked suspiciously.

"I know you're not going to, and I'm not going to make you, but I still think you should go to the police."

"No."

"Then, I'm a part of your team. You chose me, and you're stuck with me."

He could tell his declaration almost relieved her, but she said with ill grace anyway, "Sounds like I don't have any choice."

"You could still hold me at gunpoint and threaten to shoot me."

She lifted her brows in that way people do that silently asks, "Really?"

"Of the people who saw the package, which one do you think it is? The one who acted on it?"

"None of them. I don't know. Maybe it was someone at the lawyer's office?"

"Was the package opened?" he asked. She shook her head. "Move past the lawyers for a moment. Go back to the people you know who saw the contents of the package."

"Like I said, it's none of them. I don't like Lorinda at all, and my father's a cold fish, but Della . . . or Hague . . . they just . . . wouldn't. I mean, why? Hague was a baby when our mother died, and Della wouldn't care. . . ." She trailed off and Auggie's attention sharpened.

"What?" he asked.

"It's nothing. It's just . . . Hague orates. In a corner of the bar below his apartment. He holds court and just talks about everything. Rants, really."

"About?"

"Political stuff, mostly. He has followers. They come and listen to him, or argue with him, or just come to feel like they're part of a crowd."

"You think he brought up the package to his listeners?" Auggie was skeptical.

"He said he did . . . but I don't know if it's true. I upset him and he reacted. Hague gets things confused."

"If you had to put a finger on what item specifically, from inside the package, would send a killer to Zuma, what would it be?"

"The photo of the stalking man," she said. "The zombie-doctor. That picture stands out. *He* stands out." She made a sound of disbelief. "I'm sorry. I don't know why it's taken me so long. Do you want to see the package contents?"

Auggie was happy with this show of trust. "Sure."

She dragged her backpack up from beneath her chair, dropped it on the tabletop, then dug inside it and lifted out a manila envelope. Wordlessly she handed the package to him. He slipped the contents onto the table and arranged each piece so he could see each one, feeling like an intruder when he read the personal note.

"I think he was a visiting doctor at Hathaway House, but I have to wait to talk to Dr. Knudson. I don't even know if that'll work. Knudson wasn't on staff when I was there, so will he even know him?"

"There's only one way to find out," Auggie said positively. "We'll go see him together."

"On Monday . . . today's Saturday . . . ?"

"I can wait." He smiled and she just looked at him. Eventually, she nodded her agreement as she slid the items back inside the package and set it to one side.

Now, he just had to figure out a way to talk to D'Annibal without Liv Dugan overhearing.

Chapter 12

Jessica Maltona's boyfriend, Jason Jaffe, was exactly the piece of work Gretchen had said he was. He even looked the part with disreputable jeans and a wife-beater T-shirt. He was an artist who worked with metal and a welding machine and Gretchen and Nine found him hard at work in the garage of the small home he shared with Jessica, a blue flame spurting from his hand-held welder, melting metal into a bubbling liquid at the joint of something that looked like a large ball with rebar spikes that now looped down like limp spider's legs.

Such was September's appreciation of Jaffe's art.

He looked up at their approach through his welder's helmet; his eyes visible behind black mesh, the rest of his face hidden. Switching off the torch, he flipped up the helmet. He was good-looking in that lean, rawhide way with deep grooves beside his mouth and flinty eyes.

"Who the fuck are you?" he greeted them.

"We've spoken," Gretchen said, whipping out her ID and getting bristly.

As soon as he realized who they were he visibly pulled on a mask of geniality. September introduced herself and then explained a little about the general investigation, and their visit to the hospital to see Jessica.

"She's not doin' so well, huh," he said blithely.

Gretchen's eyes narrowed at his callous tone, but September sensed it might be a cover-up. She wasn't in love with the guy, but he might have a lot of feelings buried down deep that he wasn't willing to let them see.

"Tell us a little bit about her," she suggested.

"Like what?"

"How long have you and she been living here? How did you meet? Like that."

He paused for a long moment, then took off the helmet and flexed his arms and back. Hunks of metal surrounded him in disorderly bins and a wooden workbench with scattered tools stood against the back wall.

"We met in a bar. I liked the way she looked. I guess she felt the same. I was doing some landscaping for Lawn Like New. Asshole boss. Asshole company. She was workin' for that Zuma guy and makin' more money than I was. We started renting and then the bastard fired me and Jessica said maybe it was meant to be. We could squeak by on her salary for a while, and this way, I got to work on my sculptures full time."

Gretchen just stood back; she'd heard enough bullshit in her life to be bored or irritated or both. She was itching to get on to something new.

September said, "Any thoughts on why someone might have it in for Jessica?"

His flinty eyes gazed at her as if she'd lost her mind. "Hell, no. Everybody loves Jess. She's *nice*." He slid a look Gretchen's way as if making a point. "You gotta get your head outta your asses. This ain't about Jess. This is about that asshole Kurt Upjohn. He's the *asshole*. Makes tons of cash and works everybody like crazy."

"You have any specific reason to suspect the murders were because of Upjohn?" September asked.

"Wha'd I just say? He's an asshole!"

"I heard that Paul de Fore gave her a hard time for leaving on her break," September said.

"God . . ." He shook his head. "She met me at that Starbucks close by Zuma to give me my keys, which she ran off with this morning by mistake. Stop trying to pin this on her. It's Upjohn's fault Rambo came in and shot the place up." A pause, and then he said with a hitch to his voice, "That was the last time I saw her."

Gretchen chose that moment to join back in, saying coolly, "She's at Laurelton General now. You can stop by anytime. Do you have anything concrete to back up your theory that this was Upjohn's fault? Something besides just not liking the guy?"

"All I know is that Jess doesn't deserve this. Any of it." His lips started to quiver a little and he smashed them together. "It's Upjohn's fault she got hurt. That's on him . . . asshole," he added.

They left after a few more questions that earned them more of the same. In the car Gretchen observed to September, "You're a lot more patient than I am."

She observed right back, "You haven't set the bar too high."

That earned her a snap of Gretchen's head and a drop of her mouth. To date, September had been quietly taking it all in, not wanting to make waves, but her innate sense of humor couldn't remain repressed for long.

Gretchen gave a short bark of laughter. "Okay," she said. Then, "Let's get our asses back to work."

"We don't want to be assholes," September agreed.

They both broke into chuckles.

* * *

At the station, D'Annibal was just coming back from an on-site interview at Zuma with Pauline Kirby as Gretchen and September entered the station. Gretchen glared at Urlacher, whose throat worked as if he were desperate to get the words out even though he knew she'd growl at him. He just managed to keep his requests for ID to himself.

D'Annibal was entering his office, taking off his coat and loosening his tie. His gray hair was smooth, his color high, as if he'd been standing in the sun for a little too long, which he probably had been.

"How'd it go?" Gretchen asked him, stopping outside his door.

"Fair. She kept zinging questions about Upjohn's finances, his relationship with Dirkus's mother, and the secrecy surrounding his operation. I kept deflecting."

"Did you bring up the Martin killing?" she asked, as September joined her, both of them standing outside the office.

"I tried to say next to nothing except that we're on the job." He smiled thinly. "The usual. It'll be on tonight's news. Another reporter appears to be on the Martin homicide. Expect a call," he said to September, seating himself behind his desk.

It was their cue to leave and as they walked away, Gretchen said, "Ever talked to the press?"

"Not about work."

"Give 'em the basics: where the body was discovered, that the death was from a bullet wound—don't say how many shots—that the name won't be released until next of kin have been notified."

"His parents are both gone. Jo is really all he has," September reminded her.

"Don't mention her name, either. Let 'em think we're still notifying family, even if we aren't."

She asked innocently, "Do you want me to also keep it

quiet about the fact that Olivia Dugan, Zuma's missing employee, is a person of interest in the Trask Burcher Martin homicide?"

Gretchen shot her a look, realizing she was being put on. "Smart ass."

September grinned. "You and Jaffe. Big with the 'ass' stuff."

Gretchen pointed a finger at her. "I'm just sayin', when you get the call, sound like you're being overly helpful but give them as little as possible."

"How do you propose I do that?"

"Omit, omit, omit."

"What if I screw up?"

"You won't. And if you do, you'd better hope to hell you get that other reporter instead of Pauline Kirby because she'll eat you alive."

The news came on at five and Auggie, who'd flopped himself on the bed and gone channel surfing the last ten minutes, switched to Channel Seven's *News at Five*. His antennae were very aware of Liv Dugan, who had settled on the couch as if she were done for the day.

He called out to her. "You want anything to eat? You missed lunch."

"I'm not hungry," she called back.

"You should eat something."

He heard her rustle around and then she was standing in his doorway. There was something elfin about her large eyes and pale face, but her chin was stubborn, and her arms were crossed.

"Wanna go get something to eat?" he asked. "I just was going to check the news."

"I don't want to show my face anymore than I have to."

"But food . . ." He tried on his most winning smile. "It's how we stay alive."

"I don't think I could eat anything. I'm just . . ." She looked over her shoulder as if she'd heard something. "I'm just not hungry."

"There's a deli about two miles away with the best soup around. I'll go get some after the news and bring it back."

"Maybe I could go and wait in the car," she said, looking worried.

"Sure. Whatever . . ."

The lead story was a murder from the night before. Auggie looked at the screen as the young male reporter was saying that the shooting had happened around nine o'clock. The camera revealed a parking lot and then led them up to the second story where it zeroed in on a length of balcony toward one end of the building.

The gasp from Liv was almost a shriek. Her hands were at her mouth, and she was gaping at the television. Auggie's gaze slammed from her back to the screen.

". . . Laurelton police are waiting to notify next of kin before releasing the male victim's name. If anyone has information, please contact the authorities. . . ."

"What?" Auggie asked her. "What?" But he was getting that strange feeling, like electricity running beneath his skin, that said something momentous was about to happen.

"That's my apartment."

He jumped off the bed, wishing to high heaven he had a DVR at this place. "Your apartment?" he snapped. He'd seen her apartment from the backside, but then she'd appeared on foot with her backpack and he'd followed her, never actually turning off the main road and into the drive of her parking lot.

"Who . . . who . . . oh, my God . . . *Trask?* Is it Trask?" She swayed on her feet, and he took two large steps and grabbed her by the arms, steadying her.

"The neighbor? The one who saw the photos?"

"Maybe it's someone else. Maybe it's . . ." She couldn't come up with another alternative.

The news had moved on and suddenly there was Pauline Kirby, standing in a bright blue dress outside a two-story glass building with a large wooden door and thrusting a microphone toward Lieutenant Aubrey D'Annibal. The image caught Auggie unawares and he stood there in frozen surprise, his hands still clasped around Liv's shaking shoulders.

"That's Zuma," Livvie choked out.

"Lieutenant, can you give us an update on the mass murder that took place here yesterday? Do you know what precipitated this deadly slaughter?"

D'Annibal winced a bit at the word "slaughter." "We're still sifting through evidence and interviewing employees."

She jumped on that. "Has the missing employee been found? Ms. Dugan?"

The faintest hesitation and Auggie held his breath. D'Annibal said, "As soon as more information's available, we'll make sure the public's made aware. Zuma Software's owner, Mr. Kurt Upjohn, is through surgery, as is the other injured employee, Ms. Jessica Maltona."

"We understand they're both critical," Pauline said.

"Yes, ma'am."

"Aaron Dirkus, one of the deceased, was Kurt Upjohn's son. Is Mr. Upjohn aware his son is dead?"

Auggie sucked air between his teeth while D'Annibal did something similar on the screen. "Yes," he stated flatly.

"He suffered bullet wounds to his abdomen, whereas Ms. Maltona was shot in the chest?"

"We hope to have some good news about their recovery soon," D'Annibal deflected.

"Is it true Zuma Software was creating software for the

military?" Pauline leaned forward, trying to create a fake kind of tête-à-tête.

D'Annibal didn't buy it for a minute. "As soon as we learn something definitive, we'll let you know. Thank you." And he moved away. The show cut to Pauline staring directly at the camera as she wrapped up with comments about how she hoped good news would be forthcoming about capturing the gunmen so we could all sleep more soundly in our beds.

Liv had collapsed against Auggie, and he'd wrapped his arms around her. He led her to the bed and had her sit down. She seemed to be boneless, so he told her to lie down, and she did so with a blank look on her face.

"Trask," she said. "It's Trask."

"What's his last name?"

"Um . . ." Tears were forming in the corners of her eyes. "I don't . . . Martin, I think."

"I'm gonna go find out what happened," he answered, already moving, already planning.

"I'm going with you."

"Stay here," he ordered. "I'll get some more information and I'll bring back some soup."

"I don't want you to leave," she said, swallowing hard.

He'd been halfway out of the room, but now he crossed back to the bed. Looking down at her, he said tautly, "I'll be back. I promise. Do you believe me?"

She hesitated. "Yes. I don't know why you're doing this, but yes, I believe you."

"Stay put. Try to relax. I'll be back in an hour or so."

"An hour . . ."

"Or so," he said. "Don't panic. Trust me."

She nodded, and he was gone.

* * *

He phoned the lieutenant as soon as he was out of view of the house. D'Annibal answered on the second ring, as if he were waiting for his call, which he probably was.

"Where the hell are you, Rafferty?" D'Annibal demanded as an intro.

Auggie shot back, "What happened to this Trask Martin? Who's on that? He's Liv Dugan's neighbor."

"We know that. Did she tell you his name?" he asked suspiciously. "We didn't release it."

"Yeah, she told me. She nearly fainted when she saw that he'd been gunned down!"

"You know, the only reason we're not chasing her down like a dog is because supposedly she's been with you," he returned levelly.

"She *has* been with me. Ever since yesterday afternoon."

"How the hell did that happen?"

Auggie thought about how Liv had climbed into his Jeep and held him at gunpoint and decided some things were better left unsaid. "We struck up a conversation and one thing led to another."

A hesitation, then, he managed to laugh faintly. "You always get the women."

"It isn't like that." *Yet*, he thought. It isn't like that *yet*. "I haven't told her who I am, but she's scared, and she thinks the other Zuma shootings were incidental, in that she thinks the killer was after her."

"Why?"

"Mostly because of her past . . ." Auggie gave him an abbreviated rundown of Liv's mother's death and the package that was sent, and finished with, "I don't know if she's right, but I want to follow this through. Even if it doesn't pan out with the Zuma shootings, there's something there."

"What about the neighbor?"

"She was sick when she saw it on the news. She believes his shooting has to do with her, too, but doesn't know why.

That's why I'm sticking close to her. There's a connection there. Has to be."

The lieutenant humphed his agreement. "Nine's on the case," he said, answering one of Auggie's earlier questions.

"My sister?" He stared through the windshield, aware of a cop car ahead. "Hang on," he said, pulling the phone from his ear. He didn't want to be pulled over for using a cell phone while driving and he didn't have Bluetooth, or an ear bud with him.

Nine was the detective on the Trask Martin homicide? *Nine?*

The deli was on his left and he pulled over and into a spot. "You still there?" he asked the lieutenant.

"Yeah. How soon can you bring Dugan in?"

"Uh . . . She's got some trust issues, with the police. It'll happen. Just give me a little time. Believe me, she had nothing to do with Martin's death. She was with me the whole time." An eely feeling slid down his back. *But she was gone for a while last night. She went to see her brother.*

"Talk to your sister," D'Annibal said. "She can give you the particulars about the Martin homicide. Don't take too long. I want Dugan brought in by Monday."

"Okay. Oh, and have someone look into the serial strangler who was around the Rock Springs area about twenty years ago."

"I remember that case," D'Annibal answered. "What's that got to do with this?"

"I don't know. Nothing maybe. Olivia Dugan's from that area."

"All right. Monday," the lieutenant reminded him as he hung up.

Auggie sat for a moment, staring through the windshield. *But Liv didn't fake that reaction to Martin's death. That was real,* he reminded himself. Worry was scratching at his brain. He knew Liv wasn't the Zuma shooter. Knew she wasn't . . . But she'd taken her gun with her when she'd gone to see her brother, so she could have stopped by her apartment.

But no. It just *wasn't* true. Couldn't be. She was too careful and responsible and nice.

And he liked her.

He punched in the number to his sister's cell. "Well, good God," Nine greeted him with when the connection was made. "How're you doin', big bro? What's been happening in your life? Having a little R&R with one of our suspects?"

"Not one of your suspects. Maybe a person of interest. How're you doin', yourself?"

"Okay." She sounded wary.

"I *am* with Olivia Dugan," he admitted. "I told D'Annibal about it."

"And how did that come about?" Like D'Annibal before her, he gave her a quick recap of how he'd come to be with Liv. She listened silently and when he finished, she said, "So, you're bringing her in."

"Not quite yet. I've left out the part that I'm a detective."

"Oh, peachy. Why? No, I don't even want to know. Just tell her, and let's get her down here for a statement. The victim died at her doorstep, after all. I interviewed Martin's girlfriend, Jo. She thinks we oughtta be looking at Olivia Dugan."

"Any particular reason for that, other than that they're neighbors."

"Not as far as I can tell." September filled him in on what she'd learned about the murder of Trask Burcher Martin, which wasn't a helluva lot at this point.

"What kind of gun was used in the killing?" Auggie asked. He tried to keep his voice on the edge of disinterest even though he was keyed to the answer.

But his sister knew him too well. "Why?"

"September . . ." he said on a long-suffering sigh. "Just tell me."

"A Glock."

Thank you, God. He closed his eyes and exhaled. Liv had a .38. That cleared her, unless she possessed a second gun, which was about as likely as igloos in Florida.

"Auggie?"

"I gotta go. D'Annibal told me to bring her in by Monday. I'll do that."

"Why can't you bring her in now?"

"I love you, too," he said.

"Don't play with me. You've got to tell her who you are!"

"You're breaking up. Gotta go."

"Liar!"

He clicked off. When she rang back, he ignored the call. Pocketing his cell, he climbed out of the car . . . and remembered his wallet beneath his seat. He hadn't asked Liv for money, and now how was he going to explain being able to purchase the soup?

Maybe he should just tell her who he was. What would she do? What *could* she do?

Peeling back the tape that held his wallet to the underside of the driver's seat, he pulled it out and extracted a twenty, then put it back in place. He went inside and placed a to-go order for two bowls of chicken tortilla soup. A young woman served it into cardboard containers with plastic lids and placed them into a bag along with hunks of baguette. Auggie felt his mouth water as he headed back to the Jeep and then drove home.

At the house, he parked the Jeep and yanked down the garage door. He slipped the key into the lock of the back door, twisted, gently pushed it open and called softly, "Lucy, I'm home . . ." into the darkened interior.

She appeared like a wraith, standing at the edge of the

kitchen in her jeans and a light top, the color indiscernible in the blackness of the room.

"Can I turn on a light?" he asked.

"Do you have to?" She sounded uncertain.

"Are we hiding? I mean, more than before?"

"I thought maybe . . . you wouldn't return."

He flipped the switch and they blinked at each other. He realized her shirt was light pink and she had a black pullover in hand. Beside her was her backpack, zipped up and standing at the ready. The package was nowhere in sight. "You were leaving," he said.

"Thinking about it."

"Ye of little faith. Here." He set the bag of food on the table and pulled out the containers of soup. The scent of chili and tomato was enough to send his salivary glands into overdrive once again. There were plastic soupspoons inside and he handed one to Liv.

For a moment she hesitated, then said, "Did you—learn anything about Trask?"

"A few things. Sit down and eat. We'll talk afterwards."

Fifteen minutes later they were still at the table, but sated and quiet. Liv had been so certain he'd left her that she'd gone through seven levels of hell debating what to do next. Now, she felt weak and less sure of herself, all her energy used up. Trask was dead, and she didn't know if she had the strength to go on. It was all happening too fast and she couldn't put the pieces together in any meaningful way. Her head was loaded with information, none of which made sense.

She looked into the bottom of her empty soup container. "This was really good."

"I know. Sometimes I've gone there every night for a week."

Her lips tightened. "How did you pay for the soup?" she asked carefully.

He didn't miss a beat. "I stole from your purse."

"You couldn't have. It was in my backpack."

He grinned, then, looking so boyish and unrepentant that she was afraid to hold his gaze, afraid what he would see in her face. "Okay, I scrounged some money out of my car. No easy trick. Luckily there was a bunch of change in the glove box."

She hadn't noticed any extra cash when she'd popped it open, but she hadn't looked all that closely, either. She'd been so undone that he'd lied to her about the car charger.

And also he'd lied about having an ex-wife.

"Just how much of what comes out of your mouth is the truth?" she asked.

Chapter 13

For a moment she thought he was going to pretend offense, but then his gaze narrowed a bit and he inclined his head. "About 92 percent."

"So, how am I to know when we're in the other 8 percent?"

To her shock he reached over and covered her hand with his. The heat of his skin sent a prickle of warning up her arm. Dangerous. He was dangerous. To her.

"Right now, it's all about truth," he told her, sounding so serious that she wanted to jerk her hand free of his and wrap her arms around her torso for protection. "I need to talk to you about your neighbor. Trask Martin."

"You found out what happened to him. Who did you talk to?"

"There was a newspaper left at the deli, and I read what was there. Not much more than what we heard on the news. But I do believe his death, the timing of his death, has to do with you."

"You do?"

He nodded. "I want you to tell me exactly what happened between you and him. He saw the photograph. Who else knew he saw it? His girlfriend?"

She carefully withdrew her hand. "No, she wasn't there. No one else knew." She thought back to Trask, feeling a weight on her heart. Another weight, along with the one already in place for Aaron. After a moment, she told him, "Trask did say something to me."

"What?"

"After I saw Hague, I stopped by his apartment Thursday night, and we had drinks with Jo and then he walked me back to my place. He told me he'd seen someone outside my door, kind of lurking, I think. It gave me a jolt."

"Did he talk to the guy?" Auggie asked, watching her closely.

"No. The guy took off when he said something to him."

"What'd he look like?"

"He was wearing a hoodie, so Trask thought he might be young, but he really couldn't tell how old he was. The guy just turned away and Trask watched him, I guess. Anyway he left in a truck . . . a gray GMC. 2005. Trask said he noticed, because he used to have one just like it."

"When was this?"

"Sometime in the last couple weeks?"

"Before you got the package from your mother?"

"Yeah . . . I guess so." Liv stirred, uncomfortable, and got to her feet. "It just made me feel, again, like I was right: someone's following me."

Auggie also stood up, clearly rolling that over in his mind. "Maybe that's how he learned about the package, because he was keeping close tabs on you."

"I got it at work. I don't know how he could possibly know. It was always in my bag. Even the people that worked there didn't know about it, except Paul de Fore, and he never saw what was in it."

"What about when Trask saw the photos? You said no one else was around. Could there have been someone? Someone you didn't notice?"

Liv thought back to when Trask stopped by her apartment unannounced. "The door was open for a few minutes. If someone was there, they might have heard him say something about the photos? But there was no one on the balcony when Trask left. I just don't see how."

"Somebody killed him, and if it has to do with you, it probably has to do with the package, too. And that may, or may not, have to do with the Zuma killings. But there's some connection to you."

She was happy to have an ally. Happy and surprised. She knew she should ask him more questions about himself; something just wasn't ringing true. But she almost didn't care. It was just such a relief to have someone *listening* to her. "What now?" she said into the growing silence where she could tell he was thinking hard.

"You don't have a cell phone." He said it as a fact.

"No."

"You're twenty-five. I can't name you one other twenty-five-year-old I've met in the last few years who doesn't have a cell phone." He paused, then added, "I'm guessing it's another way to keep the bogeyman from finding you."

"I do have a land line," she pointed out.

He half-smiled. "You and everybody else over fifty."

"That's . . . not accurate."

"Close enough, but okay, we'll use my phone."

"Who are we gonna call?"

"Your doctor. The one who treated you at Hathaway House."

"Dr. Yancy . . ."

He nodded. "Maybe she can remember the zombie doctor, and then you won't have to go through all those bureaucratic hoops."

"I don't know where she is," Liv protested.

"I can check on my phone. What do you know about Dr. Yancy?"

"Nothing really."

"No idea where she lived?"

"Somewhere in the Portland area? Not that far from Hathaway House, I think. She mentioned something once."

He clicked a few buttons, scrolled around a bit, waited a few minutes, then said, "There are about four Yancys listed with a 'y' ending, and another three, with an 'ey' ending."

"There's no 'e'," she said.

"Okay, then, how about Buzz Yancy?"

"She wasn't married."

"What's her first name? There are some initials listed for first names here. That's usually women."

Liv pictured the slim, middle-aged woman with the gray hair and solemn eyes. Dr. Yancy wore reading glasses, which she had a tendency to set down on her desk and pick up with some regularity, even when she didn't put them on. "Her first name was Fern. I remember thinking it was a plant. There was a notepad on her desk with initials. FSY. I don't think I ever knew what the S was for."

"There's one F. Yancy listed."

Liv felt her pulse start to beat hard. "Well, that's probably her, don't you think?"

"One way to find out . . ." He dialed the number, then handed Liv the phone.

Auggie's stomach muscles were tight. He'd put his phone in her hand and there was a chance, even though she wasn't familiar with cells, that something could give away his deception. September could call back, for Chrissake. He was pushing it, but there it was.

"It's just ringing," she said after a tense moment. "If it

goes to voice mail, I can't tell her who I am. People are looking for me."

"Then name someone else from that time you were there. Use another girl's name. Say you're her."

"I—maybe Talia . . . O'Conner."

Auggie nodded encouragingly. A moment later Liv stumbled through the voice mail giving Talia's name while Auggie quietly whispered his cell number in her ear and she repeated the digits into the phone.

After she hung up she handed Auggie back the cell, which he tucked into a pocket. Then they just looked at each other.

"You're good at this," she observed.

"Eight percent of the time," he answered. Then, "What about your birth certificate?"

"What about it?"

"Why was it in the package?"

Liv cocked her head and frowned. "I have no idea. It just listed my birth parents, but I always knew I was adopted."

"Well, maybe your mother just wanted you to have it," Auggie posed, "or maybe there's something else there. Some other meaning. She had a purpose in keeping these things together, setting it up for you to receive them at twenty-five."

"You're thinking she was getting ready to take her own life," Liv said tiredly, looking away.

"Nope. I'm going with your theory that something else happened. Maybe something that set up what happened at Zuma. Or, maybe something your mother knew or suspected that put her in danger. She sent this to you, just in case. Your brother didn't get anything, did he?" he asked as an afterthought.

"Not that I know of."

He shrugged. "You were the oldest."

"I was adopted and Hague's theirs."

Auggie gave her a long look. "Now there's a difference we haven't explored. Your mother put your birth certificate in the package, and not your brother's. So, who are your birth parents?"

"I don't know them. My father never mentioned them, so I doubt he knows who they are," Liv said.

"Let's look at that birth certificate again."

"It's the hospital certificate," Liv said, as she dug into her backpack, pulled out the package and slid the contents onto the table once again. "The one with the impressions of my feet. My parents' names are written on it."

"How did your adoptive mother get this?" Auggie wondered aloud, picking it up. "Father, Everett LeBlanc. Mother, Patricia LeBlanc."

Liv took the paper from him. "Malone General Hospital. The closest one to Rock Springs."

"So, maybe your mother knew the LeBlancs," Auggie hazarded a guess. He pulled out his cell and checked numbers for Rock Springs and some of the neighboring towns. "There's an Everett LeBlanc in Malone," he said.

Liv inhaled and exhaled, her eyes huge. "Okay."

"Want to call?"

"Who should I say I am this time? If I tell them Olivia Dugan, they could know I'm their daughter. And even if they don't, my name's been all over the news the last couple days."

"We don't know what they know," Auggie said. "I'd be honest but a little careful. Tell them you're Liv Dugan, not Olivia, just in case they've been listening to the news. Say you're looking for the Everett and Patricia LeBlanc who gave up a girl baby for adoption twenty-five years ago."

He punched in the numbers and handed her the phone again. She listened as it rang and rang and then left a voice mail almost verbatim to what Auggie had told her. Auggie quietly repeated his cell number and she echoed it into the receiver. She handed him back the cell and he clicked off.

"Now what?" she asked.

"We wait."

September got the call from Channel Seven just after five-thirty. Luckily, it wasn't Pauline Kirby but an underling, trying to find out information, and since there was really nothing new to report, their conversation was over in a few minutes. When she was off the phone, September assessed her feelings about the whole thing and decided she hadn't liked being asked question after question by someone who was basically reading a script and hurrying her through the answers. She filed that aspect of the job under the heading of Try To Avoid.

It was getting later and she fooled around at her desk until nearly seven before she finally left. She would have stayed on, for lack of anything better to do with her time, but perversely she didn't want her coworkers to think she was a loser without any social life. It wasn't like she hadn't dated. She just hadn't dated in a while . . . a very long while.

She'd texted Auggie numerous times since his abrupt phone line cutoff. So far he'd been singularly unwilling to respond. How like him to play the cowboy and just run off with the investigation anyway he liked. *Her* investigation. Well, hers and Gretchen's. She kinda wished Wes Pelligree were a part of it, too, but he was busy with other things, cases that were wrapping up and a court appearance where he was a witness for the prosecution against a man who'd faked his own death for the insurance money, which his wife then promptly absconded with and he'd run her down and shot her and now they were both having separate trials and heading toward prison terms.

On her way out she passed Wes's empty desk and noticed the picture of Sheila Dempsey—something from her high school days, September guessed—which was propped up against his desk lamp. Dark-haired, in her thirties, slim and attractive, Sheila's body had been found in a field just outside the city limits, in Winslow County, though her place of residence was an apartment complex not all that far from the station. She'd been strangled and the flesh on her torso had been scored with lines that resembled letters, but maybe weren't. It wasn't Wes's case, it was county's, but he'd met her once at a bar sometime recently and her death bothered him.

Or, at least that was the word around the office. Wes hadn't said anything about her himself, but September had kept her ears open on the subject and had queried George about it a bit, at least until George had given her a look that said, "What the hell is it to you?"

There was no way September was going to admit she had a mild attraction to Wes, especially since he was deeply invested in his own relationship with a woman from his days as an athlete at a junior college. Their relationship was solid; that was fact. So, September kept her case of "the warms" to herself.

Liv lay on the couch in the darkness, staring at the ceiling once more. She moved onto her side and punched up the pillow, squeezing her eyes closed. Auggie was back in the bedroom and they were waiting for morning. Maybe someone would call them back.

There'd been an awkward moment or two when neither of them knew what to do. Auggie had finally said he was going to bed, but he was taking a shower first. Liv thought that sounded like heaven, but was too uneasy to strip off her clothes and spend a few moments naked with him around. Maybe in the morrow.

But then, before he'd gone to sleep, he'd actually walked past where she was sitting on the couch, removing her shoes. He was wearing boxers and nothing else as he strolled into the kitchen and poured himself a glass of water.

He stopped by the couch briefly, made a comment about trading places with her, the bed for the couch. She'd vehemently shaken her head, and he'd shrugged and moseyed on.

She, meanwhile, had lain back on the sofa cushions fully clothed, her mind caught on the smooth muscles she'd seen moving beneath the skin of his shoulders, the hard curve of his back, his taut, hair-dusted thighs.

She was shocked at herself. In the midst of her terror and anxiety, *this* was the overriding emotion quickening her blood? Desire? Lust? *Sex?*

With an effort, she dragged her feminine attention away from him and concentrated on the more urgent problems at hand. *Dr. Yancy. Think about Dr. Yancy.* But a pair of faintly amused blue eyes crowded her inner vision. She flung her arm over her eyes, as if that would help, and squeezed her brain shut.

"Liv."

Immediately she flung back her arm and popped her eyes open. The room was empty and dark. She was alone. Had only heard him in her head.

What? she answered silently.

The room was quiet. There was no sound anywhere. All in her head.

Then, a voice said, "You don't know what you're talking about, Dr. Yancy."

She recognized it. It was her own voice. Sullen and combative.

She saw herself at Dr. Yancy's desk and the doctor was regarding her with concern.

"You saw something," Dr. Yancy said. "Something you're repressing."

"What?" Liv demanded. "*What?* I didn't see *anything!*"

"Something," the doctor insisted. She was fading in and out, a watery vision.

"All I saw was my mother, hanging by her neck!" Liv practically screeched.

"Something else . . . maybe something that didn't actually have to do with that day. . . ."

A cracked door. A beam of light. In the glint of illumination, the wetness of an eye as he turns and sees her . . . outside . . . outside . . .

"I don't want to talk anymore!"

Slam! She was out the door. Running. Running. *Running!*

And Dr. Yancy's voice was calling after her, "It was him, Olivia. You saw him."

The memory sank away and Liv came fully awake, drenched in sweat. She heard the door to Auggie's bedroom slam open and suddenly he was there, beside the couch, kneeling beside her.

"You cried out," he said.

"I saw him. The monster. I saw him through a crack in the door. Dr. Yancy made me remember at Hathaway House but I ran away from her."

"Who is he? The monster?"

"Monster?" She blinked.

"You said 'the monster.'"

"I meant . . . the doctor. The zombie. The bogeyman. I think maybe I saw him, and he's the serial strangler. But if he's the doctor in the picture, that means Mama knew him. . . ." She swallowed. "Maybe she *knew* about him and that's why he had to kill her."

"Okay, wait. Take it slow. We'll start with him. We'll call Dr. Yancy again in the morning, if she hasn't called back. See what she knows about the doctor."

"Okay."

He smiled at her and actually had the audacity to sweep her hair back from her forehead before he turned to leave. Liv had to fight the desire to call him back. She kept her lips pressed tightly closed with an effort. The last thing she needed was to suddenly depend on him too much.

Chapter 14

The next morning Liv woke up when he walked past her to the kitchen in a pair of low-slung blue jeans and no shirt. She sat up, finger-combed her hair, then followed him into the kitchen. He'd picked up his cell and was looking at it.

"Let's go somewhere for breakfast," he said.

"I don't want to be seen. . . ."

"If you're with me, it's less chance you'll be recognized. Put on your baseball cap again."

"I guess I'm buying, huh."

That stopped him short and he shot her a look. "I . . . guess so."

She smiled faintly. "No problem. But I'm going to take a shower first."

"Do it," he said, turning back to his phone.

"Is there . . . a towel?"

"Should be. Linen closet's in the hall outside the bathroom."

She left him working through his phone and wondered if he'd lied about being such a loner. Maybe he'd contacted someone. He could be texting someone right now.

With a last look back at him, she picked up her backpack and headed into the bathroom.

*   *   *

Auggie had indeed received a text. A raft of them, actually. Mostly from his sister. At least she'd shown the good sense to move from phoning to texting. He'd turned off the text "alert" and they came in silently.

It was Sunday. He had one day until he needed to bring, coerce or drag Olivia Dugan to the Laurelton police station. He heard the taps turn on and he texted his sister, telling her to stop texting him. He would bring Olivia Dugan in tomorrow. Monday. And did she have any leads on the Zuma massacre, or Trask Martin's death?

She texted back:

New case. Short-handed. Will get back to you.

New case? Something that superseded the Zuma shooting? Not likely.

"Hmmm," Auggie said aloud.

What was that about?

September stared down at the cold, white corpse of the woman and felt ill. The woman's body had been stripped to the waist and her abdomen was carved with the scrawled words:

DO UNTO OTHERS AS SHE DID TO ME

"Jesus, somebody went to a lot of trouble." Gretchen's nasal tones were normally cool, curling around the edges with disdain, but staring down at the female corpse she sounded shaken. "'Do unto others as she did to me.' What the hell does that mean?"

"Who is the 'she' he means?" September asked.

"Or the 'she' *she* means," one of the techs corrected her. Bronson, September remembered.

"This wasn't done by a woman," Gretchen said with a cold look at Bronson.

"I'm just saying it's possible," he argued, although lamely. "She's been strangled, too. There are ligature marks."

"Anyone taking bets on whether she's been sexually abused?" Gretchen asked.

There were no takers.

"You have all the charm of a boa constrictor," Bronson said. He had a nerdy, prim look and a way of rolling his eyes that was epic theater.

"Shut up," Gretchen said, though it was almost an after-thought. She was gazing around the clearing where the body had been found while they stood on the edge of a small, wooded area filled with Douglas firs, oaks and scrub pines.

"This is a lot like Sheila Dempsey," September observed. She hoped to stall the pissing contest between Bronson and Gretchen, though they seemed to like to go at each other. She'd learned that much on her few weeks on the job.

Bronson rocked back on his heels. "Mebbe," he allowed.

Gretchen's lips grew even tighter, as if she were forcibly holding back another argument.

They were on the north side of the clearing where the shallow grave had been discovered by a couple of day hikers on a jaunt carrying a picnic basket and a bottle of wine. Now the basket was upended; the wine spilled in a red river on the ground and both hikers were sitting in bug-eyed silence on a moss-covered log, their arms entwined in a hug of support. The man's mouth was twitching as if he couldn't control it; the woman looked ready to keel over.

Sheila Dempsey's body had been discovered in an over-grown field behind an abandoned building. Unlike this one, she'd been stripped bare, where this victim still had on her

jeans, socks and a pair of running shoes. Her chest was
bare; no sign of a blouse or bra.

"Dempsey's the picture on Weasel's desk," Gretchen
said, as if they'd asked.

September nodded. For a moment they all stood in silence in the shadow of the firs while Bronson slowly rose,
brushing his palms together as if to rid himself of the taint,
all of them sheltered from the noonday heat which was blis-
tering nonetheless.

An hour earlier, D'Annibal had received the call. Neither
George nor Wes had been available while Gretchen and
September had shown up by mutual agreement to go over
the Zuma case. Gretchen wanted to interview Camille
Dirkus and September had offered to go along.

But then the call came in and they were sent out after the
hikers called 911.

Now it was September's turn to gaze past the body and
over the dry, yellow field grass that ranged north from their
large copse of mixed oak, fir and pine trees. This too, could
be the county's problem; this crime was right on the city
line, but the dispatcher had called Laurelton PD.

D'Annibal had apparently claimed rights to this case, or
maybe county was simply bowing out. Somewhere along
the line, a guy from county named Jernstadt, since retired,
had royally pissed off the lieutenant according to remarks
she'd heard around the squad room. The result was nobody
wanted to go head-to-head with D'Annibal, involving
whatever he decreed, and therefore there was no strict protocol on jurisdiction. If the lieutenant wanted a case that
could be considered county, the prevailing thought was to
let him have it. So, though September and Gretchen were
already working hard on the Zuma Software case, Laurelton PD was on this one, too. County might complain about
it, but they would acquiesce. D'Annibal did things his own

way and his attitude was, if county didn't like it, they could just go screw themselves.

Said attitude didn't exactly foster warm and fuzzy relations, but such was the way of things.

Gretchen dragged her gaze away from the body and shook her head. "Learn anything from those phone records, Nine?"

September shot a look at her partner who'd apparently detached from the scene around them. "Yes," she said. She'd been scouring Kurt Upjohn's phone records and had discovered several numbers that had yet to be identified from the myriads that he'd placed to friends, family and business associates. "I was hoping maybe Camille Dirkus could shed some light."

"Yeah, whenever that interview takes place," Gretchen grumbled.

"I was thinking about giving the list to George."

Gretchen snorted. "Good idea. He's bound to be back in the squad room now. He just always misses the calls to the field. Weasel's on something else, drugs and gangs, like your brother was."

Was being the operative word, September thought.

"I'm not stopping on Zuma. This has gotta be somebody else's, or we need some serious help."

"Yeah." September gazed down at the body again for another moment, unsettled. "I wonder who she is."

"We'll check missing persons." Gretchen made a face. "I wonder who *he* is," she added, meaning the killer.

Bronson shot her a look as a hot breeze caused the oak leaves and fir and pine needles to dance lithely, as if waving at the victim and the group of bystanders. Victims left in fields . . . the back of her brain tickled.

"Get her covered and outta here before the fucking newspeople show up," Gretchen ordered the techs.

"You do your job, we'll do ours," Bronson said. "The ME's on his way."

"Don't get all testy on me, Bron." Gretchen offered a humorless smile. To September, she added, "Maybe this second body will make our letter carver easier to find and we can get back to Zuma."

September had her doubts, but she kept them to herself.

Waiting proved more difficult than Liv had anticipated. They went to a small café and Liv ordered an omelet that she moved around her plate as the morning dragged slowly by. For all the talking they'd done, all of a sudden it felt like she and Auggie had run out of things to say to each other. As they got up to leave he really struggled with the fact that she was picking up the tab, but what could he do? She wanted to suggest they go back to Bean There, Done That and see if someone had turned in his wallet, but she couldn't.

"I can't afford for us to get pulled over," she said, to which he answered, "Okay," and the subject appeared to be closed.

Now, back at his house, they were both sitting at the table, lost in their own thoughts, when his cell phone suddenly rang, surprising them both.

He swept it up quickly and got to his feet. "Hello?" he answered as Liv's pulse began to race. He shot her a look. "Ah, yes. Talia's right here . . ."

Carefully, he handed Liv the cell and she said, "Dr. Yancy?"

"Yes," the doctor answered cautiously.

Liv could visualize the woman in her mind: small, birdlike, with short, gray hair and narrow glasses that she looked over the top of. "I was just wondering if you could maybe help me with remembering a few things."

Dr. Yancy's voice said, a bit uncertainly, "Did Hathaway House give you my number?"

"No, I took a chance on F. Yancy. I knew your first name was Fern. I—um—"

"You've been having dreams," Auggie whispered. "About the doctor . . ." He moved his hand in the "go ahead" signal.

"I've been having dreams," Liv said. "About a doctor . . . at Hathaway House. I feel like it's important somehow." Auggie was nodding at her. *Good. Good. Keep going,* he mouthed. "A visiting doctor, maybe? He wasn't there all the time. He kind of—stalked, if you know what I mean."

Dr. Yancy didn't answer immediately. "Have you spoken to anyone else at Hathaway House about this?"

"I wanted to talk to you first," Liv said.

"You know I'm retired?"

"You helped me."

"But I wasn't your personal doctor, Talia."

Liv swallowed hard. She'd forgotten that. "I always trusted you," she stated honestly. "Do you know the doctor I mean?" she asked urgently. "Do you remember him?"

"I think you mean Dr. Navarone."

Navarone!

"Dr. Navarone," Liv repeated for Auggie's benefit. "He wasn't one of the regular doctors."

"He was on staff at Grandview Hospital during that time," she said. "He came to Hathaway when he could. We were always short-staffed."

Liv felt her senses swirl. "Grandview," she said faintly.

"You know the hospital's no longer in existence," Dr. Yancy went on. "Loss of government funding. Grandview's now an elder-care facility."

"Oh . . . no, I didn't know," she murmured.

Auggie was eyeing her with concern. She could imagine what she looked like: white face, pale lips, shadowed eyes.

And she felt like she was going to faint. Gripping the phone harder, she said, "I'd like to reach Dr. Navarone. Do you know where he is now?"

"I'm sorry, I don't." A pause. "Are you all right, Talia?"

"Fine."

"I know Hathaway House is for teens, mostly, but if you're looking for a recommendation, I could give you some names, or make some calls—"

"No, no . . . thank you, but no . . . I'm . . . I've got that handled. I just wanted to find Dr. Navarone."

She said slowly, as if thinking over her words, "I don't know quite why you're so interested in him, but he might not be the right doctor for you."

"Oh?"

"His methods were unorthodox, and he was . . ."

When she paused long enough for Liv to worry she wasn't going to go on, she urged, "Tell me. Please."

"He was asked to leave Grandview. He was a fine doctor," she added quickly. "His reputation was clean. It was just his methods weren't in sync with Grandview."

"And Hathaway House . . . ?"

"He was never accused of any wrongdoing, you understand. But he was . . . his methods were deemed unacceptable at other facilities as well."

"What kind of methods?" Liv asked.

"What are you looking for, Talia?"

The doctor's voice had grown ever more cautious. Time to hang up. "I think he was the doctor of a friend of mine who really felt he'd helped her," Liv said, lying through her teeth. Her voice was starting to shake. One of those "I cannot tell a lie" idiosyncrasies that cropped up unexpectedly. "I just was hoping to find him."

"Well . . ." There was censure in her tone. "I'm not sure I would recommend the man."

"If I asked at Hathaway House, do you think they'd know where he was?"

"Are you still getting treatment?"

"I'm seeing someone privately." She glanced around the room wildly, her gaze falling on Auggie. "Dr. Augdogsen."

"I don't recognize the name," Dr. Yancy said, and Auggie shook his head in disbelief.

"He's not from the Portland area."

"Well, if you need anything, please call again, now that you have my number. I'd be happy to help."

"Thank you. I will." Liv hung up quickly, her hands trembling.

"Augdogsen?" Auggie repeated, picking up the cell phone where she'd set it down.

She ignored that. "The zombie doctor is Dr. Navarone. I recognize the name. He's the stalker in the photos, I'm almost sure of it. I never paid that much attention to him at Hathaway House. He looked different than in the photo, but I'm almost positive he's the guy." Liv hugged herself, suddenly cold even though the room was warm. "The killer."

"So, where is he now?"

"She didn't know. He used to be at Grandview Hospital, but now it's an elder-care center, and he was asked to leave anyway, something about his methods of treatment."

"Electric shock therapy? Lobotomies? Kumbaya?"

"None of the above," she said automatically. They looked at each other, and for some reason both of them cracked up. "I don't know why I'm laughing," she said after several moments of hilarity. "Hysteria, I guess."

"C'mere." He pulled her to her feet, amusement still lurking around the corners of his eyes. "You can't keep this stress up without some laughing. You'll go crazy." She lifted a brow at him, and he made a sound. "I wasn't gonna say it."

"You thought it."

"You're the one who thinks you're crazy. I'm just here to listen."

"My dad's the one who thought I was crazy," she corrected him. "And Lorinda. Later, they sent Hague away, too, though I was out of Hathaway by then."

"Your brother was at Hathaway House?"

"No . . . Hague's my father's *real* son. Not his crazy adopted daughter whose real parents were probably crazy, too. Hathaway wasn't quite good enough for blood." Liv looked into his face, so close still; he hadn't backed away from her. "To Grandview Hospital."

He stared at her. "Are you saying your brother was at Grandview when Dr. Navarone was there?"

"That's what I'm thinking." Liv moved slightly away from him. Being so close was becoming unnerving.

"So . . . does Hague know something about Navarone?"

"I don't know. Hague's hard to read."

"What did he say to you?"

They keep their hands in their pockets and wear rigor smiles. . . . He'll drill holes in your head and he'll put receivers inside the folds of your brain. . . . We both know him . . . from when we were kids. . .

She shivered, remembering.

"What?" Auggie's gaze sharpened on her.

She shook her head. "He doesn't know much more than I do. Less, probably. He's not really in touch with reality."

"You showed him the package."

"He barely leaves his apartment."

"But maybe he's involved somehow, at some level. Could he have any—"

"No!" Liv cut him off. "He doesn't have anything to do with this. My brother's sick, but not like that. He wouldn't hurt anybody. He was a baby when my mother died! And the only place he goes is to the ground-floor cantina in his own building."

"But it sounds like he crossed paths with Navarone at Grandview. Maybe something got kick-started then that involves Hague. Maybe—"

She pushed him. In the chest. In sudden fury. He staggered back a couple of steps.

"Hey," he said, affronted. He'd been so wrapped up in his train of thought that she felt he'd forgotten she was there.

"Leave Hague out of this," Liv ordered. "It's not about him."

"Well, it kinda is," he argued. "He didn't kill your mother, sure, but there's a connection there."

She wanted to clap her hands over her ears. No! Not Hague. Not her little brother.

"If this Dr. Navarone is the man in the picture with your mother, and she sent you these photos, photos you showed to your brother who was a patient at Grandview Mental Hospital about the same time Navarone was there . . ."

Liv didn't respond. She was wrestling with anxiety and a sudden fear that she might not want to know the truth after all.

"When you showed your brother, and his girlfriend, caretaker, whatever, and your father and stepmother, the photos in the package, they saw this guy. The stalking man in the photo. And you told them you were going to look into your mother's death, and so maybe . . . somehow . . . word got back to him?"

"I don't know for sure they're one and the same," Liv said, backpedaling.

"We need to find this Navarone." Auggie was certain.

"We," she repeated.

"We'll go to Grandview. So it's an elder-care facility now. Someone there might remember, or at least direct us to Navarone."

"Why are you doing this? What do you care?" she demanded, her voice rising.

He stared at her for a long moment, then slowly leaned forward, grabbing her by the forearms and pulling her gently toward him. She resisted, holding back, until her feet actually stumbled a bit as he drew her closer.

"What are you doing? Let go of me," she said in a voice that sounded high and alarmed to her own ears.

"Stop fighting. Let me help you," he stated with repressed urgency.

"Do I have a choice?"

His face was way too close to hers. "Maybe not. You dragged me into this, and now I'm committed. I have to know how it ends."

"How it ends?" She half-laughed. Definitely hysteria creeping in this time.

"I'm going to kiss you," he said.

She reared back on that one, eyes wide. "No . . . I . . ."

But her protests were lost beneath his lips on hers. Liv stood stock still, completely shocked. She told herself to move but her brain and body felt disconnected. All she could really feel were his lips molding to hers, his thighs pressed to hers, his hands sliding around the small of her back.

She didn't want him. She didn't. She didn't want any man. But her traitorous fingers were clenched on his arms, feeling taut, sinewy muscle beneath. Her mind fractured. Too many sensations bombarded her at once: his lips, his hands, his shallow breaths. No, those were her breaths, rapidly growing in tandem with her heartbeats.

His mouth was hard and soft and warm and his tongue teased at the crease of her lips.

She wasn't sure how this had happened. She didn't want it to stop.

She opened her mouth to protest and his tongue moved in, taking it as an invitation. The feel of his tongue was warm and slick and the way it filled her mouth did something to her knees. They quivered wildly and she would have sunk down, but his arm was a bar around her back, keeping her lower body hot against his.

She could feel his arousal. It was all she could think about. She'd put on her jeans and a clean T-shirt but it felt as if there were nothing between them. Her bones had turned to liquid. Her skin felt sensitized. Somewhere in her mind she knew she should resist, but she couldn't. This was nothing like anything she'd experienced before and she suddenly wanted it. *Wanted* it. If she died tomorrow, she was going to have this. Now.

He sensed her capitulation and half-walked her, half-dragged her to the couch. They didn't say a word to each other. One moment they were kissing and bending toward each other as if they wanted to fuse bodies, the next they were both naked and she was feeling the cushions of the couch meet her bare buttocks and shoulders.

And then he hesitated. As if second thoughts had finally penetrated the blinding passion that consumed them. "I—don't—" he began.

"Shhh . . ." She dragged his mouth down to hers.

It was all she needed to say. His body pressed against hers, his hands sliding along her sides, one of them caressing her left breast convulsively. Her hips rose of their own accord and his other hand slid between her legs, stroking her in a way that sent her pulse skyrocketing and made her desire flame along her nerves.

Hurry, she thought. *Hurry*. If something happened—anything—to interrupt them, she didn't think she could bear it.

And then he was poised at the brink of fully taking her and she wanted to yank him forward. Somewhere distantly in her brain she sensed that if things didn't proceed at breakneck pace they wouldn't happen. Reason would reassert itself. Auggie would remember she was a crazy, damaged fugitive and would stop himself.

And she needed this. Maybe it wasn't love. But it was desire. And she was going to have it.

"Livvie . . ." he whispered unsteadily.

"Come on," she urged, her hands running down the hard muscles of his back.

That did it. He pushed against her and she felt a joyous thrill slide into her feminine core. Her hips urged him forward and he pushed harder, entering her, wringing a gasp from her lips. He stopped but her hands were urgent, pulling him closer and then he began rhythmically moving, sliding in and out until her mind was mush and she was simply sensation. No body. Nothing. Some other plane of consciousness.

The pressure built. Her body moved with his as if she'd been meant for him. Maybe she was, she thought half-hysterically. Maybe that's why she hadn't understood the joy of Trask and Jo, why she hadn't felt anything that even vaguely resembled this pleasure.

Trask . . .

For a moment she was filled with anguish, but a pulse was beating in her head and her hips were meeting his in a delicious rhythm and before she knew it her hands were raking his back and she was convulsing beneath him, crying out. A moment later he thrust harder, stiffening in his own climax before he collapsed against her, his breath rasping against her ear, his heart galloping against hers.

Chapter 15

Liv woke up as if she'd been asleep, though she hadn't. One moment she was tangled on the couch in Auggie's arms and legs, the next she was off her astral plane and back into reality with a bang.

Her first thought was: *we didn't use protection*.

Her second: *it's way down the list of my worries*.

When she stirred, he lifted his arms, managing somehow to prop himself on his elbow and regard her lazily. She watched him push a strand of her honey-brown hair away from her face.

"I am crazy," she said seriously.

"It must be catching."

Feeling idiotic, she picked up the scraps of her clothing, eased herself from his embrace, headed into the bathroom and closed the door behind her with a soft thunk that sounded as loud as thunder to her ears.

She dressed hurriedly. Checked herself in the mirror.

Good. God.

She stepped back into the living room to realize he'd put on his boxers and jeans again. He was still shirtless and standing beside the couch.

They stared at each other. After a moment, she said, "Well."

He said, "Wanna go again?"

"Yes . . . no . . . no . . ."

He sat back down on the couch. Liv told herself to stay away from him, but she walked over and sank down beside him as if she had no will.

He laced the fingers of his left hand through those of her right. Her heart was thudding so hard it hurt. He was looking at her, she could tell, but she couldn't turn toward him.

"I want to," he said, his breath fanning her ear. "Tell me you don't and make me believe it."

The heat from his hand was radiating up her arm and through her chest, reaching toward her hammering heart. She was no proof against his slow seduction. If it was a battle, he was going to win. It made no sense to her. She should be running, planning, *escaping* . . .

When he stood up again, pulling her with him and leading her to the bedroom, she complied as if the whole thing had been scripted.

And when he turned her toward him at the side of the bed and his mouth captured hers and her hand was on his chest and she felt the light and fast beat of his own heart, she moved her mouth down to his bare chest and lay a row of kisses down his sternum that had him making a strangled sound.

A moment later they were both on the bed, their clothes being ripped off with frantic fingers and searching mouths.

Auggie lay beside Liv on the bed, his naked body spooned up next to hers. He couldn't tell if she was awake or asleep. He would guess awake, as he was. And probably just as conflicted. But happy. Or, maybe relieved. Or something.

Damn, but this shouldn't have happened. Especially as many times as it had.

Damn, but he wasn't sorry.

If he let his brain travel along the recent road of these last moments he could get all stirred up again and he knew that wasn't a good idea.

Well, not unless she wanted to again, of course.

Her eyes were closed. Her lashes lying soft and weblike against her cheek. As if feeling his intense gaze, her lids opened and she turned her hazel eyes to him. They searched the depths of each other's eyes.

"What now?" she asked.

"Grandview," he told her, and then a bit more reluctantly, "Time to get dressed."

September stood beside Gretchen at George's workstation and listened with only half an ear to his report. He'd met up with Paul de Fore's parents, who were making burial plans for their son. In the course of his one foray into real fieldwork, he'd learned enough about the de Fores and Paul to convince him that the Zuma massacre had nothing to do with them.

"They're relatively sane, hard-working, unimaginative. Neither of 'em has enough passion to break a smile. Their son sounds just like them, from all accounts. More rigid maybe. But whoever shot the shit out of Zuma . . . it ain't them."

"In your opinion," Gretchen said.

"Yours, too. If you'd talked to them."

George had also been digging into the Zuma finances and their contracts with video-gaming distributors. "Military, schmilitary. They're just developing video games. Lots of shooting and fake blood and gurgling sound effects. Rad showed me some backdoor ways to get to upper game levels. That's about the extent of their secret military involvement. And with Phillip Berelli as the company comptroller, they look like they're paying all their bills and taxes, too."

"So, you're saying this wasn't about Upjohn or de Fore," Gretchen said.

"Doesn't read that way. And it doesn't seem like this was some disgruntled employee. Most everyone who's worked for Upjohn left on their own accord." George looked at September. "You okay?"

He knew all about the body they'd discovered; September and Gretchen had reported all they knew to D'Annibal with George standing by. D'Annibal had gone to talk to someone at county.

"I keep wondering where Wes is," September said. "He met the first vic at a bar."

"He was miles away. On his way back," George said.

Gretchen's desk phone rang and she walked over and scooped up the receiver. "Detective Sandler."

"You look like hell," George observed.

"Thanks."

"Don't mention it."

"Who would you look at?" September asked him. "As the target for the Zuma shootings?"

"Possibly the receptionist. He shot her twice in the chest and that's pretty serious business."

"But he kept on going," September pointed out. "He shot de Fore. Then Maltona. Then he went after Upjohn and Dirkus who were together in Upjohn's office. Maybe he made a try for the upstairs."

"I hear your brother's contacted the other one, the bookkeeper. She's damn lucky she wasn't there on Friday. Maybe she's the target and that coulda been her Waterloo."

Gretchen slammed the receiver into the cradle. "Nine," she said shortly.

September looked at her.

"Camille Dirkus is with Upjohn at the hospital. Let's roll."

* * *

Grandview Senior Care was a squat, brick hospital with wings sprouting like spokes from a central hub. Some of those wings were connected in the back, and Auggie imagined hallways that turned off hallways that turned off hallways until you were back where you started. He also suspected that when the facility had been a mental hospital, its halls and rooms weren't quite so tired looking. Or, maybe it was just that with so many wheelchairs, walkers and elderly residents the place had picked up that sense of being in another time. Somewhere slowed down. Out of rhythm with the goings-on outside their doors.

"Hello," a middle-aged woman with a lean, outdoorsy look greeted him. Her narrow face had a windburned quality to it, etched by lines around her mouth and eyes.

Auggie glanced back, through the sliding glass doors to the parking lot. Liv was sitting in the passenger side, staring at him through the window, her eyes covered by sunglasses. She'd been afraid to come in, and she'd been even more afraid to let him go alone, but in the end she'd allowed it, saying simply, "Go on."

She was discombobulated, he knew. Making fatalistic choices. The only way he'd been able to penetrate her defenses and make love to her.

To the woman, he said, "I need to talk to someone about one of the doctors who was here when Grandview was a mental hospital."

She lost interest immediately. "Oh, that was a whole different company. They've been gone a while."

"Is there someone, though, who might know about that company?"

"I guess you could talk to Sofia," she said reluctantly. "She didn't work for them, but I believe her sister did."

"Is Sofia here now?" Auggie asked. Inside his pocket,

his cell phone was feeling very heavy. He needed to call D'Annibal again. He needed to make certain the lieutenant felt he was actually working the job. In truth, he wondered if he really was. He'd sort of lost perspective on his own directive. From putting a tail on Liv Dugan to becoming her hostage, and then her lover . . . well, that wasn't exactly in the playbook for detective work.

The receptionist pushed a button and said into the receiver, "Sofia? Are you available? There's someone at the front door for you." A few moments later the phone buzzed back and she picked it up. Her gaze met Auggie's and she nodded. "She'll be right up."

"Thanks." There was no chair but there was a short bench along one wall. Auggie sauntered over to it, casting an eye toward the door and Liv who was still looking his way. He gave her a surreptitious thumbs-up.

Ten minutes later a large woman with short, gray hair above her ears, wearing green surgical scrubs, her breath heaving as she half-waddled, half-strode into the waiting area, skewered Auggie with a look. "You wanted to see me?" she said with a trace of disbelief as she looked him up and down.

Her voice was gravel. Her expression was bland, but he sensed a certain disapproval coming from her. "I wanted to talk about Grandview Hospital, before it was a senior-care center."

"I don't know anything about it."

"I understand your sister worked at Grandview?"

She cast an eye toward the receptionist, who met her gaze blandly and shrugged. "She did. For a short time."

"Can you help me, or should I talk to her?"

"What do you want to know?"

This was normally where he would haul out his identification and suggest they go in a room and have a talk. Most people, upon realizing he was with the police, fell all over themselves to give him what he wanted and get him on his way. Unless, of course, they had something to hide.

But without the ID, he was relying on Sofia's cooperation out of the goodness of her heart. Her very large heart, in a very large chest. And he didn't want to take a chance that Liv would find out who he was before he was ready. Especially after what they'd now shared . . .

"I'm actually looking for a Dr. Navarone," Auggie said, cutting to the chase.

Sofia's eyes glared down at him. "Why?"

From across the room the receptionist was looking at them curiously now, too. Auggie said, with a mixture of fact and fiction, "I think he treated my brother when he was at Grandview. The treatment didn't help him. I'm not interested in a lawsuit. I just want to talk to the man, find out what Dr. Navarone's treatment was."

Sofia snorted and it was a loud noise. "Treatment," she said with a curl of her lip.

"I heard it was unconventional," Auggie encouraged her.

"That's a nice word for it."

"What would you call it?" he asked.

"Dangerous. Stupid. Maybe even criminal. That's what my sister said, and she would know."

"What kind of things are we talking about?"

"What's your brother's name?" she asked.

"Hague Dugan," he answered without hesitation.

She seemed to think that over. "Dr. Navarone used psychotropic drugs. Deprivation techniques. He experimented. Got his hands slapped for it, too, according to Andrea, my sister. To his credit, Navarone seemed to really believe he was helping his patients. A lot of people bought into it for a long time . . . until they didn't."

"What happened?"

"Somebody died. They couldn't prove it was because of Navarone outright, but he was booted out as soon as they could figure out how to get rid of him. Andrea thought it was the beginning of the end for the facility."

"Do you know what happened to the doctor?"

"He was a visiting doctor at different places. Maybe one of them took him. He still has his license . . . at least as far as I know."

"You remember his first name?"

"I didn't know him," she reminded him, but she thought it over anyway. After a moment, she said, "Frank, I think. Frank Navarone. Google him," she said, turning away.

Auggie fingered the cell phone. He fell in step beside her and when she looked at him askance, he asked, "The men's room?"

"Take that hallway and where it turns to the left you'll see the restrooms."

It was in the opposite direction she was going, so he stopped as if he were heading the other way, waiting until she got far enough ahead of him. She'd already forgotten him, however, and was aiming toward a room farther south. Auggie yanked out his cell and quickly placed the call to D'Annibal's office.

"D'Annibal," the lieutenant answered.

"It's Rafferty," Auggie said. "Anything new on Zuma or the Martin killing?"

D'Annibal didn't waste time with preliminaries. "Nine and Sandler interviewed Camille Dirkus, mother to Aaron Dirkus, Upjohn's son. Apparently the son and a couple of the whizbang Zuma techs who worked the computers had this little marijuana-growing operation. Upjohn found out about it and threatened to fire Dirkus's ass. Camille was fighting with both of them, but it's possible some other player with a bigger operation took offense."

Auggie stared into the middle distance, stunned. He hadn't expected there to be an answer. Could that be? He immediately wanted to refute the lieutenant's words. Could he have been so wrong about Liv? Had he blinded himself to the fact that her personal dramas were just that, personal dramas? Was he so completely *wrong*?

D'Annibal was still talking, telling him how the department was following leads, plucking threads, finding this big one smack in the middle of Zuma's fabric. He finished with, "So, bring in the Dugan woman and let's get on with it."

"Okay," Auggie said, but the reluctance in his tone reached D'Annibal's ears.

"Whatever the problem is, fix it."

"I will. Hey, put out the word to look for a 2005 GMC truck. Gray. Trask Martin mentioned it to Liv. Said a guy was looking for her at her apartment and that's what he drove."

"Liv?"

"It's what she goes by," Auggie answered evenly.

"Got a license number?"

"I woulda given it to you."

"Not much to go on," D'Annibal reminded him tautly. "While you've been playing house with one of our suspects, we got all kinds of stuff breaking around here."

"She's a suspect?" Auggie challenged him, but the lieutenant just ran right over him, "I sent Nine and Sandler out on another call this morning. A dead body found in a field . . . a woman . . ." Quickly, he brought Auggie up-to-date on the homicide that had taken over the station this morning.

A field. A woman. "You think it has anything to do with Zuma?" Auggie asked, his mind racing.

"That'd be a stretch. But it's a copycat of the Dempsey homicide about a month ago."

Auggie knew about as much as the public on the Dempsey murder; he'd been wrapped up in his Alan Reagan persona and hadn't been following it too closely. But the particulars were ringing other, distant bells. "Did you put someone on that cold case, the serial strangler around Rock Springs twenty years ago?"

"I said I would. Got a lot of stuff coming down here, Rafferty. I'll check on the truck, but I—"

"Who're you talking to?" Liv demanded in his ear. Auggie whipped around. She'd pulled on her baseball cap and was staring at him from beneath the brim with wide, wounded eyes.

He clicked off his phone and dropped his arm. "The lady I was talking to, Sofia . . . her sister used to work for Grandview. She gave me her number. I was trying to reach her and follow up." The phone rang in his hand and they both looked at it. Auggie felt his pulse escalate. D'Annibal. The ass.

Liv's gaze was like a laser on the phone. "Are you going to answer it?"

Hell. No. Shit. He glanced at the number and realized it wasn't D'Annibal. It wasn't even in this area code.

She was waiting for him to answer and he did so like a man facing the gallows, in slow motion, his mind screaming through excuses and explanations when she learned he was with the police.

"Hello," he said into the phone.

"Oh . . . uh . . . I got a call from someone named Dugan? About Everett LeBlanc?"

Auggie snapped to attention. "Uh, yes. Ms. Dugan is right here." He held out the cell to her and mouthed, "LeBlanc."

"What?" Liv whispered, but she took the phone.

He looked around. There were no cameras here but he wished they were outside of Grandview, in the privacy of the Jeep.

"This is Liv Dugan. Is this Mr. LeBlanc?"

Auggie put a hand on the small of her back and guided her back outside as she spoke on the phone. He lifted a hand in a silent good-bye to the rangy receptionist as they stepped back through the sliding glass doors. He could tell Liv was not talking to Everett LeBlanc himself. Sounded like the man might be renting LeBlanc's home and was using his phone.

They were at the Jeep when she hung up.

"What?" he asked.

"He's staying at the LeBlanc home. Everett was married to Patsy—must be the nickname for Patricia—but they're divorced." She shook her head and looked around the grounds. Dappled sunlight lay on the grass, filtered through three large oak trees. "He gave me Everett's Portland number."

"What is it? I'll plug it into the phone." Liv recited the number and Auggie added it to his call list under LeBlanc. "You want to call him now?"

"I don't know."

"C'mon." He put his arm through hers and led her to the Jeep. When she was safely inside, he went around to the driver's door.

Liv watched him slide into the driver's seat and start the engine. She was fighting the conflicting desires to run far, far away or throw herself into his arms. The last few days had been jagged peaks and low troughs, and she felt that same out-of-control sensation that had swallowed her up as a teenager and sent her to Hathaway House.

She'd never had sex like that. Never. But then she'd barely been sexual at all. It had all been so embarrassing and messy and uncomfortable, and now she knew it had been partly because of her; she couldn't give of herself. Couldn't let herself be transported away.

Until yesterday. When he'd said, "I'm going to kiss you."

For a heartbeat she'd thought it was sort of a joke. Ha, ha, ha. Just kidding. Except when he'd looked down at her through blue, blue eyes as he captured her mouth and her knees had buckled. *Buckled.*

She was still having trouble putting the memory of his body moving inside hers to some other part of her mind. Every time her brain touched on it she got a sexual thrill just from remembering it. No wonder people raved about sex. She finally *got* it.

And those dancing, jolting thoughts were superseding her paranoia, keeping it locked down as if it had been physically subdued.

She'd agreed that they should go to Grandview together, but she'd still been floating inside with thoughts of their lovemaking. Then when she'd watched him enter the building and talk with first the receptionist, then the larger woman, then disappear around a corner, she'd suddenly gotten scared, certain she'd been had.

She'd smashed on the baseball cap, entered the building, offered the woman at the desk a smile, then walked past as if she knew where she was going, had been at Grandview a hundred times before. She'd been blind. Her brain fed with images of Auggie calling the police, or sneaking through the back corridors, looking for an escape, or something.

And then she'd caught him on the phone and she'd nearly come undone.

Who are you talking to? she'd wanted to scream. Luckily, her voice had sounded normal when it came. A bit strained. But normal.

And he'd answered her easily. She'd scarcely been able to remember because she'd been consumed with thoughts of his mouth and tongue and hands working on her skin, and she'd focused on his lips and *couldn't think*!

And then the phone rang again and it was about Everett LeBlanc, and he'd guided her outside and they'd had a conversation and she still couldn't think, but something that shot through everything was the feeling that she was being played and nothing was what it seemed.

He was looking at her now. Those eyes intense.

She remembered the way he'd sighed and groaned and laughed softly at different moments of their lovemaking.

Lovemaking . . .

"There's something wrong with me," she blurted out, unable to stop herself. "There must be. I feel out of control."

He glanced away from her, as if it hurt to look at her.

"What about your girlfriend?" she asked. "What was it like with her?"

"Ex-girlfriend," he reminded her. He looked back at her. "It wasn't like this."

She collapsed against the Jeep seat, spent. She was still holding his phone and she saw him look at it, slide a hand her way, palm up, asking for it. She put it into his hand, careful not to touch his skin. She was way, way too susceptible.

"This isn't going well," she said on an expelled breath.

"Isn't it?"

"No." She choked out a laugh. Then shook her head. "Are you going to call the sister and ask about Navarone?"

He hesitated a moment, then said, "She told me to Google him. I think that's what I'll do." And then, "We need to talk to your brother."

A shiver slid down her spine. She was trusting him some, but it felt dangerous.

He glanced at the Jeep's clock, said, "Let's get something to eat," then pointed the nose of the vehicle back on the road. As they sped away from Grandview Senior Care, he said, somewhat ominously, "We don't have much time left. I want to find out as much as I can before things change."

"Before things change . . ." she repeated.

He slid her a look, a frankly assessing look that was full of repressed sexual energy. Her heart jolted. So, he was feeling it, too. She gazed back at him, suddenly wanting to pull over and make love in the Jeep. As fast and furious as possible.

As if picking up her vibe, he hit the gas and growled low, "Look at me like that again, and we won't make it back to the house."

With that she sank back into the seat and wondered if she were truly losing her mind.

Chapter 16

The mood around the station Sunday afternoon was gloomy and restrained. Gretchen was on the phone to missing persons, trying to get a lead on the new vic, George was looking through Zuma Software records, though more desultorily now than before, as he'd become convinced there was nothing there, and September was still reviewing her meeting with Camille Dirkus and the woman's belief that the shootings were drug-related. There was the smell of revenge and retribution to her insistence, however; Camille was distraught over her son's death and she wanted to blame both Kurt Upjohn and Aaron Dirkus's roommates for everything.

It didn't help that both Upjohn and Jessica Maltona had taken a turn for the worse.

September walked down the hall to the water cooler and poured herself a cup. She stood in the hallway, smelling the scents of floor wax and Pine-Sol, drinking slowly. She hadn't liked the way Gretchen had handled Camille Dirkus; she was too brash, too impatient, too everything. Camille hadn't appreciated the treatment, either, and her short, blond hair had bristled as her pinched mouth bit out answers and finally spewed her theory about the drug operation. She was certain Kurt Upjohn and the roommates had sparked a retaliation from a bigger fish up the chain. That's who they should be looking for. Not wasting time talking to her!

When September and Gretchen related Camille's theory to D'Annibal, he'd taken in the information and, from what September had gleaned, had asked Wes Pelligree to look into it. Personally, she didn't think it was the root cause of the shootings, but maybe . . .

Returning to the squad room, she overheard a few of Gretchen's terse remarks into the phone, then tuned her out. She and Gretchen were never going to be simpatico; they were just too different. As she looked out the window, her mind drifted again to the woman's body found in the field. DO UNTO OTHERS AS SHE DID TO ME. The words, carved into the vic's skin, were an extra violation that bothered September deeply.

"Okay," Gretchen said, slamming down the receiver. She leaned back in her chair and ran her hands through her curly dark hair. "From the description, I think our vic is one Emmy Decatur. Her roommate called her into missing persons this morning. She and the roommate, whose name is Nadine, work at a tanning salon in Laurelton. The Indoor Beach."

"Let's go," September said, glad to get moving again.

"Helluva way to spend another Sunday," Gretchen muttered, heading for the door.

"Overtime," George said from his desk, not looking up, to which Gretchen merely snorted.

They got to The Indoor Beach in twenty minutes. It was at the end of a strip mall, painted a virulent shade of puce, and announced in big black words across the front window: TAN, TAN, TAN!!! IMPROVE YOUR APPEARANCE!!! IMPROVE YOUR LIFE!!!

There were two young women behind a podium that served as the reception desk. They both looked vaguely at

September and Gretchen, their thoughts clearly elsewhere. Their attention sharpened when Gretchen showed her badge and asked, "Nadine Wilkerson?"

The taller of the two started as if she'd been goosed. She had light brown, straight, flattened hair, the kind that comes from seriously removing the curl through a procedure. "That's me . . . are you here about Emmy?" she asked tremulously.

"Do you have a picture of her?" Gretchen asked.

"Oh, God, have you found her?" She looked ready to faint.

"Why don't you sit down?" September suggested, motioning to one of two white, wicker chairs for waiting customers. Nadine walked on wobbly legs and collapsed into the chair. "She's dead, isn't she?"

"We don't know anything yet," Gretchen said.

The other girl said, "Oh, golly." She was blond and petite with a dark tan that looked like it had been painted on. Maybe it had.

"I've . . . uh . . . I've . . . got a picture . . . in my purse?" Nadine said. She sat a moment longer, then stood up and walked around a partition. A moment later the sound of a locker slamming shut was heard, then she returned with a snapshot, which she handed to September.

In the picture were two girls in bikinis waving from a boat. One was Nadine; the other was their victim. September handed the photo to Gretchen, who said, "Do you know how to get in touch with Emmy's parents?"

The color drained from Nadine's face. "Ohhhh . . ." she cried, collapsing back in the chair. "It's her. It's her. Oh, God, God, God!"

The other girl said, "Oh, golly." Blinked, and then said, "Her parents live around here somewhere. I've known Emmy a long time."

"Anything else you can tell us about her?" Gretchen pressed.

September urged Nadine, "Put your head between your knees."

"Um . . . oh, golly . . . I don't want to be mean or anything, but she was kind of a man hater."

"No!" Nadine lifted her tear-stained face to glare at her coworker. "She was just a loner. Her parents live on Sycamore Street," she said to September. "Not far from here. Street ends in one of those circles and they're the yellow house at the end." Her face screwed up, more tears forming. "They kicked her out when she was a junior. They probably won't even care!"

"Don't believe it," Gretchen said, and they left for Sycamore Street

There was no one home, so Gretchen took down the address and phoned the station, asking for someone to get her a number. It took a few minutes, but Gretchen got the cell number of Mrs. Decatur, who fell apart like Nadine when she was asked to come and identify the body.

"Now, we know who the vic is," Gretchen said. "We just don't know who killed her. Jesus, at this rate we're gonna need some more detectives. Where the hell is your brother?"

Good question, September thought. *Hurry up, Auggie. Bring Dugan in and get back here.*

"Huh," Auggie said, seated at the table, his gaze on the screen of his cell phone. "Dr. Frank Navarone was last employed at Halo Valley Security Hospital. Google. Who knew?" Liv was staring at him, wide-eyed. "You okay?" he asked.

She seemed to shake herself out of a reverie. "Remains to be seen."

Auggie scrolled through his numbers. "You ready to call LeBlanc?"

Her answer was a short bark of humorless laughter. She held out her hand for the phone and he held up a finger. Finding the number he'd entered earlier, he pushed CALL and handed her the cell. She put the phone to her ear slowly, as if it weighed a ton.

He leaned close to her and she cocked the phone so he could hear. The line rang four times before a man answered, "Hello?"

"Mr. LeBlanc?" Liv asked.

"Yes?"

She drew a breath. "My name's Olivia Dugan and I was adopted by Deborah and Albert Dugan from Rock Springs." The strangled sound he made said he knew where this was going. "I guess you know why I'm calling. . . ." she trailed off.

"You're looking for your father. Well, you found him." He didn't sound pleased.

"I don't want to bother you, but I got this package from my mother, my adoptive mother, Deborah Dugan . . ." She went on to explain how it had arrived after she turned twenty-five and that her birth certificate was inside. "I'm trying to figure out why she sent it to me. Could I meet with you? Just for a few minutes?"

"You could," he said reluctantly.

"Is Patricia around?" she asked.

"Nah. Patsy and me, we were married but we were so young and it was over before you were even born. We had to give you up. Neither of us knew anything about anything. We couldn't raise a kid."

Auggie pulled back and mouthed for her to find out where he lived. Liv asked LeBlanc for his address and he grudgingly gave it to her, a condo on Portland's eastside.

Liv told him she could be there in a half hour, and LeBlanc grunted an assent.

The LeBlanc condo was in a large complex with units facing outdoor balconies, much like Liv's apartment complex. Liv's legs were leaden even while her insides were thrumming, a kind of anxiety building with the thought of meeting her biological father. She'd never really cared, or wondered about her birth parents. In point of fact, ever since her mother's death she'd felt disconnected from her family except for Hague. But Hague's problems had prevented her from any kind of closeness with him, so she'd basically always been on her own.

Everett LeBlanc's condo was on the third floor. They took an elevator up that let them out on a gallery that faced west, toward a common area the condominium complex enclosed. They walked to the door together and Liv hitched her backpack on her shoulder, feeling a brief moment of wonder that she had Auggie as an ally. She'd given up questioning his motives. She didn't really care. He was with her now and she was grateful.

Drawing a breath, she rapped on the door with her knuckles. Momentarily, she thought about what she looked like: jeans and a dark blue T-shirt and sneakers. The baseball cap had smashed her hair and belatedly she fluffed it with her fingers, then dropped her arms. What did it matter now?

LeBlanc opened the door, a man in his late forties with brown hair and a pair of hazel eyes that caused Liv's throat to close briefly. She could see a resemblance, the genetics obvious. It was slightly eerie and for a moment she and Everett just looked each other up and down.

"Well, come in," he said gruffly, and she and Auggie walked inside.

He gestured them to a well-worn couch and sat down in

a chair opposite them, moving some magazines to the floor. "I don't know what you're lookin' for or how I can help ya, but fire away."

Liv hardly knew where to start. It was Auggie who asked, "You watch the news, Mr. LeBlanc?"

"If ya mean, did I see Olivia's face, yes I did."

"I didn't have anything to do with what happened at Zuma," Liv said quickly. "But I think . . . I don't know . . . maybe it happened because of me. We won't stay long. I just . . . would you look at these pictures?" She yanked the package from her bag and slipped out the photos, handing them to him. "You lived around Rock Springs, too, right? I was born in the hospital in Malone."

"That's right." His head was bent to the photos. He looked each one over carefully, then set them down.

"The man walking toward the camera, reaching for it. He's a doctor, we believe. Dr. Frank Navarone."

"I don't know. My memory for that time's not so good. You should really check with Patsy. Your—er—mother."

"Can you give us her address or phone number?" Auggie asked as Liv absorbed his words.

"Sure thing." He went into the kitchen, yanked out a drawer, and pulled out a small, leather-bound book. "Want me to write it down?" he asked, but he was already dragging out a tablet and pen from the same drawer and scribbling it down. He ripped off the top sheet of paper and handed it to Liv. "You think this doctor's behind the shootings?" he asked.

"I don't know. Maybe. Maybe I'm wrong, but I feel like it has something to do with me. Like he's after me."

Everett picked up the photo of the stalking man grabbing for the camera. "He sure doesn't want his picture taken."

Auggie glanced at the address on the paper Everett had given Liv. "Patsy Owens? She's remarried."

"Uh-huh. To Barkley Owens." Everett made a face. "We

don't keep in close contact anymore, but if you see her, say hi for me, okay?"

"I will," Liv said. An awkward moment passed and Liv looked at Auggie, who got to his feet. She followed suit and so did Everett. They gazed at each other and then he nodded and gestured toward the door.

"Be seein' ya," he said as he showed them out.

In the elevator on the way down, Auggie said, "Do you want to call Patsy?"

Liv nodded. "Yep."

"Still think we're on the right trail?"

"You think I'm wrong?" She gave him a long look. His T-shirt was starting to stick to him in the afternoon heat and she had to drag her eyes away, her mind thinking about how she would like to rip his shirt off and press her own over-heated flesh against his.

"I think we're running out of time," was all he said.

September returned to the station in the afternoon to find Wes Pelligree at his desk. The rest of the room was quiet. There was a distant humming from the air conditioning that cycled on and off when the temperature reached the eighties, but otherwise the place was like the proverbial tomb.

"There you are," she greeted him. "I was beginning to think you were a figment of my imagination, Wes."

"Everyone calls me Weasel," he reminded her.

"There's nothing 'weasel' about you," she said.

Wes smiled. He leaned toward a cowboy style with leather boots, low-slung jeans and black shirts that made his six-three seem even taller. Today he was in "uniform" and his smile moved slowly across his lips. He'd been under-cover like her brother for most of the time September had been with the force.

"If I looked like a weasel, then I would be gettin' upset," he said. "But I don't."

His grin widened and there was the trace of a dimple. He'd been looking at some photos of Emmy Decatur and September saw the picture of Sheila Dempsey had been moved to his desktop and placed alongside the crime scene photos of Emmy.

"What do you think this is about?" she asked him, gesturing to the line of pictures.

"Some sick white boy carvin' up his women."

"White boy?" September lifted her brows. "No chance he's black?"

Pelligree snorted. "This is your people kinda crazy shit. No offense."

"None taken. Are you serious?"

He nodded once. "I know a lot of brothers who do a lot of bad, bad things. Drugs, killin', rape . . . as bad as it gets. But this carvin' writin' thing. That's a different kind of sick. Gotta be a white boy, for sure."

"You sound kinda racist, Wes."

"I'm just sayin' . . . we got our shit, you got yours."

"I'm not going to actually agree with you, but I'll take your point."

"And it's Weasel, not Wes." After a moment, he added, "Nine."

She laughed.

"Why're you called that?" he asked. "What kinda nickname is that? I'm Weasel 'cause my brother named me and it stuck."

"I heard that. You sure it's not because you weasel out of things?" she asked.

"Ah, ah, ah."

He wagged a finger at her and she smiled and said, "I'm surprised you don't know about the Nine thing, since you've worked with Auggie."

"Your brother doesn't tell me nothin'. And he's been outta here for months bustin' Cordova's ass."

"Okay, well, I was born on September 1. Right after midnight. The ninth month, so I'm Nine."

He looked disappointed. "Must be somethin' more to it. Nobody calls Auggie Nine, and he's your twin. Born the same day."

"We were born within minutes of each other," September agreed. "Auggie's real name is August, as you undoubtedly know."

"Nobody calls him that."

"My family does." She made a face. "Don't get me started on them. But here it is: my brother—August—was born at eleven-fifty-seven on August 31. I was born six minutes later. We're twins, but we were born different days and different months."

He gazed at her in mild horror as her words sank in.

"I know," she agreed. "It's—flukey. To make matters worse, my father insisted we each be named after the month we were born."

He shook his head in disbelief. "Wha'd I say about white people havin' their own weird shit?"

"I won't condemn my whole race," she said, "but my family? They definitely have their own weird shit."

"How many of you Raffertys are there?" he asked.

"Five. Oldest brother, March. Then my sisters May and July. Then Auggie and me. My mother died in an automobile accident when I was in fifth grade and my sister May was killed in a botched robbery. My father's still alive."

She stopped suddenly and he eyed her cautiously. "The way you say that doesn't bode well for daddy-daughter relations," he observed.

September let that one go by. She'd said about all she wanted about her father. "I suppose Auggie's nickname could have been Eight."

"Knew a guy named Crazy Eight once."

"Drug dealer?" September guessed.

Weasel's smile was faint. "Close enough." He pressed a finger to one of the photos and moved it to the side. September glanced past the array to the folder on the right side of his desk. It looked like an older homicide report; the print on the corner of one page that was peeking out was from a typewriter, not a printer.

Wes caught her look. "D'Annibal asked me to research the killer who strangled women around Rock Springs and Malone more than twenty-five years ago."

"What for?"

"Don't know. Got the impression someone asked him for it."

"Who?"

"Maybe Crazy Eight?"

"If you mean Auggie, I wouldn't be calling him that. What would he want with that information?" September mused, thinking hard. Then, "Please don't tell me it has something to do with Olivia Dugan. I've got this wild idea that he's falling for her, losing perspective."

"Nah," Weasel said, but something in his careful expression made her realize he was just placating her. She sensed he might have already had these thoughts himself.

Peachy.

She picked up the picture of Sheila Dempsey. "You knew her? Or, met her, somewhere?"

"She was a semi-regular at The Barn Door on Highway 26, on the outskirts of Laurelton, headin' toward Quarry."

"I know it," September said, recalling the red barn-shaped building with the white trim and the sliding door that entered into a shit-kicker bar complete with mechanical bull and wood shavings on the floor.

"They have that seventy-two-ounce steak. You eat it all,

it's free. Course you have to eat the potatoes and green beans that come with it, too."

"Don't tell me you tried that."

"Sure did. Ate it all, too. Threw up right afterwards in the alley behind the place and woowee, did it ever piss off my old lady. I was apologizin' for a month. But Sheila was right there, cheerin' me on with some of the other regulars. Afterwards, she clapped me on the back and said I was a man, regardless of the spewin'. I got an earful about her from Kayleen all the way home that night. Two weeks later, Sheila's body turns up in that field."

September glanced at the crime photos from this morning and suppressed a shudder. "Are you going to take over this case, then?"

"I don't want to step on any toes, but I'd like to. I want to find the bastard who killed her and this new one." He glanced at the crime photos and pressed his lips tight. "I talked to Sheila's husband after they found her. It's county's case, but I felt connected."

"I get it."

"He was . . . they were estranged and he wasn't all that helpful. I kinda wanted it to be him, but maybe that was because he was such a bastard. Fuckin' narcissist. Once they narrow down the time of death on this new vic, I'm sure as hell gonna check his whereabouts for the time of the killin'."

"They were both strangled. . . ." September slid a glance toward his file. "You think there's some kind of connection with the Rock Springs strangler?"

"Mebbe. But I was asked to pull this file on Saturday, before you found that body. I thought it had something to do with the Zuma case, but D'Annibal just said get the information. I took a trip out to Rock Springs this mornin'.

Talked to some retired cops who were on the case at the time. Got this file." He tapped it with a finger.

"Find out anything?"

"The Rock Springs strangler killed a bunch of women, mostly prostitutes. Left their bodies in fields. Strangled 'em by hand, but didn't mark 'em up. Then he stopped. Cops on the case think he was killed or incarcerated for some other crime or just went to ground. Hard to know."

"Doesn't really fit the m.o. for Sheila Dempsey or Emmy Decatur," September said.

Weasel sighed. "That's what I thought, too. I'll ask D'Annibal what it's all about when I give him the file."

His desk phone rang and he frowned at it. "Now, who'd be callin' my direct line?"

He snatched up the receiver, said, "Detective Pelligree," listened for a moment, then said in a surly voice, "No comment," and slammed down the phone. "Jackals," he muttered. "Don't ever let 'em get you on camera."

"I take it that was the press."

"Bastards," he muttered harshly.

Gretchen came into the squad room at that moment, her expression dark. "The girlfriend of Martin's at the front. For once Urlacher's fuckin' protocol is working. She's asking for you."

"Me?" September asked.

"Yeah. Jesus. Will this day never end? I see George isn't here." She threw a dark glance toward his desk.

"I'll go see what Jo wants," September said. She realized Gretchen's surliness was a cover-up for her own emotions. Meeting Emmy Decatur's parents at the morgue and having them definitely identify the victim as their daughter had been a low point. Mrs. Decatur just wept into her hands and Emmy's father kept saying, "Emmy was such a beautiful girl. Such a beautiful girl. So, beautiful . . ."

Gretchen wandered over to Wes's desk as September started out and asked him, "What do you think of the Dempsey and Decatur killings? Different than Zuma. More intimate."

"They're just different flavors of the same sickness," Weasel said. "They feel like revenge. Payback."

"Y'think?" Gretchen asked, interested.

"The Zuma guy goes in all balls out. Blows 'em all away. He's rampant nuts. Somethin' set him off and maybe he's coverin' his ass or maybe he's just all-out crazy and pissed off. But this one . . ." September looked back to see him frown down at the photos on his desk. "This one's smaller, more intimate. He's cagey about it. At least so far. He's sendin' a message but it's obscure and personal and he's not sure yet how far he'll go. He's testin' the waters."

September walked to the front where Jo Cardwick was pacing the floor of the reception area. Upon seeing her, the girl just collapsed into September's arms and bawled like a baby. Under Guy Urlacher's worried eye, she led her to a chair and simply let her cry, remembering as she did that Jo said Trask had seen some old pictures of people at Olivia Dugan's apartment just before the whole Zuma massacre, and that Olivia had been sorta crazy about them.

What did that mean? Who was in the photos?

I can't think. My head hurts. I had to kill her. I couldn't wait. I had to take her out to the fields and dispose of the body. My fingers tremble from the feel of those soft bones at the base of her throat and I harden just remembering. But she knew too much. She knew my plans for Olivia.

I've lost Olivia . . . lost her . . .

But I can find her again.

Olivia . . . Olivia . . . Lllliiiivvvv . . .

I close my eyes and stroke myself, feeling the heat.
I imagine her cool, white throat in my hands.
I scream her name as I climax. "Lllliiivvvv!"
You are mine.
You can't realize the truth. I have to stop you.
Stop you.
Stop you . . .

Chapter 17

They drove through the town of Rock Springs around four o'clock, the August sun hot on lawns of bleached grass and two-lane asphalt roads shimmering with heat, giving the illusion they were slick with water. The original clapboard buildings from the late 1800s had been mowed down and replaced along the edge of the small stream that ran behind the buildings. Garrett Hotel had been rebuilt in its original style though the Garretts were long gone and the Danners, the other family so prominent when the town was first getting started, had all but moved away, too.

Liv knew of the local history from placards around parks and street names and varying school pageants that had celebrated the town and its inception. Now she looked out the Jeep's window, her chest constricted. She hadn't been back since she was sent to Hathaway House. Albert and Lorinda had moved while she was a patient, and she'd never seen fit to return.

But Patsy and Barkley Owens still lived here. Not all that far from the small house where Deborah Dugan had supposedly taken her own life.

They passed the east end of the town and Liv got a glimpse of Fool's Falls as it rushed in a froth down a cliff-face into the stream that ran behind the town and meandered on its way to the city of Malone.

It was strange to be here. She felt disembodied. Moving through a place she'd only lived in a dream.

Auggie pulled up to a curb near Patsy and Barkley Owen's address. "You ready?" he asked as he switched off the engine.

"As ready as I'll ever be."

Liv had placed a call to Patsy, saying she'd been given her address by Everett LeBlanc and that she was Deborah Dugan's daughter. Patsy had sucked in a short gasp of breath, waited five seconds, then choked out an invitation to come by.

So, here they were.

She stepped out of the car and shaded her eyes. There weren't many trees on this street, but from the looks of the roots and stumps, there once had been. Her T-shirt was sticking to her back and she was glad it was dark blue, so maybe her sweating was less noticeable to others.

Auggie's T-shirt, dark gray, was also sticking to him. It was growing ever hotter as the day moved on.

Liv searched her feelings and realized that dread was the overriding one. Meeting Everett had taken a lot of energy and now with Patsy, she just felt zapped. Maybe it was an improvement over paranoia and fear, although those emotions were just below the surface along with an abundance of sexual desire. She was awash in emotions after trying for years to forcefully shut them down.

The walkway to the front porch was tidy, the dry grass edged, clipped short, and sporting more brown patches than green. The Owens weren't wasting water, except maybe on the two window boxes of petunias that flanked the front door and looked a little worse for wear from the beating sun.

Auggie rang the bell and stepped back and a few minutes later a trim, middle-aged woman with brown hair and green eyes opened the door. The cautious, almost bruised look around her eyes was hauntingly like Liv's own expression; one she'd seen many times in the mirror. Liv looked at Patsy and she stared right back, and only when Auggie said, "May we come in," did she seem to come to herself and step aside.

"You're . . . ?" she asked Auggie.

"Olivia's friend," was his terse reply.

"Barkley—my husband—is . . . um . . . coming home from work. He does maintenance at the golf course in Malone and usually sticks around on Sunday in case something goes wrong, but . . . he thought I might need him . . ."

Liv drew a deep breath and said, "I'm really sorry to just burst in on you." Then she handed her the package, explaining about the birth certificate and photos within it. She'd transferred the note from her mother to a pocket of her backpack, deeming it too personal to share with her birth parents.

Patsy seemed glad for the distraction of the birth certificate and photographs. She was apparently finding it as hard to meet Liv's eyes as it was for Liv to meet hers.

"I don't know any of them," she said at length. "Well, other than your adoptive parents. I've always known who they were."

"I'm looking for Dr. Frank Navarone," Liv added. "I believe he's the man trying to grab the camera from the picture taker."

She sifted through the photos until she found the one Liv meant. Frowning down at the picture, she said without lifting her head, "I don't know him."

"I was thinking he was maybe from around here. . . ."

"I wish I could help you." She handed the pictures back, then clasped her hands together so tightly her knuckles showed white. After a moment, she said, "I didn't want to give you up, y'know? Everett and I were so young, and we were penniless and didn't know the first thing about building a life. We were kids!"

Liv regarded her helplessly. "It's fine. I didn't mean to stir things up." She wanted to add, *It doesn't matter*, but since it clearly did to Patsy, she knew how insensitive that would sound. Even though Deborah had only been Liv's mother for a few short years, she would be her mother forever. Patsy was a stranger.

"Would you like something to drink?" she said. "I've got fresh lemonade."

"Thanks, but I don't want to trouble you. . . ."

She was already gone, and while they heard her open the refrigerator Liv looked to Auggie.

In her ear, he said quietly, "I think we've hit a dead end. She's on her own track."

"I can't just up and leave," Liv whispered back.

"Okay. But I sense minefields ahead. . . ."

Patsy returned with a tray holding three glasses of lemonade. Liv and Auggie each took a glass and thanked her. "Sit down," she invited. "Please."

Liv took a chair across from the loveseat where Patsy sat after putting the empty tray on the coffee table. Auggie sat on the only other chair, a wooden rocker with a needlework cushion.

"I had serious second thoughts about adoption. I told myself I was doing the right thing, but how do you ever know? After you were born, I went to the adoption agency to . . . I don't know . . . *change* things, if I could. I wasn't thinking straight, and I didn't have money for a lawyer. There was a young woman at the agency who got the files confused and thought I was the adoptive mother, not the birth mother. She said Deborah Dugan's name before she realized her error. I pretended not to notice. She hustled me out of there, was probably afraid she'd lose her job and all that, but I just left. I didn't forget the name, and I . . .

well . . . I followed Deborah for a while. I kept tabs on her and your father and you." She half-smiled. "Everett and I split up soon afterwards, but I always thought I had the Dugans, y'know? Like they were my friends. I could see you from afar, and your little brother?"

"Hague," Liv said.

"He was so cute. And you were so lively and outspoken. Fierce." She smiled, remembering.

Liv shifted uncomfortably. Oh, how things had changed.

"Then Deborah . . . died . . . and Albert remarried, and I had to let it all go. It wasn't healthy for me, either . . . so . . ." She drew a sharp breath. "Then I met Barkley and changed my life. I never really expected to meet you. It's all so long ago now . . ."

Liv drank the lemonade down. It was cool and tart and puckered her mouth a bit. When silence fell among them, she said, "This is really good," and Patsy struggled up another smile.

Auggie said, "Can I ask you some questions about that time?"

Patsy didn't seem to hear for a moment, then she nodded.

"There was a serial killer, a strangler, in the area," Auggie said.

"Oh, yes. We all locked our doors and windows at night. It went on for a few years." She drank from her lemonade, her gaze shifting from Auggie, to Liv, then down to her hands. "They were mostly prostitutes from the Portland area. He dumped their bodies in Rock Springs."

Auggie flicked Liv a look, then asked, "Were any of them from around Rock Springs?"

"I don't . . . recall . . . You could probably look it up."

Liv's feeling of otherworldliness continued. It was hard for her to believe this woman gave birth to her. She'd always expected to feel something more when she met her birth mother, but she just felt off-kilter and eager to escape.

A big, fat, yellow tabby cruised into the room and fixed Liv with its gold eyes. Her dream came back to her. And her conversation with Aaron. She reached a hand toward him and the tom sauntered forward and allowed her to slide a palm down his back.

"He never does that," Patsy said with mild surprise.

"Fat cat," Liv whispered to him affectionately and he started to purr.

A few moments of awkward silence ensued, and then Auggie got to his feet and said, "It's getting late. Thank you for your time."

"And the lemonade," Liv said, standing as well. The cat slid back and forth between her legs. She'd never had a pet growing up, hadn't really thought about them. Now she wanted to pick up the purring beast and bury her face in its fur.

She felt Auggie's hand at her elbow and amidst some last good-byes, he guided her out to the porch. Squinting up at the sun, she said, "My father always called the doctors who treated Hague and me fat cats. He hated them. I always thought it was a derogatory term until now."

"That was a nice fat cat," Auggie observed. "They're not all that way. I'm a dog guy."

"Auggie Doggy," she said, almost by rote.

"Dr. Augdogsen to you."

She tried to muster up a response, maybe even some of that fierceness Patsy had commented on, but she couldn't do it. They got back in the Jeep and Liv looked back at the house, hoping to catch another glimpse of the tom, but he was inside, out of the heat, and they drove away from the neat house just as a blue Chevy Blazer pulled up and a middle-aged man climbed out and watched them leave. He was short and balding and a bit paunchy and he lifted his hand in good-bye, looking a bit perplexed. Barkley Owens.

"I'm glad I didn't have to meet him, too," Liv said.

"I hear you. You met your biological dad and mom today. That's more than enough for a decade or two. Family . . ." He shook his head.

"Are your parents still alive?" she asked.

"My father is. Don't ask me about him. My mother died in an automobile accident a lotta years ago."

"You have any sisters or brothers?"

He made a face. "Not that I want to talk about."

Auggie drove through a Burgerville on the way back and Liv bought them each a hamburger and fries, a Coke for him, a Diet Coke for her.

"I'm going to pay you back with interest," he said as they headed up the freeway to the turnoff to Highway 26—called Sunset Highway at this stretch—and to the Sylvan exit and his home.

"If you want to go to Bean There, Done That and ask about your wallet I can stay in the car," she said, but the thought of being so close to her apartment sent shivers down her nerves. She wasn't ready to turn herself in yet. She asked herself, honestly, if she ever would be and didn't have an answer.

"Nah, but I think we should go see Hague."

"Now? What about the burgers?"

"We'll stop at the house. Eat. Then go see your brother, okay?"

"Okay."

Auggie pulled into the garage a few moments later and gathered the two drinks while Liv grabbed the bag of food and followed him inside. They sat at the table like an old married couple, like they'd been doing it for years, and dug into the food. At least Auggie dug in, Liv forced herself to eat some of everything then sipped at her Diet Coke.

She didn't want to go see Hague. She wanted to stay right here. With Auggie. Forever. "What's your last name?" she asked.

He thought a moment, then said, "Rafferty."

"Auggie Rafferty."

"August Rafferty," he corrected her. "I think . . . tomorrow we're going to have to go to the police."

"No."

"Liv, if we don't find out anything from your brother or—"

"I need more time. Just a little more time. Please. August . . ."

"Nobody calls me that but my family. Auggie'll work just fine." He sounded depressed.

"I'm sorry. Let's go see Hague. And tomorrow we can go to Halo Valley and see if we can find out more about Dr. Navarone. Then we can talk about the police. Not tonight, okay?" She felt desperate. Their time together was coming to an end and she didn't want that.

"Everything changes tomorrow," he said, and he sounded so sober that her heart clutched.

"Okay. I—I can . . . okay . . ." She swallowed hard.

"Let's go talk to Hague," he said, getting up and tossing the crumpled bag into a trash can by the back door.

She couldn't decipher his mood as they headed across the river to Hague's condo. Her anxiety ratcheted up as soon as they drew near; she would have to see Della, most likely, and Hague's companion was unpredictable. She probably knew that the police were looking for Liv, and was just as likely to turn her in as help her.

Pulling the baseball cap from her backpack, she smashed it on her head and down her forehead so she could scarcely see.

"Put your hand through my arm," Auggie said once they were parked and on the street. "Lean in. More people will remember you if you're alone."

"You know a lot of tricks for a fisherman."

"Human nature," he said, and then they were inside the building and pulling back the bar on the elevator. Auggie closed the door and they rattled their way to the third floor.

"Della won't like this," Liv warned. "She might even turn me in as soon as we leave."

"We're going to the police tomorrow anyway, right?"

"That's the plan," Liv said, but the lack of conviction in her voice caused him to put his hands on her shoulders and turn her toward him.

"I mean it, Liv. You've been playing a dangerous game with a killer. I've been playing it with you. But the best thing we could do is go to the police."

"*After* we go to Halo Valley."

"Just don't tell me something different after we've been there."

Liv was no proof against those intense blue eyes staring down at her. She twisted away and knocked on the door. He made her heart race. From the fear of taking an irreversible step, like going to the authorities, but also at a more feminine level.

Della answered after a few moments, her own icy blue eyes raking over Liv and landing on Auggie. Her blond hair was pulled back into its ubiquitous bun and her expression was hard to read.

"Liv," she said after a moment, her voice just short of a sneer. "Did you forget to tell me you were wanted by the police last time you were here?"

"I'm still wanted by the police," Liv snapped back, "so, go ahead and call them and let's get it over with. I want to see my brother."

"Well." She reared back at Liv's tone.

"I'm Auggie," Auggie said, reaching out a hand.

Della took it in hers and seemed to thaw a bit. "Where did she find you?" she said with a lilt.

Oh, brother, Liv thought, seething. She realized maybe there was some fierceness there after all, which helped restore her humor a little. "Auggie's a friend who's been helping me on my quest to find out what happened to Mama."

"Really." Della stepped back from the door, allowing them entry. The three of them walked to the back toward Hague's room where he was sitting in his chair, glaring at some loose-leaf pages in his hands.

"Who are you?" he demanded of Auggie.

"Auggie Rafferty." He started to put out a hand to him as well, but Hague didn't set down the pages so he dropped his arm.

Hague regarded Auggie suspiciously and rubbed his scruffy beard as if he were comparing himself to him. Auggie had shaved in the morning but was, like Liv, looking a little used up after their long day. Still, compared to Hague, he could have been heading for the board meeting of a major corporation.

"Hague, I need to talk to you," Liv said.

"I don't think I want to." His eyes never left Auggie.

"It's about the doctor. The one with the rigor smile?"

Hague's gaze jumped to Liv. "The doctor doesn't have a rigor smile."

"You said, 'They keep their hands in their pockets and wear rigor smiles.' That's almost verbatim. And you said we both knew him from when we were kids. Did you mean Dr. Frank Navarone?"

Hague's eyes slid around in their sockets, as if he were trying to look around the room but couldn't control the motion. "The zombie," said Hague.

"The zombie stalker is Dr. Navarone," Liv said. "That's right, isn't it?"

"I can't talk with him here." He slapped the papers onto a table by his chair and gestured in Auggie's direction. Then, in an about-face, he turned to Auggie and said, "I saw you at the Cantina. I saw you."

"The Cantina?" Auggie repeated.

"You were watching me. Listening. You were with the others. You want to hurt Livvie, don't you?"

"No," Auggie said, surprised.

"No, Hague. He's with me. He wasn't at the Cantina. Was Dr. Navarone at Grandview when you were there?"

"Out of the sides of my eyes . . . he's there . . . he's watching me, but he wants you, Livvie. He wants you."

She blinked, feeling tense. "Dr. Navarone?"

"He wasn't my doctor. My doctor was Dr. Tambor. He was Jeff's doctor, though, and he was Wart's, and some other guys. They were all zapped." Hague gave a huffing laugh, then said in a lower, conspiratorial voice, "It's the government, you know. He worked for the government. That's what happens when you work for them. They put receivers inside the folds of your brain. In the creases, where they can't be found. The mindbenders, they're at the hospitals. That's where they are. At Grandview and everywhere."

"But Dr. Navarone worked at Grandview when you were there," Liv repeated, seeking to clarify and keep Hague on track.

He suddenly sat up straight, slamming back the flipped-up leg rest and jumping to his feet in one motion.

"Hague," Della said uncertainly, shooting Liv a look.

He grabbed Liv and dragged her to the other side of the room so fast, she stumbled and had to cling to him for support. "Sister," he said on a breath near her ear. "RUN!!!!"

His bellow reverberated throughout the rooms and Della's head whipped back and forth between Hague and Liv, as if she couldn't decide whom to handle first. She chose Hague, rushing to him and tugging on his arm. "Hague, Hague! Don't let her upset you!"

Liv was shaking inside. She stared at her brother in

horror. Then Auggie was there, on Liv's other side, watching Hague intently. "Let's all take a deep breath, here," he said.

Hague croaked out, "He's coming," and then his eyes rolled back and his knees buckled. Auggie caught him and Della slid under one of Hague's arms. Together they took him back to his chair.

As soon as he was settled, Della whipped around and glared murderously at Liv. "You always do this! It always happens! I don't want you anywhere near him anymore! I told your father the same thing. He came here to talk to Hague about *you*. Like Hague knew where you were and would talk you into turning yourself in!"

"Did Hague go into one of his fugue states then, too?" Liv asked, looking down sorrowfully on her brother's unconscious form.

"Yes! Just the mention of your name and *poof!* He's gone." She threw a glare at Auggie, too. "I'm not going to call the police. I'd never hear the end of it from Hague, if he found out. I don't know what you're doing with her, Mr. Rafferty. Maybe you can get through to her. No one else can."

"Someone is after her," Auggie stated tersely. "Even Hague feels it."

"You're as bad as she is!" Della stalked to the door and held it open. "Don't come back," she said tautly as Auggie and Liv walked into the outer hallway. The slam of the door was a sharp report in the otherwise quiet building.

They stared at each other tensely for a moment, then Liv said through her teeth, "What was your complaint about your family?"

A spark of amusement entered his eyes, and he drawled, "I'm having a hard time remembering right now."

"Yeah." She headed for the elevator and he climbed in beside her. Liv was torn between laughter and tears, but

Auggie crowded her to one side, pulled up the brim of her hat and kissed her hard on the mouth while they descended. When she came up for air, she said, "I don't think public displays of attention are a good idea."

"Don't care," he said, and kissed her again.

By the time they reached the first floor Liv felt flushed and weak and some of her hurt and fury had receded. In the Jeep, he reached over and cupped her chin, forcing her gaze to his. "It's gonna be okay. We're gonna figure this out."

"Why is it that you feel more like family to me than my own brother and father?"

"Because I'm on your side. Remember that. No matter what happens."

She gazed at him through eyes filling with liquid. He was a gift. "How did I get so lucky when I picked you?" she whispered.

"Meant to be, I guess," he said hoarsely, then he dropped his hand and dragged his gaze away, turning his attention to the Jeep and the trip back home.

Who is he? How did she get with him?

She came to see her brother. Is she onto me?

I have to run to keep up with them, to see where they've parked. I have to hurry to catch up with them in traffic. But I've found her again!

Something's wrong inside my head and I thump the steering wheel with my palm in frustration. But there they are. In a gray Jeep, moving through the streets and over the bridge to the west side.

It's hard to keep them in my sights, but I will . . . I will . . .

I should have never shown my hand and killed all those people. Killed them all with a fucking gun! I wanted her . . .

to take her with me . . . but they were all staring at me with dead eye sockets and slack mouths. I took them out quickly, one by one. Bam. Bam. Bam-bam.

But Olivia wasn't there! I couldn't have her!

And then her neighbor came after me. He saw me. The gun was with me and I shot him. Bam. Bam-bam! *I had to. He was in the way.*

It doesn't matter . . . I've confused them all and they can't find me. It's not my pattern. They can't find me, because it's not my pattern!

But Olivia, I've found you again.

Who is this stud you're with? Are you fucking him? Lovely, crazy Liv Dugan . . .

I can smell the sex from here.

I follow them at a distance and wind through the west hills behind them, keeping a vehicle between us at all times. Luckily, there are cars ahead of me when they finally turn into a driveway and I speed on past, two cars back, unnoticed.

I turn around a few blocks farther on and drive past the house once more. They are out of the car and unlocking a back door, crowded together in an embrace. Kissing!

My rage blinds me. A few miles later I pull over into the empty parking lot of a church, burning up inside. I am shaking all over. I sense liquid running from my mouth. Spittle.

My brain is full of worms. I will have to kill her soon.

Like the other one, she asks questions. Questions and questions and questions. I inhale, remembering with a sizzle of pleasure her face turning purple beneath the pressure from my hands.

My hands . . .

I look down. She scratched me and there are angry red lines on the back of my right hand.

But Olivia . . . he's fucking her, isn't he? Sticking his cock inside her?

Moaning, I unzip my pants and stroke, stroke, stroke.

I see her throat. The ridges of her windpipe.

I close my eyes and hear the questions. More and more questions! She can't stop! I must kill her soon, like the last one whose life escaped in a sigh through blue lips.

Suddenly I come. It's a release, but not enough.

"Lllliiivvv," I whisper.

I know where you are now.

Chapter 18

September gave Guy Urlacher the evil eye as she entered the station around seven on Monday morning. She whipped out her badge and silently dared him to ask for more as she passed by. It looked like it took a good deal of self-control for him to just let her pass, but he did. It felt good to win that battle of wills; she wasn't the newbie she'd been last week. A lot of things—*a lot of things*—had happened since, practically none of them good.

She'd slept poorly and had fallen asleep hard around four, blasted awake by her alarm clock at six. She'd woken up slowly in the shower, then had wolfed down some strawberry yogurt and half a bagel with cream cheese. Coffee she would get at the station, sludge that it sometimes was. Still, it had the power to jolt you awake and she was counting on that as everyone involved with the Zuma case was attending an impromptu meeting in D'Annibal's office around ten.

Foremost in September's thoughts was Trask Burcher Martin. It appeared he'd stumbled into something involving Olivia Dugan, and it seemed likely whatever it was had something to do with the Zuma Software massacre, too. The press had gotten hold of that angle last night; they'd interviewed Jo Cardwick and managed to get her to scream that it was Olivia Dugan's fault her boyfriend was dead. She'd come to the station directly afterwards and broken down. That bit had been breaking news at eleven last night.

It was a damn good thing Auggie was bringing her into the station today.

Gretchen was yawning at her desk, cradling a cup of coffee. September went straight to the staff room and poured herself a cup, too. When she returned to her desk Gretchen was standing beside it.

"I called the hospital," she said. "Jessica Maltona's taken a turn for the worse. Upjohn isn't doing much better."

"That's depressing," September answered glumly.

"Weasel wants to run on the Decatur killing, since it looks like the same doer killed Sheila Dempsey and he feels connected to her."

September nodded. "Fine by me."

"I want to make an arrest on the Zuma shootings. The press is already calling it a massacre, as are we, but if Maltona and Upjohn or either one of them dies, it really will be." She looked angry. "God damn. I hate these bastards who go in shooting. The carnage."

George had joined them, catching her last remarks. "You're still on Zuma? I thought maybe you got moved to the serial strangler since D'Annibal sent you out there."

"Yeah, we're still on Zuma," she snapped back. "Why wouldn't we be? Somebody's gotta keep looking under rocks for this slimeball."

"I thought it was Rafferty. Isn't he with Dugan?"

"He's bringing her in today. Maybe we'll finally learn something." She went back to her desk and slammed open a drawer, reached inside and pulled out some ChapStick, rubbing the waxy end over her lips. "Sunburn," she snorted.

They went over the case and what they had so far. By a process of elimination they'd crossed out Kurt Upjohn and

Paul de Fore as the target of the Zuma killings. They just didn't seem to fill the bill. Add Jessica Maltona to that list, although Gretchen still felt her boyfriend, Jason Jaffe, deserved a second look.

Aaron Dirkus and his stoner buddies were still being considered, and Camille Dirkus was still floating around the periphery.

But the missing Olivia Dugan had risen up the "prime suspect" list with Trask Martin's murder.

Yes, when Auggie brought in Olivia Dugan, September had a lot of questions to ask her.

Auggie lay spooned up next to Liv, his face in the cloud of her light brown hair, his naked body touching hers, one arm possessively slung beneath her breasts. They'd made love twice and he was surprised at how much of a thrill it was to feel her soft breath on his face, her warm body pressed urgently to his, her eager tongue and exploratory caresses. He struggled for the right word to describe the way she reached for him so eagerly. Insatiable was all wrong; it sounded sleazy and borderline psychotic. But there was a hunger inside her, a need, that had been there a long time, he suspected; maybe all her life. Something she couldn't disguise when they were making love; something she didn't try to.

It also made him afraid. Not because it scared him away. No . . . afraid because when she learned the truth about him, the betrayal might be too huge for him to explain away. What had started out as a tiny omission, a small gap in the truth, had turned into a gaping abyss.

He tried to think how to tell her. Just come out with it and rip off the Band-Aid? Or, ease her into the station and let it come out after her fear of authorities had lessened a little. He wouldn't be able to do the latter without the cooperation of D'Annibal and the other detectives, and that wasn't going to happen.

He was going to have to tell her. Today. This morning.

She stirred and turned in his arms, her eyes lazy with sleep and satiation. "I like this," she said. "It's a fake world where I feel safe. I'm trying to stretch out the minutes before I have to get up."

Dread filled his heart even while he kissed her forehead and temple and eyes. "I don't want to get up either," he said regretfully.

She picked up the tone of his voice and pulled away slowly, reluctantly. "It's Monday," she said, and then added on a note of wonder, "I feel like I've known you forever."

"Liv . . ."

When he didn't continue, her eyes searched his face. Whatever she saw there shut her down and she climbed out of her side of the bed and picked up her clothes, holding them to her breasts as she skirted the bed. "I'll take a shower first," she said, and she was into the bathroom and running the water while he stared at the ceiling, watching a thin slice of summer sunlight sneak through the curtains of the bedroom and streak across the walls.

She sensed something was coming. While they were on their quest, they hadn't discussed their own relationship at all. They'd just gone head down and worked like an investigative team, something he understood completely. But after two days of going headlong into her past and on the trail of the sinister Dr. Navarone with his unorthodox medical practices, they had slowed down long enough to look at each other.

Everything would shift today, and Auggie wasn't eager for that to happen.

He leaned up on one elbow, looking for his cell, then realized it was still in his jean pocket. He'd charge it in the car as they drove to Halo Valley Security Hospital.

And after that. After Halo Valley. Then he would take her in. They were on the same page on that. That's what she'd said, and there was no more time to fool around. The police needed to debrief her and get her take on the Zuma killings and Trask Martin's murder, and Auggie needed to be brought up to date on the case. It hadn't been a full three days since the shooting, but a lot had happened.

When she was finished she came into the bedroom with a towel around her torso and one around her head.

"I like this look," he said. "Drop the towels and I think I'd like it better."

She almost did. He could see the twitch of her lips and the glint in her eyes. But her built-up walls of reserve won and she merely arched a brow at him. "Nope. We have things to do."

Growling, Auggie climbed to his feet, naked, and grabbed his clothes and cell phone and headed into the bathroom, but not before squeezing past her and running a hand across her bare shoulder.

When he was through in the shower and had shaved and brushed his teeth, he examined himself in the mirror.

You're a coward, he told his reflection silently.

His own blue eyes were full of accusations.

"Shit," he said softly, under his breath, then he walked back to the bedroom where Liv had finished putting on a pair of black pants and a dark green blouse, which she was yanking on, trying uselessly to pull out the wrinkles.

"Have you got an iron?" she asked.

"Uh-uh."

"I'd like to look a little more presentable."

"The police aren't going to care. Trust me."

She stopped tugging. "I was thinking of the hospital."

"Oh."

While Auggie put on his jeans and a blue shirt, she pulled off the blouse and grabbed a black, short-sleeved

T-shirt, which she yanked over her still damp hair. When they were both dressed, he said, "You want to catch some breakfast on the way?" though he could scarcely stand making her always pay.

"I don't think I could bear more fast food," she said.

"I've got cereal. And the milk's still good, I think."

"Let's do that," she said.

Ten minutes later they were sitting at the table, each with a bowl of cereal in front of them. She didn't have much of an appetite, as usual, and this morning he didn't have much of one, either.

The effect of a guilty conscience.

It was nine A.M. when they hit the road and began the hour-and-a-half drive to Halo Valley.

The detectives all squeezed into the lieutenant's office along with a researcher and the uniform who'd been with September when they'd found Trask Martin's body, Don Waters. It was crowded enough that D'Annibal shooed them all back to the squad room and they moved as if choreographed toward Wes Pelligree's desk, where he had the photos of the two female strangulation victims on a bulletin board with their names and the dates and locations of where they were found.

"County giving you Dempsey?" George asked D'Annibal, who answered tersely, "We're working with them. But I want to concentrate on Zuma. I just got word from the hospital. Jessica Maltona died this morning and Up-john's still in critical condition. The press are going to be all over this."

Died, September thought with a wrench.

"When the hell is Rafferty getting here?" Gretchen demanded.

D'Annibal looked like he was going to say something

rude, but pressed his lips together instead. "Today," was his clipped response.

September surfaced from her funk. For once she was in complete agreement with Gretchen. What was Auggie doing? She could scarcely stand to wait one more minute!

They reviewed the case quickly, but there wasn't much they didn't already know, apart from the ballistic report that proved the Glock used in the Zuma massacre and the one that killed Trask Martin were one and the same. The researcher added a few more documents to the pile concerning Zuma Software's business. Don Waters related what he and September had found at Olivia Dugan's apartment, which was little more as well, apart from an empty box of ammunition for a .38. George commented that he was getting pretty darn eager to interview Olivia Dugan, which D'Annibal ignored. At the end of the discussion Wes pulled out the file that had been on his desk, the one with the typewritten pages that looked like an old case. He handed it to D'Annibal and told the lieutenant about the trip he took to Rock Springs to gather the information he'd asked for.

D'Annibal didn't open the file, just said, "Thanks."

It was George who asked, "That got to do with any of our cases?"

"Detective Rafferty requested it," the lieutenant answered flatly.

They all looked at September, who wagged her head slowly from side to side and asked carefully, "My brother wanted information on the strangler? Why?"

D'Annibal lifted a palm. "I took it to be something to do with Olivia Dugan. She's originally from Rock Springs."

Gretchen made a strangled sound in the back of her throat, and demanded, "What's he doing?"

"We'll know soon enough," D'Annibal said, effectively ending the meeting. He was clearly bugged about Auggie's failure to bring Dugan in and was reacting to the tacit feeling of the detectives that the lieutenant had been too lax in this regard.

"Has Jason Jaffe heard about Maltona's death yet?" Gretchen asked.

"The hospital's waiting for us to deliver the news." D'Annibal walked back toward his office, opening the file as he closed the door.

Gretchen said to September, "Let's go see how Jaffe takes it."

"So Auggie did ask for the file," September said, more to Wes than anyone else. "Damn it. He's off on some tangent and thinks that makes it okay not to bring her in!"

"Hey, ruleser. You sound like Urlacher," Gretchen observed on a drawl.

"He's my brother. I can go there." She opened the drawer to her desk, pulled out her Glock and ID, and slammed it shut. "Are you ready?" she demanded of Gretchen, who got her gun and ID and waved September ahead of her in the universal "let's get moving" gesture.

September could tell her partner was getting some secret enjoyment out of her pique with Auggie. Go right ahead, she thought, as they climbed into the Ford Escape.

"This case bugging you?" Gretchen asked as they wheeled out of the lot. "Or, the other one."

"Both."

"You know, since you've been here, we got a lot more than our quota of homicides."

"Yeah, I'm the reason. It's me."

"Take it easy, Nine. I'm just saying. Both Dempsey and Decatur turned up since you've been with LPD, and the Zuma killings and Trask Martin. Almost like from the moment you came on board."

September didn't answer. It was a meaningless fact. As a partner, Gretchen was fine, but she sure could be a pain in the ass, too. She suddenly, fervently wished she could bounce ideas off Auggie; she could talk to him.

If he would let her.

With a dark cloud building over her head, September settled back in the seat and tuned out Gretchen, concentrating on the task ahead.

Halo Valley Security Hospital. Liv had heard tales about it, with its two sides, A and B; Side A for the mentally challenged; Side B for the criminally insane. When she was at Hathaway House it represented the next step. If you can't get well here, Halo Valley awaits. . . .

It was nonsense, of course. Halo Valley was a private mental hospital, a modern facility that was funded by both donations and wealthy patients' families and bragged about an impressive success rate, at least on Side A. One of the Side B inmates had escaped a while back—a real psycho— and the resulting bad press had hurt the hospital's reputation some. Still, Halo Valley was considered a first choice by anyone seeking more one-on-one help than the state-run mental hospital could provide.

The landscape flashed by: furrowed fields with milk-chocolate colored earth, stubbles of hay, bent and dry, Douglas firs framing large plots of land. Halo Valley was in the center of the Willamette Valley and down I-5 about eighty miles from Portland.

Auggie turned off the freeway just outside Salem and drove west. Liv looked out the window and noticed Vandy's, a rambling building with a shake roof bearing a scripted sign that sported its name in red neon. She'd heard about it somewhere before. Ah, yes. Kurt Upjohn had met a woman there once and carried on a torrid affair for a couple of weeks, which had brought Camille Dirkus into the office, screaming. Aaron had told Liv that this kind of thing happened at least once a year. He'd started smoking dope as a means of pushing reality away.

Liv slid a glance at Auggie. He was watching the road with concentration while his cell phone, sitting in an accessories slot in his dashboard, was charging away. His knuckles were white on the steering wheel, which put a niggling worry in her head. He was looking no more forward to this interview with the powers-that-be at Halo Valley than she was.

The entry to the hospital was unprepossessing: a small metal sign at road level just inside the lengthy drive with HALO VALLEY SECURITY HOSPITAL painted in black letters.

They turned in and drove for a quarter of a mile before the hospital loomed into view, a concrete and redwood block with razor wire peeking out from the roof of the back building, which was brick, dividing it from the first.

Auggie pulled into a space two parking sections over from the main portico. He switched off the engine and looked at Liv. "How do you want to play this?"

"I don't want to go in there," Liv answered, the words popping out before she could stop them. Flushing, she added, "Geez, I'm a chicken. Sorry. I'll go. Now that I'm this close, I'm just—dreading it."

"I'll go," Auggie said, unplugging his cell phone and pocketing it as he started out of the Jeep.

"No, no. I'll go." Liv unbuckled her seatbelt, but Auggie turned around, leaning in the door.

"I may get stonewalled," he told her. "Wait here."

"I should go. You're dreading this almost as much as I am."

He frowned. "No, that's not . . ." He dropped his gaze for a moment, then said, "We're going to the authorities later today. Let's not have someone recognize you and send the posse out before we get there."

"I'm not . . . sure . . ." But he was already walking away, covering the distance with ground-devouring strides.

Auggie's insides were churning with tension. He could scarcely look at Liv, and yet his eyes wanted to drink her in as if she was the last sight he would ever see. This wasn't going to be good. Nope. Wasn't going to be good.

He pressed the buzzer at the main entrance, looking through the glass doors. A woman sitting at a long desk asked him his name. "August Rafferty," he said, deliberately leaving off *Detective*. He didn't want Liv finding out before he was ready to tell her.

He heard a double-click and pushed through. Ahead was a room with couches and a television, where several people were sitting around. No one seemed to be watching TV, and none of them seemed to be interacting, either.

He felt a cold feeling between his shoulder blades. Nerves.

The woman at the desk regarded him impassively, waiting for him to tell her why he was there. "I'm trying to locate Dr. Frank Navarone who worked here for a while. I think he's been gone a few years."

"There's no one by that name working here now. . . ." She glanced toward a computer monitor, then slid to it, pushing rapidly on the keyboard.

"Is there someone here who was working at the same time he was?"

"Let me call the director's office." She placed a call and said quietly that a man was asking about one Dr. Frank Navarone. Was there someone who could help him? When she clicked off, she said, "Nurse Champion will be right here."

Nurse Champion. That didn't sound good, somehow. And when Nurse Champion with her black pantsuit, iron jaw, barrel torso and squinty eyes appeared, his fears were realized.

She spoke in a surprisingly soft voice. "May I help you?"

Auggie tried on a concerned expression. "I hope so. I'm looking for Dr. Frank Navarone who used to work here."

"He's been gone for three years."

"Can you tell me where he went?"

"'Fraid not. I understand that he may no longer be in the medical profession."

"He was a visiting doctor to other facilities around Portland while he was here," Auggie said like he knew, though he was carefully fishing. "Hathaway House . . . Grandview Hospital . . . maybe others . . ."

"I believe that's correct."

Auggie's badge was in the car, taped under the front seat with his wallet. He wasn't going to get anywhere with this woman who, though she was regarding him mildly, would be a wall of resistance if he pushed.

"I'm guessing he lost his license because of something that happened at Halo Valley," Auggie said.

There was a long silence while she studied him closely. He almost told her he thought she would be a good interrogator, but decided that might be counterproductive.

"What is your purpose in finding Dr. Navarone?" she asked.

"I'm not planning to sue him. I'm really looking for information."

"May I ask what kind of information?"

He thought for a moment, then shook his head. Nope. This wasn't going to get him the desired results. It would be better to come back with the power of the law behind him. He'd known that before he set off this morning. He'd just been delaying telling Liv the truth.

"Thank you," he said, turning back to the front doors. The woman at the desk had to buzz him out again and when he was outside he sucked in a lungful of air. Jesus. What a place. It felt like the walls were moving in on him.

Liv's eyes were round pools of anxiety as he slid into the driver's seat. "Nada," he told her regretfully.

She'd been sitting rigidly and now she collapsed back like a punctured balloon. "They didn't know where he went?"

"They didn't want to tell me if they did, so I don't know." He put the Jeep in gear, reversed, then headed back down the long drive to the road.

Liv felt inordinately let down. She wanted answers and a resolution. Closure. As they drove back toward Portland, she tried to think of a course of action. She needed a plan. It just felt imperative, and she sat with her hands in fists as the miles sped by beneath the Jeep's tires.

"It's noon," Auggie said as they turned onto the 217 juncture, which would take them to Sunset Highway and his place. "I know you don't want fast food, but maybe we should eat before going to the police?"

She clenched her jaw, then relaxed it. "Fast food's fine," she said, reaching for her backpack and her wallet.

"I'll go through KFC," he said. "Chicken. It's what's for dinner."

"I think that slogan is for pork."

"Yeah?"

"I don't know." She looked out the window, feeling anxious and itchy. She didn't want to go to the police. She didn't think she would. She wasn't ready and maybe never would be, but if he forced her? Coerced her? What would she do? All she wanted to do was run, just like Hague had urged her. *RUN!*

They went to the KFC less than a mile from his house. Her hand scrabbled around in her backpack, touching the cold barrel of her .38, before closing on her wallet. She set the backpack down in the well at her feet and looked in her wallet, pulling out a twenty. She was going through her money. She really should insist Auggie go back to Bean There, Done that, or head to his bank and figure something out about accessing his own cash.

"I think I need to talk to Dr. Knudsen at Hathaway House. That's where it all started for me. She's back today."

"After we go to the police."

Liv didn't answer. He looked at her, and she gave him a nod, hoping she could go through with it.

They reached the window and Auggie looked at her for her order. She just shook her head. Food. She needed it for sustenance but her appetite had all but disappeared.

"Two individual meals with cole slaw and mashed potatoes . . ." He glanced her way and she simply nodded.

"How many pieces of chicken?"

The cell phone, plugged into the charger, suddenly lit up. There was no ring; Auggie had it on silent, but Liv's eyes slid to the screen. A text message showed:

Bring Dugan IN!!!!

"Three pieces," Auggie said.

Liv dragged her eyes away, confused. Dugan. He'd told someone about her? Who? *Bring her in?* What did that mean? Someone was urging him to take her in to the police? But who . . . how . . . ?

She froze, staring through the windshield, barely aware as he took the twenty she'd pulled from her wallet and paid for their order.

He didn't want to tell you who he was.

He doesn't have any ID and doesn't seem to worry about it.

He jumped onto your side pretty fast and stayed there.

Liv glanced down briefly as Auggie pulled back into traffic. The screen from the phone was dark again.

"I got the standards, cole slaw and mashed potatoes. I

coulda got french fries." In her peripheral vision she saw him glance her way, smiling.

Oh, God . . . oh, my God . . .

And her mind jumped to their lovemaking. The tender touches and soft sighs and pleasure.

Her heart was pounding so hard she thought he might be able to see it.

"Did I do all right?" he asked.

"What?" Her voice was a whisper.

"Mashed potatoes instead of fries."

She was going to be sick. Sick. The smell of the chicken, normally such an enticing aroma, nearly emptied her stomach.

You jumped in his car. You did that.

But he was there . . . waiting . . .

He was watching her now, a line forming between his brows. "You all right?"

"Mashed potatoes are great," she said with an effort.

"You look kinda pale."

"I'm exhausted," she admitted. "I just need to lie down, I think."

"Okay."

Later, she couldn't remember how she got out of the car, how she managed to act normal enough to get inside the house, how she mustered enough energy and bluff to put him at ease enough to sit down in one of the chairs and start digging into the sack with their food, putting the plastic covered plate with her meal on her side of the table.

The twine was still on the counter. She walked over to it, still holding her backpack.

"I'm gonna make this up to you, y'know," he said. "I've got a running total in my head of how much you've spent on our meals."

"You've provided a place to hide," she said, shocked by

how normal her voice sounded now. Adrenaline was coursing through her veins. Why hadn't she seen it before?

Carefully, she set down her backpack and pulled out the .38. It wasn't loaded. Did he know that? She had ammunition. All she had to do was pull it out.

"Are you gonna sit down?"

"I just want a glass of water."

"I got you a Diet Coke."

"I'll just get water, too." Her fingers, though quivering, found the small box of shells inside her purse. She quickly opened the chamber and put the ammo inside.

When she turned around he was staring at her, alerted by the sound of her loading the gun.

"You know that sound, don't you? Loading a gun?" She pointed the .38 at him and his eyes moved from her face to the end of the weapon.

"What are you doing?" he asked cautiously.

"I'm going to tie you up. I'm sorry. You won't be able to 'bring Dugan in.'"

"What happened?"

"You! You happened!" She could feel her control slipping a little and forced herself to get a grip. "You happened along right when I needed someone, didn't you?"

"At the coffee shop?"

"DIDN'T YOU! Don't LIE. Don't you lie!"

"Yes," he said, holding up his hands at the wavering gun.

"Who are you working for?"

"I'm a police detective," he answered. Then quickly, "I'm on your side, Liv. I didn't expect you to jump in the car, but you did and—"

"Don't say my name. Don't say *anything!*"

"—and I wasn't sure what your part in it was. But I believe you. There's something about your past that—"

"Shut—up."

"—has something to do with the Zuma killings. And Trask Martin's death."

"You've been reporting in all along, haven't you?"

"I've—yes—I've called in."

"I'm going to tie you up, and I'm going to leave. I will shoot you. Don't think I won't, this time. I will. I want to."

Her lips were quivering. She'd slipped the leash on her own control and she wanted to hurl herself at him and pull out his hair and claw his face. Betrayal. It was everywhere.

"Okay, okay. I'm going to turn the chair around. You can tie me up." He carefully did as he said he would and put his arms around the back of the chair. Liv grabbed the twine and stood in front of him, still holding the gun at him. "Trust me, I'm gonna let you tie me up. I'm not gonna fight you for the gun. I'm not gonna risk either of our lives."

She took the chance that he was telling the truth and walked behind the chair, setting the gun on the table as she quickly wrapped the twine around his hands. He didn't move a muscle. She tied his legs to the chair as well, although halfway through her hands and arms were shaking so badly she wasn't sure how good a job she did. Then she swept up the gun and held it in both hands in front of him.

"I'm on your side," he said again, his expression totally sober.

"I'm the only one on my side," she answered, then she walked out the door and headed for his Jeep.

Chapter 19

Liv drove directly to Hathaway House, her insides wrenched in turmoil. Part of her wanted to go back and slap Auggie, or kiss him, or kill him. All of the above.

But she couldn't think. She was ill. Sick . . . lovesick . . . Strange little mews of torment spilled from her lips. She'd trusted him. And he'd set her up!

It was beyond bearing. No wonder he'd been so eager to take her to the authorities: they were clearly waiting for him to bring her in.

Oh, *God*!

Liv shook her head violently, wanting to run his car off the road, smash it into something, cause him pain. But she wasn't an idiot. She couldn't afford to foolishly wreck his Jeep. She had to get away . . . get away . . .

She was on her own. Again.

And she couldn't leave him there indefinitely, either. She had to go back eventually and free him, or something. But he could damn well sit there a while! Maybe she'd find a pay phone and call the Laurelton police and tell them where to find him. He hadn't said where he worked, but since he'd been assigned to her, apparently, that was the right jurisdiction.

She *hated* him!

No, you don't, the rational side of herself said.

Yes I do! the irrational, wounded side of herself answered.

She slammed her palm on the steering wheel hard three times in a row, feeling the impact bruise her skin. Good. She wanted to feel physical pain.

Tears burned her eyes. *I could just die!* her inner self cried and that brought her up short.

She roughly brushed the tears aside with her sleeve. She was trying to stay alive. That was the purpose of all this. Keeping ahead of a killer who'd slain Aaron Dirkus and Paul de Fore and shot Jessica Maltona and Kurt Upjohn and probably Trask Burcher Martin.

Damn Auggie Rafferty. Detective August Rafferty. *Damn* him.

She was at Hathaway House much too fast. She parked, grabbed her backpack and swung out of the car, loose and staggering. Crazy. Just the way they liked 'em here.

She felt disembodied and oddly empowered. This time when she walked toward the reception area under the pools of diffused light, she didn't give a rat's ass what anyone thought or if they called the cops or anything.

"I need to speak to Dr. Knudson," Liv said to the woman in a tone that brooked no argument. "Right now."

The receptionist was the same as before. Same shagged gray hair. Same pinched attitude, as she said, "Well, I'm sorry, Miss. But we only accept appointments for our staff."

"Dr. Knudson is the director," Liv stated flatly.

"Yes, but he's very, very busy." She looked down her rather long nose at Liv.

"Yeah? Well, tell Dr. Knudson my name's Liv Dugan and that I used to be a patient here of Dr. Yancy's. Now, I'm on the run from the authorities because I should have been shot at Zuma Software last Friday, but I got away. I think it has something to do with one of the doctors who used to be connected with Hathaway House. Dr. Navarone. You can call the cops, if you like. Go right ahead. They undoubtedly know where I am or will soon. But I am going to speak to Dr. Knudson today, if I have to walk down every hall screaming his name until I do."

With that she turned blindly toward the corridor on her right. "Dr. Knudson?" she yelled at the top of her lungs. She turned back to the receptionist who was reaching quickly for the phone. "That crazy enough for you? Dr. KNUDSON!!! Dr. *KNUDSON!!!*"

Doors flew open along the corridor and heads peeked out. One of the rooms' occupants, a man with silver hair moussed back slickly from his scalp, eased into the hallway a step or two later, probably having just picked up the page from the receptionist. He walked slowly Liv's way with what looked like false confidence.

"Dr. Knudson?" she demanded as he neared.

"Let's take a moment," he said with a practiced smile. "Please . . . Ms. . . . ?"

"Dugan. Liv Dugan. You didn't get that when she called you?" Liv inclined her head to the receptionist.

"There's a bench right over by the wall where we can sit down and talk."

"Afraid to have me in your office?" Liv smiled coldly. To hell with them all. "I don't have time for this shit. Was Dr. Navarone a visiting doctor here when I was a patient here seven years ago?"

"I think it would be best—"

"Yes or no. It's a simple question." She hitched her backpack up her arm. "I have a gun," she added mildly. "Make of that what you will. Just give me the information."

His eyes jumped to her backpack. "That sounds very much like a threat."

"You're quick. Call the police. Go ahead. I'm a lunatic.

Not responsible for anything. Hey, who should know better than Hathaway House?"

"Ms. Dugan . . ." He was starting to panic, his lower lip trembling a bit.

"Did he work here?"

He nodded, gulping.

"Where did he base from? Or, where did he go from here?"

"I'm not certain. . . ."

"Guess!"

"Halo Valley Security Hospital."

Liv felt her own energy start to dwindle. They'd given Auggie the runaround at Halo Valley, like he'd said. Or, he hadn't passed on the information to her because he worked for the *police department*.

Either way, the answer was at Halo Valley.

Liv turned on her heel and pushed back through the front doors, aware they knew where she was headed and it was down to minutes how long she would be free before the authorities caught up with her.

Auggie slowly worked himself free of the bonds, a little surprised at how long it took him. He'd expected Liv to do a half-assed job in her emotional state but she had managed to make it damn difficult.

His cell phone lay on the table, mocking him. Piece of goddamn garbage. Who had texted him? September?

He swore solidly for about a minute and a half, pulling out every word he knew as he struggled with the twine. He'd told Liv the truth about his compliance: he didn't want her accidentally shooting either herself or him. It was safer to let her go.

But he was in a dark fury.

He wrenched his right thumb free, then seesawed out

the rest of his hand. The fetters dropped and he was on his feet, sweeping up his phone. Another text came through just as he switched the screen to his caller list.

When?

September. Yup.
God. Damn. It.
Pulling up her profile, he hit the CALL button with repressed savagery. She answered after one ring and started in a surprised voice, "Well, well, well—"

"She saw your text. And now she's fled. I asked you not to. I wasn't kidding around, Nine!" he bit out, cutting her off. "When I ask you to do something, I expect you to do it!"

A pause. Then, "What do you mean she's fled?"

"Liv took my car. She left me at the safe house. That's where I am. Do you know where it is?"

"Um . . . no."

"Find out from D'Annibal and get over here. I need your vehicle, and I need it now."

"I soooo appreciate your high-handedness, Auggie. We've got tons of time to indulge you," she said sardonically. Then, "You think I'm not involved in this investigation? We all are. We're waiting on *you.*"

"Bitch at me later. I don't have time. Liv's in trouble and now she thinks I'm the enemy. Either get over here, or send someone fast. I'm not kidding, Nine."

"So, you're through pussy-footing around?"

"Are you listening to me?" he ground through his teeth.

"Fine. Jesus. I'll figure it out."

"Good."

He clicked off in a fulminating fury. He loved his sister, even thought she might make a good detective . . . someday. But not today. Not . . . today.

Then he sat down at the table and stared straight ahead,

a clock ticking inside his skull. She said she wanted to go to Hathaway House. That's where she was.

Did he dare call them? Tip her off? Tip them off? Have someone find her and drag her into custody?

The thought of her loaded gun made his stomach drop and his limbs go cold.

He needed to find her.

"Goddammit, Liv," he whispered aloud. "Be . . . careful . . ."

She drove with repressed fury. A little out of control, not a lot. This time the fields of stubble and turned earth were a blur that barely registered in her peripheral vision. Would they call Halo Valley and alert them? Maybe. Though they would probably call the police first. Put the problem of Olivia Dugan in their capable hands. Auggie's hands.

She thumped the steering wheel again; this time with less force. Hurt her bruised palm a little, but it was a tiny little pain on the edge of a much larger one.

She kept to the speed limit. Didn't need to pick up a trooper for any reason other than she was in Auggie's car. A stolen car, actually. The felonies were just piling up, weren't they?

She was half-surprised when she made it all the way to the hospital without being pulled over. Minor miracle. She screeched to a halt with a little *burp* of the tires, grabbed her backpack, which was starting to feel heavier and heavier as her energy waned, headed for the front doors.

The hospital receptionist had to buzz her in. She asked Liv her name and without really thinking, Liv answered: "Jo Cardwick."

Bzzzzz.

Liv clicked through and then stopped and inhaled a long, long breath. If they knew about Olivia Dugan's meltdown at

Hathaway House, she didn't want to give herself away by losing control.

But suddenly, she was done. Her knees trembled violently and she couldn't even get herself to the chairs grouped against the wall opposite the reception desk. She just melted into the floor, put her hands to her face, and sobbed.

September had barely gotten out of her car when Auggie was demanding the keys and commandeering the Pilot while she sputtered, "I'm coming with you! Where the hell are you going? Damn it, Auggie! Stop being such a cowboy!"

"I'm taking your car, and I'm heading south to Halo Valley Hospital. I'm not taking you with me."

"Portland PD contacted us. They got a call from the director of Hathaway House that a Liv Dugan threatened them with a gun."

"*What?*"

"You heard me."

"Liv pulled a gun on someone?"

September lifted a hand. "Yes. No. There's some confusion about that. She definitely said she had a gun."

"Jesus Christ." Auggie reached to slam the driver's door shut behind him and September shoved her way between the door and the car, stopping his momentum.

"Stop it. I'm going with you."

"The hell you are. I'm chasing Liv down before she gets in worse trouble."

"She's a loose cannon, Auggie. And you're clearly personally involved. Let the department—"

"Get out of my way." He met his twin sister's gaze, two sets of coldly furious blue eyes dueling with each other.

"Ballistics came back. Same Glock for Zuma and the Martin killing."

"Shit. I knew it."

"I'm going to walk around and get in the passenger side."

"I'm not taking you with me."

"And one more thing: Jessica Maltona died a few hours ago. And Upjohn doesn't look good."

Auggie's lips became a thin line of determination. "Back up, September."

"You're taking me with you."

"No."

"Auggie!"

"You've got your cell," he bit out. "Text somebody else."

His implacability finally reached her and she stepped away from the vehicle, holding up her hands and shaking her head to let him know she'd ceded but she thought he was a complete madman.

He reversed and burned out of the driveway.

Swearing like a truck driver, she inwardly called her pig-headed, gotta-save-the-damsel-in-distress-at-all-costs brother an idiot to the nth degree.

They took Liv into a quiet room and actually lay her down on a bed, still clutching her backpack. They spoke in soothing tones. Maybe they'd seen enough nervous break-downs to establish a protocol. Probably. Not that this was what that was. This was physical collapse from overwhelming mental stress.

He betrayed you. You trusted him, and he betrayed you.

One of the women was a doctor. Dr. Norris, by the tag on her lab coat. She was slim and dark-haired and regarded Liv with concern. Liv's ears finally seemed to start working again, picking up her words.

". . . you hear me, Ms. Cardwick? Nurse Champion is putting on the blood-pressure cuff. Just lie still and—"

"No," Liv said, pulling her arm away from the nurse.

"It's not painful. We just want to check what's going on with—"

"I need information. Not medical help." She struggled to sit up and was practically pushed back down by the overbearing nurse. Glaring at her, Liv said, "Get your hands off me."

Dr. Norris held up a hand to the nurse. "What kind of information?"

"Dr. Frank Navarone was on staff here once, correct?"

Dr. Norris peered at Liv and frowned and the nurse sucked in a breath and said, "I told you about the guy who came in just a few hours ago asking about Dr. Navarone," the nurse said to the doctor.

"Auggie," Liv said through her teeth. "Detective August Rafferty. Yes, I know. I was in the car when he came in." She glared at the woman.

"He didn't say he was a detective," the nurse defended herself.

"Well, he is." She addressed Dr. Norris. "We're looking for Dr. Navarone as a person of interest in a series of murders."

"Dr. Navarone was on staff here once," Dr. Norris admitted, her gaze searching Liv's.

"And he was a visiting doctor to Hathaway House and Grandview Hospital, before it was elder-care, and he hailed from the Rock Springs–Malone area?" Liv pressed.

"I'm not sure about all that, but we can easily check it."

"Are you humoring me, Doctor?" Liv demanded.

"You haven't asked me anything I can't tell you. I'm not really giving away state secrets here. What series of murders are you referring to?"

Liv shook her head. She hardly knew where to start. "Do you know where Navarone went after he was terminated from Halo Valley?"

"You seem better informed than we are."

"I think he's a killer," Liv stated flatly, tired of pussy-footing around. "I think he strangled women around Rock Springs twenty years ago, and I think he's responsible for several deaths now, including the Zuma Software attack on Friday. Can you give me any information about him?"

Dr. Norris thought a moment, then asked, "Are you sure your name isn't Olivia Dugan?"

Before Liv could respond, the doctor's cell phone started ringing. Her gaze never left Liv's as she answered. "Hello." She listened several long moments while the person on the opposite end of the call went on for a bit. Finally, she said, "Okay, I'll be right there." Clicking off, she frowned at Liv. "Your Detective Rafferty appears to be here. He wants you to give me the keys to his vehicle. He says his identification is strapped to the underside of the driver's seat."

Liv lay back down on the bed and drew her arm over her eyes.

I hate you, Auggie, she thought, as tears leaked out and dampened the skin of her inner elbow.

He waited impatiently in the reception area, pacing and growling beneath his breath like a caged beast. He didn't know where Liv was but his own Jeep was parked outside, so she was here somewhere. He'd told the suspicious-eyed receptionist to tell whoever was with Olivia Dugan to get the Jeep's keys from her, so he could retrieve his identification and maybe, finally, induce SOMEONE to talk about Navarone. September had been right about one thing: he was through pussyfooting around. It was time for answers.

And to set things right with Liv.

It took another twenty minutes before an attractive, dark-haired woman appeared from a south-running corridor beyond the reception area and headed his way, her hands thrust deep inside the pockets of her white lab coat. He read her nametag: DR. NORRIS.

"Detective Rafferty?" she questioned.

"Yes. But I don't have the ID to prove it."

She pulled his keys from her pocket and held them out to him. "I believe these are yours."

"Where's Liv . . . Olivia Dugan?" he demanded, taking the keys.

"Resting."

"Resting?" he repeated slowly, wondering what the hell that meant. "She gave you the keys, though. She's all right . . . right?"

"Yes."

"She doesn't want to see me." He got it, but it pissed him off anyway. "Well, I want to see her."

The doctor clasped her hands together and said, "Bring back your identification and let's see where we stand."

Auggie stalked to the front doors, throwing a look to the receptionist who buzzed him out. He race-walked to the Jeep, opened the driver's-side back door, reached under the seat and ripped off the tape that held his identification. His Glock was also there, and he stuck it in the back of his jeans' waistband, then thought better of it and put it back for the moment. He needed to let the hospital personnel know who he was, but intimidating them with a firearm might backfire, so to speak.

Not that Liv didn't have a gun on her, he reminded himself darkly.

When he was buzzed back inside Dr. Norris was waiting for him. He handed her his identification, which she examined carefully, then handed back to him.

"Well?" he demanded impatiently.

"Ms. Dugan doesn't really want to see you," she said slowly, as if she were turning the idea over, checking it for flaws.

"She's a—person of interest—in a murder investigation," he clipped out. He was going to say *suspect*, but for him, at least, that was so untrue that he couldn't force himself to speak the word. "You can call my superior, Lieutenant Aubrey D'Annibal of the Laurelton PD, and he'll say the same."

"No, I believe you, Detective."

"So?"

She seemed to be having a conversation with herself inside her head. Clearly there was something going on. Some kind of war. After a few moments, she nodded firmly. "All right. But you need to pull yourself back a little," she said.

"What do you mean?" he asked, swinging his head to look at her hard as they started toward the corridor from where she'd appeared.

"You're emotionally charged. It's coming off you like heat. So is Ms. Dugan. I don't want to see you two explode when you get together. Bear in mind, this is a hospital. . . ."

Liv had pulled herself together enough to give Dr. Norris the keys and now she was sitting up, turned away from Nurse Champion, whose take-charge personality seemed to be filling up the room and then some. She wanted to leave. Had actually glanced at the door a time or two, thinking of jumping up and taking off, but there was something about Nurse Champion that suggested that might not work too well. The woman felt like a jailor, more than a nurse.

As she was weighing her options, the door opened and Dr. Norris walked through . . . followed by Auggie.

She stared at him, her heartbeat increasing so rapidly it felt as if she were free-falling. She pressed her fingers to her temples to stop the sensation.

Don't cry . . . don't cry . . . don't cry . . .

"Liv," he said, and just the sound of his voice broke something inside her.

She had to struggle to even speak. "Am I under arrest?" she managed to ask in a voice much stronger than she felt.

Dr. Norris and Nurse Champion stood by like sentinels. If she had to pick sides, she'd choose the doctor. There was compassion there. The jury was still out on Champion.

"No," he answered.

"But you're 'bringing me in,' aren't you?" She didn't bother driving the sarcasm from her words.

His blue eyes held hers for long seconds. She thought she saw a flash of pain, or guilt, or remorse, but it could have been her imagination. He glanced away, to the doctor, and asked, "Can you tell me anything about Dr. Navarone? We're looking for him."

Dr. Norris flicked a glance at Liv, then at Auggie. "Nurse Champion told me about your earlier visit. Lori, our receptionist, said you gave your name as August Rafferty and were asking about Dr. Frank Navarone. I looked up everything we had on Dr. Navarone. I don't have any information about where he went after he left Halo Valley."

"After he was asked to leave," Auggie corrected her.

"Dr. Navarone's employment contract was terminated," she admitted. "That's all I'm going to say about that. What I can give you is the name of the person listed as an emergency contact: his sister, Angela Navarone. The address is Seattle." She reached in her pockets again, withdrew a piece of paper and handed it to him. "It's over five years old."

"We'll find her. Thank you," Auggie said. He turned back to Liv. "You ready?"

She almost laughed. *For what?* Instead, she slid off the table on legs that were still a bit wobbly, but now that she'd faced Auggie and hadn't completely collapsed she felt stronger for it. She picked up her backpack once more, gazed at him coolly and said, "Sure."

They were buzzed out of the hospital together and walked into vivid sunlight and late afternoon heat. When Liv realized Auggie wasn't heading to the driver's side of the Jeep her steps slowed. "How did you get here?" she asked.

He pointed to the silver Honda Pilot parked next to his dark gray Jeep. "My sister's," he said.

"The one you didn't want to talk about?"

"Yeah, that one."

"You really must have had a long laugh when I jumped in your car. Talk about the bird flying into the cage. So glad to be a source of amusement for you, in every way." Liv exhaled slowly, hanging on to her composure as best she could. "This part of your m.o., Detective? Follow 'em, get 'em to trust you, have sex with 'em."

He was leaning tensely against the Pilot. "You can blame me for the deception, but you were a willing participant in the lovemaking."

"Lovemaking. That's what you're calling it?"

His lips tightened. "Would you rather I use some crude term? Would that make it more my fault than yours?"

She flinched and turned away.

He came toward her suddenly and she backed away. But he went around her to the driver's side of the Jeep. "I've got to get my gun."

Liv walked around the back of the car and watched him dig around under the seat. "So, your ID and gun were in the car all the time?"

"I was just off a case where I was hiding my identity," he said. "I hadn't had time to leave the 'safe house' and go home when the incident occurred with Navarone or whoever shot up Zuma. My boss asked me to check your apartment and . . . there you were."

"Where do you live?"

"In one half of a duplex I own in Laurelton." He shut the

back door of the driver's side and looked at her. He held a
gun loosely in his left hand. "It's a Glock," he said, seeing
her gaze light on it. "Like the shooter at Zuma used. Ballistics came back: the Zuma shootings were by the same gun
that killed your neighbor." He hesitated, then added in a
softer tone, "Jessica Maltona died this morning."

Chapter 20

Died? Jessica was *dead*?

"Oh, my God . . . oh, my God . . ." Once again Liv felt her knees struggle to hold her and she placed a palm against the Jeep's hot back fender for support, feeling her skin burn. Auggie automatically moved toward her but she jerked away.

He stopped short. "I believe someone's after you," he said in a low, urgent tone. "I'm sorry I lied. I wasn't sure how to get you to accept the police. But now . . . now that everything's out in the open, I can ask the department to run down Navarone. We need to find him. He could very well be the Zuma Software killer and even if he isn't, he's somehow involved with you and your past, and that past intersects with the serial strangler around Rock Springs."

Liv couldn't take it in. She was emotionally overwrought and this was . . . a case to him. She felt betrayed and angry and foolish.

You fell for him, her cold-eyed inner self reminded her. *You let him in.*

"Liv . . ."

"I threatened Dr. Knudson," she stated flatly, feeling as if it were a long, long time ago, not just hours earlier.

Auggie froze. "Did you hold him at gunpoint?"

"No. I told him I had a gun, just to let him know I meant business." She swallowed. "I was, out of control . . ."

"Liv, listen." He stepped forward and it took all her willpower not to shrink away. "You have a right to be mad at me, but . . . us . . . *this* . . ." He motioned between them. "It's real to me." She made a strangled sound, but he barreled on, "I wanted to earn your trust and protect you. I didn't want you to jump into this headlong without me."

She held up a hand when he would have moved within touching range.

"Now, I want to see this to the end," he said. "I don't want you to get hurt, so let's go to Laurelton PD together. Yes, they're expecting me to turn you in. My sister's a detective there, too, and she's the one who texted me. She brought me her car."

"Your sister's a detective, too?" She stared at him in anguish. It was too much!

"Liv, please. I'll be with you. Come back with me."

"To the police . . . sure. Why not?" She was fatalistic. "They're going to arrest me sometime anyway. Might as well be now."

"They're not going to arrest you."

"Don't lie to me anymore," she spat fiercely. "Not anymore."

"I'm not lying." His gaze was fixed on her, willing her to believe.

Did she? No. Not really. But she was so tired of fighting. She shook her head and counted to ten, then said in a hard voice, "Fine. I'll go. I suppose you want me to follow you."

Auggie looked at the silver Pilot, then back to his Jeep. Clearly, he didn't think that was a good idea, but it was the best answer. "We could go together and come back later."

"I'll follow you," she said.

"Okay," he said reluctantly. "This isn't just about the

case, y'know," he added, as if he were reading her mind. "I'm—involved."

"Yeah."

"It isn't," he stressed, stirred by her flat disbelief.

"I'll follow you to the police, Detective Rafferty," she said. "That's all you get." Then she moved around him and slid into the driver's seat.

September sat in stony silence at her desk, fully aware that things could be worse and Gretchen could be amused at her expense over Auggie's handling of her case. Instead, she seemed more concerned about what the hell Auggie was doing.

"He gonna call in?" Gretchen asked now. She'd come to September's rescue at the safe house and had brought her back to work.

Earlier, they'd both gone looking for Jason Jaffe to give him the news of his girlfriend's death, but he hadn't been at the house he shared with Jessica, and his cell-phone number had gone straight to voice mail every time they called. Since they'd returned to the station Gretchen had called him twice more, and some of her frustration with being unable to connect was mixing in with her feelings about Auggie and his relationship—whatever the hell that was—with Olivia Dugan.

Wes shot Gretchen a half-amused look, then smiled faintly at September. Gretchen wasn't even trying to hide her interest in Auggie. Maybe she just didn't care. "He said he'd bring her in today," Wes reminded her. "I suspect that's what he's doin'."

"Goddamn that Jaffe," Gretchen muttered, shooting back her chair and stomping into the hall.

When she was out of earshot, he asked September, "How you doin'?"

George had been focused on his computer screen, but now he glanced at Wes. "Who're you asking?"

"Nine."

George looked at September. "Still steaming over having your car highjacked?" He chuckled and shot a glance to Wes for encouragement but Pelligree just shook his head.

September tried hard to make it appear as if she wasn't bothered, though having her car commandeered by her brother and needing someone to pick her up was embarrassing in the extreme. Momentarily she'd considered asking one of her other siblings to do the honors, but that would have been even more galling. Neither March nor July had supported her when she'd followed Auggie's footsteps into law enforcement. Her father had been apoplectic that August had joined; September following in her twin's career choice had been too much for Braden Rafferty, who, unable to hold his head up in the rarified society of acquaintances he called "friends," promptly disowned his youngest two children, telling them not to darken his door until they'd come to their senses.

Like that ever worked with Auggie.

She almost smiled. Almost. Had to bury that wayward thought and concentrate on how pissed she was at him.

D'Annibal came in, looking again wilted compared to his usually put-together self. His suit coat had creases at the elbows and his tie had been jerked loose. It was sweltering outside, so maybe that accounted for it, but then the lieutenant barked out, "Rafferty and Ms. Dugan are on their way here now. Rafferty's working a lead to the Zuma killings. Dr. Frank Navarone. A psychiatrist who was last booted out of Halo Valley Security Hospital. We need a warrant for his records. A Dr. Norris at Halo Valley coughed up the name of his sister: Angela Navarone. Seattle area. Weasel . . ." He looked to Wes who, after a pause, turned to his computer to do a search.

September blinked. "Lieutenant, umm . . . I'm on Zuma with Sandler."

"Not anymore. I want you exclusively on the Decatur case, Nine. For God knows what reason—better ratings, probably—the press has been all over us about this one. I want you to be the face for this investigation. Be ready to make a statement."

"But—" She cut herself off. Had she really been going to say, "That's not fair!"? Like, oh, sure, D'Annibal would really respond to that. Instead, she said, "I thought Wes wanted the Decatur case?"

"He does. But right now, you're on it." D'Annibal's usually easy manner was completely missing.

"This is because of Auggie," September said, flushing. She knew she should just shut up, but she couldn't seem to make herself. "My brother got you to remove me from Zuma. He thinks I'm incompetent."

"Don't make this personal. Auggie's on the Zuma case now with Sandler," D'Annibal stated firmly. "You're with the Decatur and Dempsey victims. This is a big case and Pauline Kirby from Channel Seven is already all over it. I need you to be the department's voice. Can you do that for me?"

September said, "Yes," and fought back the rest of her objections.

"Good. Your brother got on the inside with Olivia Dugan," he added as an explanation.

"I'm sure he did," she said coolly.

The lieutenant shot her a look, but let it go. "The press doesn't know about the message carved into Decatur's skin. We're trying to keep that under wraps."

Gretchen, returning with a glass of water, caught the end of his words. "It'll get out," she warned. "The hikers know and they'll tell someone."

"Well, for the moment, it's not for public knowledge."

D'Annibal's exasperation escaped his control. "When Rafferty gets here with Dugan, I want all of you here."

"When will that be?" George asked.

"Within the hour."

"I'm going over to Jaffe's," Gretchen said. "Stake out the bastard, so I can deliver the bad news about his girlfriend."

"I'll go with you," September said, daring anyone to object. No one did, and she followed her partner back outside to the Escape. Zuma might not be her case anymore but she'd been with Gretchen when they'd first interviewed Jaffe, and she didn't feel like waiting around for Auggie anyway.

Liv drove back up the freeway toward Portland again, keeping the silver Pilot directly in front of her. If Auggie pulled into another lane, she slipped in behind him. If he slowed his speed, she did the same. She didn't want to give him any reason to think she wasn't doing exactly what he wanted. She did, after all, intend to follow through.

Sighing, she glanced across the wide strip of grassy median that divided the north- and southbound lanes at this part of the freeway. Rush hour was upon them and each mile that drew them closer to the city meant heavier and heavier traffic. Not so much her direction, as she was in the northbound lanes and more commuters would be leaving the city, not heading to it.

She barely noticed the landscape again. Her thoughts were too chaotic. She was truly living in the moment because every time her mind opened up and questioned her about her own future, panic set in. She had no job, no friends, no place she could go back to. If and when the authorities caught up to Dr. Navarone the threat against her might end, but where would she go from there?

Shivering violently, she shoved that thought aside.

And Auggie . . . she was giving him everything he wanted on a silver platter! It angered her, but mostly just hurt. She wasn't so naive as to believe what they'd shared meant anything to him. He'd been soothing a schizoid personality, so that he could keep her in check until he could reach his own ends, that's all.

Movement in her rearview mirror caught Liv's eye. She glanced up in time to see the front of a gray truck rushing to her right rear end. *Slam!* The Jeep's steering wheel leapt from her hands! She grabbed at it, but it spun around as the Jeep sailed west off the freeway, bounding and thundering across the median toward the southbound lanes.

Shrieking, Liv gripped the steering wheel hard, holding firm, slamming on the brakes. The Jeep's speed propelled it like a rocket toward the oncoming traffic. The front tires bounced onto the shoulder, jumped the Jeep into the fast lane and stopped.

BWWAAAHHHH!

She heard the horn blast and saw the semi coming straight for her. On automatic, she slammed the vehicle into reverse and smashed her foot to the accelerator.

Blam!

The Jeep spun backward and around, clipped on its front fender.

Liv's head smacked into the steering wheel and she saw stars.

Oh, God . . .

Auggie's gaze was on his rearview mirror more than it was on the road ahead of him. He half-expected her to do something rash. Tear away from him, or lag way, way back. He just didn't believe in her complete capitulation.

She'd lost trust in him, and who could blame her. He'd lied to her and kept that lie going long past its pull date. It was bound to blow up in his face. He'd just thought if he could get her to the department and prove to her they were on the same side . . .

But it hadn't happened that way. Still, it was just a matter of doing damage control. At least he hoped that's all it was. He couldn't bear the idea that they would solve this case and she would walk out of his life forever. Yes, her safety was the most important thing, but his imagination was working overtime and the picture of her thanking him for a job well done while shaking his hand and then turning away felt as if it were a vision of the future.

He switched to the inside lane, needing to pass a truck pulling a trailer full of rakes, ladders, hoses, mowers and other handyman and landscaping tools. He glanced back to his Jeep and was gratified to see Liv follow suit.

With a touch of the gas, the Pilot surged forward. He kind of liked his sister's rig, although it had a couple of pairs of shoes tossed on the floor in the footwell of the front passenger seat and assorted jackets and papers in the backseat. He kept his vehicle neater, but that didn't—

His gaze flicked to the rearview where a gray truck was tearing toward the Jeep's rear end. "Hey, buddy, slow down!" he blasted out just as it smashed into the Jeep and sent it careering over the grassy medium like a bullet toward the opposite lanes.

"Shit! Goddamn! *Asshole!*" Auggie couldn't stop. Had to move forward. The truck that hit Liv shot past him and up the freeway. He had the presence of mind to look for a license plate—none on the back—before he wrenched the Pilot to the right and sped forward, chasing the older, gray GMC truck.

"Damn . . . Damn . . . Damn . . ." He scrabbled for his cell phone, which he'd flung on the passenger seat after he'd called D'Annibal and told him that he and Liv would be at the station soon. The Pilot swung into the next lane and a horn bleated behind him.

With a wrench, he straightened the wheels and the cell phone went flying to the floor.

The GMC truck was racing hard. He couldn't chase it. He had to get off the freeway. Had to turn back to Liv.

"Shit!"

It was the guy. The guy who'd gunned down Trask Martin. That was his truck! The guy with the same Glock used to kill the Zuma employees. *The guy!*

But he couldn't chase him. Had to pull off and call. The next exit was coming up and he could cross the overpass and circle back. He jockeyed aggressively to the ramp and slipped in behind an elderly driver, right on his ass. Jesus. H. Christ! Auggie got around the slowpoke, raced across the overpass and down the southbound ramp, merging with rush-hour traffic that luckily was still moving at a fairly good clip. He worked his way to the inside lane, fighting for space, earning a middle finger from a young male driver, who traded lanes with him.

Suddenly he had to practically stand on his brakes. Traffic was stopped.

Liv, Auggie realized. The accident. Rubberneckers were creating a traffic snarl.

Oh . . . God . . . please . . . let her be all right. . . .

When he couldn't move forward anymore he pulled onto the shoulder and drove past the stopped cars that were now on his right. He could feel their outrage but he didn't care. The Jeep was up there. On the shoulder. Out of harm's way. He slammed the Pilot to a stop half on the shoulder, half on the grassy median, and ran for the Jeep, where some well-meaning, good Samaritan who'd pulled to the shoulder in front of Liv was at the driver's side window.

"Livvie!" Auggie yelled, spying her through the windshield.

She put a hand up, reaching for him, touching the glass. He practically shoved the good Samaritan aside and yanked at the driver's door. It opened with a squeal of metal and then Liv was in his arms, her face buried in his neck, her arms around him.

"Shhh . . . shhh . . ." he said, though she wasn't saying a word, just trembling in his arms.

"I called 911," the would-be helper said.

"Good. Thanks. I'm with the police," Auggie said with a sharp nod.

"Okay, then." He looked a little dubious, but he turned back toward his car.

"Liv, it was the GMC truck. I've gotta call it in."

"What?" she asked dully.

"The 2005 GMC truck. Gray. That's what your neighbor said, right?"

"He tried to kill me."

"Yes." Auggie reluctantly pulled her back and held her at arm's length. "It is about you, Liv. This whole thing. It's about you."

The sound of a siren split the air. Exhaust fumes were starting to overwhelm them, so Auggie helped Liv back in the Jeep. "The cavalry's coming," he said. "Take it easy. We'll get you to an emergency room."

"No. No. The police," she said. "I want to go to the police."

"I've got to call the truck in. Just wait . . ."

He rapidly punched in his sister's cell phone and when she answered, he quickly related the information about the truck, then added, "Get an APB out. Front-end damage. Catch this bastard!"

"A license number would help," she said.

"Goddammit, Nine. If I had one I'd give it to you. He ran

Liv off the freeway and damn near into oncoming traffic!
Just—take care of it!"

He hung up and turned to Liv, noticing how pale her skin
was. "You really need to be looked at. You've got a cut and
swelling on your head." He pointed to her hairline above her
right eye.

She reached up, touched the knot and winced. "I can't do
the circus, Auggie. When my name gets out there, and all
the questions and everything . . ."

He saw the wisdom of that. "We'll go in the Pilot. I'll
take care of it." With that he helped her to her feet and
though her legs wobbled, they made it to the Honda.
Auggie tucked her inside, then climbed in the driver's seat,
fired the engine and merged into the slow traffic, heading
southbound. He called D'Annibal's line and left a message
asking him to run interference as they'd just left the scene
of an accident.

Fifteen minutes later, they took another exit and crossed
back to the northbound lanes. Forty-five minutes after that
they drove into the Laurelton Police Department's parking
lot, still arguing if she should go to the ER or not.

Auggie got out and came around the car, opening the
passenger door. Liv looked at the building for long moments, her breathing escalating. Then she lifted her chin and
climbed from the vehicle.

"Let's do this," she said grimly, and Auggie led her
inside.

September and Gretchen sat in the Ford Escape across
the street from Jason Jaffe and Jessica Maltona's home for
over an hour with Gretchen muttering under her breath
about douche bags masquerading as "artistes." September
was trying very hard not to start up her own rant about her

brother and Lieutenant D'Annibal and the unfairness of the universe.

Though she'd opted for this stakeout in a fit of pique, now she was having serious second thoughts. This was taking far longer than it should, and she could feel time ticking away. Now, she wanted to be there when Auggie brought in Olivia Dugan. She wanted to get her eyes on Dugan; needed to see for herself what about this woman seemed to hold her brother in thrall.

She shifted in her seat and wondered if she would ever feel that way about anybody. The last truly meaningful relationship she'd had was in high school, and it was basically a one-night stand her senior year with a handsome jock and a lot of months spent mooning about him, wondering if he really liked her. She wondered now why it had mattered so, as this was the same guy who'd teased her in grade school, mainly because her family was wealthy and his father worked for hers for a time, and who'd wanted to score with a virgin, or so her friends had warned her after the fact. At least that's how September remembered it.

The whole thing had been torture and had pretty much soured her on relationships and men ever since.

"Goddamn, there he is," Gretchen said. "As much as I can't stand the guy, it's not gonna be good telling him his girlfriend's dead."

"Wait." September grabbed her arm, stopping her from opening the door.

Jaffe was pulling into his driveway and putting the brakes on his Trailblazer, but he wasn't alone. Another head was visible in the passenger seat.

Gretchen sat tensely, as did September. "That look like a woman to you?" Gretchen asked.

As they watched, the passenger door opened and a long-legged blonde with a very short skirt and heels stepped out. She carefully walked across the sloped driveway, clasping Jaffe's hand as she tiptoed up the broken asphalt. They disappeared inside the garage.

"What do you make of that?" Gretchen asked.

"Nothing good."

"Let's go."

September fought back her urge to get to the station and met up with Gretchen as she strode across the road and toward Jaffe's house.

The man door was open and Gretchen didn't bother knocking though Jaffe and his girl were already in a heated embrace with hands yanking her blouse and his shirt from their pants.

"Sorry to bother you," Gretchen said, and the girl squeaked out a half-scream, jerked away and yanked her blouse down in one movement.

"What the fuck?" Jaffe asked, glaring at them.

"I've been trying to reach you all day," Gretchen said. "You don't turn your phone on?"

"What the hell do you want? I'm busy." He had the grace to color as he looked over at his "date."

"It's about Jessica Maltona. Your—girlfriend. I'm sorry to tell you that she did not survive her wounds. She died this morning."

You could have heard a pin drop. Jaffe's friend turned scared eyes to him. "Oh, shit, Jason."

Jaffe just stared at Gretchen as if he hadn't heard her correctly. "That's not true," he said. "Jessica's *nice*."

Gretchen frowned. She'd gone in loaded for bear, but Jason was clearly pole-axed. "Death doesn't discriminate," she pointed out.

"No . . . she can't be dead . . . how . . . why . . . no, she's supposed to survive!" The color leached from his face and he swayed on his feet. September moved forward to catch him, but he took a step back, holding up his hands as if to ward her off. "Upjohn killed her! He killed her! Arrest him. It's his fault!"

"Jason . . . ?" the girl said on a trembling note.

He swung around, looking at her through hollow eyes. "I love Jess. I do."

"Yeah . . ." Gretchen said, sliding September a look.

The blonde didn't know what to make of that. "You want me to go?" she asked in a small voice.

But Jaffe had forgotten her the moment Jessica Maltona's name was mentioned. He didn't even bother to respond.

"I need to see her. Can I see her? I need to see her."

Blondie gave a hurt little cry then tottered out, half-tripping on an uneven piece of asphalt just outside the garage man door. Gretchen looked at Jaffe, calculating the sincerity of his response, then said on a sigh, "I'll take you to the hospital morgue."

"Swing by the station first," September reminded Gretchen.

Liv sat in a chair beside Auggie's desk. He actually had a desk, although he said that he rarely used it; he was usually undercover. They'd entered the station through the front doors, and Auggie had pointed a finger at the guy at the desk who looked as if he wanted to protest them passing by without checking with him, but Auggie's finger quelled his objections.

As soon as they were in the squad room Auggie demanded to know if the gray GMC truck with front-end damage had been found. A roundish detective with his face tuned to his computer monitor looked his way and shook his head. Auggie had some choice words to say about that, then introduced Liv to his superior, Lieutenant Aubrey D'Annibal, who came out of a glass-walled office to greet Liv and interview her. Like Auggie, he suggested she get checked out at the hospital first, glancing at the injury to her head, but Liv assured him she was fine.

Was she fine? That was definitely a matter up for debate. But she wanted this interview with the police to be behind her. In her head, she kept replaying her interview with the officer from Rock Springs after her mother's death, and she could still feel how small he'd made her feel during the worst time of her life.

"The Portland PD got a call from the director of Hathaway House, saying a young woman came in demanding information on Dr. Frank Navarone," D'Annibal said, causing what little color Liv had to drain from her face. "She threatened them with a gun."

Auggie inserted calmly, "That was Liv, but she didn't actually threaten them with a gun. She just said she had a gun. She didn't show one. It was a comment, nothing more."

"What are you, a lawyer now?" the lieutenant asked him.

"I'm just saying she didn't hold anyone at gunpoint," he answered.

Except you, Liv thought.

D'Annibal shook his head and flapped a hand in the air, as if swatting the whole mess away. "I'll give Portland PD a head's up. Let's move on."

Liv hadn't realized she was holding her breath until D'Annibal turned back to her. She expected him to start asking questions, but he turned that job over to a lean, black detective named Wes Pelligree. Pelligree ran her through the events of the previous Friday, before and after the shooter entered Zuma's front doors. She could tell Auggie wanted to intervene; that he was worried about her, but the lieutenant had designated Pelligree and there was nothing to do but for Liv to review the sequence of events that had led her here.

She told them about Zuma, and about jumping into

Auggie's car. Before she could even wonder how much to tell about that, Auggie broke in, saying she had a deep-seated fear of the authorities and that he'd spent a lot of time earning her trust. That was why it had taken them so long to come to the station. To Liv, he said, "Tell them about the package."

He was trying to protect her, she realized, and though she felt a spurt of resentment after the way he'd betrayed her, she decided to let him guide her discourse. No reason to get into deeper trouble than she already was. If Auggie was okay with it, then so was she.

Still, her heart was heavy as she told them all about how she'd received a manila envelope from her mother shortly after her twenty-fifth birthday and that ever since the package arrived, she'd felt a heightened fear that she was being followed, that someone was after her. When asked about the contents of the envelope, she explained about her mother's "suicide" and the serial strangler who'd been terrorizing Rock Springs at the time.

"The strangler could very well be Dr. Frank Navarone," Auggie put in when Liv wound down. "He knew Liv's mother and brother. He worked at Grandview Mental Hospital when Hague Dugan was a patient there, and he's the man identified in one of the pictures that was in the package." Liv reached for her backpack and handed it to Auggie who unzipped it, pulled out the package, then laid out the photographs.

Pelligree stood beside Auggie's desk, looking at the spread-out pictures. "You think this same guy shot up Zuma?"

"I think he was after Liv," Auggie said. "He knows she got the package and he thinks she's a threat to him."

"And that's why he went to Zuma?" Pelligree's voice was full of doubts. "How did he know about the package?"

Liv said, "I don't know. I told my brother and father and

stepmother about it, and my brother's caretaker was there when I showed the photos and my birth certificate to Hague. My neighbor, Trask Martin, also saw the contents, and then he was shot . . . and killed."

"By the same Glock that was used in the Zuma shootings," Auggie reminded her. "There's a connection between the two crimes."

"And a serial murderer . . . ?"

"I don't know," Auggie admitted. "But it's all pieces of the same puzzle."

"My brother orates at the street-level bar in his building," Liv added. "He may have inadvertently told Dr. Navarone about the package during one of his—rants. He has followers . . . maybe one of them is Navarone? Or someone who's close to him?"

"What have you got on Navarone?" D'Annibal suddenly clipped out to the black detective.

"Not much," Pelligree answered. "I've been workin' on findin' the good doctor most of the day, but it looks like he's gone to ground. Isn't practicin' anywhere that I can tell. At least not under Navarone. I have his sister's cell and address in Seattle. You want me to call, or are you plannin' a face-to-face?" he asked Auggie.

"I'll make the call."

Two more detectives entered the room, women. One had dark, curly hair and slanted blue eyes that were focused laser-like on Auggie. The other was also looking at Auggie, but her expression was harder to read. She had dark auburn hair and blue eyes and Liv realized with a jolt that this must be his twin sister.

"Guess I missed the interview," she said, and Liv picked up her underlying tension.

Auggie dug in his pocket, pulled out keys to the Pilot,

then lifted his hand in readiness before lightly tossing them to her. "Thanks."

"What about the Jeep?" she asked.

"It's been towed."

D'Annibal said, "We'll get you one from the department. Nine, Pelligree can fill you and Sandler in about this interview. What happened with Jaffe?"

Sandler lifted a hand in good-bye and said, "I'm on my way to take him to the hospital morgue now. Nine'll tell you." She left a moment later.

"Are we done for now? I want to get Liv checked out," Auggie said.

She would have protested again, but the headache that had been hanging on the edges of her brain was turning into a rager. Might as well agree to see a doctor. Beyond that, she didn't have a plan. Where was she supposed to go? Back to her apartment?

As if reading her mind, the lieutenant said, "Ms. Dugan, we would like you to be available for further questioning. Where will you be staying?"

"With me," Auggie said. "This killer's after her. He must have followed her to Halo Valley somehow. I want to keep her safe."

"Somebody musta talked," his sister suggested. "Got any idea who?"

"No." Auggie's gaze met Liv's but she let her eyes slide away. She didn't want to like him so much.

"Always gotta play the hero," his sister muttered, earning a glare from him.

"Thank you, Ms. Dugan," D'Annibal said, straightening and smoothing his tie, effectively ending the interview. With relief, Liv got to her feet, and Auggie stepped toward her, placing a hand on the small of her back, guiding her to an outer hallway.

"We'll go out the back, pick up a Jeep and head to the hospital." As he showed her the way, he added in her ear, "The police aren't so bad. We do want to help you."

Liv didn't answer. The Laurelton police had definitely treated her with more respect than the Rock Springs force, but Auggie himself had used her as a pawn.

I listen to my heart as it pounds in my ears. My mind is full of sludge and I can't think.

She went to Halo Valley! She drove there and her stud followed her!

I saw them. In the parking lot. Standing by the vehicles.

You could smell the sex from where I hid. I could see them in my mind scratching their clothes off each other, hear their howls and screams as they fucked.

I went after them. It was foolish, but I couldn't stop myself. And there she was following him in his car, obedient and willing, a slave. Changing lanes when he did, speeding up, slowing down, a good little girl.

I rammed her Jeep as hard as I could. Just like it's going to be later, when we're on the ground, rutting in the grasses, my cock filling her as my thumbs dig into her neck.

But I didn't think it through. My brain is full of worms. I lost her. I had to hide the truck and I lost her! But then, but then . . . I did think it through. I knew her next move would be to go to the police. Laurelton. That's where she would go.

I waited outside the parking lot, away from their cameras, down the street. When they drove by, I almost missed them, but I know HIM now. I recognize HIM.

And now they are at the hospital, at the emergency room.

Did I hurt you, Olivia?

Liv . . . Lllllliiiivvvvv . . . !

I will hurt you more.

Soon.

Chapter 21

Both sides of the duplex were stained dark brown with white trim and there was stacked stone formed into a planter beside each front-door entry. The units were basically back-to-back; Auggie's renters faced west while Auggie's porch and front door faced east.

Liv entered with trepidation. She'd scarcely said a word at the hospital and could have told them she didn't have a concussion; it just hadn't felt that severe, though her head did hurt. Auggie's solicitousness irritated her already-frayed nerves, and a part of her wanted to jump up and run as soon as she was pronounced good to go. Still . . . she couldn't bring herself to break away, and even though she told herself it was because yes, she believed he could keep her safe, she didn't trust herself around him. Her heart was tender when it came to him, and another part of her wanted to drag him to the bedroom and make love all night long, blocking out everything but the moment.

And maybe she was more shaken up from the accident than she'd allowed to herself. She was riding a roller coaster of emotion, a lot like she'd felt just before she'd ended up at Hathaway House. Overwhelmed. Frightened. Unsure of whom to trust.

She wanted to trust Auggie, but he'd proved himself unworthy of that trust.

What was she going to do?

"So, how do you think he knew you were going to Halo Valley?" Auggie asked as they walked to the front door together. "It wasn't random luck."

"He must know we're investigating him," she said, as he unlocked the door and swung it open, extending his arm in invitation.

Inside, she realized she was finally seeing the real August Rafferty. Though the living room was picked up, there was electronic paraphernalia shoved up against the base of a big-screen TV and overflowing onto the carpet. A recliner took center stage, its side table covered with remotes. Beyond the living room was a glimpse into a cream-colored kitchen with a door to the side yard. She could see a wooden deck covered with a grouping of lawn furniture and then grass beyond that had taken a beating from the sun.

"You think he found your whereabouts through your brother?" Auggie asked as Liv followed him through the living room into the kitchen. There was a small breakfast bar with two stools that looked into the kitchen, dividing it from a den/family room area that held a desk and two well-loved occasional chairs, an office of sorts.

Liv sat down at the breakfast bar and leaned her arms across it for support.

"I don't know," she said tiredly.

"You want to lie down?"

"Don't . . . be nice to me," she said with an edge.

"Liv . . ."

"My name's Olivia. Don't call me Liv. Or Livvie. Especially Livvie. Just don't call me anything."

"I'm sorry," he said, leaning against the counter, regarding her with a caring expression that filled her with torment.

She'd fallen in love with him. That's what this was, this sickness that invaded every cell. She'd never been in love before but she had no doubt that's what this was. Lovesick. She understood it perfectly.

"What?" he asked, responding to whatever emotions he saw crossing her face.

She'd had a breakdown. That's what had sent her to Hathaway House when she was a teenager. Her life had been careening out of control from emotions long buried, emotions that had affected her sleep, her appetite, her every waking moment. She was sent to Hathaway House as a last resort, and it had helped to meet with Dr. Yancy and learn her triggers. She'd learned how debilitating her own emotions could be, and she'd become careful to keep herself under control. But these feelings for Auggie . . . Detective August Rafferty . . . were huge. She felt almost swallowed up by them, and she wouldn't be able to hide her love for him much longer.

"Are you going to call Navarone's sister?" she asked now, keeping her gaze centered away from his.

"I'm sorry about the deception," he began again. "You weren't willing to go to the police——"

"I know why you did it," she cut him off, her voice brittle. "We don't have to cover that again. I just want to get Navarone."

"I have feelings for you," he said, unwilling to give it up.

"I can almost remember Navarone, from Hathaway House. Enough, anyway. He made me uncomfortable and I can't really say why. He never did anything to me. I just thought he was—not being honest."

"Liv, I—"

"DON'T CALL ME THAT!"

Silence fell between them. He closed his eyes as if in pain, then inhaled, opened them again, and said in a voice nearly devoid of emotion, "I'll phone Angela Navarone now."

She listened while he placed the call, exhaustion sweeping over her. She needed to lie down. Beyond the hard lump at her hairline, she also now felt a number of growing bruises, especially around her chest, which had rammed into the steering wheel as well.

Getting to her feet, she didn't know where to go. Upstairs? To one of the bedrooms. That felt too intimate. Instead she chose the living-room recliner and settled herself into it with a sigh of capitulation. She could do nothing about Auggie and her feelings for him, at least not now.

His conversation wasn't going well, by the sounds of it. He kept trying to attack the subject of Angela Navarone's brother from different sides, but she didn't seem to be offering up much. Eventually, she must have hung up because he clicked off his cell and came into the living room, looking down on her, his expression dark.

"She says she doesn't know where he is. Maybe she doesn't. But there was something she was holding back."

"What do you want to do?"

"Make love to you and go see her tomorrow."

Liv tightened her jaw and when he perched on the arm of her chair, she refused to meet his gaze.

"What do you want to do?" he asked her.

"Sleep for a thousand years."

"How about twelve hours? Are you hungry? I could get us something to eat—"

"Don't go." The words just popped out before she could stop them. His reaction was to gently brush back her hair with his fingers and place a warm, lingering kiss on her forehead.

She tried not to react but it was impossible. Turning her gaze up to his, she saw a blue light of desire in his eyes and suspected her own eyes reflected the same.

"God, Liv . . . Olivia . . . what the . . ." He pulled her out of the chair, grabbing her arms and bringing her to her feet.

Whatever he'd planned to say was lost beneath his mouth pressing down on hers. She clung to him for support, then from desire.

Tomorrow. Tomorrow she would be stronger.

She wrapped her hand around his neck, strengthened the kiss until they were straining against each other and sinking to the floor as one.

They left for Seattle at daybreak, stopping at a breakfast spot in Kalama, Washington, that promised "the best waffles you will ever eat," which neither of them ordered. Liv managed toast, coffee and one soft-boiled egg. Auggie dug into bacon, eggs and hash browns.

"You need to keep your strength up," he said, pointing at her with a piece of bacon.

They'd taken the department-issued Jeep, but climbing inside it reminded Liv that very, very soon she was going to have to get her own car, switch to a new apartment—there was no way she could stay there after Trask's death—and start another life.

But not today.

"This is more than enough," Liv told him, gesturing to her meal.

"If you're six years old, maybe."

Auggie had kept a close eye on the rearview mirror, just in case someone had somehow learned of their plans, though he didn't see how that could be. He hadn't told anyone in the department what they were doing. He'd just related to Pelligree that he'd made contact and was following up, so that he didn't double up the work. Liv had asked him if they expected him to come in, but he'd said that he would let D'Annibal know later.

It didn't appear that anyone was following them. No suspicious vehicles were loitering around the restaurant and none had taken the off-ramp after them for a good ten minutes; Auggie had stopped and counted.

Liv was specifically shoving thoughts of last night's lovemaking to one side of her brain. If her mind touched on moments with him, her attention shattered and though she would love to relive what they'd shared, she knew it was a lie and would only be a sweet torture. She had to let it go. Especially now, when her attention needed to be on the matter at hand.

The department Jeep was equipped with GPS and they found Angela Navarone's apartment on the south side of Seattle fairly quickly. She wasn't home. Undaunted, Auggie checked in with the department to see where she worked, which turned out to be Southcenter Mall at an upscale boutique that specialized in women's clothing. As they walked in, a dark-haired woman in her fifties was showing a younger woman a leather handbag by Michael Kors. There didn't appear to be anyone else around at the moment so it was a good guess the saleslady was Angela Navarone.

Auggie waited until their transaction was finished; the younger woman plopped down payment with a credit card, then grabbed her package and headed out. Liv and Auggie moved to the register as one and the woman turned her attention to Auggie, the fish out of water in this scenario.

"Ms. Navarone? I'm Detective Rafferty. I spoke to you on the phone yesterday."

She went utterly still, then turned her dark gaze to Liv, her eyes sliding to the backpack Liv had slung over her arm. Inside was the package Liv had gotten from her mother, though Auggie had removed her gun and put it in a drawer in the kitchen before they'd taken off.

"I told you I don't know where my brother is," Angela said, turning her attention back to Auggie. "I'm working."

"Maybe we can talk on your break," Auggie said easily.

She lowered her eyes, obviously thinking hard, then stole

a glance at the slim silver watch on her left forearm. "Julia comes on at eleven. I suppose I could take a break then."

"Almost that now," Auggie said. "We'll be outside."

They walked out to a bench in the mall.

"What if she's telling the truth, and she doesn't know where he is?" Liv asked.

Auggie was already punching a number into his cell phone. "I'll check in with Weasel."

He had to leave a message with Pelligree, then he phoned D'Annibal and talked to the lieutenant for a bit. A scowl crossed his features and after he hung up, he swore under his breath.

"What?" Liv asked, her heart clutching a bit.

"My sister. She's . . . not happy with me."

"Because you took her car?" Auggie had given Liv the recap of how he'd wrangled his sister's Pilot from her.

"More because I took her investigation. Not that she's not wrapped up in something else, but she hasn't liked the way I've handled things." He shot Liv a smile that sent a thrill through her veins. Dangerous, dangerous stuff.

"Why is she called Nine?"

"Ninth month. When she was born. That's why she's September."

Liv stared at him. "She was born in September? Aren't you twins? I thought you were named August because . . ." She trailed off in confusion.

"We are twins, born on each side of midnight, August 31. It's a crazy, crazy thing."

"I know crazy," she said, and he smiled and pressed a kiss into her hair, which elevated her pulse.

"My parents just happened to like naming their children after months. My older brother and sisters were named March, May and July. Of course, my parents realized they were going to have to break that tradition when they found out they were having twins, but nope. Guess again. According to my mother, we could have both been born in August, but my father . . . has a way of getting what he wants, so they delayed the process just long enough for my sister to be born in September."

"What if you'd been born last, your sister first?"

"My guess is, my name would be September. There's no logic to it."

"Are you close with your family?"

"I'm close with my twin," was his careful answer. "At least most of the time."

Angela Navarone stepped from the boutique and spied them sitting on the bench. Auggie got up and offered her a seat. She wanted to refuse, but after a moment she sank onto the bench gratefully, taking off one shoe and massaging her foot. "I knew I was going to regret wearing these today. The heel's too high to work in."

Liv wasn't much of a fashion maven, but after seeing the purse, she made a stab at it. "Are those Michael Kors?"

"Ferragamos." She wiggled the toes on her free foot and sighed. "Okay, Detective, why are you looking for my brother? I'm not on good terms with him." She arched a brow at Liv. "And how do you fit in?"

I think your brother's a serial murderer who's been stalking me.

Liv shot Auggie a look, wondering how she should respond. He opened his mouth to answer for her, but she decided to take things into her own hands. "My name's Olivia Dugan. I think your brother was a visiting doctor at Hathaway House when I was there in my teens."

She considered. "Hathaway House . . . it's possible."

"You know of it, then," Liv said.

"Frank worked at a number of hospitals, never long anywhere. His methods were controversial, and honestly . . ." She hesitated, chewing on her lip a bit before she caught herself. "My brother's brilliant. There's no question about that. But he's always been too *invested* in his own brilliance. Do you understand? There's an arrogance there. He won't listen to anyone else. It's always been his downfall."

"He was working at Halo Valley Security Hospital the last we know," Auggie said.

"He was fired for nearly killing a patient," she stated flatly. "Some experiment that went wrong. Then the patient died and he lost his medical license, and now I don't know where he is. Glenda hasn't seen him, either."

"Glenda?" Auggie asked.

"My daughter. His niece. My marriage lasted about five minutes, but the one good thing that came out of it was Glenda. She never had much of a relationship with her father, but she connected with Frank. This was all before his mind started failing him, you understand. I thought maybe he'd contact Glenda after he lost his license, but he hasn't. Glenda lives in the Portland area and that's where Frank was, the last I heard."

"Can you give us her address?" Auggie asked.

She made a face. "I suppose. Do you have a notepad, or something?"

Liv reached into her backpack, her hand closing over the manila envelope from her mother. She pulled it out and a pen and invited Angela to write her daughter's address and phone number on the face of it.

"Laurelton," Liv said in surprise.

"Yes. Why? Something wrong?" she asked quickly.

"Her last name is Tripp," Auggie observed.

"Yes, that was my husband's name." Angela was focused on Liv, a frown on her face. "What is it you want?" she demanded. To Auggie, she asked, "You think my brother's done something . . . criminal?"

Liv opened the package and pulled out the photographs, passing the one with the man stalking to the camera to

Angela. She reared back a bit, holding the picture away from herself as if it could harm her somehow.

"Where did you get this?" she demanded.

"My mother sent it to me. She's—"

"Dugan," Angela said as if it were a revelation. "Your mother's Deborah Dugan. The woman who hanged herself," she said, pointing to the picture of Liv's mother.

"The man in the photo . . . is he your brother?" Auggie asked when Liv didn't immediately respond.

She nodded slowly. "Yes, that's Frank." She turned to Liv again, staring at her. "So, you're Deborah and Albert's daughter."

"That's right." Liv's heart was fluttering with a nameless fear.

"How do you know the Dugans?" Auggie asked.

"Oh, I didn't. I knew of them from Frank. He was still in love with your mother when this picture was taken."

"Still?" Liv asked.

"Albert stole her away from Frank, and he never forgave him."

"What?" Liv asked faintly.

"Ah, you didn't know. Hmm . . . maybe your mother wanted you to know. Maybe that's why she sent these to you?" She flipped through the other photos, and said, "That's poor Sylvia Parmiter, and that's her husband . . . um . . . Dan, I think. Maybe Don. They all were part of a larger group of friends. I don't see the LeBlancs here, though."

"The *LeBlancs?*" Liv repeated. Her ears were roaring.

"Everett and Patsy LeBlanc. They were friends of Frank's, and that's how they met Deborah."

"I know the LeBlancs. I just didn't know my mother did," Liv heard herself squeak.

"Well, I think so. At least Patsy and Deborah were friends. Frank said as much to me, once, when he was in one of his dark moods." She inclined her head. "There was a time I thought Frank was seeing your mother again. Something he said clued me in, but when I asked him about it he flatly denied it. Deborah was married to Albert by then, so maybe not."

Liv's head was reeling. It was more information than she could take in all at once.

"Why did you say 'poor' Sylvia Parmiter?" Auggie asked.

"I don't know if you remember, but there was a serial killer in the area of Rock Springs about that time. He strangled a number of women and left them in fields and ditches and in the foothills." She lifted a hand and dropped it into her lap, unaware of both Auggie and Liv's shock. "Sylvia was one of his victims."

As if she suddenly heard the accusation in her words, her hand flew upward. "That's not what this is about, is it? My brother did not kill those women! That was hysteria. Nothing more!"

"At the time, there was the suggestion that your brother was the serial killer?" Auggie asked carefully while Liv gripped the arm of the bench.

"Oh, people were hysterical. All kinds of accusations were thrown around! It was a witch hunt, and I always thought Albert was behind it!" Angela practically cried. "He was jealous of Frank. And I'm sure Patsy had something to do with it, too. She didn't like Frank. But my brother was innocent of all charges!"

"Patsy didn't like Frank?" Liv repeated.

"And he didn't like her much, either. Why do you think he's coming after her for the camera? He didn't want her taking his picture."

Everything rearranged itself in Liv's head. Her parents. Their relationship with each other and with their friends. Patsy LeBlanc Owens. Angela was a wealth of information but she didn't seem to know that Patsy was Liv's birth mother.

"You're saying Patsy LeBlanc took this picture?" Auggie repeated.

"I've seen this picture before. It's from Frank's camera. He must've given the photos to Deborah." She looked from Liv to Auggie and back again. "Patsy has always wanted to crucify my brother. I'm surprised you haven't talked to her yet. She still lives in the Rock Springs area, as far as I know. Married another guy. Owens. Barkley Owens. Go ask her, if you want more information, just don't believe a word she says about Frank."

The trip back down the freeway from Seattle to Portland was about three-and-a-half hours, but it went by in a flash. Liv was full of questions that she didn't know how to start asking. Auggie kept looking at her, checking to see how she was doing, but she was incapable of knowing. He alternately checked with Wes "Weasel" Pelligree, who had asked for a warrant for Navarone's records since Halo Valley Security Hospital had been less than approachable without one.

Liv could hear both sides of the conversation, and when Pelligree said, "I've got a theory," though Auggie tried like mad to learn what it was, the detective wouldn't say. "I should know by the time you get back," was all he would answer.

They were crossing the Glenn Jackson Bridge, which spanned the Columbia between Washington and Oregon, when Liv finally said, "I want to go see Patsy Owens."

"Now?"

"She lied to us about Navarone. Maybe she knows where he is."

He checked the clock on the dashboard, then phoned Pelligree once more. "I'm going to be a little later than I originally thought. Come on. Tell me what you've got." A pause, while he listened, then, "Damn you, Weasel. I'm taking a detour to Rock Springs and when I get back, you're talking."

"I should call my father, too," Liv said. "See what he has to say about my mother and . . . Navarone." He handed her the cell, but she didn't use it. "I'll probably get Lorinda, and I just don't think I have the energy to talk to her."

"Let's talk to Patsy and see where we are."

"Okay."

September stared at the bulletin board by Wes Pelligree's desk with Sheila Dempsey and Emmy Decatur's pictures. She then looked down at the opened file in her hands. The carved DO UNTO OTHERS AS SHE DID TO ME was clearly visible on the crime-scene photos of Decatur.

Wes was still making phone calls, amassing information that had to do with Olivia Dugan and the Zuma case. She couldn't help wishing she were still part of it, though D'Annibal had not been wrong. The Do Unto Others case was big, too. Very big. There was no reason to feel slighted. None at all.

"Let me ask you somethin'," Wes said to September as he hung up the phone and leaned back in his chair. "I can't stir up anyone named Dr. Frank Navarone. It's like he's dead. But there's a Dr. Frank Navato who does psychological counselin' out of his home. I thought it was an office, but it's a rental house on the east side. A separate buildin', a garage, that the home owners apparently renovated and rent out for some extra income."

"You think Novato is Dr. Navarone." She'd been given

the basic outline of the scope of Auggie's investigation, but
no serious details.

He nodded. "Suppose, after he lost his license, Navarone
decided to just fake it. Change his name and keep on goin'.
Sure, he's vulnerable to discovery, but maybe his clients
even know. Or, don't care. He's unorthodox, and there's apparently enough negligence or disregardin' of the rules or
whatever to yank his license, but he was never convicted of
a crime. So, he hangs out his shingle and starts up again.
Maybe not with all the accolades, or hospital trappin's, but
the guy's gotta make a livin', right?"

"And Navarone is the guy Auggie likes for Zuma and
the Trask Martin homicide."

"Crazy Eight thinks he could also be the serial strangler from Rock Springs about twenty years ago," he reminded her.

"Don't call him that. Please, Wes . . . Weasel. I'm mad at
him. I don't want him to be mad back."

"Chicken." He grinned.

"Aren't you a little upset that our cases got switched?"

"Nah, your brother's gonna crack this one with my su-
perlative help, and I'll be back on the case with you before
you know it."

September managed a smile. "You think Navarone's
good for the Zuma massacre?"

"I'm leanin' that way."

"Where is Auggie?"

He glanced at the clock. It was three-thirty. "Rock Springs."

Chapter 22

Liv rang the doorbell to the Owens house, shaking a bit inside. They'd wasted valuable time and Navarone had run her off the road since Patsy had *neglected* to tell them what she knew.

"She could be at a job," Auggie pointed out.

"Maybe." Liv pressed the bell again, listening to the chimes.

It took longer than it probably should have; Patsy was apparently in no hurry to answer the door. But then she did, swinging it slowly open. She was in shorts and a tank top and sweat was beaded on her face. Liv felt a wave of sweltering heat hit her from the inside.

"The air conditioner wasn't much, but it died for good last night," Patsy said, standing back to allow them inside.

"You don't seem surprised to see us," Auggie observed.

Patsy gestured for them to take a seat, but Liv ignored her and jumped right in. "You knew the man in the photo was Frank Navarone. Why did you lie?"

"The mad doctor?" Patsy smiled faintly. "I just didn't want to relive those days, I guess."

"You took the picture!" Liv accused her.

The stuffiness inside the house was horrendous. Patsy

had the windows open from the kitchen, but there was no breeze. Liv felt practically starved for oxygen and she could feel a trickle of sweat collect between her breasts.

"Please sit down," Patsy said, taking her original chair from the last time they were there. Auggie complied, and Liv reluctantly followed suit. "This is embarrassing. I just really didn't want to talk about it. I had a real thing for Frank, but he was in love with Deborah. It was obvious."

"You had a thing for him?" Liv questioned. "Angela Navarone said you didn't like him, and not to believe anything you said about him."

"Unfortunately that's not true," Patsy wagged her head slowly from side to side. "I did like him. Too much. Sounds like she's just trying to protect him."

"You were friends with the Dugans? Liv's . . . Olivia's . . . adoptive parents?" Auggie questioned.

Patsy looked at him, then down at her clasped hands, then over to Liv. "This isn't going to sound good. I'm sorry. You're . . . my daughter . . . and I just didn't want you to think bad of me. I was so overwhelmed when you came here the first time. . . ."

Liv wanted to say so much; her emotions were threatening to spill over into a fulminating fury. Auggie intervened quickly, as if aware of her conflict, "Tell us about Navarone."

"First, let me say that Deborah Dugan was a lovely person. Really. A very lovely person, and I forced a friendship on her, I guess you'd say. I never told her I was your mother," Patsy said.

"My birth mother," Liv corrected her.

She nodded. "Yes. I know. I made her acquaintance because I wanted to know you, and I wanted to know her, and I got kind of caught up in it all. Everett and I were over, and it was all I had. It felt like it was all I had, y'know?"

Liv didn't trust herself to answer, but Auggie said, "Go on."

"I took the photographs with Frank's camera and he wasn't happy about it at all. Didn't want his picture taken. But in the end Deborah must've got them somehow. I didn't know she had your birth certificate, too. I don't know when that happened. She probably got it from the hospital."

"With the help of Dr. Navarone?" Auggie guessed.

"I guess when she found out . . . that Everett and I were your biological parents . . . that's when it all sorta fell apart and we stopped being friends." Patsy's eyes closed in defeat. "I never really knew what happened. One day we were friends, the next we weren't. I always kinda thought maybe it was because of Sylvia Parmiter's murder."

"Tell us about that," Auggie said.

"Not much to tell," she said, shaking her head. "She was one of the strangler's victims. Up until Sylvia we all thought we were safe. That he was only targeting prostitutes, y'know. From the big city. Rock Springs was just the dumping grounds, out here in the boonies. But then after they found her, it was all so real. One of our own, and I started wondering if maybe the reason the bodies were dumped here was because the killer was familiar with the area. I think we all felt that way, but nobody would admit to it."

"You started thinking it was Navarone," Auggie said.

"No . . . no." She shook her head, but it was almost like she was still trying to convince herself. "But then, Deborah hanged herself, and that was the end. Frank left town. Everett and I were already broken up. Albert found Lorinda and it was just—over."

"You never thought Frank Navarone was the strangler?" Liv asked quietly.

"How could he be? I just . . ." Patsy rubbed her clasped hands together. "But I always wondered, y'know, if Deborah thought so . . . and maybe that's why she hanged herself? Because she really did love him, but thought . . . oh, I don't know."

That was not what Liv wanted to hear. She needed to believe her mother was murdered. That her death had not been a choice. "From what Angela Navarone said, my mother chose my father over him. Why would she hang herself?"

"You don't think it was suicide," Patsy said on a note of discovery.

"I don't know." Liv was firm.

A moment passed, then Patsy asked, "Angela Navarone really said she thought I hated Frank? I wonder what he told her that made her think that."

"Do you have any idea where he is today?" Auggie asked. "Any idea at all?"

"I thought he was at Halo Valley. That's the last I heard. When I married Barkley, I let all that go. I didn't really want to think about it anymore, y'know? I'm sorry I didn't tell you everything on Sunday."

Liv got to her feet. She was anxious to get out of this hot, little house. She felt slightly light-headed, and was glad to feel Auggie's steadying hand on her arm.

"One more thing, I don't know if it matters. It was just a rumor," Patsy said at the door.

On the porch Liv closed her eyes to the blinding sun and heard Auggie ask, "What?"

"Deborah told me once that she thought Hague might be Frank's, not Albert's. I don't think either Frank or Albert ever knew for sure. . . ."

"Hello, Detective Rafferty. This is Pauline Kirby from Channel Seven News. I was told you are the person in charge of the murder investigation into the death of Emmy Decatur. Is that correct?"

September held the receiver in her hand and stared across the station at Wes for help, but Wes was on the

phone, still searching for Navarone. George was tuned into
his computer, as ever, and Gretchen wasn't around. D'Annibal was in his office, but a hell of a lot of good that would
do her; he was the one who'd sicced Pauline on her in the
first place.

"Yes, that's correct."

"We understand that this homicide has similarities to the
murder of Sheila Dempsey earlier this year."

"That is also correct."

"Our team is meeting at six o'clock at the site where the
second homicide victim, Emmy Decatur, was found. We
want to invite you to take this opportunity to soothe the
public. Let them know the Laurelton police are doing everything in their power to find this sadistic killer."

September pictured the newswoman: dark-haired, tense,
pushy, brittle, with perfect hair and a perfect smile. If she
accepted the invitation, she wondered how she herself
would look on video, then immediately thrust that aside.
Who cared, really. To hell with it. If D'Annibal wanted her
to be the face for the department, she would. And she would
stop complaining.

"I'll be there," she said succinctly. Wes had hung up
and was already heading out when she ended her call.
She would have liked to talk to him, but felt a little like the
"uninvited." George gave her a questioning look, and she
answered, "Pauline Kirby."

He snorted in amusement. "You'll be the darling of television."

"Oh, goody."

Half an hour later Auggie and Olivia Dugan blew into
the police station again. They appeared to be joined at the
hip. September surreptitiously observed them as they approached. Something was going on there. She just wasn't
sure what. Dugan didn't look all that happy. She was a little
pale, a little remote, and there was a quality about her that

seemed to shout that, given the slightest provocation, she was going to run like a rabbit.

"Where's Weasel?" Auggie demanded.

"Nice to see you too," September said. "You just missed him. He's working on finding your Dr. Navarone, the last I heard."

"I know. What's he got?"

"I don't know. Give him a call. He thinks Navarone may be using an assumed name: Novato."

"Novato," Auggie repeated, glancing at Dugan. "Does he know where he is?"

"Like I said, call him."

Auggie was already punching numbers into his cell as he asked Dugan, "Can I get you some water? Coffee? I can take you down to the staff room."

Whoa, September thought. *Kind of proprietary, even for her brother.*

"No, thanks. I'm fine."

Olivia Dugan looked anything but fine, in September's opinion. She appeared tense, tired and anxious. Small wonder, if this Navarone was guilty of half the crimes they were laying at his feet. The woman was lucky she'd escaped Zuma Software with her life.

Auggie was talking to Wes, and when he clicked off, his expression was hard. He didn't say anything for an instant or two, then brought himself back to the moment. "Weasel has an address. He and I are planning to pay the doctor a visit. Liv . . . Olivia . . . I'll take you back to—"

"No, no. I'm going with you," she said, showing more spunk than September would have credited her with.

"—my place. You're not coming along."

"I don't want to leave you," she said tautly.

Auggie's blue eyes slid a glance September's way. "Don't mind me," she said, holding up her hands in surrender.

"Come on," he said to Dugan, helping her to her feet.

He was regarding the lovely Ms. Dugan with a thoughtful exasperation that did not bode well, so September reminded him, "She can't go with you."

Olivia Dugan turned and gave her a *look*.

George was grinning across the room as Auggie said tightly to September, "I can handle this."

"Fine. Have at it. I'm outta here," she said with a shrug. "I've got an interview."

"When? What kind of interview?" Auggie demanded.

"Six. Check the Channel Seven news. Maybe you'll see my bright shining face on TV."

"*Pauline Kirby?*"

"You got a complaint, take it to our boss," she said, hiking a thumb in the direction of D'Annibal's office as she gathered her identification and firearm, then walked down the hall to the staff-room lockers where she retrieved her purse with its small makeup bag tucked inside. She next headed to the women's room. No sense going on television without looking her best.

"I'm not going back to your place," Liv stated firmly when they were outside and heading to his Jeep.

"This guy's a killer. Probably stalked you for years. That's what *you* said, not me. Let me handle this from here," Auggie responded.

"I want to face him," she said. "I want to look in his eyes and tell him that it's over."

"We don't know enough. Wait till we bring him in for questioning."

"Hell, no."

"Liv—Olivia—whatever," he said through his teeth as they climbed inside the vehicle.

"You can call me Liv," she said tautly.

"Oh, now I can call you Liv. When you want something.

Keep reminding me as the rules change. I don't want you anywhere near Navarone."

"I get that, but I don't care. I'm not going back to your house."

"Then stay here at the station."

"No."

"You're not going to Navarone's," he gritted out, thrusting the key into the ignition.

"I don't want to be away from you!" she shouted back. "I'm *afraid*. Do you *get that?*"

He paused, his hand still on the key. "Liv . . ." he said.

"Please. I'll wait in the car. Down the block. I don't care. I just need to be near you until he's captured. Sorry. I know what that sounds like, and I wish I were stronger, but I can't be yet."

"It's not safe. . . ."

"It's better than being alone," she argued.

He shook his head, not looking at her. A moment later he fired the ignition and slowly turned the Jeep out of the lot.

"Where are we going?" she asked anxiously.

"To meet Weasel," he said, sounding exasperated. "That's what you want, right?"

"Thank you."

His answer was a string of swear words beneath his breath that she couldn't quite make out, which was probably for the best.

September reached the site where Emmy Decatur had been found and realized the two hikers who'd discovered the body were there and prepped and ready for the camera, too. Pauline was talking to them like they were old friends, and the videographer was standing by, his camera on his shoulder.

Uh-oh. Ambush, September thought, as she pulled her

Pilot to a stop at the edge of the gravel access road and climbed out. Spying her, Pauline waved and walked carefully across the field in her expensive-looking black pumps. "Detective Rafferty!" she greeted with a wide smile.

September did a mental inventory of her black pants, black, V-necked T-shirt and light gray, linen jacket. It was sweltering, but she sure as hell wasn't going to go on camera and have to worry about pitting out. She'd dragged the jacket out of her locker and given it a few snaps to clear the wrinkles . . . she hoped.

"Come on over," Pauline invited, glancing at her watch. "I'd like to get this tape ready for the ten o'clock news." She showed September where she wanted her to stand, then said, "We've already done the intro, so we're ready for you."

September wondered what that intro was. Since the hikers didn't seem to be setting up, she suspected they'd already spoken.

Peachy.

If there was one thing Pauline Kirby knew it was good television. When Lieutenant D'Annibal—sly politician-type that he was—had said he would put her in touch with one of the investigators on the Decatur homicide, she'd expected to be given someone who would make the Laurelton Police Department look good, in the public-opinion sense. What she hadn't expected was to be delivered someone so attractive. Dark auburn hair, large and serious blue eyes, a trim figure that looked hard, as if she worked out regularly, a wide mouth.

And young . . .

It was all Pauline could do not to touch a hand to her hair, though she knew every strand was in place because her hairstylist sprayed the hell out of it.

Little did Detective Rafferty know what she had in store

for her. Pauline had friends in high places, all over the region. Well, maybe not friends, exactly, but sources. She even had a few with the Portland PD and had curried favor with someone at Laurelton, too.

As if catching a whiff of what was to come, Rafferty said, "I can't tell you much more about the investigation than you already know."

"I just need some corroboration. Darrell . . ." She signaled her cameraman without looking at him. She and Darrell understood each other and there was no need to ask him to set the shot.

He lifted the camera to his eye. They were going handheld. Gave the video a little more jerky-but-immediate quality that played well to the public. The hikers were off to one side, out of the shot.

Pauline started slowly, getting Rafferty to reiterate the circumstances that brought Decatur's body to their attention, and also the connection made with Sheila Dempsey. When the detective was a little more relaxed, she asked, "We understand there were markings on the bodies. Words."

Rafferty's eyes slid off camera, to where the hikers stood. Then she looked directly at Pauline. "Cause of death was strangulation in both cases."

"But there were markings . . ." Pauline looked over to the two hikers whom she'd introduced in the intro. "There were words, cut into Emmy Decatur's torso. 'Do Unto Others As She Did To Me,' right?" Brian, the male hiker, nodded and Pauline felt rather than saw Darrell pull back the camera lens to include him. "Can you confirm, Detective Rafferty?"

"Not at this time."

"You're afraid of a panic? That people will freak out when they learn there's a serial killer whose signature is cutting a phrase into his victims' skin? Well, I think this is information we all need to know." She looked directly at the camera, her expression super-serious. "Young women are being murdered and their bodies used as a crude message." She turned back to Rafferty. "What are you doing to protect us, besides keeping the truth to yourselves?"

"There's an ongoing, full-scale investigation in progress," Rafferty said smartly.

"Really? Excuse me, Detective, but how can that be, given the other still-unsolved major case, the Zuma Software Massacre? Is that an ongoing, full-scale investigation, too?"

"Yes." Rafferty's lips had tightened.

"Do you have the manpower for both? We all know there have been major slashes to government budgets and that includes law enforcement as well. Can you guarantee our safety? I mean, seriously?"

"Laurelton PD, in conjunction with the Winslow County Sheriff's Department and Portland PD, has qualified personnel working hard on both cases. We—"

"But has progress been made *anywhere?*"

"Yes, of course."

"On Zuma, or the Do Unto Others killer?"

"Both," she said. "I'm sure you understand we can't reveal details that would jeopardize—"

"What about Dr. Frank Navarone?" Pauline asked, almost hearing the descending whistle of the dropping bomb. Blindsided, Detective Rafferty blinked once. Perfect!

Pauline waited, and after a long moment, Rafferty said, "Dr. Navarone is a person of interest."

"In which case?" Pauline asked, loving it.

"The Zuma Software shootings," she said after another pause.

Oh, it was delicious!

With that Pauline turned back to the camera and Darrell zoomed in on her face. "It may be just as Detective Rafferty suggests, that the police are doing everything they can—" Her tone suggested otherwise. "—but can we trust our lives to an undermanned, overworked local police force? There's a killer out there. Likely more than one. Take care and lock your doors. . . ."

Weasel and Auggie headed up the drive to the garage apartment that Dr. Frank Novato was renting in an older section of southeast Portland. Bubbles stood in pools of tar from broken-down asphalt and they stepped carefully toward the brick walkway that ran to the front door.

Auggie was tense. They had no warrant. This was really a reconnaissance trip; hopefully the doctor would be willing to talk to them. If not, they would have to go through proper channels, and Auggie was already chafing at the time waste, even though it hadn't happened yet.

"This guy Dr. Frankenstein or Dr. Feelgood?" Weasel asked.

"More like a Freud–Timothy Leary combo, from what I get."

"And maybe the Boston Strangler?"

"That, too."

The converted garage apartment was a separate building in front of the main house by about ten yards. The brick walkway was about ten feet from the asphalt drive to the front door. Pampas grass leaned forward like greeters and Auggie pushed at it as he walked to the door, his heart rate elevating. Adrenaline coursed through his veins. His Glock was in a holster under his arm, concealed by the navy jacket he kept at the station for whenever he needed to hide his weapon. With the blue T-shirt and jeans under the jacket, he supposed he looked like a guy working "casual Friday."

Except it was Tuesday.

He knocked and Weasel stood a little in front of Auggie to the left, visible but ready to push his way in if necessary.

There was a long wait, and then the door opened. A man

with oiled down gray hair and dark, suspicious eyes stood in the aperture. Dr. Navarone, Auggie thought, his pulse spiking.

"Dr. Novato?" he asked.

"I have a session. You'll have to come back later." He tried to shut the door, but Weasel moved quickly, his foot in the way. "I'm not buying anything!" Navarone shouted.

Auggie pulled out his badge and said, "Detective Rafferty with the Laurelton Police Department. We'd like to ask you a few questions."

"Get a warrant!" He slammed the door against Weasel's foot.

"We will if we have to," Auggie warned. "We just want to ask some questions!"

"Fuck you." This time when he hauled the door back to slam it, Weasel moved back. *Bam!* The door shuddered as it slammed shut.

"Did you see that?" Weasel asked, inclining his head to the apartment.

"You mean the hypodermic on the table, or the woman passed out on the couch?"

"Probable cause." Weasel was grim.

"Dr. Novato!" Auggie called through the paneling. "I'm calling 911. Open up, or we'll break this door down! You have till the count of three!"

Liv was baking in the car. The events of the past week— her head injury, bruises and lack of sleep—all made her feel physically ill. She was parked around the corner from Navarone's apartment. Part of her was glad to be safely out of range. Another part worried something awful would happen.

Bam! She heard the sound of a door slamming. She'd rolled down the window and now she stuck her head out, listening. Someone was beating on a door. Then there was yelling. Then *blam, blam*.

Gunshots.

Throwing open the door, she was running to the corner, skidding around, before she even considered her own safety. The front door to the apartment was wide open. There was a body lying half-in, half-out of it, a man's jean-clad legs visible, his upper body disappearing inside.

Auggie . . . Her heart lurched painfully. No, the shoes were wrong. *Weasel!*

Liv ran forward, then stopped, looking around for help. She wanted to run pell-mell inside, but knew what a bad idea that was.

She needed a phone. Auggie had the cell. She glanced around quickly. A house . . . a neighbor . . . everything looked hot and dead and empty.

Somewhere someone was moaning. Then shouts. She heard Auggie's voice, yelling, "Put it down! Put it down or I'll shoot. Put it down, so help me God!"

A clunk and then silence. Then a scuffle. And in the distance, the WOO-woo, WOO-woo of an approaching siren.

A moment later a middle-aged man came staggering out of the apartment, hands on his head, shrieking and sputtering, throwing spittle with each syllable. Navarone! Behind him, Auggie had a Glock aimed between the man's shoulder blades.

"Give me a reason, you cocksucker," Auggie growled through his teeth. He saw Liv and his mouth hardened even further. "Make a move toward her and I'll kill you!"

"No, no . . . I don't know what you want . . . she's fine . . . she's fine . . ." He fell to his knees on the brick path, catching himself with his hands. "You'll pay for this!"

It was Dr. Navarone, Liv thought faintly. It was. From Hathaway House. From the picture.

"Shut up! Shut up!" Auggie yelled as the ambulance

screamed down the street and came to a screeching halt.
"You shot a police officer, asshole!"

Liv looked over at Weasel, whose legs were moving in
pain. *Please,* she thought. *Please . . .*

EMTs rushed out of the ambulance and raced to Weasel.
A Portland prowler pulled up, spilling out a couple of uni-
forms who aimed their guns at Navarone and Auggie, until
Auggie carefully set his gun down, said, "I'm Detective
Rafferty with the Laurelton PD," and gingerly pulled out
his ID.

Chapter 23

By the time September got back from her interview all hell had broken loose around the station. "What? What?" she asked as George and Gretchen were crowded into D'Annibal's office and the lieutenant was on the phone.

"Pelligree's been shot. They've taken him to Providence." D'Annibal was grabbing his jacket from the coat tree behind him and smoothing his tie, his actions automatic, his gaze in the middle distance.

"Shit," September whispered. "Is he all right? What happened?"

"Gunshot wound to the abdomen," George said soberly. "He's heading for surgery."

"Navarone?" September asked, her mouth dry, her heart thundering in her ears. "My God . . . Auggie?"

"He's fine. He contained Navarone after the doctor shot Wes." D'Annibal was already halfway out the door.

"I'm going," Gretchen said.

"No." D'Annibal stopped. "Stay here. Take the calls. The press is going to be on our necks. "George, Nine . . . both of you, too."

Then he was gone.

"Jesus," George said, heading back to his desk and

dropping heavily into his chair. His phone rang and he glanced at it dully, picking up and speaking into the phone in a monotone, clearly already answering questions of the press.

Gretchen was staring at the wall, her hands clenched, her slanted blue eyes glittering with suppressed anger. "If Weasel . . . if . . . that fucker hurt him bad . . . maybe . . . killed . . ."

"Don't say it," September said soberly. "Just don't say it."

Auggie and Liv were in the waiting room, both of them standing, neither being able to sit still. Auggie's call to 911 had brought the cavalry, but he was kicking himself for not being able to stop Navarone before that first wild shot went off and Pelligree took the hit.

"Damn," he said for about the fiftieth time, but with less energy now as worry replaced fury.

"He's going to be all right," Liv said. "No vital organs hit."

"I took my eyes away. All I saw was the woman. I thought she was dead. But he reached for the gun on the shelf."

"Auggie, it's all right. She's all right, and he's going to be all right," she said, parroting the doctor. "She was drugged with some kind of mind expander. Psychotropic drugs. But she's going to be okay, and Detective Pelligree isn't going to die."

D'Annibal appeared through the whoosh of the ER's sliding-glass doors.

"He's in surgery?" he asked Auggie.

"Yep."

"Where's Navarone?"

"Portland PD took him in. I want to talk to him," Auggie said pointedly.

"It's your case. Go after him," D'Annibal said. He looked to Olivia. "Excuse me, Ms. Dugan, but what are you doing here?"

There was nothing warm and fuzzy about his tone. And while she searched for an answer, Auggie said, "I'll take her home before I interview Navarone."

Interior double doors that could only be accessed by a card key or code suddenly opened, allowing a glimpse into further hallways and rooms, and a doctor stepped into the waiting room. Spying Auggie, he came forward and directed his report to him. "Surgery's going well. We removed the bullet which was lodged in Mr. Pelligree's hipbone, and cut out a piece of disrupted lower intestine. We're now stitching him back together. Everything looks good."

"Thank you," D'Annibal answered.

"Lieutenant D'Annibal is Detective Pelligree's commanding officer," Auggie said as he introduced the lieutenant.

"We should be done soon," the doctor said with a nod to D'Annibal. "I'll let you know when he's out of surgery."

As soon as the doctor was out of earshot, Auggie said, "I'm outta here."

"I know you want to crack the bastard's head into the wall. Be careful. It's Portland's jurisdiction," D'Annibal said.

Auggie made a succinct remark, expressing his feelings, then looked to Liv. "I'm taking you home."

"To your house," she corrected him, hurrying after him through the sliding doors and to where he'd parked the Jeep sideways, taking two spots in his hurry.

"My place."

"I want to go with—"

"Hell, no. Please. Lock the doors. Navarone's in custody, so you'll be all right. I can't take you."

There wasn't a lot she could say to that besides, "Can you get him to confess?"

"I'm gonna give it the old college try," he stated stonily.

September sat at her desk, tapping her forehead with one finger, tamping down her roiling feelings. Gretchen was talking into the phone, her answers growing shorter and shorter and finally she pressed a finger to the connection, severing the conversation in mid-word, as if they'd been accidentally cut off. George was staring off into space.

"I hate this," Gretchen said.

D'Annibal had called around eight. Wes was through surgery and in recovery and everything looked good. Auggie was interviewing Navarone with the Portland PD and there was really nothing for any of them to do on their end, but nobody wanted to work on other projects or go home yet.

Gretchen looked at the phone, and then over at September. "So, how did that interview go with Kirby?"

"Oh . . ." She'd pushed it to the back of her mind. "Not great. It'll be on the ten o'clock news. The hikers that discovered the body were there, so she knew about Do Unto Others As She Did To Me."

Gretchen made a face. "Bound to happen. How'd you handle it?"

"Basically 'No comment.' Where she really got me was when she brought up Navarone."

"Navarone?" Gretchen's brows drew together in a frown. "You were doing that interview before Auggie and Weasel got to the bastard's house. How'd she know?"

September shrugged. "It took me by surprise. I said he was a person of interest and left it at that."

George said, "Pauline Kirby's got a pipeline into Portland PD. Didn't D'Annibal say Olivia Dugan threatened the director of that mental outpatient facility, Hargrave House?"

"Hathaway House," September corrected him. "I didn't hear that."

"Me, neither," Gretchen said.

George nodded. "Oh, yeah. You two were staking out Jaffe. Dugan told the director she had a gun and that she wanted information on Navarone. Scared the shit out of him."

"Dugan?" September said, surprised. "I can't picture her with a gun."

"She didn't show the weapon," George said, "so, everybody's kind of past it now with everything else going on."

"You think someone at Portland knowingly leaked that information to Pauline Kirby?" Gretchen looked skeptical.

George shrugged. "I'm just sayin'. . . ."

"Kirby'll be calling you again," Gretchen said to September. "As soon as she's sucked 'em dry at the hospital. Just wait."

"Like today?" September asked tiredly.

"They don't call her the barracuda for nothing."

Auggie's arms were crossed over his chest and he was leaning against a painted cinder-block wall inside the interrogation room. No frills for Dr. Navarone, who was cuffed and seated in a chair at a table.

The Portland detective on the case was named Curtis. Detective Trey Curtis. Cool, and gruff-voiced and willing to let Auggie run point, which was gratifying that he didn't have to fight him for it. Curtis was fully aware this was a Laurelton case that had spilled over into Portland.

Auggie had proceeded to fire questions at Navarone who, after explaining and explaining and explaining that he'd thought Auggie and Weasel were going to kill him and that's why he grabbed the gun and shot wildly, was answering them willingly enough, though he adamantly decreed that he'd had nothing to do with the Zuma shooting, Trask Burcher Martin's homicide, or anything to do with Olivia Dugan, though he did allow that he remembered her from Hathaway House. When the questions switched to Rock Springs and the strangulations, he grew visibly upset, but he swore that all those old, malicious rumors had been started by Patricia LeBlanc Owens and had nothing to do with him!

Had he been in love with Deborah Dugan?, Auggie asked, which shocked him to his socks, but he finally admitted, yes, he had. But she was married to Albert Dugan and nothing ever happened between them, despite what others may have thought. She wouldn't betray her wedding vows. Not with him, anyway.

Periodically throughout the interview, the doctor's eyes rolled around, as if he couldn't control them. When asked about his behavior, he admitted that he had to take medication himself. That he suffered from an unspecified neurological condition. Auggie recalled Angela Navarone mentioning he had dark moods and had alluded to him having mental problems.

Auggie kinda thought the doctor might just also be a drug abuser, so he brought up Halo Valley and the loss of his license and Navarone started shouting about all those pernicious imbeciles! They never understood his brilliance and technique. If anyone should have their licenses revoked, it was the quacks that worked there, not him!

At this point Detective Curtis said, with more empathy than Auggie would have credited him with, that he had a colleague who'd once felt very much the same way about Halo Valley, an ex-detective with the force. The officer in question had since had a reversal of opinion, but Curtis could understand why Navarone felt the way he did. That calmed the doctor down again and Auggie was able to run Navarone back to the Zuma shootings, but he just kept shaking his head and saying they had the wrong guy. He then asked for a lawyer.

Taking a break, Auggie met Curtis in the outer hallway. "What do you think?" Curtis asked him.

"He's a lying piece of garbage. But I don't have anything to tie him to the crimes," Auggie said, frustrated. "It took him a while to lawyer up, but we weren't getting anything anyway."

"You've got him for practicing without a license. Whatever drugs he was using gotta be illegal, too."

"It's not enough," Auggie expelled angrily. "But it'll hold him a while."

"I'll talk to Lieutenant Cawthorne. See if he can delay things as long as possible," Curtis said.

The lawyer, an officious-looking man with wire-rimmed glasses and an annoying habit of looking at each detective a full ten seconds in the face before moving on to the next one, hustled in. Apart from letting them know that calls had been placed to Angela Navarone, his client's sister, and Glenda Navarone Tripp, his niece, who lived locally, the attorney shut down the interview.

Auggie left the station around midnight and sucked in a long draught of cooler air. He left the windows down as he drove out on the Sunset and to his duplex. When he pulled into the drive his heart clutched a bit: both sides were completely dark. Though it made sense—he'd told Liv to turn off the lights and lock the doors—he had a moment of fear, nevertheless.

He'd given her his extra house key, so he debated whether to just let himself in, wondering if that would scare her. But when he got to the door the porch light went on and she flung the door open, wide awake herself.

"I saw you pull in," she said.

"Hey . . ."

"Did he say anything? Did he confess?"

"Not yet. But he's safely locked up."

"But he didn't say anything?"

"He will," Auggie stated positively.

She nodded, gulped, and choked out, "Thank you."

And then he was through the door and pulling her into his arms and she was responding. It was all they could do to get the door shut and locked, the porch light off and up the stairs to his bedroom.

He thought, inconsequentially, *I love you.*

September had one of the worst night's sleep of her life. She tossed and turned then woke at four A.M. from a dream about carving her initials in a tree, words that morphed to being embedded in the skin of a corpse. No need to look for why she'd had *that* dream. Then she'd fallen asleep again, only to wake up at five on a loud scream issuing from her own lips, a dream that disintegrated into wispy fragments as soon as she was fully awake.

She rolled out of bed and jumped in the shower, letting the water run over her hair and face. She did a quick check of her own emotional state. She was upset about Weasel. She was concerned about the case—not Zuma any longer, but Do Unto Others. Her case. She'd accepted the assignment, and now that Zuma appeared to be wrapping up, it felt like she could completely switch over. But Pauline Kirby had upped September's anxiety, and now she was itching to dig deeper.

She'd made the mistake of viewing her own interview on the ten o'clock news the night before, and had wanted to shriek and pull a pillow over her head at how young and wide-eyed she'd appeared. Her hair was dark brown, no auburn streaks at all showing, and her eyes were a brilliant crystalline blue, the camera focusing on her closely.

She looked like someone play-acting the role of detective, rather than really being one.

But that was just her, being extra critical. She hoped.

She drove to work early and saw that she'd beaten Guy Urlacher to the station. Didn't matter really. When he wasn't there, the detectives, uniforms and other employees were free to enter through the back door, which she preferred. Now, as she walked down the near empty, brightly lit hallways, she felt her jaw tighten. No matter what, she was going to investigate the hell out of the Do Unto Others case, and with that in mind, she got herself a cup of coffee, then walked over to Pelligree's desk and rooted around for all his notes.

Auggie was up around six, and though he tried to ease away from Liv, her eyes shot open and she was wide awake. "Are you going back to see Navarone?" she asked, leaning on one elbow.

He was sitting on the edge of the bed, naked and looking sleepy. Before he could answer, his cell phone gave a muffled ring. He held up a finger to her, got to his feet, went to the chair where he'd thrown his clothes, searching for the phone. "Early," he said to Liv, then answered the cell, "Rafferty," stifling a yawn. Liv could hear a woman's voice start in excitedly. Auggie said, "Whoa, Nine. Slow down. Give it to me at normal speed. What's wrong?" He listened carefully for a few moments longer, then his whole body froze. "I'll be at the station in ten . . . fifteen."

He clicked off and ran for the shower. Liv was up after him, tripping on the bed sheets, aware of her nakedness but unabashed by it. "What?" she demanded, following him into the bathroom.

"Navarone's niece. Glenda Tripp. They found her body this morning."

"Her body? What? She's *dead?*"

"That's what Nine said."

"His own *niece?* Why? Who found her?"

"One of the officers went out on a call about a possible dead body. The door to Tripp's apartment was open and she was lying on the floor. September took the officer's call. She's on her way there, but decided to include me because of Navarone."

Liv was trying to catch up. ". . . because Navarone's your case. Of course, she'd call you."

"You'd think," he said, stepping into the shower, turning on the taps, and pulling the curtain. Over the water, she heard, "But Tripp's case follows the pattern of one of September's cases more than mine. There were scratches cut into Tripp's torso like two other of the killer's victims."

"What are you *saying?* That it's *not* Navarone? That Glenda *Navarone* Tripp's murder is a coincidence?" Liv was practically shouting and had to pull herself forcefully back from the ledge. "That's bullshit!"

"An eyewitness in her apartment building saw Tripp dressed up to go out around eleven last night. Long after we had her uncle in custody. So, he didn't kill her."

Liv couldn't think. It didn't make sense. And she was downright scared that the fabric of their whole case against Navarone was coming unraveled. "I don't understand."

"I don't either," Auggie said. "I'll go meet September and try to figure it out."

Glenda Tripp's body lay on its back about three feet inside the front door. She had been wearing a short black skirt and a red silk, sleeveless top. The skirt was pulled down around her thighs, the top bunched up above a black lace bra. Only the chandelier earrings and chunky silver bracelet on her right wrist were still in place.

Across her torso were scratches that looked like they'd been carved in a hurry. The first one could have been the back of a "D" but the others were haphazard slashes with no finesse.

J.J. was already examining the body when Auggie and September arrived together. Neither of them had said much to each other when Auggie arrived at the station to pick her up. Neither was saying much now.

"What do you think?" Auggie asked the medical examiner.

"She died of strangulation. He wrapped a thin cord or wire around her neck. Same as the others, and he must've taken it with him. We didn't find it around anywhere. These marks cut into her skin. . . ."

"It looks like there's a certain urgency to them," September spoke up. "He started to write and then just started slashing."

"Maybe he was interrupted," Auggie said.

J.J. said, "I'll know more after a more thorough exam." He got to his feet and grimaced down at the corpse. Then he turned to September, "Saw you on the news last night, Nine."

"What?" Auggie asked, so September was forced to relate the gist of her interview with Pauline.

She finished with, "I stopped by my apartment and set my DVR before I came back to work."

"You watched it yet?" he questioned.

"I saw it when it ran at ten. I hate seeing myself on video."

"Wonder how Pauline gets her information," he muttered, frowning down at the body.

"The way she gets all of it: bullying," September said.

There were two crime-scene techs with J.J. and September reminded them to pack up the laptop, which they didn't appreciate, as she and Auggie walked carefully through the other rooms.

"Looks like all the action took place in the living room," Auggie observed.

September said, "Maybe he left in a hurry after being interrupted, and that's why the door remained open."

"Maybe that explains why she wasn't left in a field," he answered.

"The other bodies were just dumped there. Arranged for our benefit, but the murders took place elsewhere." She gave her brother a long look. "Why is it Navarone's niece? There has to be a connection."

Auggie shook his head and placed a call on his cell to Detective Curtis. He didn't get him, but he left a message about Glenda Tripp's death. "Curtis can break the news to Navarone," he said, clicking off.

"Why now?" September said again.

"More importantly, who?" Auggie reminded her. "It wasn't Navarone."

"Could he have an accomplice? I know that sounds nuts. But really, Glenda Tripp gets killed like Dempsey and Decatur, and she's Navarone's niece? There's always been a connection between these two cases. Something. I've felt it before, but I can't see it."

They walked back outside, past the body and onto the private, wooden deck/entry of Tripp's apartment. Each of the apartment's entries came off a sidewalk that wound through the units and led to the parking structures.

They were getting back in Auggie's car when his cell rang again. "Rafferty," he said. "Curtis. Did you alert Navarone?" He listened for a few moments, then said, "Huh. All right. Let me know if there's anything else."

"What?" September asked.

"Curtis told Navarone someone had murdered his niece and he broke down and cried like a baby. Hasn't really come out of it since. And Tripp's mother, Angela Navarone, is driving down from Seattle. She's devastated, of course."

"How . . . how did he do this?" she asked.

"He didn't. At least not personally."

"But you've got him for Zuma, and Martin, and those homicides in Rock Springs?"

"Nine, I don't have him for anything, yet," Auggie said, heaving a deep sigh. "I'm going home for a while to think. If anything breaks I'll call you. Do the same?"

"Yep."

When Auggie returned to the duplex, Liv was showered, dressed in jeans and a taupe sleeveless T-shirt and a pair of sneakers. She still looked pale, but a little less haunted than she had in all the time he'd known her. The rush of desire and affection that flooded him upon seeing her was becoming a familiar sensation.

"I don't know anything yet," he said, dashing her hopes as he plugged his cell into the charger in the bedroom.

"Can you tell me about Glenda Tripp?"

"It's gonna be breaking news soon enough. . . ." Auggie related what he knew about the Do Unto Others killer, finishing with, "It's not Navarone, and I just don't see him working in tandem with someone else. He's too much of a loner."

They thought about it for a while, then Liv said, "I think I'm ready to go get my car."

He looked at her. "And . . . bring it back here?"

"If that's okay."

"More than okay."

She nodded.

"So, we're okay, then?" he questioned cautiously. "We're past that?"

"*That*, being your deception?" she asked.

"Yeah. *That.*"

She smiled faintly. "Let's go get my car."

"All right. I'll even buy you breakfast."

"Make it lunch. I want to go to my apartment first."

They drove into her apartment complex and Liv pointed to her parking spot, feeling like a stranger at this place though it had really only been days since she'd left. She spent as little time as possible inside her unit, glad to have Auggie by her side. She glanced at her unplugged phone and answering machine. Nothing about it felt like home.

As soon as they were finished, Liv followed him back to his house in her Accord, parking next to him in the two-vehicle carport. This felt more like coming home, but she warned herself not to assume too much. Then they climbed into the department Jeep and headed to a bistro in downtown Portland.

"It almost feels normal," Liv said. "Or, at least what I think normal must feel like."

"Being together?"

"Being . . . aware that this nightmare might be over." She slid him a look. "And being together."

"You don't have to humor me."

"I'm not."

It was more of an admission of her feelings than she'd allowed to date, and he appreciated it. "We've got him, Liv. It's just a matter of time before he cracks."

"I hope so."

They finished up lunch, then went back to the house. Auggie placed a number of calls to Trey Curtis and his sister, then Curtis again, while Liv curled into the living room recliner and closed her eyes. Sometime later, she sensed Auggie come over and look down at her. "I'm gonna talk to Navarone again," he told her. "I'm tired of waiting for crumbs of information."

She wanted to say, take me with you, but forced the words back.

"Stay put," he said, giving her a light kiss. Then a little harder one, until Liv was clinging to him and it was a while later that he disengaged himself. "Lock the doors," he said, digging in his pockets for his keys.

From the window, she watched him climb into the Jeep and back out of the drive, leaving her car alone in the carport. He'd been gone about ten minutes when she wandered into the kitchen and saw his cell phone lying on the kitchen counter where he'd set it before coming into the living room.

She snatched it up and stuck it in her pocket. Good. It gave her a reason to go after him to the Portland Police Department. Grabbing her backpack, she dug around for her keys, then headed out to the car through the front door, testing to make sure it was locked behind her. Hurrying down the walk, she crossed the carport toward the driver's door, hitting the remote as she neared it.

Movement in the corner of her left eye. She half-turned. Something slammed into her head and she went to her knees, crying out. Jean-clad legs swam into her line of vision.

"Wha—?"

She was hit again. A large piece of wood. Vaguely she heard an engine and then sometime later—minutes? Hours—that engine sound was right by her ear.

And then she was on her back, being dragged. The last thing she saw before she went out cold was GMC in large letters across the back of a gray truck.

Chapter 24

He was only ten minutes out when he glanced down for his cell phone and realized he didn't have it. He almost went on anyway. He didn't know what the hell Navarone was up to, and he wanted to see for himself.

But no cell phone was simply a bad idea.

Muttering to himself, he turned the Jeep around and went back to his duplex, pulling into the drive next to Liv's Accord. The sight of it brought a smile to his lips. Things were working out.

He unlocked the front door, expecting her to meet him like she had the night before but he made it all the way inside with no sign of her. "Liv?" he called loudly as he walked toward the kitchen. "I forgot my phone."

He stood in the kitchen and looked at the empty space on the counter where he remembered setting the cell down. Realizing she must have taken it upstairs, he took the steps two at a time, saying, "I'm tellin' ya. You're gonna have to get yourself a cell phone. Especially if you keep stealing mine."

There was no one in the master bedroom. No one in the bathroom. No one in the spare bedroom.

Auggie went back to the kitchen then stood perfectly still for the space of five heartbeats, his mind racing. She was gone. But where? Her car was sitting outside and all her things were here. Except where was her backpack?

It's not Navarone, his gut told him. Then, *He's got her.*

No.

He raced back outside, suddenly galvanized into action. The ground was too hard and dry for tire tracks; he could see nothing. But then his eye caught something that didn't look right. A piece of fir bark and a disturbed place in the gravel.

And now that he was oriented, he could see where something had been dragged to the edge of the gravel drive and the edge of his lawn was smashed down from a vehicle's tire.

Panic swept through him. He had her! He had Liv. *They'd been wrong!*

But who? How?

Who could he call?

Hague.

He had no phone. Liv had his phone.

He leapt into the Jeep and burned out of the drive, racing toward the Laurelton PD. Half of him wanted to stop and demand to use some neighbor's phone, or a grocery store, but the other half knew he needed to get to the station and trace the GPS on his cell.

Liv woke up slowly. She was lying on rough-hewn boards. Her head was foggy and she sensed the concussion she'd been spared earlier was in full bloom. Her shoulders ached, and she realized her hands were tied behind her back. She tried to muster up the strength to fight but couldn't do it. The heat was overwhelming and the putrid odor surrounding her sent her into a gag reflex she did her best to quell. She could hear him rustling around somewhere outside of her line of vision, and she couldn't have him come back. Not yet. Not till she was stronger.

Where am I?

She opened her eyes to slits and saw she was in some kind of small outbuilding.

There were landscaping tools. And pieces of wood. And that *odor*! God! Like something *dead*.

And then she saw the leg, sticking out from under a tarp. Wearing a woman's shoe.

She bit down on her tongue and drew blood, holding back the scream as her mind closed down and darkness descended again.

September was avoiding Pauline Kirby's second call by taking a short drive out of the station. She'd stopped at Starbucks and gotten a soy Chai Tea Latte and was pulling into the lot when one of the department Jeeps squealed in behind her and stopped.

"Hey," she said, climbing from her car, when she saw Auggie slam out of the Jeep and run the three spaces it took to reach her.

"He's got her. He's got Liv. I need to track my cell phone. She's got it with her. Goddammit, Nine. Stop staring and give me your phone!"

"Who's got her? Did Navarone get released?"

"No. Come on." He grabbed her arm and hustled her into the station with him. "I need to get a ping off a cell tower and locate that phone."

"Okay, okay. You sure someone's got her?"

"*Yes.*"

They went down the hall to Querry's office, the department's tech whiz, who asked for Auggie's phone number, zeroed in on it in a matter of minutes, and gave them the coordinates, adding, "It's not moving right now."

"That's west on Highway 26," Auggie said.

"Toward the coast?" September suggested.

"Give me your phone," he said to September.

She handed it over and said, "I'll come with you."

"No, stay here. I need you to get me Hague Dugan's number. Probably unlisted."

"I can get another phone."

But he was already running for the door.

Laurelton was on the western edge of the metropolis considered Greater Portland. About seventy miles due west was the Pacific Ocean. Auggie's cell was located in the weeds of a ditch about ten miles outside of Laurelton and just before the eastern foothills of the Coast Range.

He found it fast. Faster than he'd expected. It was just right there. He picked it up and stared at it helplessly.

September's phone rang and she said, "Okay, commit this to memory," and then she rattled off a series of numbers and said, "Hague Dugan."

"Say them again," he said, feeling dull. Fear was squeezing him like a vice.

September repeated the digits, then said, "You need help. What do you need?"

"I'll call you."

The second time Liv came to she found herself tied to a chair, much like she'd tied Auggie. The kidnapper behind her, his breath ruffling her hair. Gooseflesh rose on her skin and she feigned more sleep. She needed time. Time.

Auggie, she thought in anguish as her mind worried at her predicament.

The shoe . . . the dead woman's shoe . . . she'd seen that shoe somewhere recently, hadn't she? Not Angela Navarone and her Ferragamos . . . somewhere else . . . in an apartment?

The phone.

It was in her pocket. If she could just get her fingers free!

But then she glanced down at her jeans and saw the pocket was flat.

A faint cry of disappointment issued from her throat and it alerted him that she was awake. He came around to stand in front of her, about five feet away. Liv braced herself but he wore a hoodie that obscured his face and jeans and sneakers. Yet . . .

He was very familiar. Then he removed the hood and she stared into the face of her own father, Albert Dugan. She blinked once, to see if she was dreaming, and yet felt a strange sense of inevitability and understanding. He was the bogeyman. So close . . . so very close.

He smiled and said softly, "Lovely Livvie."

And she said, "Lorinda wore those shoes to Hague's."

Auggie was halfway back to Hague's place. He'd called and called and called with no response. He'd gotten Albert and Lorinda's number from September as well, but no one answered there either. Hague had to be there. He never left. Unless he was at the cantina . . . Rosa's Cantina . . .

He grabbed up the cell to call September again when it rang in his hand. "Rafferty," he bit out.

"Detective . . ."

"Hague?" Auggie asked quickly. "Are you there?"

"You've been calling."

There was no time for preliminaries. "Someone has Liv! Someone took her, and it's not Navarone! Who is it? Do you know? *Do you?*"

"You're looking too far . . . he killed those women . . ."

"The strangler? Who is he?"

"Out of the corner of my eye . . . I always knew . . ." He was fading out.

"I'm almost at your place, Hague. Five minutes. Stay with me. I need to know who it is."

"My father," he said, then the connection ended.

Liv's mind raced. Her father. Her adoptive father. The only father she'd ever known. "You gunned those people down at Zuma," she said. "You killed Aaron and Jessica and Paul . . . and Trask . . ."

"You made me," he said. "Waving that package around, saying you were going to investigate. Showing it to your neighbor. I saw! I saw! You stupid girl. Stupid, stupid girl." He kept right on smiling.

She realized she'd never seen him smile before. Not a real smile ever. And this one was downright blood-chilling.

"You killed Lorinda. Your wife."

"She should have left it alone. She left it alone for a lot of years, but then she didn't."

The phone call. Lorinda had wanted Liv to call her back. Something about her father and Hague and Liv. Lorinda had been frightened, frightened of her husband.

Then Dr. Yancy's voice slipped into her head. "You saw something that you're repressing."

And then the memory came so easily. That little piece that had been floating around in her subconscious, bumping along the wall of her fear.

"I saw you," she said. "Out in the field. You were . . ."

Masturbating.

The night of her birthday. A piece she hadn't wanted to remember. The piece Dr. Yancy had tried to elicit from her subconscious.

Liv had said she'd stayed in the den the whole time, but that was a fallacy. A lie she'd told herself. No . . . she'd walked out the back door and seen her father in the dim square of light from the kitchen window, his hands working in a manner she hadn't quite understood at the time, his gaze zeroed to the place where her mother stood.

"You killed Mama, too," she said, surprised at how conversational her voice sounded. A little father-daughter chat.

"You told her that you saw me outside. You told her what you saw," he said. "And you know what she did? She accused me of killing those whores. She was going to go to the police. Stupid little Livvie. You told, and so I had to kill her. Your fault, little girl."

She stared at him. His face was the same, but it seemed unrecognizable. He was totally nuts, she realized. "I'm not to blame for any of this."

A spasm crossed his face and he rubbed his temples. "You think it's my fault? Your mother was a whore! She was having an affair with that hoity-toity Navarone. She was done with me, her own husband, and I wanted to kill her. I thought about it, but I would have let her live. I still wanted her even though she wouldn't share a bed with me. We were sleeping apart. So, I found other women to fuck, but I always thought about her . . . and then . . . you . . ."

She swallowed. Had to keep him talking. Had to. "Why Sylvia Parmiter?"

"You know about her? Of course you do," he snarled. "All your *investigating!*" He shook his head angrily and said, "Sylvia saw some scratches on my arm. Deb was having one of her fucking barbeques so she could get her lover over. She was panting for Navarone all the time! Sylvia stepped into the bathroom when I was at the sink, washing my face, cooling off. I'd shoved up my sleeves and she saw the scratches. Stupid bitch didn't get it immediately, but I knew she would. I had to stop her, so when Don was out one night I dragged her from her bed and put my hands around her throat . . . and pressed . . ."

He was breathing hard, getting an erection. Liv watched him start to reach for himself, her memories dancing, pinpoints behind her eyes.

They keep their hands in their pockets . . . wear rigor smiles . . .

Liv had thought he'd been referring to the doctor—Navarone—but maybe he'd seen something about Albert, too.

But he was just a baby!

It could have been later. After their mother's death. Maybe he'd seen something that scared him, though he didn't know what it was. Sensed, like she had, that their father was the killer, but neither of their unformed, child minds could process the information correctly.

"Mama sent the package to the lawyers," Liv said, dragging her gaze away from him.

"Bitch!" His eyes flew open and his erection failed. "A safety precaution against me!"

"It didn't implicate you," Liv said, playing for time.

"That's only because you're stupid. You and your brother. You thought it was Navarone."

"Did you kill Glenda?"

"Who?"

"Glenda Navarone Tripp?"

"Don't know what the fuck you're talking about." His hot gaze touched on her breasts, which were thrust forward as her arms were pulled back.

Desperately, Liv said, "You were fighting with Mama on my birthday. You hit her."

"She deserved it." He moved forward and reached out a

hand. She felt bile move up her throat, but instead of touching her breast, the fingers of his right hand slid around her nape and then forward, until his thumb fit inside the well at the base of her throat.

"What were you fighting about?" Liv asked.

"She suspected about Sylvia . . . I had to hit her. She said she was leaving me for Navarone."

I'm done, Mama had told Liv.

And that's when Liv had gone through the back door and seen what she'd seen, not understanding, burying the memory except for the bad feeling that haunted her soul.

"I watched her often. Through the window. From the field. I only really wanted her . . . then . . ." he said in that ultrasoft voice that sounded more menacing with each syllable. "But that night was the last. She even told you she was done. That's when I knew I had to finish it. I went back in after she sent you away. I wanted to caress her." His hand squeezed Liv's throat. "But I had to do it differently, or even those morons at the Rock Springs police would have found me. So I hung her." His hand squeezed harder, his breath raspy. "I wanted to touch her, but I couldn't." His other hand joined the first in a circle around the base of Liv's neck. Liv's heart was jumping wildly in her chest. He'd come back in the kitchen, knocked her mother senseless, then hanged her. If either Liv, or Hague, had gone back to the kitchen at that time and caught him, they would have been killed as well.

"You hit me with your truck," Liv said, desperately trying to keep the conversation going. "You ran me off the road."

"The truck isn't registered to me. Lorinda found it. She asked too many questions . . . and now this is the last time I can use it, because you damaged it!"

Liv surfaced briefly from her paralyzing fear. "*You* hit *me.*"

He yanked his hands back from her throat then slapped her. Hard. Her ears rang. She felt darkness enveloping her once more and she welcomed it.

Before she blacked out, she prayed, *Auggie, find me.* . . .

Auggie pounded on Hague's door with his fist so hard it made his whole arm hurt. It was only a few minutes but felt like an eternity before Della opened the door. Just like last time her blond hair was pulled back in a bun and her blue eyes raked him with suspicion, and it just combined to make him feel crazy. He burst past her and confronted Hague in his chair.

"Albert has Liv?" he demanded. "You're saying Albert has Liv?"

"It's the government. You can't trust them."

"Where? Where does he have her? At his house?"

"No. No. Not there," Hague said. "He'd be afraid of Lorinda. He stopped because of her. She kept the demons out for a long time, but not forever."

"He told you this?" Auggie demanded.

"No . . . in the folds of my brain. They put them there . . . and I know things. . . ."

His eyes rolled back and Auggie grabbed him and shook him. "Hague! HAGUE!"

"Let go of him!" Della shrieked. "You're hurting him!"

"HAAAGGGUUEE!"

Della's hands were scrabbling at Auggie's arms. He slowly released Hague, who flopped back in his chair. Gone.

"You bastard! You bastard!" she was shrieking at Auggie.

He turned on her. "I need answers! Don't you get it? He has Liv. *Albert has Liv!*"

Della was breathing hard, her emotions rocketing around. He watched her fight for control. "Albert?" she questioned.

"Hague says it's Albert. Goddammit," Auggie said, frustrated. "Liv dropped my cell phone on Highway 26, just before the foothills. Or, he did. One of them did."

"Trees," Della said. "Hague's been talking about his father and trees."

Blue eyes met blue eyes. Auggie said, "Forestry . . . that's his profession."

Della nodded.

"There's a forestry tower out there." He turned away, stumbling, sick with worry. He'd been so close. *Right there!* And now he had to go all the way back.

If anything happened to her . . . and he could have saved her . . .

He shot past the clambering elevator and jumped down the stairs, out to the street, into the Jeep.

"My brain is full of worms. I don't have control. There's no finesse anymore because ends must be met. Ends must be met."

Liv's ears picked up his voice. Her head was hanging forward and she kept it that way, hoping he wouldn't notice she'd returned to consciousness.

She realized he was behind her, untying her. She poised herself. This might be her only chance. As soon as her hand was free she leapt to her feet. But he was on her in an instant, slamming her against a rafter.

"Don't try that again," he snarled. "This time there will be finesse. I've waited a long, long time, Deborah. We're going to the field."

"I'm not Deborah."

"I know who you are. You're all the same . . . all the same . . ."

"You've stalked me for years."

He cocked his head. "You knew about me. Too fucking crazy to remember, but you knew about me."

"I was a kid!"

"I had to know if you'd really forgotten . . . and guess what? You didn't forget. You were just waiting to remember." He slipped the baling twine he'd used to hold her hands around her neck and yanked it tight. "We're going down the ladder, now."

They were at a forestry tower, Liv realized with a sinking heart.

"Don't make me hurt you," he warned, tugging on the twine. "Come on."

She had to move forward or be choked. "What about Hague?"

"Hague." He tried to feign disinterest but his expression darkened. "He's Navarone's."

"I don't think so. He's more like you."

"Crazy as a loon? That what you mean?" He pressed his face to hers. "I thought he was mine. Didn't wanna send him away. Not my son. But then it turned out he's crazy like Navarone, not like me. He's Navarone's."

"I don't believe Mama ever cheated on you," Liv said, and that earned her another slap as he dragged her to the ladder and she stumbled after him.

The track to the forestry tower was overgrown with dry weeds and Auggie forced himself to drive slowly though he wanted to race with sirens blaring. There was a curve about a quarter of a mile in, and he parked and slid out of the Jeep, pushing his Glock in the back waistband of his pants, pressing himself close to the Douglas firs on the west side, moving quietly beneath their green canopies. The forestry tower was at the fat end of a tear-shaped clearing; he was at the other. Parked to one side was a gray GMC truck. Albert's.

And then he saw Albert coming down a ladder from an access door in the floor of the tower. Behind him was Liv. Tethered by a rope.

He saw red. There was no way to describe it later. Blind rage overtook him and he ran forward at his fastest sprint. He was gonna kill the bastard.

Liv was giving Albert some trouble. He could hear her saying she felt faint. He didn't know if it was true or not and he didn't care.

Albert heard him coming and turned. His eyes bulged out and he yelled, "YOU!"

And then Auggie was on him. Rolling on the ground. Both of them throwing punches. Auggie trying to reach his gun. Failing. The Glock flying loose. Breaking Auggie's hold. Albert scrambled away, stumbled, grabbed for the gun. Liv was hanging onto the last rung of the ladder as if she were about to faint.

"Stop!" Auggie yelled, struggling to his feet.

Albert was heading for Liv but then jogged away, under the tower. Auggie started after him but Liv collapsed onto the ground. A rope was around her neck. Choking her.

Quickly he dropped to his knees beside her and loosened the tie. She gasped in a long breath of air.

"Auggie," she whispered, barely audible. Then, more urgently, "Auggie!"

Albert was running at them with an axe held high. Auggie leapt at him, low, taking out his knees. Albert swore viciously, kicking at him, trying to wield the axe.

In a flash Auggie yanked the axe away, then slammed the back of it against Albert's head, knocking him cold.

Silence filled the air.

Dropping the axe, Auggie returned to Liv, holding her close while she clung to him.

"It's over, Livvie," he whispered.

Epilogue

One week later . . .

"Hey!" Auggie yelled to Liv, who was taking her sweet time coming out to the backyard. He was barbequing chicken, not nearly as good at it as he would have her believe, but he wanted to bring some more of that normalcy to her world, convince her that yes, they could have a boring, suburban life together despite the rigors of his job, the trauma she'd just been through and her paranoia that, though eased, had been ingrained so deeply that she feared it would never be completely gone.

Auggie didn't give a rat's ass. He loved her, and she loved him. He believed it, even if she couldn't say the words, yet. Baby steps.

She stepped through the back door and looked at his efforts. She'd mostly physically recovered from the effects of her kidnapping, though the mark around her throat from the twine was still visible. Auggie had to tamp down a fresh round of fury directed at the man who'd caused her so much pain, but the system would take care of the bastard once and for all.

Across the fence, the other duplexers were sitting outside

as well, enjoying their own end of the summer party, and, if her nose wasn't lying to her, enjoying some marijuana.

"Aaron smoked weed, too," she said, walking up to Auggie. "It almost makes me nostalgic."

"It's for medicinal purposes," he said, inclining his head toward the neighbors. "Or, so they would have you believe."

"They know you're a cop?"

"I told 'em I was a doctor."

"You did not."

"I did. Dr. Augdogsen."

She started laughing, and then Auggie joined her, and pretty soon their combined laughter caused one of their neighbors, the one who wore a kerchief over a mass of long hair, to look over the fence and ask, "Hey, man, you guys high?" which caused them to break into another round.

Sitting in the swivel chair at her desk, September swung back and forth in a slow arc, her hands clasped behind her head, thinking. Pauline Kirby had been all over her for another interview but she'd been "unavailable," and D'Annibal had been too busy to give much thought to Laurelton PD public relations with the Zuma Software case coming to a close. The lieutenant had also been getting accolades for solving the cold case of the Rock Springs serial strangler, so D'Annibal had been even more "unavailable" than September the past week.

Navarone was out on bail for shooting Detective Wes Pelligree, and was staying with his sister at his garage rental pending trial. There were other charges pending, and he would undoubtedly return to jail soon. His business had been shut down, though a number of his "patients" were loudly protesting his arrest. Go figure.

Wes himself was recovering well. September had gone to see him in the hospital, and met his girlfriend, Kayleen

Jefferson, who told him he could just stay in the hospital 'cause she wasn't gonna be listening to his whining while he had her running and fetching for him. Nosirree. He'd grinned at her and she'd glared back at him for all of five seconds before she broke into a smile, too.

September and Gretchen had tried to make a case that Albert Dugan was responsible for Glenda Tripp's death, and maybe Emmy Decatur and Sheila Dempsey's, as well, but it had been a longshot from the outset, and Dugan himself had been repelled by the "slice and dice" aspect to the victim's flesh, to which Gretchen had commented, "Dugan's got a rule book for killing people, and this is too graphic?"

Apparently so.

Now, September got up and walked to the bulletin board where Glenda Tripp's picture had been placed beside the other two victims. Gretchen came into the room with a sandwich from the vending machine and held out half to September. "Ham," she said. "The only thing that looked edible."

"Thanks."

"Think Olivia Dugan's gonna be your new sister-in-law?" Gretchen asked, resting a hip on her desk and biting into her sandwich.

"I think he really cares about her," September said.

"Pisses me off," she said around a mouthful. "Woulda liked a shot at him. Instead, it's back to the bars with disgusting drunks and lechers."

"Maybe there's a better place to meet people," September suggested, munching on her sandwich as well.

"Church?"

September chuckled and Gretchen smiled as well. "Maybe somewhere in between," September said.

They finished their sandwiches and both of them tried to throw their wrappers in Wes's trash can. Gretchen failed, and September's lobbed in.

George appeared from the hallway just in time to see it. He clapped and said, "You're getting pretty damn good. How long've you been here now, Nine?"

"Four months?"

"Just about the time Sheila Dempsey's body was found," Gretchen said. "That's how I remember."

"Hey, Detective Rafferty."

September looked up. One of the women who worked in administration—Candy Something-Or-Other—entered the squad room, holding an envelope. "This came for you," Candy said.

"For me?"

"Says Detective September Rafferty right in the address." She put the manila envelope in September's hand and walked away.

"No return address," September said as she reached inside.

George snorted. "Must have a new fan from your television debut!"

September pulled out a birthday card. It read, "Way to go, 3-YEAR-OLD," except someone had written in a zero beside the three, making it "30." "They know my age," she said, faintly disturbed as she opened it.

Then she reached back into the envelope and pulled out a piece of children's artwork that nearly stopped September's heart. It was *her* artwork. From a grade-school project that she'd received a happy face for a job well done. The teacher had stuck several gold stars across the top of the page as well, and added a handwritten note: *Your birthday cupcakes were terrific! Way to start the school year!*

But now underneath the teacher's words, new ones had been scrawled in blood: DO UNTO OTHERS AS SHE DID TO ME.

"Jesus, Nine," Gretchen said, shocked. "It really does have to do with you!"

"No." September wouldn't believe it. The missive dropped from her nerveless fingers but fluttered down to land face up.

"What the hell is that?" George asked, getting up from his desk.

Her vision narrowed. She felt weird and dissociated. The card and artwork were from someone who knew her from her youth? How did they get it? What did it mean? "This is from . . ." *Second grade!*

"The Do Unto Others killer knows you," Gretchen said from a long distance away.

"Who . . . ?" September whispered aloud.

Who . . . ?

Dear Reader,

I'm so glad you've been introduced to Detective September Rafferty, who first shows up in NOWHERE TO RUN as a newbie member of the Laurelton Police Department and reappears in NOWHERE TO HIDE, where's she's reconnected with a high school boyfriend amidst a series of killings, and then on to NOWHERE SAFE, where she helps track down a wily serial killer. September, nicknamed "Nine" for the month she was born, also appears in several of my other books, sometimes as the main investigator, sometimes peripherally. She last helped solve the longtime mystery that surrounded the ritual deaths at Camp Fog Lake in my latest River Glen Series book, THE CAMP.

I guess it's obvious September is one of my favorite characters. From day one she just jumped off the page! What's next for her? She's partnering with one of my sister's favorite characters from her To Die Series, Detective Selena Alvarez, in the upcoming NOWHERE TO DIE. When a member of Selena's family dies in an accident in September's bailiwick,

Selena shows up at Laurelton P.D. and demands answers from September, who's already looking into the suspicious deaths of other women around the Greater Portland area. September is pretty sure she doesn't need interference from this seasoned homicide detective from Grizzly Falls, Montana and lets Selena know that she should go home and let local authorities solve the case, but over time, as the trail leads deeper and deeper into all levels of Portland society, the two detectives unravel a decades-long conspiracy and murder plot that puts both of their lives in jeopardy.

Lastly, I want to tell you a little bit about my upcoming book, THE SORORITY. In high school ex-cop Mackenzie Laughlin was on the periphery of a group of girls who called themselves The Sorority. These "sisters" were the popular crowd at River Glen High, but just before graduation one of their members cheated with another one's boyfriend. Shortly afterward, that boyfriend died in a car accident. His death affected the whole school and tore The Sorority apart. Now, ten years later, Mac is approached by one of the sisters, who claims another is missing and wants Mac to find her. While Mackenzie searches for the missing girl she learns that the sisters all pledged to kill the cheating boyfriend mere weeks before his death. Was it real? Did someone actually arrange for the accident? Or, was it just a bad joke that macabrely came true as the head "sister" claims? As Mac grows closer to the truth, and with the help of her P.I. partner, Jesse James Taft, who's embroiled in a case involving another supposedly accidental death, Mac becomes the next target for someone who'll go to any length to keep their deadly crimes a secret.

Hope you enjoyed NOWHERE TO RUN as much
as I enjoyed writing it! It was the kickoff to the entire
Rafferty series, which is listed in full on my website:
nancybush.net. You can also check me out on social
media to keep up with my latest releases, contests,
and fun!

Happy, happy reading!
Nancy Bush

Please turn the page for an exciting sneak peek of
Nancy Bush's next thriller

THE SORORITY

coming soon wherever print and e-books are sold!

Prologue

"Hi, Ethan!"

"Hey, Ethan!

"Yoohoo, *Ethan!*"

"*ETHAN!*"

Ethan Stanhope looked over at the girls waving frantically at him from the front steps of River Glen High School. *Freshmen*, he smirked to himself. He nodded toward them with his usual half-smile and chuckled as they fell all over themselves in hysterical giggles. He was a senior. And captain of the water polo team. And king of the prom this year, although he'd taken off his crown as soon as the foil and glitter piece of junk was laid on his head and then placed it atop Celine Ergon-Smith's instead. From her wheelchair she gazed up at him in adoration, her cheeks turning pink. He didn't know why she was in the chair; some kind of birth defect he never knew the name of. He then bumped fists with Celine, smiled at her, ignored his "queen," and the crowd had gone wild.

The queen was Mia Jordan, his girlfriend. Ex-girlfriend now, as she'd iced him out ever since he'd fooled around with Roxy at Gavin's parents' pool house during the senior barbecue. He'd told Mia that nothing had happened between him and Roxy, and really not much had. Roxy was a tease, which he could admit he kind of liked. It was just . . . well, there'd been less than a month of school left at that time and he'd wanted to do something else. Be with someone else before there was no more school, no more seeing everybody every day.

Sorry, Freshmen, he thought as he chirped his tires and drove his silver BMW from the school parking lot. *I am fuckin' outta here.*

Friday was graduation, and his classmates were once again gathering at Gavin's afterward. His parents had purposely left again, tacitly allowing Gavin to have the party for his class. But Ethan didn't really want to go if Roxy wasn't there, and he'd asked her if she would be there and she'd simply shrugged. He didn't know what that meant, but she'd been hard to pin down since the pool party. He just felt . . . unsatisfied. He remembered kissing Roxy in the pool house. She hadn't really kissed him back, though. She'd just stood there. And then she'd told him to back off. He was too aggressive, which had pissed him off. Who the hell was she to tell him?

But then she'd pushed him back onto the pool house cot and slowly pulled down his pants to stare at his engorged cock. And when she'd leaned over him, he'd groaned aloud in anticipation, but all she'd done was kiss his dick and then give it a friendly pat. "Not tonight," she'd said.

"When?" he demanded.

"Probably not ever."

She'd then sauntered out of the pool house and he'd had to wait a while to cool his blood before nonchalantly following after her. But then, of course, one of Mia's friends had seen Roxy leave the pool house and then she saw him coming out a few minutes behind her. From that point on there was no talking Mia out of it. Everyone assumed he and Roxy had had sex, and though Ethan had half-heartedly stated that they hadn't, Gavin had thrown back his head and roared and said, "Sure. Wink, wink," exaggeratedly closing one eye a couple of times and grinning like an idiot. Ethan let him think what he would. Why not?

Of course Roxy said nothing had happened between them as well, but Mia hadn't believed her. She'd called Roxy a slut, which had pissed Roxy off, even though she was one. A real bitch, teaser, slut. Yet, Ethan would never say so, because he still thought there was a chance they might get together tonight, again at Gavin's, now that he and Mia were unofficially through. After that last barbecue he'd gone home to learn Roxy had left red lipstick on his skin and the realization had made him groan some more and engage in a little self-love.

He wanted more.

Friday afternoon, following the graduation ceremony and his family duties, Ethan called Gavin to ascertain when to arrive. He didn't want to be the first one to show up, but if Roxy was there . . .

"Nobody's here," Gavin informed him with a disgusted sigh. "Nobody good, anyway." A pause. "Mia's here."

"Hey, Mia's good," Ethan protested. "She's always good. We don't hate each other."

"You sure about that?"

"Why? She say something?"

"It's all her 'sisters'. They're standing around like in judgement, man."

"Is Roxy there?" He tossed the question in lightly, but Gavin was all over it.

"Stop thinking about her. It's messing with your head and we're done here. School's over. Graduation's over! Foxy Roxy's probably out screwing someone else. You know that's who she is."

"It wasn't like that with us."

"So you say, so you say . . . Get over here and cheer these bitches up or get 'em outta here. I'm gonna get hammered and maybe get laid, but not with any of them."

"I'll be there." Ethan felt his hopes sink. If Roxy wasn't there, he really didn't want to go.

And he really didn't want to see Mia, and the rest of her posse. Leigh and Kristi and that Natalie. God, she was the worst. And the other one . . . Allie. Gavin had tried to make it with her, but she was needy and whiny and he'd given up after one make-out session. Ethan could have told him. None of them were worth anything but Mia, and even she had gotten on his nerves. It annoyed him off that she'd stopped talking to him, but it was a relief, too. He could go about whatever he wanted now.

And what he wanted was Roxy.

An hour and a half later he showed up at Gavin's. Maybe nothing had been happening earlier, but the party was in full swing now. Some of the guys were really wasted and loud, and so were some of the girls. Not Mia's group. They were all standing together and looking dead sober. Okay, maybe Allie was staggering a bit, but the others were grim as parents surveying the lot of them. He saw Mia's black hair, clipped back at her nape like always. She was talking to Jeremy Orsini, a total piece of shit.

Natalie lifted her chin. She'd zeroed in on him as soon as he'd entered through the back gate and was coming his way. She, too, had black hair, but unlike Mia, whose skin glowed with good health, Natalie's pallor was pale as death. Natalie was totally goth. And she was grim like that, too. Mia said she was the leader of their group. Well, good for her. She was another piece of shit.

He watched Natalie lean toward Kristi, who was the tallest and heaviest of their group. Kristi was looking over at him, too. She wore a one-piece swimsuit instead of a bikini to probably contain the flab. He waved frantically at them all, pretending to be crazily overjoyed to see them. No one waved back, although Leigh, who'd always been nice, surreptitiously lifted a few fingers. Leigh had light brown hair and was sort of cute, but she was flat-chested and Mia said she was emotional. Not as bad as Allie, maybe, but who needed the aggravation.

Roxy was nowhere in sight. How she was even part of their group was a mystery.

He got himself a beer, but then another girl, younger, he decided, since he didn't know her, talked him into a glass of punch. He drank half of it, and then set it down as some more people arrived. It was just getting dark and the air was starting to chill, so Ethan headed around the side of the house and to his BMW to retrieve his jacket. He nearly ran into Mackenzie Laughlin on the way, staggering a bit to avoid her as she was just standing in the driveway by one of the SUVs, eyeing the house, clearly thinking over whether to join the party. He'd recently seen her in the school play, *Oklahoma*, that Mia had talked him into going to. Mackenzie hadn't been half bad. He couldn't remember the name of her character, but he could remember part of the song she'd sung.

"*I'm just a girl who can't say no,*" he warbled badly, half laughing. He was no singer.

Mackenzie eyed him carefully, but didn't say anything. He started to feel a little foolish for making fun of her. As he shouldered past her toward the street where his BMW was parked, she said, "You don't want to drive in your condition."

His condition? "I've barely had anything to drink," he protested. Had his voice slurred?

That was . . . weird.

"You need a ride? I'm leaving." The words sounded dragged from her. She clearly didn't mean what she'd said.

"You just got here."

"Yeah, well . . . I'm not staying."

"Yeah, well . . . I'm just getting my coat." He heard his voice and thought he'd said those words pretty clearly.

Mackenzie gave him a look he couldn't decipher, then headed back to an older model Ford Explorer that was parked on the opposite side of the street from Ethan. He leaned into his SUV and half fell on the seat as he snagged his coat. In a way he was kinda sorry to see Mac go. She was friends with Mia and her group, but a bit of an outsider. And there was something about her parents . . . oh, yeah . . . her dad had died a few years back. That was too bad.

Back at the party Ethan grabbed another glass of punch and sank into one of the lounge chairs around the pool, which really irked Miles, who'd been sitting there apparently. The world was spinning and he lay back and fell asleep. When he came to, he realized most everyone had moved indoors. He thought about Roxy. She wasn't here, so why was he? He saw his drink and someone had put ice in it. He picked it up and swallowed about half of it. He looked toward the pool house, but it was dark. However, the plate glass windows of the main house were brightly lit from within, and he could see through the dining room to the kitchen. Mia was standing with the rest of her group. He felt a pang in his heart. She'd ditched him, and he wasn't the kind of guy who should be ditched.

Staggering up, he walked back around the pool house through the gate and down the drive. When he got behind the wheel of his rig he saw that someone had left him some food, sealed up on a paper plate beneath plastic wrap. Mia, maybe?

He started the car but sat there for a while. Maybe Mackenzie was right. He shouldn't drive. He certainly felt odd.

* * *

He didn't know how long he'd sat there before he shook his head. Fuck it. He didn't live that far away.

He pulled into the street and glanced in the rearview mirror. Someone was standing in the road behind him. Mia? Was she waving?

No. It wasn't Mia . . . he didn't think.

And they weren't waving. They were giving him the finger.

Well, shit. He threw the BMW into gear and roared away. He wanted to drive to the ends of the earth, but then remembered vaguely that there was some obligation he needed to do for his parents so he headed home.

He didn't know that he'd be dead within the hour.

Visit our website at
KensingtonBooks.com
to sign up for our newsletters, read
more from your favorite authors, see
books by series, view reading group
guides, and more!

BOOK / CLUB
BETWEEN THE CHAPTERS

Become a Part of Our
Between the Chapters Book Club
Community and Join the Conversation

Betweenthechapters.net